What people are saying about Sigrid Weidenweber

CATHERINE

"The admirers of literature and history will welcome this trilogy as a ray of light suddenly invading our age of darkness. Well researched and well written, it gives a unique insight into the tragic and fascinating story of Volga Germans over three centuries. Pasrts of it (such as volume 3) can and should be turned into an excellent movie, too.

"A reader who prides himself in his knowledge of history will still learn much from this book. A reader of most refined literary taste will still find it difficult to put down. Both will be eagerly waiting for Sigrid's next work."

— Vladimir Bukovsky,
Russian political activist and author

"With great skill and passion Sigrid Weidenweber unveils an epic and important historical journey, bringing to life the danger, violence, and intrigue of European royalty through the eyes of one of its most prominent and fascinating members."

— Tim Green,
New York Times bestselling author

"Great nations become great because of great people. Sigrid has combined her research and writing skills to trace the story of one of Russia's great leaders. Catherine is superb reading about an exciting monarch who changed the course of European history — a real 'page turner'!"

— John Van Diest, Founder, Multnomah Press;
Associate Publisher, Tyndale House Publishers

The Old Man and the Mail-Order Brides

To Marilyn,
one of the Angels,

Fondly, Sigrid
Weidenweber

SIGRID WEIDENWEBER

The Old Man and the Mail-Order Brides

Sigrid Weidenweber © copyright 2013

GreenE-Books.com
PO Box 140654
Boise ID 83714
www.GreenE-Books.com

First eBook Edition: 2013
First Paperback Edition: 2013
ISBN: 978-1-938848-33-9

Cover design by Diana Philbrook
Interior design by GreenE-Books.com
Published in the United States of America

Acknowledgments

THE WEALTH OF FLORIDA'S HISTORY and the fish lore contained in this book was bestowed upon me by Don and Mary Edwards and Paul Sarbo over a period of ten years. We spent many happy days fishing on the ocean and in the bay. My three friends spent most of their lives in the Florida Keys and on the blue waters of the Atlantic.

Another delightful part of my Florida education derived from the teachings of Jack Dunham, who imparted to me the wisdom of living life like foam floating on a gentle river.

A special thanks goes to David Henson, who resurrected my dead computer long enough to save this manuscript among other documents and scripts before the equipment totally expired.

Last, but not least, I want to thank Jason Chatraw, owner and publisher of Green E-books, who is wonderful to work with. I give the same accolade to my editor Jenn Wolf, who fully understood the essence of the Florida descriptions. Having lived in Titusville and visited the Florida Keys many times she was very familiar with the scenes. Jenn collects and writes stories for a magazine and fine-tunes manuscripts. I very much appreciate her precise work.

As always, recognition of merit is reserved for my husband who supports my work with vigor.

Last, but not least, I want to thank my friend Diana Philbrook of Philbrook & Associates for the creation of a cover that I like very much, because it captures the participants of the book as well Snake Creek with its bridge in the background.

- S. I. W.

Preface

ABOUT FIFTEEN YEARS AGO when I found myself in the doldrums of the mind, in the middle of a research project, I needed a break and began writing the tale of *The Old Man and The Mail-Order Brides*. It was summer and I idled during a Florida vacation—my mind was pleasantly at rest, my eyes followed lazily the flights of tropical birds and the changing tides.

In the midst of this pleasant lassitude I suddenly experienced the urge, an urge growing stronger by the day, that I had to write about a phenomenon that was becoming more prevalent with each month—the import of foreign brides by lonely American men.

As the women's movement had grown stronger, changing the traditional gender roles, men with deeply ingrained concepts of these roles were dissatisfied with the choices of women available, or unable to find companions willing to fulfill their wishes and demands. That characterization alone though, would not encompass the whole gamut of reasons for their wishes to marry foreign, pliable women; many psychological shades of wants, wishes and fantasies were included therein.

I had firsthand experiences with eight men who looked to Russia and Asia for possible brides. Their experiences amused and intrigued me, for I noted that quite predictably, some of their adventures ended badly, or in disenchantment, to say the least.

A few of the encounters ended in marriages that—after restructuring and adjustments as in other relationships—were tolerably beneficial.

I also perceived that in the latter cases the women in question were expertly using psychology to make the situations pleasant. With these case studies in mind I began to write this partly tongue-in-cheek tale, into which I imparted the flavor of my Florida summers.

- S. I. W.

CAST OF CHARACTERS

৯৶৶

Dmitri Pataklos - wife, Theresa
Martha Lenius - neighbor beside
Jan and Brent Sorensen - neighbors from across the canal
Ben - Fishing Buddy
Irina Petrovna Sokolova - mail-order bride
Alphonso Morales - cabbie
Raphael Mendoza - detective
Mr. Rogerson - INS detective
Dan Heminger - Second officer Intrepid, wife Ada
Petros Avarikidze - head of Georgia mafia in Florida
John Morrell - Petty Officer of Intrepid, wife Kelly
Robert Butweiler - seaman first class, no wife
Ignacio, Angel - detective working with Raphael
Manny - detective
Angel (Lenin) Correal – Raphael Mendoza's nephew, detective
Anthony Li - Customs Agent, Japanese American
John Brandeis – Head of Miami Customs Office

Part One

Nightmares and Dreams

ॐ⋙

IN HIS LATER YEARS Dmitri suffered occasionally from nightmarish dreams. Dreams, in which he invariably found himself standing, pressed against the railing of his boat, searching the dark waters below for a woman's body. The night was always warm, the sea calm; the sky above and all around was very dark.

Toward midnight a bright moon rose into the black sky reigning supreme in the starless firmament as it bathed the scene below with a mild white light. Dmitri always knew with certainty that the boat was positioned below, or close to, one of the long bridges that strung the Florida Keys together. Some nights the dream was so vivid that he identified the boat's proximity to be at Duck-Key or Little Pine Key. At other nights, when he was dreaming very vividly, he knew that the boat was drifting in the middle of Moser Channel.

In his nightmares he always held a large gaff in his hands; a gaff, powerful enough to hook and pull a shark or marlin into the boat. Unvarying he used this murderous instrument to hook into the woman's black diving suit when he finally spotted her.

Sometimes the dream ended at this point; sometimes the scene played longer. Whenever that happened, other characters appeared in the boat. Long-time friends of his would become part of the woman's capture. They would be by his side, ready to help him. He needed help every time, for the woman once gaffed and pulled aboard, fought like a demon from the bottom of the sea. Sometimes the struggle would be so fearsome that he awakened bathed in sweat, fighting for breath.

At other times, a U.S. Immigration and Customs Enforcement (ICE) agent named Rogerson, would be present. Leaning against the tall mast of the sailboat, he would be laughing as if possessed. There were times, when Rogerson spoke, or rather, ghastly whinnied like a horse.

"I told you so! I told you that you would be responsible!"

Rogerson's words immediately echoed back from the water's expanse.

"Responsible, responsible!"

Of all the dream scenarios, the last was the most horrible. Upon awakening, an overwhelming feeling of sadness and dread imprisoned him, a feeling he had to combat with rational thought.

It all began when Theresa, his wife of forty years, died. She passed away after long years of illness, fighting lymphoma. He had dutifully supported her, cared for all her needs. However, secretly, he began to long for regular, vigorous companionship while tending to the invalid. He needed a woman to take on fishing trips, a mate when sailing his yacht to the islands of the Caribbean, a deck hand to help in rough seas. But most of all he longed for sexual pleasures to relieve the needs assuaged only in his fantasies. In one of these secret dreams, he once again fathered a child; a child to love and teach, a child to whom he could pass the wisdom of his life.

His neighbor, Martha, a widow and his senior by five years, suggested that he might not need a wife at all. "If it is companionship you are looking for, there is plenty within shouting distance. You are deluding yourself with this young wife business. I have observed you closely for a long time now. You have thought, and said so many times, that there has to be more to life. Perhaps what you really need is a spiritual experience, a tuneup so to speak for your soul, a soul that has been buried beneath cares and worries. Come to church

with me and speak to my pastor. I think he can help."
Dmitri, however, treated her rather insightful suggestions dismissively. His needs screamed louder than ever that he needed a woman. Who would have thought to deny him a new happiness? Was he not a good man, always faithful, never thinking of abandoning his marriage as long as his wife had lived? He thought, therefore, that no one could blame him, when not long after his wife's death he went every night into Miami in search of a suitable woman. Although, his neighbors, especially the women, believed that there were plenty of fine choices to be made from the local eligible females.

And so it was inevitable, when his wife was interred for only three months that urgency set him to pursue a particular woman. The object of his pursuit was a shapely, sultry-faced Cuban lady in her thirties, whom he had met at a Cuban restaurant. Yet, this, his great romance, begotten tempestuously, was not destined to flower.

The lady's two almost adult, mercenary children ruthlessly nipped the flowering relationship in the bud. Apparently both precocious youths learned at an early age how to exploit their mother's single state to exact favors from the men courting her. They knew how to manipulate the array of suitors to provide them with electronic gadgets, clothing and sweets. The ferret-faced seventeen-year-old boy in particular had the loathsome habit of blackmailing the men in his mother's life, thereby destroying every chance of marriage for her.

At one point, Dmitri was threatened with bodily harm by the young thug for his refusal to pay him off. Mind you, Dmitri was a military man and could have, even at his age, trounced the Cuban pup. He understood, however, that the pup's numerous accomplices, hovering nearby, were too much for him to handle. Finding valor in an organized retreat, Dmitri chose to gently and cleverly extricate himself from his Cuban entanglement. He made doubly sure that the errant son of his former beloved was kept in the dark as to his residency.

His second attempt at romance also shattered resoundingly when a well- meaning fishing buddy informed him that the sweet little librarian he was dating had infected three of their acquaintances with bad cases of the clap. His disappointment went deep. The lady in question was a perky, blond forty-year-old with a solid, proud bust and nice slim legs. He had greatly enjoyed their few dates, for he could talk with her about a great many subjects, a rarity in the islands. Upon reflection though, he was grateful that fate had spared him a deeper involvement, which could have ended with a visit to the doctor.

However, despite these close calls, women haunted his mind at all times. Whether he shopped for his food, mailed letters at the post office or went for his customary bike rides or walks, he encountered females in all shapes, sizes and ages. The best female specimens he found were already married unfortunately. Others, still unattached, had allowed themselves to become unappealingly sloppy or fat. Fitness and looks were important after all for a man dead set on an active life. There were plenty of single, good-looking women of the right age within reach. Unfortunately, they held no charm for him. For he had a dream—she must be pretty, young enough, and willing to have children.

Because of this obsessive dream, he was ready to follow a most unusual piece of advice. A friend came to him with a magazine. "Here, old man," smiled his fishing buddy Ben, a man amply familiar with Dmitri's dreams. With the flick of his wrist he opened a slick publication, while announcing, "This here is the candy shop of our former enemy. You can now further good relations with the Russians by showing their females that capitalism is vastly superior to socialism. In this magazine of Russian women you will surely find your dream." A wicked smile flickered across his face as he continued, "Any woman in here is between eighteen and twenty four, long legged, blond or dark, and willing."

"How would you know that? I haven't seen you with any of them," poked Dmitri at him. "I still see you drinking rum and Coke and chasing women at the Tiki Bar every evening, and you aren't having any luck there either."

Ben, fifty-five, beer-bellied, his skin browned by the sun to look like roast chicken, fingered his thatch of reddish hair. "If only I had your money, old man, I would have sent for one of these delectable chicks pronto."

"You can't have women, live human beings, ordered in like take out dinner," objected Dmitri. "It is somehow indecent."

Looking like a big, fuzzy St. Bernhard, Ben set his brown eyes on his friend, "Trust me. It's for real. Guys do it all the time."

"So you say these women actually come and marry any kind of guy who wants them?"

"Pretty much so. You can go and check them out over there in Roosia, or you can have them visit, and if you click—who knows."

"You seem to know much about this stuff. So how are the marriages faring or whatever ménages men have arranged with these women?"

"It's like everything else. Win some—lose some. Some of the gals try to trick a guy into marrying them, and then, after they get their citizenship papers, they divorce the guy and take him to the cleaner. I've seen this happen. But you can have a prenuptial and be fine."

Ben, the devil, having set the hook went his way, laughing as he walked. For himself, he was going to pursue willing American chicks and stay single.

Highly intrigued, Dmitri paged through the glossy magazine with ever increasing interest. My, oh my! He had never considered that women, looking like American models, would be interested in a guy like him. Picture after picture fired his imagination. There was Tatyana, looking like she could star in a major motion picture. Tamara, sultry, dark, slim and riding a horse, reminded him of the steppe and adventure. On and on he looked—each picture a dream.

For fourteen days he studied the photographs and biographies of the Russian beauties with academic thoroughness. Then he made the decision that he would invite Irina Petrovna Sokolova, a blond, blue-eyed, twenty-four-year-old to come to Miami, so that he might study her in America's bright light.

This, however, was easier said than done. Immigration took a dim view of trial affairs and suggested he go thither to meet her in Russia. In particular, an (ICE) agent, Rogerson, was of the opinion that this was a hare-brained scheme.

"Mister Pataklos, let me tell you, in my many years working for the Immigration Service, I have seldom come across a great love involving those seeking to come to this country. Mostly these brides are after one thing only—permanent residency. The moment they have attained it, you become expendable."

It was only after long palavers and his personal pledge to deliver the damsel after the visit to the gates of Aeroflot, that his beauty was granted a visitor's visa, allowing Dmitri three weeks of discovery. Mister Rogerson, having finally succumbed to Dmitri's persistence, sighed resignedly, "Well I tried my best to save you from yourself. Go ahead and make a fool of yourself. I give up! They don't pay me for counseling services anyway."

After this long sad exhalation, his parting words were rather harsh and peremptory, filled with admonitions to keep an eye on the bride at all times.

The highly anticipated day came when the former first officer of a navy vessel, dressed himself in his best outfit, a gray suit, set off by a blinding white shirt and a steel-blue tie. He tamed his unruly dark hair, which was woven through with bristly gray, by applying pomade and other hairdressing until it gleamed. It was slicked back, tame, but unbecomingly so. His still handsome, tanned face with a prominent nose and commanding brown eyes would have been better off without the severe treatment, but he did not know that. To complete his effort at perfect appearance, he put on a regular pair of well-shined brown shoes instead of his ubiquitous boat loafers. The job completed, he admired the result in the big mirror that covered the inside of his closet door.

Not too bad for my age, was his thought. He was pleased with the outcome of his labors. Yes, Dmitri at sixty-five was in fine shape, ready to get married again.

And so, on this the appointed day, sweating with anxiety and excitement he stood at the exit gate of Aeroflot, holding a sign with her beloved name as the plane disgorged its passengers.

First to appear, looking like seedy lawyers, were several leather-clad, swarthy men of different heights, carrying fat, black pigskin briefcases. On closer examination, they could have belonged to the KGB—if its members were that obvious—or possibly, adherents of the Russian mob. Closely following this unsavory bunch was one of the most stunning women Dmitri had ever seen.

The woman turned out to be his Irina. Bashfulness or diffidence were not Irina's hallmark. Dmitri's Russian flower was not shy. Having spotted him, she walked straight into his arms and kissed him with practiced ease on the cheek. Dmitri almost died right then and there. He definitely felt his heart stop for a moment. When the faintness left him, his heart resumed work with a resounding thud.

Dear Lord, he prayed silently, *allow me to live a little longer and I shall die happy.*

Irina, Irina, sang his heart while he forced his trembling voice to obey. "Welcome to America, Irina," he managed to rasp, adding sheepishly, "You look just like your picture."

To his less-than-eloquent effort she replied in good English. "Thank you. You also do look like yours."

As they passed through the long, carpeted corridor leading to the baggage claim, Dmitri felt blessed, anointed even, that among all the young and old men surrounding them, he was the chosen one. Irina's long, wheat-blond hair was gathered at the crown by a broad tortoise-shell clasp, allowing it to free-flow down her back. Thus leaving her face nicely framed yet unobstructed. And what a face it was. Between high cheekbones emerged a straight, most-delicate nose. It looked down upon a large, generous, crimson mouth that smiled at him with perfect teeth.

Blue, clear eyes assessed him competently. She was taller by at least two inches than he was and Dmitri stood six foot three. However, she wore very high- heeled, elegant croc-leather shoes with ridiculously long pointed toes, which added much height to her frame. Irina was very slim. Her svelte figure was even more exaggerated by the severe, tailored cut of her expensive, turquoise rawsilk suit.

She had moved into his arms with such practiced ease that he, feeling momentarily uncomfortable, surmised that she had done this many times. "Dmitri, dahling," she breathed, sounding exactly like Eva Gabor in Green Acres. It was a show she had watched over and over again in her Moscow cubicle to practice English pronunciation. Now her English was almost perfect.

"It is so nice to get to know you in perrrson after the letterrrs and phone calls; I know that we shall become grreat frriends."

She rolled her "r"s in a very sexy Russian way, advertising her motherland proudly. Upon this promising pronouncement they kissed each other three times on the cheeks in Orthodox fashion. Benumbed by her presence, he murmured simply worded greetings and gladness at her safe arrival. As they walked together Dmitri was aware of the stares other men directed at his companion. This observation caused him to walk with straighter posture and more bounce in his step. Improved posture gained him additional height and new self-confidence swelled his breast. Yes, this was the way a man should feel, uplifted as if by angels' wings.

They claimed Irina's four substantial—perhaps one should more correctly say enormous—suitcases, leading him to think, *She carries clothes as if she wants to open a business with the stuff.* His searching eyes could not locate a porter, but found a smart cart, which he loaded to the hilt, topping it with Irina's very stylish Coach Sateen Tote. Leaving the airport for his car, Irina walked alongside the cart with long, hip-swinging strides worthy of the best model on a runway.

He had booked two rooms at the Fontainebleau at Miami Beach, hoping that soon they would require only one, because the place was obscenely expensive. The least expensive rooms were eight hundred dollars each. It went enormously against his thrifty Greek grain, having to pay so much money just to sleep in a place. But Irina had requested that they stay here because she had heard so much of the Fontainebleau. To impress the girl, Dmitri acquiesced and bled.

Once in the car they made small talk. It was the kind of awkward, polite talk interspersed with silences, usually reserved for strangers. Irina was suitably impressed with the views Miami presented, emitting little cries of, "Verry prretty! Lovely! Oh, look at this mahhhvelous carr!"

She had great taste. The "carr" was the newest model Jaguar. It was a silver predator—the very top among many other pretty, sleek beasts which, bathed in sunlight, roared along broad streets.

Dmitri savored the way the doorman's eyes popped when Irina, unfolding her length, stepped from his well-kept, still beautiful, but aged, dark-blue Chrysler Town car. The doorman motioned excitedly to a bevy of bellboys, who descended like a flock of practiced vultures upon the Chrysler. The uniformed doorman, in an exalted class by himself, opened the sparkling cut-glass doors for the odd couple. He deigned to bestow only a swift glance at the male model of the odd couple. Dmitri didn't care. He relished being the escort of beauty. Although in the deepest recesses of his soul, the place where honesty resides, he understood that he must come off beside Irina like her grandfather.

The patches of gray in his hair gave away much of the story; the rest was offered by his presentable but outdated attire, the lines in his face, and the slight paunch he could not keep at bay anymore even with the most vigorous exercise and the strictest diet. Of course, he had to shower the flock of busboys with cash—but for once he did not mind.

To Dmitri's astonishment, the girl showed neither awe nor delight when she saw the famous, opulently appointed lobby or the grand staircase. Disappointed to the core, he asked her why this was so.

"Dahhling," she sighed by way of explanation. "I have seen some of the best lobbies in Moscow, in Rome, in Berlin and in Paris."

"So, you travel quite a bit?"

"No, really not much, but as an escort to the minister of Trade, I went a few times abroad."

"In what capacity?" Dmitri wanted clarification on the escort thing, wanted to know if they were thinking of the same thing.

"Oh, arranging things, making sure that all goes well. Rooms, taxis, tickets, everything." To which Dmitri replied with obvious wonderment, "If you have such an important, interesting job why would you be interested in a marriage with an older foreign man?"

Irina laughed aloud, delighted by his frankness. "In Russia you have no—what do you call it—jobsecurity. Tomorrow they may find a prettier, younger girl and I am finished."

The elevator delivered them to the fifth floor where they had rooms with a view of the ocean. They agreed to freshen up and meet at six for cocktails in the bar before leaving for a quaint place overlooking the beach to have dinner.

Later that evening they enjoyed a large, expensive seafood dinner which, at Irina's suggestion, they washed down with two bottles of Veuve Clicquot. As Irina informed him, Madam Clicquot became internationally famous after her wines, and especially her champagnes, were a grand success in Russia. They topped off the champagne with a few mixed drinks at the bar, and awakened next morning in Dmitri's bed. He could barely remember having gotten into the room, never mind having gotten into his bed. Irina, however, assured him that he had been the perfect companion and a very, very viril man!

For three days in a row this scenario repeated itself. They went sightseeing, shopping, which meant buying clothes for Irina, and eating in fancy restaurants, ending the evening in one of their rooms.

By God, thought the old navy man, *this girl is so much fun, so easy to be with*. Anything he suggested they do, she was happy to try. Most of all, he liked the afternoons they spent lying on the beach under an enormous umbrella, talking, swimming and napping. He was the most envied man on the beach, for Irina in a bikini was a sight to behold. It seemed as if sunlight was made only for the purpose of illuminating her supple, lithe and elegant body, and to make her hair glow.

Everything developed so splendidly that Dmitri believed himself to be in love. He was convinced that he finally had found the woman he wanted to be with for the rest of his days. He did not, however, deceive himself into believing that Irina loved him. That was not what he needed. If she could just accept him as her husband—and treat him as such—that was all right. Perhaps affection and yes, maybe even love, if he could bring her to respect him, would grow later when she knew him better. At times though, when he devoured her lovely face and body with his eyes, little nagging doubts crept into his mind. Could she really live with him as his wife down in the laid-back Keys where all was casual, natural, rough even? Would a woman of her caliber be satisfied with fishing, boating, backyard parties and little else?

But the bewitching minx laughed delightfully when he brought such thoughts to the fore.

"No, I am quite sure that we will have a great marriage. I will learn to be a good wife. To go out on yachts and have lovely parties sounds like a lot of fun. I will learn how to fish to please you."

So he put his rational thinking on hold and enjoyed what had so graciously fallen into his lap. However, already on the fourth day, after a long luxurious lunch and a stroll through a local gallery, Irina's face clouded as if she was in pain.

"What is it? Irina, you seem to be in agony."

"Oh, it's nothing. I sometimes get these headaches. I never know when they strike."

"Poor baby." Dmitri was all over the girl, solicitous and concerned.

"Don't worry, Dmitrri. I will be fine if I just lie down a little while. I know how to deal with these things. A little Aspirin and some rest will take care of it."

Off to bed she went, leaving the old man standing alone in front of her bedroom door. Deeply disappointed he decided to seek his supper at a more reasonably priced place for a change. After driving around for a while looking for a suitable restaurant, he ended up in a squalid place on the beach where he was served a remarkably decent fried lobster tail with French fries and coleslaw. He returned to the hotel, toting a few beers in a brown bag. The miniature bar in his room was much too pricy for his blood. Still fully clothed, he threw himself on the bed and clicked on the TV. However, as he was lying there on his Damask coverlet amid the luxurious surrounds of his room, watching a deadly boring rerun of Miami Vice, a disturbing thought came unbidden. Irina was a superbly healthy girl who had not mentioned any illnesses until late in the afternoon. If she was indeed ill, it must be something serious. Food poisoning could act quickly and begin with the symptoms she had described. Or, perhaps being unused to the hot Florida sun, she had succumbed to a heat-related ailment.

An Unpleasant Discovery

❧❧

BY HIS VERY NATURE Dmitri was a considerate man, solicitous even, and so it occurred to him that it was rather unchivalrous to allow a damsel in distress to suffer alone. He must therefore go at once to her side, and see for himself what she might need. He had to get her assistance, perhaps medicine or a doctor. Poor girl, here she was in a foreign country, maybe unwilling to ask for aid. Or perhaps she was shy, afraid to appear burdensome. Following this train of thought, he convinced himself that his Russian flower was going to expire on the spot without his intervention.

He jumped off the bed with the vigor of bygone days. Adjusting his rumpled clothes, he set out for Irina's room. He knocked on her door, delicately at first, pounding forcefully moments later. Yet, no answer was to be had—not even a cry to stop the pounding.

There was utter silence behind her door. His worries multiplying, he raced back to his room and hastily dialed her number once he was seated beside the phone. Alas, to no avail, Irina did not answer. His worries rose to a fever pitch. Once more he left in a rush what he had come to call the "eight-hundred-dollar folly," taking a lift to the lobby.

"I have a problem," he told the desk clerk. "I think my lady friend in room number 580 is very ill. She doesn't answer the door or her phone. I am deeply concerned, as she earlier complained of feeling ill."

The clerk, a young man in his late twenties, tanned and very athletic looking, had been watching the world with bright, alert blue eyes. He now contracted his handsome, somewhat square features thoughtfully.

"Are we speaking of the blond, elegant Russian lady on the fifth floor?" he asked.

"Yes, we are," said Dmitri, amazed that the clerk seemed to know Irina.

"Well, don't worry Mr. Pataklos. That lady is just fine. I saw her leaving the lobby about half an hour ago. I called a cab for her because the doorman was busy with arrivals."

The clerk's face lit up appreciatively as he continued, "And if I may say so sir, the lady looked absolutely fabulous in a stunning, little black dress."

For a moment Dmitri thought that he discerned a glimmer of Schadenfreude crossing the clerk's features. Perhaps it was just his imagination that he read on the young face: "She is not for you, old man." That look was so fleeting, however, that he must have been mistaken.

Twenty dollars slipped covertly into the doorman's hand bought Dmitri the intriguing knowledge that the cabbie transporting Irina to her playground had returned. He was now waiting for new fares in line at the taxi station. His name was Jorge Hernandez, the third in line. Another twenty to Jorge got Dmitri the name of the club Irina had been taken to.

Bitterly disappointed with his lady Dmitri descended by elevator into the underground garage. He trudged along the narrow exit lane, staring at the tire-marked concrete floor, and collected his trusted old car. He navigated carefully, at times plowing his way through the crowded streets, seething with tourists and fun-seeking natives. Thirty minutes later he reached Club Hispaniola. Admittance to the club presented a problem. Hispaniola was a private club. Membership was required to enter the club.

༄~✌

THIS NEW DEVELOPMENT SET Dmitri's mind in renewed uproar. How could Irina have come here unless she already knew a club member who was meeting her? Furthermore, how could she have set up such a date? From the moment she arrived they were together almost every moment. There had not been time for her to meet people and make dates. Or could it be that she had been out at night when he slept? "A devil in every woman," he fumed under his breath. He had not been a military man for nothing. He offered the doorman a deal he couldn't refuse. Money changed hands and Dmitri became a temporary club member.

As he entered the main part of the club he was blown away by the décor. The floors and walls were marble clad while the ceiling was a firmament of Moorish arches and arabesque tile work. Palmetto palms in grand urns were placed becomingly along the walls and throughout the rooms. On one end of the room, a low platform held disco equipment alongside instruments belonging to a band. A grand piano and a harp stood standoffish to one side, lending a sophisticated elegance to the stage.

One enormous wall sported a bar. Bar was a word wholly inadequate to describe what was perhaps better entitled a great work of art. Mirrors, glass, and chrome shelving allowed the exotic wine and liqueur bottles to be arranged in artistic, wild patterns. The counter, too, was constructed from heavy glass. The shiny glass shimmered in melted-in pastel color patterns. One of the Latino bar tenders was in constant motion wiping and polishing the glass marvel.

Very impressive; lots of money in this place, thought Dmitri, while he scanned the crowded room for the elusive Irina. When he finally spotted her, she was the center of a flock of young men. One man in particular, a tall, dark-haired, olive-skinned fellow with classic facial features and fiery eyes seemed to have a claim on her. Dmitri ordered Scotch and soda. "Twenty dollars," said the bartender. Dmitri almost spilled the pale golden liquid changing hands.

"What did you put in here? It better be gold," he joshed, with a sour undertone.

"You are paying for the ambiance, Sir," laughed the bartender good-humoredly. He had heard similar lines many times before.

Dmitri decided to frugally nurse the Scotch for a long time. He turned his back to the crowded room and the flirtatious Irina. He planned to remain unobserved while spying on her. To accomplish this feat, he found a miniscule table for two in a small alcove. Hidden behind a Palmetto bush, he could watch the crowd to his heart's content. He owed his good fortune to the remarkably good band. The band had begun to play by this time, drawing the crowd to the dance floor, leaving tables unoccupied.

Irina looked glamorous in the black sheath he had bought her only two days ago at an Oscar de la Renta boutique. And yet, to him she seemed achingly vulnerable. She danced in turn with all the fellows in her group. However, he noticed that she favored the "Spaniard,"—thus he had dubbed the fellow· with the burning eyes—with many more dances than the others. Adding to his agony was his observation of the fellow's very proprietary air, putting his hands on Irina in sure ways, as if he had known her for a long time.

His possessive behavior infuriated Dmitri to no end. He decided, however, that he would play it cool. Let her have a little fun. Deep down though, he fervently wished she should have fun with him. Did he not dance? Dashed well, too, for a fellow his age, and when it came to drinking, he held his own with anyone. He knew he could. *Well*, he made the concession reluctantly, *maybe not quite like the old days. As to the affair at hand, he opined to self, I will see how this plays out. When I know it all, I will decide.*

As the night turned into morning, Irina danced only with the Spaniard and drank from his glass. Twice Dmitri broke his vow and replenished his drink—at twenty bucks a shot—while conducting an internal dialogue on the foolishness of his behavior.

The music, a nice mixture of DJ-work interspersed with a live Latin band, suddenly stopped. The great hall emptied, as if the tide swept everyone outside. In the stampede, he lost sight of Irina and the Spaniard. Slinking toward the door, he hoped that he would beat them back to the hotel to see her arrival.

To take this passive action was his first inclination upon leaving the club. But then he saw both of them standing by the curb to the right of the door, almost melting into each other. Watching Irina's blatant deceit aroused his passion once more. He changed his mind in an instant. What if Irina were to accompany the Spaniard to his house or hotel? Fired by the drinks and the unfairness of the situation, Dmitri felt like a cuckolded husband.

Had he not paid for her airplane ticket, the visa, the hotel, food, wine and an extraordinary array of clothes? Had she not agreed to a contract stating that they would honestly and openly decide if they could live with each other? How dare the Russian minx go behind his back and play fast, loose and false? Now that he knew of her betrayal he wanted to know the whole story. How long had she known the Spaniard? Did she know him before she came to Miami? What was their previous connection and where were they going?

He stipulated that he needed a cab to do his detective work following the faithless hussy, because she knew his car. So, here he was once more settled with another unnecessary expense. His frugal soul recoiled at this terrible realization. As his woes wound their way through his mind, he watched as Irina and her darkling beau jumped into a black, chauffeured limousine, which an arrogant chauffeur had driven up to the curb in an ostentatious display of exclusivity and bravado.

Throwing caution to the wind, Dmitri jumped out into the seething thoroughfare, scintillating with lights, and hailed a cab. Noting his eagerness, a cabby pulled up to the curb. Dmitri jumped into the vehicle before the car was fully stopped.

"Follow that limo!" he shouted.

"Make sure they don't spot us following. I just want to see where he takes her!" he added, looking into the cab driver's face. The cabbie was a middle-aged Cuban with pleasant, wide-open features and deep, dark eyes. With eyes trained to take in everything in his field of vision, the cabbie had naturally noted the beautiful young couple entering the limo.

"Your daughter is it?" he asked, with the wisdom of a father of three blossoming girls for whom he was forever on the lookout.

Dmitri was slightly insulted. *Isn't there anyone capable of believing me to be the lover or husband of this woman?* he thought. But instead of correcting the driver's perception, it was easier to just agree with the concept.

"Yes," he said, "It is my daughter. I don't trust the man she is with."

"Why don't you just go and tell her to come home with you?" asked the Cuban with logical directness.

"Can't," prevaricated Dmitri "She is twenty-four and can get married if she wants to without my permission. If I confront her, she will be angry and embarrassed, and hate me."

"You are a good man, Dmitri," the Cuban said with approval.

"I promise you, we will not lose them," vowed the cabby, whose name was listed as Alphonso Morales on his posted license.

Alphonso was as good as his promise. He stayed just far enough back to remain unsuspected, and yet, they never lost sight of the limousine. They drove for a long while. First, through the convoluted squares by the club, later on the coastal US 1 south. The limo left US 1, also called S. Dixie Highway, cutting over to the beach, stopping on the pier in front of the Princessa, a 200-foot luxury yacht.

"Damn, your kids are not going home. They are going to lose some money. This here is one of the finest and biggest gambling establishments in Miami, ten-thousand square feet of any game you want to play," Alphonso informed him.

Dmitri groaned. "Now what are we going to do?"

"Nothing," said the practical Cuban. "I am a father. I know how you feel. May the devil take all good-looking young men!" He turned to his fare and a gentle smile covered his wide face. "I am turning off the meter. So this will cost you nothing, nada. When they come out I will turn on the meter and we will follow them again."

"Thank you. Thank you very much for being so nice to a perfect stranger." Dmitri, humbled by so much good will from a cabbie of all things, was deeply touched.

"De nada! Business is slow tonight anyway, and I have three daughters. I know you would do this for me."

Alphonso backed the cab away from the ship and parked under a palm tree. They had a nice view of a slice of Biscayne Bay, shimmering with the reflected lights of the city, and a great view of the ship, lit up glitzy like a Christmas tree. Savoring the view, they sat companionably for a while. They talked about fishing: It was lousy in the bay where all the eelgrass was dying and not that great oceanside anymore either.

"Too many damn tourists and the charter boats taking them out are after fish. Every day that God makes these boats go out to fish—damned, it never ends."

"Yea," growled Dmitri, "and a few miles out float the real menace. There are the boats, which haul in anything their illegal nets catch."

"The Coast Guard is too busy catching dope smugglers and Cubans to pay attention to the fishing," laughed Alphonso. He admitted, "Many years ago I, too, came illegally to Miami on a small fishing boat. Thank God I escaped the Communist pig, Castro."

Dmitri commiserated, and they sat silently for a moment listening to a Cuban radio station. Irina and her beau chose this exact moment to sway, while tightly joined, down the gangway connecting ship and dockside. Halfway down the ramp their bodies separated, and although it was close to sunrise the girl almost danced beside the tall man walking down the ramp.

"Ah," sighed Alphonso, "they are so beautiful and full of energy when they are young. Not like we are—gray and tired." Had he only known how deeply he wounded Dmitri with these words. Worst of all, there was nothing Dmitri could say in his defense. After all, he was playing the roll of father, and damn it all and truth be told, he had a daughter older than Irina.

Once more they went off in pursuit. Cautiously they followed the limo through two side roads back onto South Dixie Highway, turning north, then south. They traveled about six miles when suddenly the limo turned toward Coconut Grove, a very exclusive old area of Miami. Once off the main drag, the taxi followed an old, established, gently curving road. Huge old trees, gnarled and rich with large leaved foliage, hung over both sides of the street shutting out most of the morning's early light. Wide lawns swept from the curbs to beautiful mansions, some of them old and stately like women of a certain type whose looks intensify with age.

They followed the limo into a new drive, and found it parked a third of a mile down.

They saw Irina and her beau leave the car, walk across an expanse of lawn, and disappear behind a high white wall. The limousine drove off. After waiting for a while, Alphonso eased the car down to the exact spot of the couple's departure.

"I think that is the house," he said, pointing.

"Yes, that is the one."

The building, a huge mansion, built from coral rock like so many homes in the area, was half hidden behind a tall wall. Inset into the wall, flanking the driveway, were two colossal lions, holding an ornate, black, wrought iron gate in their paws.

Dmitri wrote down the address, 21578 Palm Ave. They waited a while to see if this was only a temporary stop for the couple. However, when all lights had been extinguished in the house they decided their vigil was over.

The sun rose listlessly, amid a cloud bank over the Atlantic, as Dmitri, beaten and tired, crawled under the soft damask covers of his bed. Forced to conclude that Irina was not cut out to be the kind of wife he had hoped for—if, indeed, she would be any kind of wife to anyone, duplicitous as she was—he just wanted to sleep, clear his head, confront her and send her home.

After a few hours of dreamless sleep he awoke, showered, shaved, dressed and went in search of breakfast. Waiting for his food on a sunny terrace with a grand view of the beach and a goodly strip of water, he checked his watch and found that it was already eleven. *I am checking out of here,* he promised himself, *as soon as I get a hold of that woman.* How remarkable that overnight the adored girl had become "that woman."

Everything annoyed him this morning. Finding Irina to be a faithless, deceiving wretch had destroyed his usual sunny, albeit obsessive disposition. He found fault with perfect eggs, critiqued superb fruit and even complained about the innocent milk. No wonder that the waiter, a polite young man in Fontainebleau blue livery, finally looked askance at him.

Having devoured breakfast with his usual good appetite—his stomach never let him down, a very good attribute when you are in the Navy—he signed the bill presented by his spotlessly garbed and groomed waiter and walked with alacrity to the lobby. The lobby—all marble, oriental carpets, precious wood, and humongous flower arrangements—was seething with a crush of people.

From the babble of the crowd Dmetri learned that most of the ahs and ohs emanated from the mouths of a group newly arrived from Kansas. These good people were so impressed with the Fontainebleau they could hardly contain themselves.

Today four pretty, sophisticated looking young women manned the front desk. He introduced himself to one of the seemingly unoccupied sophisticated-looking maidens as the occupant of number 521.

"Ah, Mr. Pataklos," replied the well-trained receptionist. She was perhaps twenty-five years old, of medium height and slender. Her black hair was severely brushed from the face to show a pretty widow's peak, making her large brown eyes appear more dominant in her Hispanic face.

"I would like to have a look in Miss Sokolova's room, please," he announced. "Can you have someone come with me and open up?"

"I am sorry; sir, but I can do no such thing. Under no circumstance can you get into another guest's accommodation," frowned the Cuban maiden. He had pondered that she must be Cuban. Skintone, Spanish lilt and big eyes, she just had to be Cuban. He liked Cubans and was enormously attracted to their women. Perhaps his Greek blood responded to the kinship of shared sunny homelands, with the resulting dark, seething eyes and tempers. At this moment, however, he snapped waspishly, "Let me set you straight on a few things, miss." He took a deep breath of cool lobby air and continued.

"First of all, I am paying for that room—so it's mine to look through. Secondly, the person occupying it is in my custody. That is to say, I am responsible for her whereabouts and she seems to have disappeared. I need to see the room for clarification. If her belongings are there, fine, then she will be back. If they are gone— I am in trouble."

The receptionist looked uncertain as to what to do. Her sweet face, above the collar of an immaculate silk blouse, tightened with a frown. But her discomfort was fleeting. Her features straightened as if pressed by an iron into a commercial masque, and with obvious relief she sang out, "I will call the hotel manager instantly. I am quite sure he can help you with this." She sighed softly, another crisis passed on to the higher ups.

Moments later the manager crossed the lobby with long, seemingly unhurried steps. He was a man in his forties, endowed with Scandinavian blue eyes and blond hair, sharply parted on the left. He wore a more expensive, sharper version of the hotel's ubiquitous suits for the staff—dark blue instead of the lighter fountain blue, and approached with a "can do" air.

Without the slightest hesitation he said, "Mr. Pataklos, how can we help?"

Apprised of Dmitri's request and without waiting for long explanations, he commanded.

"Ms. Careras, the master key, please! I will escort Mr. Pataklos to the room in question."

"Careras, I was right," thought Dmitri. He followed the manager who walked before him across the intricately woven oriental carpets of the lobby with measured, elastic steps.

Arriving in Irina's room, they found that every mote of her four-day presence had vanished. The room had been thoroughly cleaned and looked untouched by any mortal. It was a neat trick to make all the guests think they were the first to stay here. Dmitri wandered into the bathroom where a flotilla of perfume, foundations and clarifying lotion bottles had until recently made their home under the mirror. Gone were the suitcases that seemed to have sprouted young in Miami, and gone were the uncounted pairs of shoes to which Irina was so attached

A huge sigh escaped Dmitri's breast. "How on earth did she get all her things out unobserved," he mused. "I should have noticed something. Such a thing can not be accomplished at a moments notice."

With a desperate air he explained his predicament to the sympathetic manager. "I am responsible for the damned woman," he moaned. "What am I to do now?"

The manager, used to countless heartbreaks, turned to him with the manner of an undertaker comforting the bereaved.

"Terrible, terrible, Mr. Pataklos! I shall go and see what the staff might have observed. Anything unusual shall give us more of a lead."

"I will be on the terrace, having an espresso," said Dmitri, sounding depressed.

"I will be reporting shortly, but I cannot promise anything." With these vague words the manager left. Dmitri retraced the steps he had taken earlier for breakfast. The same waiter as before, his face set, came to take his order. Dmitri felt ashamed for his earlier boorish tiff and said, "Espresso, please, and my apology for my surliness earlier this morning. I had some very unpleasant discoveries."

"No problem, sir," said the waiter with just the slightest smile. He came across jerks all the time, but this one did not seem to be one of them. He expected a guilt-sized tip that would make up for the guest's earlier behavior.

Dmitri surveyed the happy, tanned people surrounding him on the terrace. They had pre-lunch cocktails, were chatting while watching the tide come in on the beach. All of a sudden he felt terribly alone. Today the waves were larger than usual. *There must be a disturbance somewhere in the Caribbean,* he thought; as an old sailor, he paid attention to such things.

But this was only the fleeting observation of a mind preoccupied by weightier concerns. It had finally dawned on him that Irina's disappearance presented more than just a missed opportunity for marriage. No, as tragic as that was, and as used and as hurt as he felt, more troublesome was his problem with the ICE.

He knew that he was pledged to deliver the unscrupulous woman back to these powerful people in three weeks, but moment-by-moment his hope faded that she might return to him. Her escape from him had obviously been planned, perhaps as long ago as the day she put her ad in the bride magazine; just as a poor American clown like him had planned for a foreign bride. He had been preordained to procure a visa for her, getting her into the Promised Land. America was a land so free and unobservant of its own laws that foreigners planned with impunity to get there illegally and disappear into the population without further consequences. This casual freedom was very unlike Russia, where such a deed would be savagely punished.

The thought that he had been nothing but a pawn in another's game, to be discarded at the pleasure of the queen, depressed him even more. Into his gloomy thoughts slid the impeccable figure of the manager.

"Mr. Pataklos, I am glad to find you comfortable. I had good luck with my inquiries."

"Please, have a seat while we talk," begged Dmetri in a subdued voice.

"Thank you. I shall sit a moment. This might take a while and I shall be glad to be off my feet." He sat across from Dmitri where he could observe most of the guests on the terrace and a sliver of blue ocean.

"It seems that Miss Sokolova has been observed by our staff, leaving the hotel every night between three and four in the morning. She always carried a suitcase, returning thirty to forty minutes later without a case. My men thought this was suspect, but they are trained to allow our guests the utmost freedom and never interfere unless they think there is a crime involved. Since Miss Irina only removed her own things, the men had nothing to object to. However, they thought she was acting highly irregular."

"That explains it," moaned Dmitri, touching his forehead as if in pain. "That's why I slept like a log and felt so groggy and hung over in the morning. It wasn't the liquor; I can drink with the best of them. She must have slipped me something."

"Permit me the question. What was your relationship with Miss Sokolova?"

"I was going to marry her. We were looking to determine whether we were suited to each other. Looks like she thinks she isn't. I suspect she made other plans a long time before coming here." Dmitri sighed—long and despairingly.

"I feel like a fool now, but I thought that there was a possibility. She is Russian, you know." The last statement was not posed as a question—more as an explanation for the play that had unfolded before the hotel manager and his staff.

"Oh, I understand!" the manager's inscrutable face suddenly showed empathy.

"We have a huge Russian émigré population in Miami, especially from Georgia and the Black Sea region. They love the sun with the same fervor as we do. Some of these people are assets to the US; many more are unsavory elements of the Russian mafia."

He got up from his seat and said in parting, "Be careful Mister Pataklos. I hope they did not get too much of your money."

Left to stew by himself, Dmitri came to the conclusion that the situation needed to be handled immediately. He had facts. She had deserted him, fled clandestinely with all her belongings, including his lavish presents. He had only one clue to go on—an address. He checked out of the hotel, collected his car and drove straight to the offices of the ICE. Located in the heart of Miami, the offices were part of office complexes—huge, rectangular concrete boxes, dominating this part of town. The ICE building distinguished itself by a broad walk-up. Twenty wide steps or more led to its large, dark, brown doors where golden seals proclaimed that behind their symbol the offices of the Immigration and Customs Enforcement and Naturalization Service could be found.

Dmitri knew the routine to be followed; however, it was close to the noon hour when the place closed for lunch and he needed to see Irina's caseworker in a hurry. Therefore, he anxiously approached one of the uniformed officers walking the marble entry hall.

"I must see Mr. Rogerson as soon as possible. This concerns a Russian citizen that fled my custody and is now on the run."

The officer, an older man with the soulful eyes of a blues singer, briefly considered the matter. He then said with military precision "Please, wait here, sir. I will be right back."

He returned a moment later. "That better be important," he admonished. "I got you three minutes with Mr. Rogerson, so be brief!" He gave a slight wave with his hand in the direction of Rogerson's office.

Taking the hint, Dmitri trotted more than walked to the office and knocked. Asked to enter, he walked up to a massive but scarred desk behind which the agent sat in a deep leather chair. Rogerson was seated before a window that almost took up the entire wall. He threw Dmitri a look that said, "This better be good!" He was a man in his late fifties with a receding hairline, a broad face and a build as massive as his desk. It was well known that in his younger years he was in enforcement and had taken down many a strong man going wrong. From these times stemmed his delight in teaching law-breaking punks that there could be real power in enforcement. His steel-blue eyes gave the message, "Don't bullshit me! I have heard it all! No, overstaying your visa will not gain you citizenship!" He gave Dmitri an exquisite look of distaste and said, before Dmitri could open his mouth, "Oh, it's you! So the bride took a powder already, or so I was told."

"Yes, Mr. Rogerson." And before he could be interrupted Dmitri spilled out his sad tale ending with, "I have the address. You can just send some agents over there and apprehend her."

As he listened, Rogerson got redder and redder in the face. So that by the end of the tale he was almost apoplectically blue. He had been appalled by the whole silly bridal business in the first place. These stupid men with their asinine dreams of foreign bliss, who brought their troubles into the lives of Immigration officers made him and his fellow agents sick to their stomachs. Who were these besotted, ill-begotten outcasts anyway that they could not find a woman of their own breed and culture? Why were they so imbecilically incapable of perceiving that most of the damned brides were nothing but whores willing to lay their bodies down for perverts, old goats and misfits to gain citizenship and monetary gain?

That, at least, was Rogerson's perspective. During the length of his long tenure he had seen very little to discourage this rather bleak view. He had a German homosexual, an American whore in tow, apply for a lengthened visa to marry the hired "bride" who had been paid off with three thousand dollars as investigators found later. He had seen some women trying twice to get married to foreigners in four years time. And then there were legions of love-starved men and their mail order dreams. Picking out wives in picture magazines was obscene—and that was that! Holding this view, his mounting anger now came to bear on hapless Dmitri:

"You say what? You have an address and we can pick her up there?" he roared with a force that rattled the huge window and sent papers flying across his desk. She can be with the fucking Russian mafia for all we know! I am not sending my men into a shoot out with the Russian mob for your mail-order plaything."

Dmitri felt once again like a young inconsequential, stupid navy sailor in front of an irate captain.

"Do you remember, sir," Rogerson hissed the "sir" like a cobra ready to strike, "that I tried my damndest to dissuade you from this harebrained scheme. I told you that I could not withhold the visa from you, but that I would, however, hold you personally responsible if any funny business occurred.

Before his blazing anger, Dmitri shrunk to half his size. Rogerson drew an enormous breath and went on with deadly calm, "Here is what's coming down, my man: You go and get that woman back to my office so we can put her on a plane back to Russia after the obligatory hearing."

Dismayed, Dmitri mumbled that this would be too hard to for him to accomplish, which drew a new gust of ire from the agent.

"I don't give a flying leap how you accomplish the deed," he roared. "Do you understand me? Just get her here! If you don't, by God, I will have you in court for alien smuggling. Who knows, maybe you are in cahoots with her. Good day!"

Rogerson reached for the disordered papers on his desk, and Dmitri found himself dismissed. He reached his car not knowing how he had gotten there. His head was reeling with the responsibility that had just been heaped upon him. Russian mafia! Not sending his officers into a shoot out …! Dear God, this sounded serious. No, much more, it sounded damned dangerous.

What on earth could he do to get Irina back and in front of Rogerson's desk? He was nothing but a fool duped by a Russian beauty with a plan to join what appeared to be her lover, using him as the proverbial mule to pull the cart out of the dirt. As he pondered why the Russian lover might not have applied for her visa, the believability of the mafia thing became more certain. Of course, a man with a record would not step into the limelight; chances were that Irina's lover was also illegal and perhaps wanted by the FBI or the police.

Oh God! Oh my, what to do? He was nothing but an aging re-
tiree. All of the connections he once had and could have drawn on
for help were gone. In his younger years he had known a bunch of
rough and ready guys who would have looked upon the tussle to
rip a woman from the Russian mafia's clutches as an opportunity
for a lively Saturday night's entertainment—but now, he knew nada,
nothing, no one.

The house in Coconut Grove into which Irina had disappeared
looked patrician. Yet, why was an upstanding citizen's home fortified like a prison? Dmitri realized that he would never make it past
the front gate. How many people were living in the house anyway?
What was the chance that Irina would willingly walk out of there
with him if he came to call on her? Zilch! She had drugged him,
giving him the illusion that he actually had sex with this goddess.
She had deceived him as to her status and standing in the world and
then, adding insult to injury, fled in the deep of the night feigning
illness. Traitress! He realized how much it suddenly mattered to him
that she must be brought to justice. Back to Russia with the Communist Jezebel! Have her marry KGB instead of Russian mafia.

Steaming thus, he was still sitting in his car, both hands on the
wheel to keep himself from trembling with fright and anger. He
had only felt like this once before in his life. When, as a young en-
sign, he had become distracted and thrown all engines on his ship
into reverse for just one fleeting moment. That moment, however,
had been long and hard enough to foul up all of the ship's operations, causing chaos among all ranks.

On that occasion he received such a frightful dressing down that
it seemed to be the last judgment. Today's problem ranked right up
there in seriousness. However, the consequences were easier to deal
with then—at least, that is what he thought in retrospect.

As he sat and stewed, it had escaped his notice that a cab pulled
up in the spot before him. An amply endowed Cuban matron left
the confines of the cab and grandly walked up the impressive staircase to the ICE offices. The cabbie left his vehicle. He stretched

his square, muscular body in the bright sunlight, walking back and forth. He passed Dmitri's car twice before he noticed the features of the occupant. But once he did, he stopped short and knocked on the tightly closed window, because inside the air conditioning was going full force.

Dmitri looked up and saw with pleasure and relief that it was Alphonso from the night before, and not some meter-enforcing maid.

"Alphonso!" he cried out, lowering his window. "What are you doing at the ICE offices?"

"Not me, it is a cousin I am bringing here today. She needs to finish some paper work before she is totally citizen. But what are you doing here?"

"Do you have a moment? Yeah? Well, then come sit in the air for a while and cool off and I'll tell you everything."

Dmitri hung his head as they sat there and said, "I owe you an apology because I lied to you when I saw you last. I left you in the belief that the young woman we followed to Coconut Grove was my daughter. Well, she isn't. She is a woman from Russia I had hoped would marry me. I felt like a cradle-snatcher when you spoke of a daughter and so I said nothing, leaving you with the wrong impression."

Embarrassed Dmitri looked down, studying his brown, work-worn hands.

"I thought something like that was going on," said Alphonso, "because at one point you talked like an angry husband and not like a father at all."

Relieved that the burden of lying had been removed, Dmitri brought Alphonso up to speed on his predicament. They sat for a moment in thoughtful silence until Alphonso interrupted the calm saying, "I think I know what you need. You need a detective, someone who can find out things for you. Who can spy in places where your face is known. Someone has to keep an eye on the illusive Irina before she skips out for another place."

"Damn! You are right that is just what I need! Help, I need help."

"If you trust me, I know the perfect man. It's my wife's cousin, Raphael Mendoza. He works for a detective agency in Homestead and I would trust him with my life. He is a solid, honest man who knows right from wrong and likes to be on the side of the good Lord."

"Oh, God, I do need someone like him. How do we find him in a hurry? There is little time to lose. The sooner I deliver Irina to Rogerson the sooner my trouble is over"

It turned out that hiring Raphael Mendoza was easier than getting home that day. Alphonso used his cell-phone to make a number of calls and an hour later they met Raphael under the thatch of a Tiki Bar by the ocean.

"Can do," said the detective after he had been briefed in great detail. Of course, he, too, was of Cuban descent. He was a tall, thin man, with well-groomed, healthy black hair laying about his oval face. His eyes were enormous, burning into the very soul of the person he eyed. He was dressed inconspicuously, tan Dockers, a yellow T-shirt and brown loafers.

He had the amazing ability to fold himself into a small space, making him seem to disappear. When Dmitri shook his hand he found amazing strength in the grasp, leading him to believe that the detective was very strong. Despite his emaciated appearance, Raphael was good looking. Dmitri thought he was the type of man whom some women find very attractive. He seemed energetic. Yet he also had a thoughtful streak, hinting at a trustworthy, resourceful and intelligent mind. Dmitri was well pleased with Raphael.

"I charge four hundred a day plus expenses. That okay with you? In return I give you every evening a detailed report on all developments. I work with a group of people to whom I look for backup if trouble develops. That's extra, of course. I will check with you ahead of time, if I can. Also you must agree to cover expenses arising from logistical problems and perhaps needed machinery, this could be tricky. We once had to use a crane to enter an apartment in a high-rise."

"That's fine with me," agreed Dmitri, who would agree to any amount to bring back Irina, finishing the entire horrid tale. A while back he had calculated the cost of his failed marital adventure, toting up a cool thirty-five thousand dollars. His frugal soul groaned under the burden. Visa and document costs had been only the beginning. Added to that came the charges for airplane tickets, hotel, food, clothing and presents. The little voice of reason in the back of his brain wailed, *You idiot! You could have bought the Boston Whaler, the expensive model, you always wanted, for that money. Now it's gone, thrown at an unthankful, cheating tramp. And that is not even the end of the spending yet!*

Outwardly he smiled, however, and voiced that there should be no concern about the money as long as they got Irina back.

"Well, since you agree to my terms, and I believe that I can deliver Irina into your hands, there is only one thing to be done. I need you to sign this document after you read the terms." Raphael left the Tiki hut to retrieve the contract from his car and a moment later presented it to Dmitri saying," I can begin working for you today, if you want me to. My agency just finished a big case, and although I wanted to take a week off, I will work your case, because it should not take that long."

Dmitri was only too glad that the investigation commenced at once. "This suits me perfectly," he agreed, while signing the document and making out a check for a five-hundred-dollar retainer.

After paying their tab the men left. Their shoes were crunching the ubiquitous white crushed coral rock that covered the walkway to the parking lot. By now the temperature had climbed to ninety-four; the humidity was high. It was time to retreat into air-conditioned shelters. Before parting, the men agreed that Dmitri should return home and receive, if possible, his first report at nine in the evening.

It seemed to Dmitri that never before could an old navy officer have been so happy to see his home among the Palm trees, as he was that day. Carrying his small suitcase into his own bedroom, he sighed with pleasure and relief. He ticked off the reasons for his well-being: there was no Irina here now for one. There was comfort, clean, simple, functioning simplicity for another—that was the ticket for an old salt. Although Dmitri was frugal, he was not penurious. His furniture, bought under the watchful eye of his wife, consisted of lovely rattan pieces, cushioned and upholstered in colorful island chintzes and heavy Egyptian cottons. On the walls hung some good seascapes and lifelike replicas of great trophies. They were both replicas of fishes he had caught a long time ago and taxidermies of marlins, dolphins and bonefish. These trophies were so outstanding that today few people could catch anything of this size in the waters of the Atlantic.

He dropped his suitcase, changed into faded, slightly torn shorts; into a shirt, sporting splotches of brown marine stain, and his oldest pair of loafers. Attired thus, he suddenly felt better. Somehow the well-worn, comfortable clothes removed the unpleasant taste of the last few days from his palate. He felt nurtured, restored, surrounded by ease, by everyday calm.

In the kitchen he made himself a sandwich composed of thickly sliced Cuban bread, cold chicken, two slices of ham and for good measure, a slab of provolone. After he added sliced pickle, mustard and mayonnaise to the sandwich, the resulting culinary work could have easily fed three people. He cut his prize into three pieces for easier consumption, and carried it on a platter out to the screened porch, accompanied by a glass of beer and a bag of potato chips. This was his favorite spot where he could eat and see blue water, swaying trees and his trusty old boat.

At his neighbor's house, Martha's garage door closed. A moment later he saw her carrying two grocery bags up her steep steps. He had long ago set aside the old-fashioned customs of chivalry, finding that widows even as old as Martha preferred not to be a burden. They managed quite nicely on their own. Women of this independent type also knew when they indeed needed help, and were in no way ashamed to call volubly for assistance.

"I see you have safely returned from the "Brautshau," quipped Martha, using part of her long-forgotten German. "And I see you are still in one piece. So what are the Russian women like?" Martha laughed uproariously as she lugged her burden up the open, steep staircase.

Oh, damn, thought Dmitri. *Now she will be right over, giving me not a moment's rest until I tell her the whole shebang.*

He knew Martha well, because she came over in a flash. The moment she had stored her food, she joined him on the porch. He had barely managed to eat half of his treat when he was forced to relate the whole sordid story between bites. There was no way he could avoid leveling with his old friend.

Martha was a good listener and had the good grace not to laugh at certain comical points. After a while it felt quite nice to talk to her about the wretched trouble. He could tell her delicate things that he could not divulge to men. Best of all, at the most humiliating points, like the moment when he found that Irina had absconded with her possessions, leaving him without even so much as a good bye, Martha gave him sympathy and a smile instead of men's deprecating grins.

"Well, I am sorry," she said when the whole miserable tale had been concluded, "but as you well remember I thought that these communists should marry their own, instead of polluting our marriage pool. They only come here for material things—not for the love of you and the country."

Dmitri said nothing. What could he say?

"Would you like me to bring you some dinner later? Martha asked solicitously.

"No, no thanks, Martha. I am fine. I think I will make a batch of Cuban black beans, rice and jerked chicken."

"Fine by me," sang Martha as she skipped through the fence posts at the end of their properties. "Have a good night!"

Dmitri took a long nap. Then, with an ocean of time stretching before him, he busied himself with odd tasks around the place. He cleaned and oiled his ten-speed-bike and clipped the bougainvillea that grew on the south side of his house. He raked the coral rock by the street and then, bored, he began to cook his dinner.

After all the fancy stuff he had eaten with Irina, his heart and stomach required solid, earthy sustenance. During all his desperate puttering around, thoughts of his predicament never left him. As he mulled the facts over and over again, he began to feel like a hapless fool—stupid, gullible and old.

Had it been so wrong for him to want youth and beauty in his life again? Oh, he had heard over and over again that youth and age do not mix; that youth takes advantage of the achievements and the wealth age has accumulated. Yea, yea, yea, it all was true—and yet, he wanted it! He wanted youth! He ached to procreate again. The thought of a small child in his arms, a child to love and teach, made him desperate for new life. What was happening to him? He could not understand himself anymore. Could it be that he was just afraid of the inevitable—of death?

Was he trying to overcome his waning strength, the drying of his body's juices with the softness, beauty and strength of the young? *For heaven's sake,* he thought, *I am beginning to think of myself as a vampire, a bloodless creature seeking to fuel a dying carcass with another's strength?*

He shook himself vigorously, like a dog leaving the water, as if thereby he could shake off these morbid thoughts. *My God, I would sound like a ghoul were I to put these thoughts into words,* he quaked. *Am I getting altogether perverse?*

He probably would have continued his depressing introspection much longer had not a sharp odor awakened him to the fact that his black beans were turning to charcoal. He raced into the kitchen and put the pot with the sizzling, popping remains of his bean dish under the spigot, pouring water over the black mess.

With great detachment, yet filled with pleasure, he watched when the black crust hissed, shriveled and separated from the bottom. It came up, swimming in pieces atop the water. Under normal circumstances, ruining a dinner would have greatly annoyed him. However, since the incident served to end the fruitless examination of his psyche, he was almost pleased. Normally he was not introspective at all. Self-examination and ruminations about soul and spirit were quite foreign to him.

He was a man of facts, of real things; things he could hold in his hands, fix, use or on occasion break. However, waiting for news deciding his fate made him unusually anxious and thoughtful.

All the puttering, the preparing, cooking and eating his dinner—he started with canned beans the second time around—only saw him to 7:30 PM. By that time he was almost itching to hear from his detective Raphael.

"You hired a detective based on a cabdriver's word?" Martha had wailed earlier. "You are getting foolish, Pato," she said, using his nickname to show just how foolish he had been. His wife had used Pato only when he committed a major faux pas.

"No," he defended himself. "Not just a cabby's word. The agency Raphael works for is a major outfit in Miami. I have seen their ads, and they seem to be well regarded from what I read on the Internet only moments ago."

But now that he was alone at home with time on his hands to doubt his decision, he wondered if he had chosen well. Nervously he cleaned his dishes. He walked down to his boat, the Estrella, a sixty-five-foot motor sailing yacht. He checked the bilge pump and the mooring lines. All was in order. Back in the house he fixed himself a rum and coke to drink in front of the TV.

Barely submerged in the plot of a crime story, he heard the phone ring, shrilling him back to sordid reality. The ring sounded ominously loud in the quiet night air, because the stillness of the night added to his state of negative arousal.

"Mr. Pataklos," the operative's voice sounded excited, stressed even.

"Things are very interesting here in Coconut Grove! I checked with some area people, and here is what they know. The owner of the house is a Georgian Russian by the name of Petros Avarikidze. The neighbors do not know what to make of the people inhabiting the place." Here Raphael's cell phone went out. Dmitri cursed roundly. But it was only a moment later that Raphael came back on line.

"Can you hear me? Can you hear me?" he yelled at the top his lungs. "Yes, good, I am through the trees. Where was I?" Raphael recapped, "Oh, yes the neighbors. They don't know what to make of these people. There are loud parties, often. The neighbors are never invited. That's a big no, no, in Coconut Grove." Deep silence followed this remark.

Dmitri once again was cut off. When he came back on line, Raphael said, "There they are! Ten-four good buddy! I'll call back when I'm stationary. Right now I am in pursuit of Petros and Irina."

The line went dead and Dmitri felt as if he was caught in the middle of a suspense movie, when at the crucial moment of discovery the projector breaks down. He was still staring at the silent phone when a rebel yell from his neighbors across the canal shook him awake.

"Hey buddy, stop looking at the phone! Come over and have a drink! I just came back from Atlanta. Ten hours straight and I need a night cap."

"No, thanks, Brent! I had a rather interesting day myself, and need to take a rain check."

"Suit yourself, old man! You are missing fine rum but the offer stands for later."

Dmitri waited up until eleven, but there was no more interruption from the phone.

He crawled into his bed with agonizing slowness, having prolonged his ablutions ad nauseam. But it could not be helped, there would be no more news coming in tonight. Surprisingly, he fell asleep faster than he thought he could. He slept until late in the morning. He awoke with an almost guilty start and did, indeed, feel guilty when he saw the clock. It was already eight in the morning. Seldom had he slept past 5 a.m, the sailor's hour. It is the time when the watch changes; when the sea breathes, stretching itself like an awakened giant before the new day; when the dew begins to fall and all is becalmed.

This is also the hour which determines the problems that will befall the new day. It is the moment when winds, tides and rising warmth from the ocean conjure the beginnings of a hurricane or tropical disturbance. It is the hour when fish feed best. They use the morning gloom to look for food, after a night of dark, silent death by large predator's feeding on the unwary—the sleeping. Perturbed, he showered and shaved. He registered with annoyance a pain in his left shoulder. Damn, the same bursa acting up—inflamed once more.

Usually he had a good cooked breakfast of bacon, eggs, toast and fruit. Today, he wasn't in the mood. He was just about to carry cereal, milk and a grapefruit out to what he proudly called his "Lanai," when the phone rang.

"It's me, Raphael! I have to tell you some interesting things. I spent almost the whole night on your case and want to report before going to sleep. My wife, Isabella, is going to kill me. Instead of taking a vacation with her I am out all night again."

"Who is watching Irina when you sleep," asked Dmitri, alarm in his voice.

"No worry! Another guy from the agency is on it. We spell each other all the time, but to get back to important stuff. There is no doubt whatsoever that Irina is involved with the head of the Georgian mob. I watched the house round-the-clock. People coming and going all the time and the place is heavily guarded." Crackling in the phone announced a breakup of the connection.

A moment later Raphael's voice came back shouting, "Shit! Of all the things I have to deal with, the damned phone is the worst. Never mind, where was I? Oh, right, security. Yea, I counted at least four armed men circulating inside the perimeter of the wall. Also there is an armed guard at all times by the gate. Worst of all, they have three Doberman dogs running about."

Raphael spoke fast trying to avoid another break in communication. The phone hissed into Dmitri's ear. Raphael finally caught his breath. Returning, his voice sounded clearer. "Just as well that you never went there by yourself in her pursuit. You would have never made it past the gate. But you would have given away the fact that you are onto her. It's a plus for our side that they don't know that we know where she is."

For a moment both men silently processed this fact. Raphael broke the silence saying, "I have been wracking my brain how to get your girl out of there; but short of an outright armed assault, I don't know yet how to do that."

Dmitri envisioned having to storm the Russian mafia-fort and imagined the small army he might have to hire. A super-sized sigh escaped audibly from the depth of his breast.

"Don't sweat it yet, man. I will figure something out. I am going to consult with a few people on the matter. In the meantime we can just watch and see if they follow some pattern in their daily life, some regular proceeding, a weakness that we can exploit to launch a surprise action."

Raphael yawned loudly, adding comfortingly, "Don't be anxious. These things just take time. This is only day one," he laughed amusedly and shouted, "Hasta la vista," and hung up.

Compared to Dmitri's earlier feelings of depression the wave of despair now engulfing him was a monster. He thought back to the other time when he felt a wave would swallow him.

Once, when he and a buddy ignored the signs of a brewing storm while fishing at the edge of the Gulf Stream, they were surprised when suddenly amid the already high seas a wave came at them that looked to be twenty-five feet tall.

"Mother of God," yelled his friend Don. Then he steered straight into the towering wall of water. They came out alive thanks to the fine boat they had been using. It was small at twenty-eight feet.

Today his gut felt knotted up—just like then. Things had deteriorated from bad to terrible. The Russian mafia, five armed guards, if one counted the gate-keep, Doberman Pinchers and whatnots were surrounding the false bride, making recovery an impossible task. As he sat there worrying, brooding and mulling over the facts, there arose within him the will to see this thing through.

Dang it all, he probably could take the coward's way out and wash his hands of the whole thing. What could or would the courts do to him anyway? Look how they judged real horrible criminals—monsters who had killed multiple times or raped and robbed innocent citizens. Judges were lenient. They did not sentence the killers to the length of time deserved. In no time murderers were out on the streets again, looking for their next victim.

So, at the very worst, what could he expect? A fine? Community service, at most! Rogerson, had buffaloed him, sent him on an emotional stampede that could have been averted by rational thought. However, the stubborn streak in him came to the fore and he said to himself, "I was an idiot. I did this to myself and I will be damned if this woman gets the better of me. I may be older but I am not in my dotage yet. There has to be a way to get her back."

His depression lifted as he began to think how he could be an important part of the operation. After all, this might turn out to be a bit of fun and excitement, and wasn't that what he had craved these last years?

If only the cursed mansion bordered on water there would be ways to launch a naval operation. But unfortunately the fortified mansion sat in the middle of prissy Coconut Grove. As the day wore on his military training and the old fighting spirit asserted itself.

"Don't give up the ship," he hummed as he began to make plans for "eventualities."

It would not hurt to alert his friends, fishing buddies and navy friends. Once the thought hit him, he wondered how much water had flown through his canal since he had last heard from any of them.

The last reunion of his last command, the "USS Port Royal," a Ticonderoga class cruising vessel, had been five years ago. Regretfully, he considered that men were lousy when it came to keeping relationships going. Always busy, always thinking to make the call to a friend, and then forgetting it. It would not hurt to have his friends alerted. First off, he should call his friend Dan Heminger from long gone navy days. Suddenly the phone in his hand became heavy. Indecision wracked him. A little voice, stemming from a guilty conscience, fed his conflict.

The temptation to capitulate and allow the sordid affaire to run its course was overwhelming. Why did Rogerson make such a fucking deal about Irina anyway? Daily, thousands of illegal Mexicans, Cubans, Haitians and South Americans from any country in that hemisphere assaulted the borders of the good old USA with impunity. Once across the border, they disappeared into the fabric of the most tolerant but perhaps also the most stupid nation and were never found again. Unless they killed, raped and robbed—which they did more often than was reported in the local papers—no one cared what they did.

It did not matter that the illegals used falsified papers, false social security numbers and drivers licenses. Why should he, a law-abiding citizen sweat the little stuff and be concerned about just one woman? Why should he invest even more money in this stupid matter? At this point he had almost talked himself out of any responsibility for the running-amok Irina.

However, his fruitless ruminations soon ceased. He was an officer and a gentleman and this flagrant disavowal of duty, responsibility and honor did not fly on his flag. There was nothing for it; he had to get Irina back. He had signed for her—and that was it.

Besides, it irked him that this foreign babe had been running circles around him, and no one did this to him unpunished. No siree, Bob. Furthermore, she had a lover in a Russian mob. Ye, Gods, how much more criminal a case had to present itself before he took action? There was nothing for it; he needed help.

Phone in hand, he considered the changes in his life during the last five years. He was astonished by the magnitude of his life's upheaval. Yet, since things had happened incrementally over time, change also had been perceived almost imperceptibly. Examined in retrospect, however, these changes were impressive.

In a span of just five years he had retired from the Navy as a first officer. He could have had a captaincy if it had not been for just one unfortunate incident early in his carrier denying him the chance to rise to the greatest office, forever. Shortly after retiring he and his wife moved permanently to his present house on Key Largo. It had been their vacation retreat for many years before. He had enlarged the small structure, fighting the powers that controlled construction all the way. For many years Florida municipalities allowed any form of development. Their devil-may-care attitude led to unspeakable atrocities committed upon the environment. Building proceeded unchecked until the hapless keys were encrusted with human abodes, like a rock in the tide pool bristles with barnacles.

When the effects of the abuse of unlined septic tanks, crudely and cheaply dug, began to show up in the waters surrounding the keys; when the oily, chemical runoff from the roads, pounded daily by uncounted vehicles, was washed back into the mangroves by the tides, then attitudes changed. Suddenly the bureaucrats became the righteous keepers of the land. As always in officialdom, they went from one extreme to the other becoming ridiculous with their imposition of rules and fees.

Although advised by the neighbors to bribe the properly larcenous persons, he chose instead a knockdown, drag-out fight for what had once been adequate as a winter retreat but was confining when lived in permanently.

Having accomplished the remodel, there came a truly fine hour, when he went to Miami and bought the boat of his dreams. He picked her from hundreds, having finally located a private seller who had to sell because ill health forced him to move north. Many men sold their prize boats so they could move to where access to specialized hospital care was available. He remembered seeing her, "Estrella," sit there in her slip. Her proud main mast reached for the sky, her mahogany deck and railings were gleaming with immaculate marine finish. He noted her rudder, the motors that would propel her through blue waters should she become becalmed—and he wanted her with a powerful desire, as he had wanted few things.

Forever after he marveled at the ease with which he acquired the boat. Her previous owner, a fine old gent, with eyes as blue as the ocean on a cloudy day and thin white hair, still stood tall although leaning on a cane. He had found in Dmitri a kindred soul and let the beauty go for less than Dmitri could have hoped for.

Settled, with a larger house and boat, he and Theresa made more friends than they had been able to during their limited vacations. Then—disaster! Without warning Theresa was struck by lymphoma. Suddenly the relaxing, joyous life they had become accustomed to—the interesting shopping trips to Miami, the casual backyard parties, the exciting fishing trips, (when the fishing was good), the beautiful, calm sunset cruises in the Bay while sipping Chardonnay—all came to an abrupt end.

Instead of these pleasures, rushed commutes to Jackson Memorial Hospital three times weekly became the norm. Visits and treatments consumed most of the day. Afterwards, there was the two-hour drive back to Largo during the worst of the rush-hour traffic. Yet, he never grumbled or even felt put out by the demands made upon him. After all, Theresa had been the love of his life, the mother of his four children—until he made a mess of their marriage.

Looking back on his life he realized that he lost the wonderful life they had together, when he went and had a meaningless affair on the West Coast. The thing had lasted for one half of the year he was stationed in San Diego. In his mind he had excused himself, *You were an animal in heat. That's all.*

Theresa found out. He never forgot the look she gave him. She didn't cry, didn't say anything. She walked away, her head bowed and her shoulders sagging. No matter what he did, he could not get her to talk. He knew that she carried a grief too large to put into words. He was sorry, wanted to explain. She said, however, "I don't want to hear excuses. Absolution can be had only from priests."

She forgave him, said she wanted to stay married because of the children. And that was it. But from that day on she punished him in the worst way he could have imagined. She fed her body until it swelled and she became ungainly. It is unlikely that the unhappy woman did this deliberately. Perhaps she was just feeding the hole in her soul. But Dmitri could not know that. Psychology was not a subject he had ever studied. And so he chose to believe that she fed herself into obesity because she knew that he hated fat women.

Over time he came to see himself as the victim of her revenge. All he had wanted was to be forgiven and have his slim, beautiful wife back, the one his friends had envied him. She, who had prided herself on being pert, fit and slender always—had chosen to offend him every day with her distended body.

He confided to a friend, "It is not for her to get a divorce, and remove me, the object of her hurt and anger. No, that would destroy her family and that is unthinkable. For her children and grandchildren matter more than anything in the world. There could be no disruption in their world, a world complete with perfect grandparents, parents, aunts, uncles and cousins. But I, I suddenly don't seem to matter anymore."

Whenever he was in his other mind he reminded himself that he was the cause of the problem. He grumbled, he groaned—he stuck it out. They learned to patch the crumbling ruins, learned to make the best of it. And after years of pain, recrimination and finally apathy—Theresa died.

The horror! When he was in his "other" mind, he blamed Theresa for her illness, although he knew it was not so. But every so often the devil played with him, insinuating that being so fat must raise havoc with her body's systems. She had brought on ill-health with too much food and too little exercise. Furthermore, she had incurred heart problems. Combined with the obesity, wouldn't that be enough to bring on even further illness?

Somewhere along the way his love for her had dried like a plant in the desert, and been replaced by a sense of responsibility. By the time Theresa died, he almost felt relief. It was about a year into her illness that dreams at night began to haunt him, and daylight fantasies began to take over his days as well.

He would find himself working on the boat's machinery, dreaming that he had sex with lovely women and he began to talk to himself.

"By Jove, I deserve to live again," was one of his favorite beginnings. "It's time to take care of Dmitri," was another.

Thinking back to those days it dawned on him that his friends' lives probably had also been changed considerably. Bifurcated thinking prevented him from making the calls immediately. He agonized. What if by calling he became the confidant and recipient of lengthy family dramas. He recoiled at the thought. Did he really want to hear of other people's problems? Wasn't it enough that he had his own dramas, and did he want to make his friends privy to his own awful dilemma?

While ambivalently dithering about in his uncertainties, he had been sorting fishing lures, putting weights into the correct containers and spooling fishing line. His collection of fishing rods numbered in the thirties. Like some women, who can't control their desire for shoes, and possess many more pairs than they can ever wear, he owned more fishing rods than he would ever use.

In his shed, in wooden holders stood special rods for marlins and wahoo, the large pelagic fish. There were thin, delicate rods with fine low-gauge test line for snapper, yellow tail and complaining little grunts, and different rigs for bottom fish at great depth. He had them all. Fishing was his greatest delight. Whenever he found a very productive mound, hole, or rock pile in the ocean he carefully wrote down the coordinates of the spot and, over time, would visit it again. Some of the best environs he sought out many times during the year. Unfortunately, other skippers did the same thing. The competition for good fishing was fierce.

Finally, he stopped this mindless activity. With disgust he put the reel-checked rods back into the shed. He walked to the house and fixed himself a large cup of cocoa and drinking it on the porch he changed his frame of mind.

What's wrong with you? he chided himself. *These are your friends. They were very close to you not long ago. So why would you not want to share in their present circumstances.* He convinced himself that he could overcome his distaste of delicate, uncomfortable confidences if he had to; and perhaps talking personally about some matters would not be so bad after all. Had he not learned to open up to Martha and the Sorensens from across the canal?

He was suddenly convinced of his ability to deal with some other guy's personal problems if they were to bring them up. He reached for the phone, but before he could dial it rang.

"Hello Dmitri! Guess who? Your nephew, Jeremy." Dmitri held the speaker shut with his thumb and sighed. It was as if the devil ran this man's life. He would always turn up when least wanted. Damn it all to hell! Jeremy was his sister's son, and although he disliked him immensely he could not brush him off like the pest he was, because he adored his sister.

He had gotten to know Jeremy well for the first time after a few years spent at sea. Then the boy was already fourteen years old. A gangly youth of medium build, sandy haired and snooty, he had instantly awakened Dmitri's ire. Boy that kid had a mouth on him! He was bossy, impolite and an all around know it all. No topic could be broached without him knowing all and nothing about it.

Over the years not much had changed. Jeremy had become a medium-sized, tennis-playing—he always had to win—sandy-haired, twice-divorced, arrogant doctor with the ability to make saints reach for a weapon with which to smite him.

Gathering forbearance about himself like a cloak, Dmitri intoned with false enthusiasm, "Oh, hallo Jeremy. How are you?" After all, one cannot afford to alienate one's favorite sister by strangling her offspring with the phone cord; an act contemplated by Dmitri many times. Instead, he said politely, "What can I do for you today?"

"Oh nothing, Dmitri. You have done enough already! I cannot thank you enough for giving me the tip for the Russian brides."

Dmitri was thunderstruck. When he found his voice he yelled, "Whoa, hold on here! What are you trying to tell me? I should tell you my story first!"

"No, uncle, I must thank you. Thank you again and again. I followed your advice and looked at the bride magazine, and damned if I did not see one I fancied."

Dmitri groaned aloud. When he had given the idiot this information they had just had a conversation about nothing. Well, they talked about women and the lack of good ones; women that would fit a man's expectations, who still kept house and knew how to please a man. Like a mindless twit he had mentioned the damned Russian magazine and here were the unpleasant results.

"Jeremy," he shouted, "Don't tell me you contacted one of these women!"

"But of course I did. Why did you ever think I would not? And I am devilishly glad that I did. I thank you, because of you I am now married to the most wonderful woman in the world, and I wanted you to be the first one to know."

"Oh, God! Not that," groaned Dmitri. He didn't dislike Jeremy to the point that he would wish an Irina on him. Ignoring his uncle's groans, Jeremy mercilessly went on:

"You must remember Tatyana, page five, upper left?"

"Yeah, I do remember, the one on horse back?"

"The very one. I went to Russia, met her, fell in love and married her there."

"Oh, God, I will never be forgiven for that," cried Dmitri. That finally did it. Jeremy lost his patience. "What is all the groaning about? I thought you'd be happy for me! Where are some congratulations instead of all this negativity?"

Mustering a commanding voice, Dmitri informed Jeremy, "My dear boy. You were very, very hasty. Let me tell me what is happening to me right here in Florida." And then he proceeded to expound on his troubles in great detail, trying to impress his hapless nephew.

"Dmitri, old man, you have it all wrong," exclaimed Jeremy cheerfully. "Our situations are quite different. I am young and desirable. I am a doctor and a brilliant tennis player, while you, forgive me, are an elderly washed-up guy. Don't you see? No commonality."

"You fool!" bellowed Dmitri enraged by the merciless characterization. "Think again! The commonality is citizenship, getting into the country and money, of course. I bet my boat that the lovely Tatyana doesn't care one whit about you or the nation."

"Now you are insulting me and my beautiful wife," huffed Jeremy. "If you are like that I can't talk to you, much less invite you to the grand reception I have planned at the Beverly Hills Hotel. By the way, that was the reason why I called!" he snarled and slammed the receiver down with a resounding crash that reverberated in Dmitri's ear drum as he was left hanging on the line.

"Oh, dear, what have I done? I should have never told Jeremy anything. Particularly nothing to do with brides of any kind."

Jeremy was a general physician, with a decent practice in Riverside, California, who over time had become quite wealthy. He had married the head cheerleader of his high school; a feat all the more astounding, since the girl had never given him a second look until he had become a doctor. Then, when the girl against all odds had tried to make the marriage work, he had negated her efforts through his controlling behavior and arrogance.

At some point Claire realized that she would never have children or a normal family, for Jeremy had to be the Number 1 in the house—husband, child—God. At that time a good attorney helped Claire to get a divorce with a settlement hefty enough to have Jeremy yelp, "Castration!" Dmitri had met Claire only superficially, but he and his wife had liked her. Theresa, who had a feel for such things, thought Claire was a very nice woman and too good for

Jeremy. She had been proven right.

As Dmitri began thinking about the situation loud laughter overcame him. This affair was too precious. Yes, Jeremy, his sister's spoiled brat deserved the likes of Tatyana, Irina, Olga, or Elena … whatever her name might be.

He, for one, would be taking large bets that Jeremy was in for a deserved drubbing. Why did the fool have to go to Russia and marry the dame? Could he not have waited to find out more things? Like his uncle's miserable experience? Well, maybe the lesson taught by such a Russian teacher would be life changing.

Closing the Jeremy chapter, he went back to the chapter entitled Dmitri's Trouble. He finally dialed Dan Heminger's number. Heminger, a fellow officer serving on the Intrepid, had, upon retiring, moved to Jacksonville, Florida, where he owned a gorgeous house on the St. John's River.

To his surprise, Dan answered after the third ring. Dmitri had expected a machine, thinking Dan would be fishing—out and about on the ocean. Instead he heard Dan's genuinely pleased voice booming, "Dmitri, Jesus it's good to hear your voice again, old man." He had called Dmitri "old man" since the day Dmitri made first officer. Dan ended his carrier as second. Dan's navy life had been of much shorter duration.

The two friends had shared many adventures, a few frightfully ferocious storms, and an attack by gunboats off the coast of Vietnam. They participated in several rescue operations, aiding distressed and sinking ships. They did, to make a long story short, such deeds that bond men.

Then, of course, there had been the shore leaves. They went drinking together and had to defend themselves on a few occasions against assaulting thugs. A stress on their friendship was Dan's addiction to sex. He was always tempting Dmitri to follow him along on the seedy path to fornication. There were always willing women to be had wherever the ship went into port. But Dmitri, secretly appalled by the sleaziness of such encounters, and deeply in love with his wife, had resisted.

The one time Dan had succeeded and gotten Dmitri entangled with a woman, he deeply regretted the deed, for it changed Dmitri's wife and his life terribly and forever, and Dan had adored Theresa.

"How is it going? Are you alright?" By that he meant to subtly inquire how Theresa's death affected Dmitri.

"It's going alright. I am getting used to a new style of living. What's new with you?" Dan caught him up on his last years of life in a hurry. His wife was now a career woman. She had used the time after her children left home to go to college and get an MBA in accounting, and now owned one of the most successful businesses in Jacksonville.

"Would you believe Ada now makes the money and I stay home and cook her dinner?" Dan's booming laugh rang out like cannon fire. He proudly announced that he was a grandfather. His daughter, Katie, had two adorable daughters who had become the light of his days. On and on he went about all the glories in his life.

A moment later he grew quiet though, for no life shall end without a deep drink of pain, grief and bitterness. He recalled the death of his only son, a twenty-eight-year-old fighter pilot. "The thing that I cannot get over is the fact that Michael did not die in combat, for a great cause or even for something he loved doing. No, he had to be cut down by a good-for-nothing drunk." His voice still reverberated with pain after all the years that had passed.

"I know. Mike was a great guy and I know that it still must hurt like hell," commiserated Dmitri. He knew fully well that such memories never fade. At the time of Mike's death he had been nursing Theresa and, therefore, felt the young man's death more deeply than he would have otherwise. He went to the funeral and tried in his awkward way to comfort Dan. He understood that Dan sought validation for the hurt he still felt, that he needed to mourn his boy one more time.

"Hey, we are getting gloomy, old man!" Dan shook himself free of the emotions that had against all odds overwhelmed him.

"What's the purpose of your call? I know you didn't call to chit chat."

"Well," intoned Dmitri, "it's this dilemma of mine," and then he spilled the whole demeaning fiasco with Irina the Russian bride.

"The worst is that she not only made a fool of me, but that she is the bride of a Russian mafia chief. That just brings up gall in my craw. Would you be up for a spot of adventure and/or mischief?" Dmitri took a long breath and then delivered the hard stuff.

"Could get rough though. I haven't figured out any details yet, but I would like to know who might want to give it a go." Dan never hesitated, even for a second.

"Count me in, old man. I am dying of boredom here. Can you imagine that my day is filled with shopping, cooking and frigging vacuuming? Once in a while I get to fish, but most of the time it's driving the grandkids from Little League to piano lessons."

Friends

⊱⊰

DMITRI GRINNED WICKEDLY AS he hung up the phone. What a delightful picture! He could picture Dan in an apron vacuuming and cooking his wife's dinner. Hot damn, he was made to pay back for all his sins. The last time he had seen Ada she looked like a million. Once plump, shy-looking—like a pretty, faded rose—she had transformed herself, like a butterfly slipping from her chrysalis into a slim, svelte, coiffed woman in designer clothes and a strong will in her face.

Best of all was that he could count on Dan. Suddenly, a funny realization made him smile, cracking his face wide open. So he was an old fool—a total idiot perhaps—but that was okay. For the last two weeks, beginning with Irina's arrival, he had been more alive, feeling shocked, excited, titillated, elated, angry, abused, detested and abandoned in a big emotional stew, than in the last five or ten years.

So, perhaps the experience was worth the many hassles, the upheavals—everything—just as long as the ending would be a happy one with the girl on a plane back to Russia. Dmitri was happy with the world. So happy, that he needed sudden strong hunger pangs to make him aware that it was way past his lunchtime, almost mid-afternoon.

Hastily, he slapped an indifferent sandwich together, searching the fridge for a hard-to-find Coke. He loved to drink rum and Coke in the evenings when there were no women around; otherwise, he would gladly have a glass of wine with them.

After sating his appetite, he began calling old friends once more. Next on his list was the petty officer of the Intrepid.

John Morrell was a marvel with all things mechanical. What he was unable to mend in the engine room necessitated a trip to a navy facility. The skipper knew his talents and appreciated Morrell's qualities. He gloated to other skippers about his few maintenance calls in port, other than those scheduled.

As he dialed Morrell's number, Dmitri's mind conjured up his face. John Morrell was a small, wiry man. He seemed to be made of bone, long, stringy muscles and tough brown skin. Sparse, thin, red hair thatched his head above a broad, high forehead that seemed to take up half his face. But the most riveting thing in his face was his eyes. Brown with green flecks, they were alive, searching, probing, forever solving problems and puzzles.

His personality matched his spare physical features. Taciturn and reserved he moved focused through life always doing, fixing, achieving. On the few occasions when he chose to speak on a subject, he expressed himself thoughtfully, knowledgeably, and with brevity. At times, when relaxing with a beer in his hand, the right company and a light mood prevailing, he could come up with surprisingly ironic and funny comments.

Dmitri remembered that John's wife, Kelly, whom he had met once, could have been taken for his sister. On that occasion Kelly had picked John up in Key West, for a vacation. The entire ship's crew, present at the meeting, was struck by their similarities.

Kelly was a redheaded wraith, whose hair in contrast to John's was abundant and curly. She was slim and spare and had the same searching brown-green eyes flanking a cute, upturned nose. She had the perfect, delicate, white skin of an Irish redhead, and a small, upward curved mouth, giving her a delectable, pert and pretty look.

Like her husband, she was an over-achiever. While John was a mechanical marvel, Kelly was a culinary wonder. She owned a restaurant in St. Petersburg that she had acquired long ago when it was a rundown joint. Faithfully each month she deposited the pay John sent her, and over time turned the restaurant into the best seafood restaurant in the area.

John, much like Dan, was glad to hear from Dmitri. "I just told Kelly that it is a crying shame that we never see anyone from the ship anymore. And she cut me short saying, "If you want to see them, you have to invite them. That will do it." She thinks that we should meet for dinner, here in the joint."

Dmitri could not figure how John could denigrate Kelly's lovely restaurant "Frutta del Mare," appointed in rustic Italian décor, with the horrid sobriquet "joint."

Catching up on family details, Dmitri heard that the Morrells had a boy and a girl both studying engineering at MIT. There were no grandchildren yet, nada.

"Well, the two of you are young and can wait," quipped Dmitri, alluding to the fact that Morrell at fifty was the youngest of the group.

"Sure, sure, yet often I don't feel so chipper and frisky any more. But forget age, what's up with you Pato?" John remembered the nickname Theresa bestowed upon Dmitri when she was annoyed with him.

Once more Dmitri had to project the ridiculous, strange turn of events in his life—the Russian bride. To his chagrin, the usually serious, quiet John began laughing like a loon.

"Oh, Pato, that's rich. A Russian beauty and gangster bride and you fell for her!" By now he positively roared with amusement.

"Come, come now! Contain yourself. This could have happened to anyone."

"Yes, but you are a grandpa, Pato. You ought to know better!" Slowly, after a few guffaws, his hilarity subsided. Then, in his normal sober tone he said, "Count me in! I need a break. Since I left the Navy, I have been running a car repair shop and it is like this—cars bore me to death. Give me a nice, big engine room any time." He sighed, "When is the thing to go down?"

"Don't know yet. The detective will tell me when we have a pattern established. I'll stay in touch."

The Final Choice

❧

BETWEEN THE THREE FRIENDS, consensus was established that they would invite only one other man from their ship's crew to be a part of what they hoped to become an adventure. This chosen one was seaman first class Butweiler. Robert Butweiler, by rank a seaman first class, would not have been a fellow in this group. He had, however, won the liking and respect of the others with his knowledge of the ship, the way he performed his duties, and last, but not least, for his sense of humor and his bravery.

Etched in their memory was one occasion when in foul, rough weather a man went overboard. The poor devil was a new seaman on his first tour of duty whom everyone knew as Jimmy D. Fortunately for him Butweiler had witnessed the event, for no one else had seen him going into the drink. Robert reacted without losing even a moment. He raised the alarm—Man overboard!—while simultaneously tossing floating devices into the churning sea in the direction of the barely visible bobbing head.

The captain instantly executed rescue operations, which meant that all engines had to be stopped. Then, with the starboard engines and the powerful bow thruster alone, he turned the ship; and with all engines racing, he ran full force in the direction where Jimmy D. had last been spotted.

In the meantime, the hapless young man had managed to swim

to a circular float to which he precariously clung. Besides gaining a bit more safety, he had also gained more visibility to the spotters on the ship. The waves were huge, so that at times he disappeared in the vastness of the troughs. As the ship came closer the men could see that whenever he emerged from the ocean valleys his face was rigid with fear and his eyes looked wild and despairing.

They tried the maneuver of turn and return three times and failed. They got no closer to their man. It seemed as if at each approach the bulk of the ship pushed him farther away. That's when Butweiler could stand it no more.

"Permission to go in the water and rescue," he yelled to the captain. "Permission granted," came the reply.

By now the deck of the Intrepid was crowded with every man not needed below to run the ship; all of them were filled with gut-wrenching pity for the kid in the water. Each and everyone could well imagine himself to be in the hellish cauldron and desperately wanted Jimmy D. safely back on board. Morrell was among them, watching as Robert was stripping his clothes off as fast as he could.

Stripped to his shorts many an envious glance fell upon his perfect body. He appeared to be a Greek sculptor's model in antiquity. He was perfectly proportioned along Greek rules of perfection. Of medium height, well-muscled, without appearing muscle-bound, with clear-cut features, a straight nose and well-defined mouth, he filled the bill of a very attractive, yet powerful man.

Morrell, never idle, had meanwhile located a likely rope and harness. Robert slipped on a life-vest and the harness and Morrell attached him to the rope. Once again the captain called out commands to the engine room, and the ship's engines whined as they were pushed fore and into reverse in short order for the sharp turn needed to close on the sailor.

At the right moment, the ship closed on Jimmy D. yet was not too close, and Robert jumped over the side. It was a dangerous thing to do, for the waves could push a man into and under the ship or into the churning propellers. But Robert got lucky and began to swim with mighty strokes toward the exhausted Jimmy.

As the ship's bulk had kept Jimmy from approaching, it now served to push Robert away, toward the kid. A few times he disappeared in the huge waves. The crowd watched breathlessly as he powered his way through the waves. A cheer went up among the men when Robert finally got a hold of Jimmie's float. Moments later he was able to attach Jimmy with a line to his harness.

Attached to the float and each other, the two men began the horrific swim back to the boat. The captain idled the engines in an attempt to keep the boat steady. Men on board had taken hold of the towline and began to pull the two men toward the boat. In their excitement they pulled too fast almost losing the men in the waves.

"Easy, easy does it," shouted Morrell conducting the rescue with the delicacy of a symphony. Long ago he had directed the men to toss a long rope ladder over the side, now it bobbed in the waves. Closer and closer the swimmers came, encouraged by their shouting, hooting and howling shipmates.

There still were plenty of anxious moments because getting a hold of the elusively swishing ladder seemed impossibly tricky. The captain's superb knowledge of the roiling seas and the huge ship came to the fore as he maneuvered the engines, steadying the ship as much as possible. At last Robert got a hold of the ladder that seemed to have a life of its own, and began to push the exhausted Jimmy upward. An impossibly long time later, helpful hands were finally able to pull them aboard.

They got their backs slapped, were cheered, covered with warm blankets and carried by eager hands to the mess for hot drinks and medical attention. The captain himself came to thank Robert and express his gladness to have Jimmy D. safe aboard. A man's man, he knew what men needed and ordered drinks all around for a job well done.

Yes, thought Dmitri, awakening from this memory, *Robert Butweiler is definitely the man we want in our group*. The phone rang before he was able to contact the worthy man.

"Dmitri, this is Raphael. I have some interesting news. The man doing my off-shift reported that two cars left the compound shortly before eleven this morning and went to Key West. He followed them all the way down but lost them in the confounded traffic snarls of that city."

Raphael sighed disgustedly and resumed, "However, my guy was thinking. Because there is only one road in and out of the Keys, he stationed himself at the exit of Bahia Honda State Park and waited. Two hours later they came back."

"What the deuce would they want in Key West? One does not go there just to have lunch. It's too damn long a drive for that," growled Dmitri.

"Who knows? To pick up a load of dope, smuggled things like Cuban cigars, rum perhaps? We shall find out whether this a regular run."

"I assume Irina was with them?"

"Yes, and she was the only woman so one assumes this was not a social event."

Dmitri informed Raphael that he was organizing a small force for extra man- power should it be needed.

"That is excellent, but something tells me we might need even more clout. My man, Ignacio, said there were nine men besides Irina making the trip. Avarikidze, Irina and two others rode in an Infinity Q 45, while six of them traveled in a Lexus SUV."

Dmitri and the detective agreed they would watch, wait and look for more professional manpower. "In the meantime, I am glad that you can count on your friends."

When Dmitri called Robert in the evening the guy was almost delirious to have a chance at mischief, a brawl, a rescue—anything at all that promised excitement. He had been divorced for the last eight years. His girlfriend just left him because he did not want to get married right now, and his job at an export-import firm was ex-periencing a seasonal slump.

"Hell, yeah, we will get the Russian babe back," he avowed, "and it will be interesting to see what the Georgian mafia looks like."

Dmitri went to bed that night feeling content, sated with satisfaction in the knowledge that his trust and friendship had been placed in the right people so long ago. His friends were real—not of the fair-weather kind that one finds so often.

The Plot Thickens

❧❧

COMPARED TO THE PREVIOUS weeks, the next few days were anticlimactic. Nothing happened on the mafia front. The daily reports told of Irina walking the neighborhood, always accompanied by a leashed Doberman; they told of a few shopping excursions to Miami and dining at fancy restaurants.

The van with two of the men had left the compound a few times; however, since Irina was not with them, Raphael decided to stay put and watch that she stayed put, too.

Dmitri busied himself with anything that would divert his mind from his bothersome yet intriguing problem. Distraction arrived in the imposing form of Brent Sorensen, swimming from his dock across the canal to Dmitri's moorage. Without great effort Brent heaved his powerful, muscular body onto the high dock, disdaining the barnacle encrusted metal ladder, which allowed easier access to the less athletic and less strong.

It was as if Brent's maker had designed him to brave and conquer the earth. His large, squarish head rested on a solid neck with muscles so developed that they went straight into his shoulders, fusing both, as if there was no neck at all. Taller by half a head than Dmitri, with long muscular arms and legs, he appeared to be Goliath visiting David. Being outrageously big and strong made Brent totally fearless. There was nothing in the world that the man thought he could not lick.

Once, fishing in the bay, their propeller became entangled in fishing line left floating in the water by careless anglers. Brent plunged into the water and was unwinding the line when Dmitri saw in the clear, shallow water a ten-foot bull shark approach the boat. Grabbing a gaff, Dmitri screamed for Brent to get into the boat. He danced like a frustrated dervish, brandishing the gaff, willing his friend to climb aboard. But Brent eyed the fish and kept working. The shark circled, coming close twice more. When the shark returned for the third time, Brent had finished the job and heaved himself into the small, shallow-bottomed vessel they used in the low bay waters.

"What the hell were you doing there?" complained Dmitri. "You almost gave me a heart attack. What would you have done against the beast? He was larger than you and definitely had designs on your body."

"I'd have punched him in the nose or poked out his eye," said Brent without as much as a smile to hint that he was joking. Yes, the man was a great companion in a pinch.

At the moment Brent's steel-gray eyes were fastened on Dmitri. Shaking himself dry like a St. Bernard leaving a river, he announced loudly, "I am off for two days and want to go fishing. What about it? Want to go?" His voice was as deep and strong as the rest of him.

"Bay or ocean?" asked Dmitri.

"I don't care. I have a case of beer and every kind of bait a man could want."

Dmitri's heart sang. Here was the answer to his prayer. Fishing with Brent was to a perfect day what scones and clotted cream were to a tea party.

"Just tell me when and what to bring." He knew they would make the trip in Brent's boat, a twenty-eight-foot fishing vessel with a high tower for spotting and a broad platform at the stern to fish from. Brent was as proud of his ten-year-old Bayliner as he was of his wife. They both were his girls, Jeanette and Jan. Brent had purchased the boat named Early Girl, and promptly renamed her, while Janette had liked the original name.

"How is it that the boat has a better name than I do?" complained Jan. "You never call me Jeanette anymore. It's always just Jan this, Jan that," she griped.

"I don't talk to my boat," was his answer. "If I would call for her constantly she, too, would be Jan. You should be proud that I named her after you; she's got a great body."

Dmitri remembered that Jan had shaken her head, laughed, and taken the comment as the compliment it was meant to be. She knew her man; he liked things tidy and solid and by glory—she was that.

If Dmitri had heard the Bayliner story once, he had heard it a hundred times. Brent never tired of retelling the stroke of good fortune by which he acquired the Janette.

"Among boat owners one could make large bets that everyone in the group had a tall tale to tell about the wonderful deal which had brought him his expensive toy," thought Dmitri.

Brent managed to sneak into most conversations references of her prowess—she made 22 knots—her dependable, economical diesel engines, her perfect condition and the incredible price of only 45,000 dollars he had spent on her. Fortunately he was not a very talkative man or their friendship could have gone sour very soon.

Of course, Dmitri deeply empathized with his friend's prideful garrulity. He understood his friend perfectly, for he had the same feelings for his fifty-five-foot sailing boat Estrella, the star. She was a grand boat, but he preferred to fish from Brent's Jeannette. She was much easier to anchor, to fish from and to clean up afterwards.

They made their plans over a few rum and cokes. Later in the evening Raphael's daily report told of suspicious activity at the compound in Coconut Grove.

"All day long strange men are coming and going. They are dressed casually in shorts, T-shirts, tennis shoes and loafers, but they look as if their T-shirts are large enough to conceal shoulder holsters."

"I swear they are packing heat. Looks like they are up to something. I wonder if they will do the Key Largo trip on Thursday again," he added.

"I am going fishing tomorrow," announced Dmitri, "thought I'd let you know that I am gone. But Thursday I will be back if you need an extra body."

"No! Thursday there will be three of us going to Key West. So we will cover all possibilities. No reason to risk that the goons recognize you."

Ouch, thought Dmitri, *three of them; that will cost me.* However, what was he going to do?

"Might as well enjoy myself fishing then," he said, resigned to a large surveillance bill.

"I want you to take a cell phone with you out on the ocean. I might need to talk to you in a hurry, and I want you to be available. Good luck! Catch one for me!" cried Raphael cheerfully and hung up.

A Perfect Day

꙼⚬꙼⚬

THE ALARM RANG MUCH too early for Dmitri's taste. Was there a chance that he was getting old? Never before had it felt quite so hard to leave the pillow at five in the morning. He groaned when a pain in his right knee made him stumble. "No, and no again, I am not going to give in. I am the same man I once was. Basta! Enough is enough!"

Having given himself orders, he went into the bathroom and performed his morning ritual. He reasoned that it was a waste of time to shave because Brent cared a rat's tail about the beauty of his chops.

Breakfast was eggs, a piece of ham, toast, and lots of coffee with milk and sugar. He filled a cooler with sandwiches, a couple of bananas, and soft drinks. For good measure, he threw in a jar of mustard and a bag of salt pretzels. They would go good with beer. Feeling much more chipper, he hurried down to the fishing shed, for time was a wasting.

He picked his favorite rods—one, a solid, strong instrument with a line capable to withstand the tussle with a large denizen of the deep, and two lighter rods for smaller fish. About to leave, he could not resist grabbing another of his favorites. There was absolutely no reason to pack all these rods because Brent, without fail, would have four to six rods already on board. Heaven forbid they should break one, or the reels would malfunction and they'd be stuck without the means of fish pursuit. Never would there be a fisherman at large without a bevy of proper instruments to catch fish.

As he bustled about, Dmitri was not too jaded to appreciate the loveliness of the early morning in the Keys. This was the only time of the day when calming stillness permeated the isles. Very soon the never-ending traffic would roar into full gear, ending the moment. The air was soft as silk; the water was calm, reflecting the green palm trees, the blinding white houses, the boats, the clouds and a few large herons sitting on boats or docks. Each bird had one leg tucked into its body. His eyes noticed the pearly sheen of pink clouds reflected in the water and he was very happy all of a sudden.

Although he knew that he would duplicate Brent's supply of chum, bait and shrimps, he had to bring more in a special cooler that despite repeated cleanings with Clorox still stank of old fish oils. Last of all he carried a bucket of oats down to the dock where Brent was already waiting with the Jeanette.

They loaded his coolers, buckets and rods. He jumped aboard. The motor purred as Brent pulled away from the dock and performed a nice U-turn in the canal. Off they were into the bay. Once in the bay it was necessary to go south until they reached Tavernier creek, which they traversed to reach the Atlantic.

Leaving the creek, with immense sand flats stretching along on both sides of the channel, they had their first view of the vastness of the ocean. The sun just began to rise on the horizon, inching toward the sky, casting sword-like rays into the blue.

The two friends, standing high in the tower, silently took in the gorgeous spectacle. It was an event they never tired of. A flotilla of Pelicans flew by, skimming the water. An old navy joke came to Dmitri's mind upon seeing the birds. "There goes the Mexican air force!"

"I wonder why the Mexicans call a flock of Boobies our air force?" A few flying fish caught their attention. That was a sure sign that something large was hunting. A little later, a family of bottlenose dolphins joined their boat. The animals loved to race ahead of the boat just ahead of the bow, performing a maneuver that looked deadly to the beholder.

As if anticipating Dmitri's thoughts, Brent remarked, "Never saw one hit by a boat. They are the most remarkable creatures." After a few antics performed around the rushing Jeannette, the dolphins tired of the game, veering off to do serious feeding.

The moment the sun stood in the sky, the feeling of the open ocean changed. Where before the water had been becalmed, the boat gliding along as if on a glass surface, now wavelets began to curl, pushed up by a playful breeze.

Brent had set the coordinates for an outcropping about half a mile from shore, hoping to start the day's catch with yellow tail and snapper. They had good luck there before. If no snappers were to be found they could try for grouper and other bottom fish. Dmitri kept a lookout for other boats. It was important to arrive at a promising spot well before other boats did because, by consensus, later coming boats had to fish from a discrete distance without the benefit of the best environment beneath the waves. Finding their mound, they ascertained with a fish finder the depth and the availability of fish.

"The mound is loaded, but they are all in the rocks. We are going to lose gear," said Dmitri, as he monitored the Lawrence equipment, while Brent prepared to anchor the boat. This was a tricky maneuver, because they wanted to be on top of the mound. By the same token they felt responsible not to drop the anchor into rock and coral formations. That maneuver accomplished, Dmitri chummed the water with the stinking, oily chopped-up remains of baitfish and his beloved oats to bring fish to the boat. Next they baited the hooks on four rods and prepared the bait on a table attached to the railing, easily within reach of both men.

At last they got their lines into the water. From that moment forth the pleasant feeling of suspense held them enthralled. Would there be fish and would they bite? Brent barely had his gear properly set when he sounded, "Fish On!" A moment later he landed a healthy looking yellowtail, which he quickly measured on the tape measure pasted to the bait table. Responsible fishermen followed the rules, never keeping an undersized fish. They carried with them a pamphlet with all the rules and regulations specified by the State of Florida.

From then on both men were in heaven. They could barely take the fish off the hooks before another rod showed a strike. Hardly believing their luck—usually you had to work like the devil for yellowtail—they concentrated on making the best of their fortune.

Half an hour later one cooler, ice in the bottom, was filled with the best eating they knew. Both preferred yellowtail and wahoo above all other catch. Suddenly, only a moment later, their rods idled.

"Dang, they moved on," complained Dmitri.

"Time to change our gear and go deeper."

They put heavier weights and sturdier hooks on the lines, dropping them down deep. From the fish-finder Brent got a measure of the depth. Above the formation below he ascertained an assemblage of fish. Suddenly, Brent yelled, "Get your line out of the water. A big fish just showed up. This thing is huge. I can make out a single large shape. No reason to feed him."

Both men knew what this meant. If they had caught anything, whatever was down there would have taken their fish like candy, ripping off hook, line and sinker. Instead of leaving their position, they both went into overdrive. Whatever was down there—-they wanted it—badly.

Pursuit called for the special heavy rods, heavy lines, huge hooks and interesting large bait. Early on Dmitri had caught an amberjack about a foot and a half long. Although he did not care for the fish as food, he'd kept him for just such an occasion. While he prepared his hooks, Brent pulled a few mullets from the bait cooler making them look like one solid fish by hooking them on several hooks, one above the other.

Lines in the water, their excitement rose to fever pitch. What the heck could be down there? Whatever it was probably scared all the fish to take cover. They used every trick they knew to entice the fish to take the bait. Nothing. Wily Dmitri moved his line through the water, making his amberjack appear to be a live fish.

Their talk and banter had ended. They fished with the silent absorption of the hunter creeping after game. *This is what I love about fishing,* thought Dmitri. *You never know what you will catch.*

Wham! A mighty jerk almost pulled the rod out of Dmitri's hands. Something had taken his bait and was running away with it.

"Brent, Brent, Brent, holy cow, I got him on the line and he is running me out of line!"

Seeing his reel emptying at lightening speed, he calculated the moment when he needed to fight the fish. Seeing Dmitri almost go overboard, Brent ran to him and clamped his powerful arms around him. Both men struggled trying to stay on board. At last the fish tired a little. Brent pulled Dmitri into a special chair bolted to the ship, which was used for trophy fish. Sitting, his legs up, pushing against the back of the boat gave Dmitri more leverage. What a struggle it was.

In hopes of a tussle both men had girded their waists with leather harnesses that contained a pocket in front for planting the grip of the road; thereby, they gained much more power. However, for this monster Dmitri had to use a steel holder bolted to the floor of the boat, close to the seat. Just when he thought he was gaining in the fight and the fish was close to the boat, the beast, seemingly invigorated by yielding to the pull, was running away again.

"I am afraid he is going to snap my line or break the chain," Dmitri complained to Brent. But Brent, standing by, enjoyed the tussle tremendously.

"I think you will be fine. I saw the chain you used for the hook; it should hold."

Smiling contentedly, for this was the sort of holiday he truly loved, he took a swig of beer from a can clamped firmly in his hand.

His bulky frame was resting against the railing.

"What do you think you have got there? Marlin or wahoo?" he speculated.

"Most likely a shark," groaned Dmitri, straining against the road.

"Perhaps it's one of those scalloped hammerheads that we sometimes get during June and July."

"Yeah, quite possibly that. They come and feed on the breeding stingrays."

"I know, the shallows are full of them. A few days ago a woman went swimming and stepped on one. It slashed her leg cleanly from ankle to knee, much as a filleting knife does."

Throughout their shouted and groaned conversation, Dmitri managed to reel the fish within thirty feet or so. Suddenly his nemesis broke through the surface. They saw the triangular fin and were certain—shark, hammerhead.

"Hot damn," Brent exploded. This boy looked to be nine or ten feet long.

"A big one, Lord it's a big one. Good job, reel him in," he encouraged the sweating, struggling Dmitri. Among fishermen it is understood that no one interferes with a man bringing a fish to the boat. Only then he might be helped with a gaff if the fish is very large and cumbersome. Only when defeat threatens, when the prize is in jeopardy, only then can help be given.

The impressive shark swam almost languidly back and forth like a dog on a leash. At the turn, the scalloped head, looking like a bonnet on the beast, was discernible.

"I think you can get the gaff, Brent, I'll try to bring him along side now." Brent crossed the deck for the gaff. He'd barely turned his back when he heard an immense splash and Dmitri's "Son of a bitch, I lost him!"

He turned around and found Dmitri fiery red in the face, cursing a blue streak, while stomping on the deck. His useless rod had been carelessly tossed on to the deck.

"The wily beast was just resting for his last hurrah," he complained bitterly. "The moment I got taut, he ran at the boat like a torpedo, went under and out the other side. That did it—he snapped the line."

Brent knew how his friend felt; nothing like losing a big one—a fighter. He knew of men who compared this feeling to breaking up with a girl they had begun to care for. He did the manly thing to comfort Dmitri by bringing him a beer. Knowing that comfort is to be found in food, he ambled to the coolers holding their lunch and dragged them to the fighting chair. Dmitri sat gloomily, beer in hand, and eyed sadly the mistreated rod plundered of tackle, which he had reverently placed back in the holding cup.

Despite his grief, Dmitri managed to partake of a good-sized lunch. Sandwiches, chips, bananas—they all were washed down with Lowenbrau. Their repast, complete with rehash of all details about the "one that got away," was rudely interrupted by the ringing of Dmitri's cell phone. It was Raphael.

"Hey man, I know you are fishing and it's Wednesday, but things are spinning out of control. We really need a boat for surveillance. Do you think you could get down to Key West in a hurry?"

"What's the problem?"

"The mob left Coconut Grove this morning and came down here. They all moved into a rented house, about ten or fifteen men. We couldn't make all of them because they moved erratically." He paused. "What, Manny?" he cried in an exasperated aside, coming back a moment later, "Oh, okay. Manny just told me that there are fifteen for sure. The most curious thing is that they have been down to the harbor's private mooring farther down, where they have a yacht stashed and a cigar boat."

Raphael breathed deeply for emphasis: "Apparently Mr. Petros is the proud owner of a very hot, expensive yacht. You should see this baby! It must be worth two mil, at least. Eighty feet—trimmed like a Christmas tree.

After another long pause he came back on line, "From my vantage point here I can see that Irina, Petros and some staff have settled on the yacht. Perhaps there is not enough room in the house with all the thugs—every one a dark-haired, brown-skinned Georgian. I don't know what's going on. But I am willing to make a bet, however, that they will go by boat wherever they are going. By the way, the dreamboat's name is Prekrasnaya Irina. What would you bet that it means gorgeous Irina?"

"Call me back in five minutes," said Dmitri, thinking on his feet. "I need to talk to Brent. This thing could take time, a day or so, couldn't it?"

"Yes, can't say how much though."

While they finished their lunch Dmitri drew a picture of his predicament for Brent. Since he had been away, Jan had filled him in on only a few details. Brent, hearing the full extent of his friend's horrific blunder sat wide-eyed, mouth agape.

"You sly, old fox," he finally blurted out admiringly. "You unbelievable, old relic! You still have got the old itch, have you?"

Dmitri almost blushed. Brent's comments were to be taken as high compliments.

"Russian beauty and Russian-mafia-boss-bride! Oh, man, you sure know how to pick them. That really spiced up your boring Key's retiree-life, eh?"

Brent was positively gushing. That was the spiciest bit their community had heard since Mrs. Simon, a delectable forty-five-year-old, made off with the diving instructor after emptying her husband's bank account.

As soon as Dmitri had calmed him down and assuaged his enormous appetite for details, he began laying out Raphael's request for reinforcement in Key West, giving special weight to the amount of time that might be involved.

"You want to take your boat and go with me? That would save immensely on time and fuel, because we don't have to go back to Largo for my boat. But that would be the end of your fishing."

In case his arguments were not persuasive enough, he mentioned that Brent's boat was faster, more maneuverable and much more inconspicuous than the Estrella.

"Give me your phone!" Without preamble Brent dialed his wife. "Jan, honey, the fishing is fantastic. We already have a cooler filled with yellowtail. We almost caught a shark, a hammerhead. Hey, would you mind, honey, if I used my time off to spend a few days with Dmitri on the ocean?"

There was a long pause on the other end. Then Jan cheerfully piped, "Of course you can, bear. You work so hard. I am glad you guys have fun." Then, ever the caring, practical wife, she said, "What about food?"

"Not to worry, we have two coolers filled with stuff, and can cook fish in a pinch on the propane stove."

"All right, fine by me! Just watch the weather. It's hurricane season. Listen to the radio."

"I will, honey, I will. Don't worry."

Brent returned the phone to Dmitri saying, "Jan is a splendid gal. Couldn't have a better wife! And—she fishes, too."

"Be that as it may, but you sly, old dog told her nothing of our probable adventure," Dmitri sounded-off, gleefully defusing Brent's bragging.

"Why worry her? She is a good woman and at the right moment I will tell her everything." His last words were drowned amid the ringing of the phone. Raphael was on the line: "So what is it? Are you coming?"

"We will be down there as fast as we can get there. Let me see, from here to Key West it's about 86 miles. At twenty two knots I figure it will take us about 3.4 hours."

"That's good, very good. So far, they have been staying put, monkeying about with the cigar boat and the yacht. Seems they are getting ready for something; perhaps not just today, because the beauteous Irina is sprawled on a towel on the high deck soaking in the sun. Just come straight to Little Smugglers Cove. I will meet you there. You know the place?"

Everyone was clued in on the plot. Brent pulled the anchor while

Dmitri stowed and fastened the gear. Moments later the engines roared, pressed into service at a high rate as they flew southward.

The Florida Keys are one of nature's marvels. Eons ago, this Florida area was a shallow, warm sea, teaming with fish and different forms of marine creatures and abundant types of coral. For millennia tiny calciferous life-forms built empires in those pleasant waters. Their success was astonishing, encompassing an enormous expanse. However, nature changes with a vengeance, and every time their world flourished magnificently, a big freeze would grip the world, depositing more of the world's ocean waters as snow on the polar regions and on every mountaintop. Solid buildup of ice and snow, miles thick, stored whole seas atop hapless continents that groaned under the load.

As the seas receded—the coral died. Again the world warmed—the seas rose and the coral empire revived. Many repetitions of this process shaped the isles, monuments to the industrious lives of small polyps.

As the men sped by the islands that were connected to one another by bridges, they marveled at the loveliness of the narrow, white area bordered by flats of white sand and blue-green water. They looked like precious stones in a necklace, an emerald setting of palms and water. No matter how often the men saw the "Islas" they always saw them with a deep appreciation.

"If someone offered me millions to leave the Keys and settle elsewhere, I would refuse. I love this place," said Brent. Dmitri concurred. Nowhere else in the world could islands be found, standing with their feet in two major bodies of water. However, such was the Keys magic that they presented a mild and gentle face on the Bayside, and the windblown, put-upon look of an easy woman on the Atlantic side. Yes, the Keys are special.

The day remained as pleasant as it had begun. Warm, breezy, small waves racing toward shore. The ocean was at its kindest, its most alluring. The boat made good time and soon they saw on their right the seemingly endless expanse of the Seven Mile Bridge.

"Every time I see this bridge I think of the men who built this engineering wonder," said Dmitri. He remembered the barbaric conditions under which these men worked as they sank pilings into shifting ocean sand. By late afternoon they approached Key West, speeding by Smather's Beach and the salt ponds where salt was made.

Raphael had explained in greater detail where in the ship's basin the yacht could be found. "Just look for a copper-colored cigar boat. The thing so shines in the sun that it blinds you. It seems as if they want to get all the attention possible with this boat. This leads me to believe that we need to watch the yacht closely because the Coast Guard will surely keep an eye on this speedy, shiny number."

No Argus eye was needed to spot their target. They noticed the shiny racing boat right away. Cigar Boats got their name from their hydrodynamic shape that makes them look like Cuban cigars. They have super hyped-up motors that growl like a pride of lions ready to be unleashed at a moment's notice. They roar dully even when slowly traversing canals or natural channels.

As they came closer, Dmitri could make out Irina in a bikini on the upper- most deck. For just a moment she allowed every male within viewing range to get a good look. Then, she disappeared below deck. Seeing her so suddenly again after days of turmoil, Dmitri's heart jumped in his breast. What a woman, what a prize! "What a bitch," said Brent unmoved, for he read his friend's thoughts. He had noted his friend's hypnotized stare and thought interference was needed or she'd hook him again.

"I think it's best for you to stay out of sight. Anyone on the boats might spot and report to Petros. Don't you think they all studied your pictures? Pictures she took so lovingly for just that purpose?"

Dmitri agreed and hid beside the fishing tower. Amazed, he contemplated how quickly Brent had fallen into the spy-game. Without a doubt he had known that the figure aboard the ship was Irina and instantly perceived the danger of identification. "Thanks, buddy," he mumbled grateful for his friend's support.

"Don't mention it; just get me a bottle of Costco's best Tequila."

How easy it is to get along with male friends, thought *Dmitri—so uncomplicated.*

They docked the boat, securing it well, and began to talk of hot food.

"Got to talk to Raphael first." Dmitri looked about for the presence of Cuban faces. Before he found anyone, Raphael appeared magically on board.

"We were looking for you! How come we never saw you?"

"Because I jumped on board when you both were busy inspecting the juicy Irina."

"You mean you have been watching us all that time?"

"Sure, I hid below and heard every word. So, you two want dinner, eh?"

"Sure would be nice. Think there is time?"

"Yes, not far from here is a very good Mexican Cantina. Comida authentica, muy delicioso."

"Just what the doctor ordered," said Brent. Leaving the boat in Raphael's care, the two friends went to dinner.

Angel

ॐॐॐ

RETURNING ON BOARD LATER in the evening, they were surprised because they found Raphael and two other men on board. One of the strangers sat up in the fishing tower camouflaged like a bundle of tarp. Called to come down by Raphael, the man slithered subtly as a shadow down the ladder to join the others.

Having assembled his crew on the floor of the fishing deck in deep darkness, Raphael made introductions. His crew of three consisted, apart from himself, of the stranger from the fishing tower and the often-mentioned Manny. He was a small, wiry, brown man with a lively face in which every feature at one time or another seemed to be in motion. His nose twitched smelling the air, his eyes moved constantly, his mouth reflected every nuance of the conversation and even his cheeks moved in concert to his interest.

Dmitri compared him in his thoughts to a small dachshund—alive, alert, ever-pursuing prey—and he was well pleased. The man who had descended from the tower was the third in this odd trio. He was a tall, broad shouldered, slender, beautiful young man in his early twenties who sat cross-legged on deck. He had large, velvety Cuban eyes fringed by heavy lashes, a well proportioned face with a straight, nicely shaped nose and a generous mouth with full lips.

Dmitri thought uncharitably, *What's pretty boy doing here? Can he re-*

ally be of any use to us? He is also awfully young. He looked at Brent and saw the same uncertainty in his friend's eyes. It was as if Raphael heard their unspoken questions because he walked to the young man, raising him to a standing position. He placed his hand on the tall one's shoulder and said affectionately, "This is the mainstay of the operation, my nephew, Angel."

He looked with such obvious love and pride at Angel that it dawned on Dmitri that the young man must be capable of pulling his weight because by now he knew that Raphael was a hard-working man and would not tolerate anyone incapable of pulling his load.

"In Angel we have the perfect decoy," explained Raphael. "He can look like a young, rich, spoiled loafer, which opens a multitude of avenues into society for him. He is smart, too, and evaluates situations correctly; lastly he is brave, not afraid to get into a difficult situation or even a brawl. By the way, he was the one who found out about Petros Avarikidze."

Later he told the men more about Angel. Angel's story was very interesting. As the son of Raphael's sister, he grew up in a divided family. After the Communist revolution most of the family resented the new regime of the few hundred privileged Castro tyrants and became strongly anti-communist, anti-Castro. They fled to America.

Raphael's sister, Blanca, however, had married a young revolutionary who converted her to his radical beliefs. This couple was so indoctrinated, blind and believing that they named their only son Lenin after the deceased Soviet revolutionary. Although young Lenin grew up in a home where the revolutionary ideals were daily espoused, he grew up to be an independent thinker. Already as a young boy he discerned that communism was a flawed ideology. It was an ideology riddled with inequalities and a stranglehold on individual achievement and advancement. It was obvious to him that the system did two things; on one hand it deprived ordinary citizens of a comfortable living or accumulation of wealth by robbing them of the fruits of their minds and bodily labor. On the other hand it provided total power and great wealth to a small group which relished their obvious control over the rest of their fellow citizen.

When his uncle, together with most of the family, escaped Cuba in a small fishing boat and set out for the Florida Keys, Angel was not given a chance to leave with them. Everyone was so afraid of Blanca's zealous obedience to the regime that they dared not disclose their plans to little Lenin who might have tattled to his mother. Wind and current conspired to carry his uncle's small boat safely all the way to Isla Morada where the family went ashore and was accepted by the authorities.

"Here begins Angel's story," explained Raphael. "After little Lenin heard that the family, uncle, aunt, grandparents and cousins had escaped and that everyone was safe in Florida, he thought and dreamed of ways to join them. It was almost impossible to escape the spying eyes of the regime anymore. Security was tightened to the utmost. Years passed. By the time Lenin turned fifteen, he had become a man. Labor in the fields had made him strong and angry. He had a great mind, yet was deprived of schooling. The party punished those belonging to traitorous families—families who had escaped the regime."

A solitary youth, Lenin studied maps, currents and winds. He worked out with homemade weights and rode the waves on a homemade sailboard every evening. Then came the day when he believed all conditions were felicitously arranged in his favor. Instead of going to work that morning he went to the beach and got on his sailboard. The wind filled his enlarged sail. He pushed the board into the seas the way the compass strapped to his wrist directed.

For hours he rode the board in the merciless sun. He thirsted. Taking supplies along for the ride had not been an option. There were times when he wanted to stop and rest. His burning anger and Cuban machismo, however, did not allow him to give in to weak temptations.

"I am the best on the board there is. I can do it. I will succeed," he prayed his mantra.

Many hours later he was still on his feet, his arms still clutching the sailing mast, keeping the sail filled with the wind. Around this time the people on the eighty-foot pleasure cruiser Morning Song, returning from a fishing trip, thought they witnessed a Fata Morgana. With mounting astonishment the owners and crew of the vessel doubted their eyes' veracity. Here they were, many miles from any beach, and yet, like the Flying Dutchman, there flew across the waves a lonely, little sailboard with a worried-looking teenage boy aboard.

This tale might have ended badly, had it not been for the ship owner's initiative, curiosity and genuine caring. A man in his fifties, he was the director of a large electronics company. He was a man used to taking charge. Directing the captain to head his boat straight for the sail was his instant command. Together with his blond, comely wife and most of the crew, he stood pressed to the railing as they approached the youth on the sailboard.

"Are you lost young man?" he shouted through a megaphone.

"Sen`or, ayuda, por favor!"

After this cry for help, a stream of Spanish followed that no one understood. Everyone aboard ship admitted that they were at a loss to understand the young man. But they all saw the extreme exhaustion expressed in the boy's face and his tired body. He looked spent. The crew threw him a line and motioned him to tie it to the sail mast and then pulled him alongside where strong hands and arms pulled him and his sailboard onto the ship.

It seemed there was not an ounce of strength left in the youth, for once hoisted safely aboard, his legs buckled and he fell onto the glossy flooring of the afterdeck. Before her marriage, the owner's wife had been a nurse. She was a woman in her mid-life, tanned, and well cared for; nevertheless, she had not become soft. Taking charge and caring for people were still her main attributes. Upon seeing the recumbent, exhausted form on the ground, she rushed to him. What a pretty boy he was, laying spread out before her. She was the mother of just such a boy—young, vulnerable and brave, and her son's picture came instantly to her mind.

Taking charge, she directed the men to bring her the electrolyte-charged fluids they used for rehydration, which she administered to the boy in small sips.

"Carry him to the shower and rinse the salt of his skin." she ordered, "The poor kid must be fried. God only knows how long he has been out there."

After the shower she continued to feed the youth fluids. Young Lenin, feeling better, began talking again. He repeated certain phrases over and over, but they understood little. The only thing of which the people on the boat were certain was of his wish to go to Miami. "Miami, Miami," he said again and again.

"He must be a Cuban runaway, "said one of the men.

"Impossible," shouted others. "On a sailboard? No one could do this for so tremendously long a distance." They argued. What were they going to do with him?

"He must be going to a hospital," insisted the owner's wife.

"Nonsense, he doesn't look that bad," said her husband, a crew cut, square- faced man. "Look how much better he looks already."

"What a story." cried Brent, "This is worthy of another round of this nice Chivas Regal I have been saving for just such an occasion." With the exception of Manny who was on night duty, they refilled their glasses and sipped with reverence. Breaking their silence, Raphael went back to spin his tale.

During the argumentative conversation of the people aboard the yacht, the youth had shed the sheet they'd wrapped him in. He was now standing before them in his bleached out, ragged swimming trunks.

With exaggerated care he pronounced, "Por favor, no hospital. Playa, playa—por favor."

"I think he wants to be put on a beach. Playa means beach. I know that much. But why? I don't get it."

"Oh, my God, I know why," cried his wife. "He is from Cuba and came all the way over here on this flimsy board. Now he is afraid that they will find him aboard a ship and send him back. Have you forgotten about the dry land rule? If Cubans make it onto the shore they are safe—if rescued at sea they go back."

All the while the boy had followed her words closely. It was as if he understood what she was saying, nodding his head vigorously, yes.

The Americans were kind people; as soon as they reached Key West they sought the closest beach. They hugged him, pounded his back and placed the lonely boy and his sailboard on the sand. Once they were away at a safe distance they called the Coast Guard and reported a Cuban illegal on the beach. This way the boy would get instant medical attention. All aspects of his arrival would be taken care of; thus, Raphael ended his story.

Turning to Angel, he said, "Tell them the rest, my mouth has gone dry." Angel laughed, a laugh that raised the corners of his mouth, as he began speaking.

"The Coast Guard arrived almost instantly. I told them through an interpreter what I had done. You should have seen their eyes. They did not believe it at first, but after a while they came around. I think my strange board and faded trunks together with my blistered hands and sun-burned skin convinced them"

Thinking back on the day of his arrival in America he grinned broadly with a fond expression. "Oh, Dio, the coast guard guys are something. They gave me Gatorade and then, when I kept it down for half an hour, they fed me. As men, they understood that I must have been dying of hunger. They rushed into their kitchen. And so it happened that I tasted my first hamburger with fries. Their cook made one monstrously large, just for me. With ketchup, mustard and onions, it tasted like it was made in heaven. I finished and they could tell I wanted more. They called to their kitchen for more. I also drank my first Coke that day. In Cuba only the rich can buy it."

Finally sated, Angel asked the interpreter to call his uncle in Miami. Raphael picked him up the next morning. His saga ended in front of a Miami Immigration judge, where his identity was certified and he was presented with papers. Right then, he made his first independent decision.

Raphael finished the tale for him: "He said to the judge through me, "Your honor, I have hated my name all my life. I am not a communist. Please, can you change my name for me?"

"I most certainly can," said the judge. "What name would you like to have?"

"I would like to be called Angel."

"Any reason why?"

"For the angel that got me here."

Raphael finished proudly, "Now you know the stuff my nephew is made of."

The Hunt

❧❧

MORNING CAME EARLY for the men on the Jeannette. The wiry Manny had shared the night watch with Raphael and came to wake them before the sun was up.

"Up and out with you guys. Go, get moving, wash and get breakfast. We want to be ready the moment the enemy goes into action."

Manny tried to infuse the sleepy men with enthusiasm that he himself did not feel at the moment. "Move it, move it," he urged them on. "I still have to wake the others and get forty winks myself if I want to be useful today."

Dmitri and Brent gingerly crawled off the cramped bed they had shared. At five in the morning adventure was definitely lacking in appeal.

Moments later they were joined by Raphael and Angel. Angel took one look at Dmitri and said disgustedly, "Put on some sort of hat and sunglasses for Pete's sake; anyone seeing you would recognize you from your picture."

Dmitri rummaged about in the untidy cabin and came on deck looking like the bad man in a sordid murder mystery.

"Madre de Dios," complained Angel, appraising the slouchy cotton hat, "now you look like a giant mushroom. Everyone will notice."

"Don't pay him any mind," murmured Raphael sleepily, "he always exaggerates. It's so Cuban. No one will pay attention to you, it is too early."

However, he was wrong on that account. As they ambled along the sidewalk to the Mexican cantina, which they had been told opened early, they were closely observed by a lookout stationed on the upper deck of the blindingly shiny, white yacht.

"He is watching us through binoculars," said Angel, whose keen eyes noticed everything. Angel was watching the big ship out of the corners of his eyes, seemingly uninterested in anything except the pavement.

"He stopped paying attention to us," he announced a minute later. Everyone somehow felt better, although there had been no direct threat coming from the yacht. The mobster just did his duty and they were in his field of vision.

After a grand breakfast of carne asada, huevos con chile, tortillas, salsa and mucho coffee, they returned to the Jeannette and divided their forces. Dmitri and Brent were to stay on board, with Dmitri keeping out of sight.

Angel was leaving, to hang out close to the yacht. He was curious to see what was on board. "He can change his appearance at will, that boy, much like an octopus or a sea slug."

"Thank you kindly for comparing me to the lowest forms of sea life," complained Angel, miffed at the denigration, although an unintended one.

"I meant it as compliment, hombre," laughed Raphael, making the young man smile again.

Raphael slouched off like a drunk hungover from last night's party to spy on the cigar boat. He strongly believed that all action would start with this speedy toy. Manny was sleeping below. Brent and Dmitri had been told to stay put but be ready at a moment's notice. If Manny was not awake by ten, they had orders to awaken him.

As the minutes ticked by and nothing happened, the friends became bored. They readied the boat. They fastened, stowed and bolted down everything capable of rolling about in fast pursuit. They had taken on a supply of food, water, soft drinks, and a very necessary case of beer that they were told not to touch by Raphael. To avoid attracting attention—someone suspicious might wonder why they were not out on the sea fishing—they cleaned the deck and washed the salt off all the exposed parts of the vessel. Their puttering killed about an hour fifteen minutes, and then they woke up Manny. The small, wiry man looked tired and discontented, arriving on deck. He flopped into a deck chair and growled, "Is there any coffee?" After two cups of the strong brew his disposition became sunnier.

As suddenly and as mysteriously as before, Angel appeared among them.

"Things are heating up," he announced. "I just visited the yacht of Mr. Avarikidze, and heard that they will make a pick-up run in a couple of hours. I already told Raphael. He will be joining us soon, and then we will wait."

"How on earth did you get aboard the Russian's boat?" asked Brent.

"Simple, I saw a delivery truck pull up and stopped the driver before they could see him from the boat. He told me that he was supplying the yacht with water, soft drinks and whatnots. Fifty bucks and a good attitude bought me a company hat plus twenty minutes of employment, pushing a dolly of water cases up on board. Once I was among the enemy, I spotted some Cuban crew members. I followed the driver, delivering my water to storage. When I came up I asked in passing what this pretty boat was up to today, and the youngest answered with a lascivious grin, "Picking up a puta, (a prostitute)." It was obvious that he was afraid to talk yet wanted me to know that something was up. Using this double entendre, he let me know that a pick-up was going to happen."

Angel's cool demeanor and bravery awed everyone. No one in their party would have dared to slip into the midst of the gangsters.

"Now we have to wait," he said. Waiting was not a word our friends were particularly fond off. Raphael came aboard and the waiting began.

The morning slowly transformed itself into the perfect day for adventure. It was warm, yet a light cloud cover promised pleasant coolness later. In the boat basin, all around the Jeannette, lively activity took place. Serious fishermen had left hours ago, at sunrise. Last night's revelers had gotten over their hangovers by now, and were leaving the basin at a leisurely pace.

At two lookout stations, Raphael in the fishing tower on board and Manny at the boardwalk, every move aboard the suspicious vessels was observed. Ralph suddenly made it known that the pace at Avarikidze's yacht had picked up and was at frenzied speed.

"Get ready to take off at any minute because I want us to be slightly ahead of both of their boats."

Brent started the engine, as Manny came at a run. He untied the boat. Brent eased the boat into the middle of the basin, picking up steam as he went. They were almost in open water when they heard an awesome roar, because the shiny cigar boat passing them kicked the engines into full drive. They had seen the boat approach from the moment it left its mooring. Promptly Dmitri, Angel and Manny had gone below. To be recognized could be deadly or end the mission prematurely.

Irina and Petros, looking the part of a young couple having the time of their lives in a speedboat, sped by the Jeanette as if she was not moving at all. They were smiling. Irina's hair was flying in the wind. Their boat was leaving a wake that could easily tip a small fishing boat.

"We will never catch up to them. We don't have that kind of power," moaned Dmitri.

"I don't think we need to follow them," said Raphael. "They are so obvious that I think they are the decoy. The action will happen with the yacht."

"Just look over there," cried Angel. "The Coast Guard is already after them. They have a little power of their own. Bet you that is what they wanted to do. Draw the Coast Guard from the real action."

"Perhaps! However, I think that another coast guard boat will shadow the yacht," mused Raphael.

"Well, if they won't, we will," said Manny with emphasis. With the onset of action he carried about him the aura of a hunting dog. All of him had become tension and focus.

They reached a point in their travel on the ocean when they had to decide how to set their course. "I would guess that the yacht will head in the opposite direction the cigar boat has chosen," remarked Brent.

"Well, that's not a chance we can take. The yacht is equipped with very powerful engines and if we make a mistake we cannot catch up to her."

They decided to idle at heir present location, pretending to be fixing a problem with their anchor chain. The tension aboard the Jeanette silenced all idle talk, making the men jumpy with nervous anticipation.

Fortunately they did not have to wait very long. Gliding like a swan on a pond, the elegant boat came into view, passing them by. The crew of the Jeanette pretended to be busy a while longer; they were represented by Brent and Raphael while the others hid below deck.

"They are heading toward the Marquesas," surmised Brent, "But why? It's heavily protected as a wildlife sanctuary and therefore watched closely."

"Who knows? We will just have to follow at a decent distance and see what develops."

"What are the Marquesas?" asked Angel. "Good question," skipper Brent said, taking it upon himself to inform the young man.

"Not many people know of this small group of islands. Keys, is perhaps a better term, because they are nothing more than glorified sand banks overgrown with Mangrove. These keys belong to the Florida Keys chain positioned 50 km west of Key West. They were declared a sanctuary, and in the waters around there one can find some of the best fishing. Most tourist fishing boats won't go so far for their clients, which makes this an unspoiled place."

Having a course to follow, they began to run the boat at full speed because the yacht was close to the horizon. They managed to follow unobserved for some time, when Dmitri, sitting in the tower, called down to the crew that it looked like the Prekrasnaya Irina was changing course, going sharply farther west.

"What the devil are they up to?" complained Brent, looking at his instruments. "Now they are running toward the Dry Tortugas."

Everyone on board knew about the Dry Tortugas. The Tortugas, too, are an assemblage of small keys, 113 km west of Key West. The largest of the keys among them is Garden Key, sporting Fort Jefferson, the most westward and southward fortifications of the United States. Once it was a bulwark against an enemy approaching from South America or Cuba.

Today, tourists alighting from their vessels step onto a boat pier; then they proceed to admire the officer's quarters, soldier's barracks, the powder magazines and the lighthouse. So popular is this tourist destination that even Angel had been here already, although he had to work very hard to make a living in Miami and did not have much money to spare.

Running along in mindless pursuit, it took a while before Dmitri from his lookout post called, "Stop engine, stop. Our bird quit flying and is sitting seemingly motionless."

Angel grabbed an extra pair of binoculars and joined Dmitri. His keen eyes spotted some interesting things. "Hope they don't have someone with exceptional eyesight and can make us out," he opined. "I can see a small, apparently very fast boat approaching from the horizon. Now, the Irina is putting two pangas into the water." Pangas are small motorized, blow-up rubber boats, which one person can manipulate.

The men below stirred with excitement and curiosity. What was taking place out there? Although burning with zeal to know more, they knew they could not get closer. A closer approach would reveal their purpose.

A moment later Angel called down, "Now the pangas are being manned—two men into each boat. The pangas are motorized and are taking off for the speedboat coming toward the yacht."

"Is the approaching boat perhaps the cigar boat?" asked Manny.

"No, I can quite clearly make it as different, but fast. It's not very large. Twenty-five feet, maybe."

For a while profound silence enveloped the boat. It was so still that the wave's softly breaking against the Jeannette sounded disturbingly loud. Angel broke the silence, reporting, "The speed boat is dumping huge bales of floating stuff into the water. Damn they are fast. They have offloaded perhaps twenty of these floating things and now the boat is racing away. Whoever is in this boat wants to be gone in a hurry."

"What is going on now?" asked Raphael impatiently.

"The guys in the pangas are collecting the bales, pulling them in with gaffs. They are almost done." A moment later he announced that they had collected every one of the bales and were heading back to the yacht.

"They are lifting the pangas aboard."

"Let's get out of here!" Ralph wanted their boat far away from the area, to be innocently fishing, or to be tied up to the dock in Key West when the Yacht caught up with them. Brent made engines whine for a quick start and then handed the wheel to Dmitri.

"You will have to keep below deck anyway, friend" he smiled. "You might as well make yourself useful."

He climbed above where he quickly and expertly readied four rods, baited them for trolling and got them into the water. He showed the three detectives what to watch for when trolling.

"If we get lucky we will have fresh fish for dinner; meanwhile, we look legit to the enemy."

Cruising along at medium speed they remained out of Prekrasnaya Irina's view. As luck would have it, something hit the line Angel was watching with the force of a torpedo. Angel had fished plenty in Cuba, mostly from shore for the family's dinner. Few people owned boats in Cuba; those who did were watched closely when fishing. For that reason, Angel had never experienced the force of a pelagic fish striking at bait.

He quickly grabbed the rod as Brent had instructed him to do and began the eternal epic battle between fish and man. This battle almost sent him into the drink. Had it not been for Brent's quick action, pulling him back and pushing him into the fighting chair and strapping him in, he would have been swimming with his fish.

"Madre mio," he cried. "What kind of fish is this? He is running away with all my line. How do I stop him?" Excitement cut off his breath. He pushed hard against the side of the boat while trying to reel in what he considered to be a monstrous fish.

"Is it maybe a shark?" he wondered.

"No, I don't think so," declared Brent, "although it could be. All bets are on the table when you are fishing in deep water. Though the way this fish struck makes me believe you have a fine yellowfin tuna on the line."

"No matter, it's big and fights like a tiger," screamed Angel joyously. No one could have expected such extraordinary luck. Before Dmitri could stop the boat to aid Angel, a second fish hit the line Manny was watching. This one, too, began running away with a vengeance.

"Stop, Dmitri, stop the damn boat!" bellowed Brent. The words had barely left his mouth when a strike on the rod he held nearly took his arm off.

"Fish on!" he rejoiced, "Dear Lord, look at the damn fighting fish." For a moment he lost his calm composure as his excitement was getting the better of him.

"We are sitting in school of whatever it is we are catching!"

With the boat at rest, gently rolling in the waves, the men could finally plant their legs and tend to business. Angel was already installed in the fighting chair doing his best against a fish seemingly supercharged with strength and energy. Whenever the young man thought he had gained even the slightest advantage, he had to acknowledge only seconds later that the fish had won back every inch of hard fought line. The fish seemed to tease him, going deep one moment, flying upward the next, changing sides quicker than Angel could move his rod.

For a while now the three men had been frantically trying to keep their lines from getting tangled. The fish swam back and forth seeking to escape the horrible force pulling on their mouths; a force, seemingly capable of ripping off their heads.

Meanwhile, everyone had a wonderful time on board. Even Raphael, just standing by watching the age-old struggle between man and the creatures of the sea enjoyed the tussle. Shouted commands flew about seasoned with a few salty curses.

"Keep your fish starboard side!"

"Put a fighting belt on Manny or he will lose his fish. He might go overboard!" Brent shouted with glee to Dmitri who had come to help. Somehow the idea of rescuing a man in the middle of fishing struck him as exceedingly funny. It was obvious to all that Manny had never fished in all his life. He was so caught up in his tussle with the fish that he had totally forgotten where he was. He babbled breathlessly and with incredible speed in Spanish. Raphael, totally engaged, replied in staccato Spanish.

DMITRI LOOKED ABOUT—happy pandemonium allover the ship—and he thought that nothing could be better in life! If his stupid mail-order bride could bring such happiness to a group of men, strangers to each other only days ago, then it was worthwhile to have blown a wad of money.

Angel's struggle had been going on for a while now, and it looked as if finally he might be winning. By chance and ingrained habit he scanned the deep blue water to the horizon, and promptly emitted a loud howl and a few unprintable Spanish words.

"The Irina, eh, she is coming! I must get this fish in the boat and go below. They saw me only this morning on their ship."

Frantically, he began reeling the fish in, dipping the tip of the rod down to the water, giving the fish the illusion that he was gaining ground, only to pull up and reel only harder. He wondered whether the men of the Irina could detect his face with field glasses.

"Dmitri, please, scan the Irina with binoculars and see if you can make out faces."

Dmitri, facing the same problem of recognition, did as he was told. "I can see figures but no faces, yet."

With quiet desperation Angel fought his fish within twenty feet of the boat. The fun had somehow gone out of the moment. Concealing himself in the deep before, the fish now changed strategy by breaking through the surface.

"Madre Dios, look at him!" cried Angel.

"Hot damn, Yellowfin!" shouted Brent. "A big one!"

"Oh, Tuna, my Tuna," sang Angel with renewed spirit, "I must get you out of the water before the enemy comes close!"

"I can see their heads but not their features, yet," reported Dmitri, cutting into the babble.

"Go below deck, Dmitri, and you too Raphael," ordered Brent.

"These people can count. If they get here and two bodies are suddenly missing they might get suspicious. They have seen Manny walking the planks like a tourist, so that's okay, but Dmitri and Angel are known faces and must be below when they arrive. So be a good chap Raphael, and go below."

Raphael easily saw good reasoning when it was offered. Although he had a great time watching Angel and Manny fight, he followed Dmitri into the cabin.

Angel's fish, finally played out, was pulled alongside. Brent, who himself had a fish on the line, secured his rod. This allowed the animal to float hither and yon like a dog on a leash. Pulling the big gaff from its hold he went to Angel's side.

"All right now! Pull him close," he instructed. Angel pulled and reeled until for just a moment the big Tuna could be reached.

Brent's gaff struck with the force of a lance striking the armor of an ancient knight. The gaff's vicious hook went deep into the fish just below the gills.

The blow was deadly. All fight left the animal. Brent's big biceps bunched, becoming enormous, as he lifted the fish into the boat.

"Nice, Angel. Damn nice! I would guess you have here about ninety-to-a-hundred pounds of fine yellowfin tuna; it's one of the best fighters swimming in these waters. Congratulations!"

Angel admired his magnificent catch silently. A silly, happy grin on his beautiful face gave him the look of a twelve-year-old. Finally he said, "Man, that's the fish I always dreamed about in Cuba and never caught."

His reverie was destroyed by Dmitri's shout.

"Get your ass below deck, Angel! I can almost see their faces."

Brent hustled Angel down the stairs to the cabin

The joy left the young man's face.

"I am coming," he said going below as Raphael climbed up in his stead. At the end of the stairs he turned back, facing Brent with a pleading look.

"Don't chop up my fish!" he begged.

"No way! I will not mutilate a trophy. But I will bleed him when I have time."

Brent, meanwhile, had become busier than a whole crew.

"Watch my rod," he instructed Raphael. "Call me if there is trouble. I have to help Manny."

After dispatching the flopping-about tuna with a few blows, because the fish had almost broken his toes in a last struggle as he slapped his tail against the floor in effort to fling himself over the rail, Brent rushed to Manny's aid.

Manny's fish was very lively and had managed to wrap the line around the tiller. Hanging precariously over the railing while encouraging Manny to keep his rod up and steady, Brent managed to disentangle the line. Then he supervised Manny as he brought the fish close.

By the time he had gaffed and landed another healthy forty-pound tuna, the Prekrasnaya Irina laid close by with a bevy of men standing on the railing. They watched all proceedings on the Jeannette with the greatest interest through field glasses.

Brent dispatched Manny's fish as skillfully as the first, shouting to Raphael, "Watch your footing, the deck is awash in blood and gore."

He kicked one of the bodies aside and positioned himself beside Raphael. "I know, buddy, that you have never fished before. However, you must be bring this one in by yourself. Remember, you are supposed to be a tourist."

Raphael's face turned the shade of olive green, "Madre de Dios! I hate fish. I will mess this up."

"No, you won't. I will tell you what you must do and you will be fine."

To the stares of the men on the Prekrasnaya Irina, Raphael reeled, dipping the rod reeling up, playing the fish-following its erratic dashes to Brent's murmured instruction until he had the fish close. Then, as before, Brent gaffed Raphael's prize, yanking him aboard.

Brent slapped him on the back a hearty grin on his wide face, "Well done, buddy! Another yellowfin, amigo, thirty or more pounds, I would bet."

His travail and angst forgotten, Raphael grinned widely, exposing rows of shiny, white, perfect teeth. "Perhaps," he opined cautiously, "this fishing is not so bad after all."

Closely observing the actions on the Jeanette, the Irina approached until the yacht lay within forty feet of Jeanette's starboard side. Her captain, a short, burly, swarthy man boomed at them in a heavily accented voice through a megaphone, "Good fishing today?"

"Fantastic," boomed Brent back. "At first, we trolled the waters without a strike, but then, here look," he bellowed, lifting Angel's trophy fish with the gaff. "And we have more of the same." He lifted the two smaller tuna with one motion groaning under the weight.

"You have done verrry well," came from the Russian's megaphone. "Would you sell us one for dinner?"

"Sorry, no can do. My customers would kill me if I let you have one of those fish!"

"OK, then," the Russian struck his megaphone and walked away. Soon the ship began to glide toward Key West once more.

"What was that about?" asked Raphael, "They can buy any sort of fish blood- fresh in Key West."

"The Russian was just testing, just making sure that we are what we are pretending to be. No sports fisherman would sell a great fish. These folks pay to get out on the ocean. They pay a lot and every fish they catch goes home with them, frozen in a box or prepared for taxidermy and mounting."

Shortly thereafter began the gruesome ritual of bleeding and gutting of the fish. Dmitri came aloft again. Between the two friends the smallest of the fish was filleted, chunked and chopped.

"Fresh tuna for dinner." They smiled happily working amid the blood and gore. They threw guts, fins and the head overboard, putting the prepared fish and the two large tuna on ice.

They finished the rite of mariners by sluicing off the deck.

When all was shiny-clean and ship-shape again, Brent called the men onto the deck for a ceremony. Flipping open deck chairs, which they pulled from a rack where they had been securely stored, they were soon comfortably seated with two coolers in their midst. Brent produced a bottle of fine, aged whiskey, a bottle of Scottish Laphroaig. He encouraged everyone to drink his measure, which he served neat.

"Drink and enjoy, for none of us will ever be able to pronounce, or worse even, spell the name of this whisky. I saved this fine old brew for a special occasion. Well, one man catching his largest fish ever and two others never having fished at all, I call that a special event." He raised his glass, toasting the men.

The taciturn Manny took a deep draught and smiled, "I never had so much fun in all my time as a detective." Looking at Raphael, he suggested tongue in cheek, "Perhaps we should be paying Brent and Dmitri." Angel nodded his head in agreement.

"Best time I have had in ages," he said wistfully. "Last time I felt like this I was a kid."

Suddenly everyone was hungry. They devoured Dmitri's sandwiches—almost a full cooler of food. Fishing had made them hungry. Brent set the course toward Key West and gave the Jeannette full throttle.

Great Guns are Needed

‿✄

"SO WE KNOW WITH certainty that the Georgians are involved in a dirty business. Smuggling of sorts, probably dope. That however does not get me Irina Petrovna Sokolova back!" Dmitri was not sidetracked from his mission by a few lovely tuna.

"I have been thinking about that." Raphael was instantly all business again.

"We cannot take on this mob on our own. I guess we need to enlist the services of the US Customs Office. Customs has clout."

"What about the FBI?" asked Angel.

"Smuggling is the domain of customs. Perhaps they will call in other guns, but that is not our worry."

Next morning the Jeannette left Key West for Key Largo. The mob left the yacht like rats leave a sinking ship and dispersed into their respective vehicles with great fluidity. After observing their actions closely, Angel and Manny, disguised with hats and sunglasses, tailed them by car.

During a brainstorming session lasting half the night, the men had decided that Ralph and Dmitri were to seek out customs officials and get the ball rolling. After berthing the Jeanette in her cozy slip, Brent went home and back to work. Angel and Manny took up station in Coconut Grove.

That afternoon Dmitri and Raphael walked into the customs offices in Miami. The first agent to whom they explained their unusual situation had a peculiar look on his face when they were finished. He was young man, with a crew cut and intense eyes. He was also a very attentive listener. The moment they finished their tale he got on his cell phone. After walking out of earshot, they saw him speaking rapidly.

He returned in an instant and directed them to another building. To the surprise of the detective and his client, they were directed away from the official, imposing building to a smaller, two-storey boxy house. It sported peeling blue paint and looked dirty and neglected.

"I thought we made it quite clear that our information is very important. So, why would they send us to this derelict place? No one important with any power would have their office in here," grumbled Dmitri.

"Beats me," smiled Raphael cheerfully, "this is my first time with customs. Usually I deal with Miami Vice."

They found the particular office without a problem; number three, second floor. Inconspicuous door, dirty brown carpet in the hallway.

A deceptively mild, well-modulated voice bade them enter. The voice gave both of them a start, for the man behind a regular, standard issue desk, was huge. "Three hundred pounds, six foot six, at least," thought Dmitri.

Thick, dirty, yellow curtains obscured the window behind the man; the brown carpet in front of the desk had a hole in it. Three sad metal chairs with even sorrier looking seats stood in no particular order before the desk.

Introductions were made; everyone sat, after Dmitri and Raphael pulled their chairs back a distance for comfortable eye contact. The fat man did not stand on long formality,

"So, what brings you to customs?" asked agent John Brandeis with mellifluous inflection, as if he had not been briefed already. Dmitri started hesitatingly.

"Sir, it's a long and strange story that I am going to tell you. However, in the end you will find why we need to involve customs. Please, bear with me! I promise it's important that you know the beginning too."

Brandeis was an exceedingly patient listener. His round, fat face, in which intelligent, brown eyes sat like raisins in yeast dough, featured a large, almost voluptuous mouth. He showed concentration at interesting points by a tightening of the lips. As the tale was alternately told by Ralph and Dmitri, his interest perked up so that one could almost discern the thoughts flying behind the broad forehead.

"So, I am to understand that the Russian mob is doing business with Cuba? Is that what you want me to believe? How often have you observed these pick-ups?"

Raphael decided to stretch the truth just a touch.

"Twice, sir. Every Thursday. The second time we got close enough to see bales containing, God only knows what, being delivered and received." He paused for emphasis, continuing,

"Whoever delivered did not take the time to make contact, but just dumped the load and ran. The Russians bore the brunt of getting caught in the transaction."

The fat man behind the desk stretched his legs, leaning back in his chair. He reposed in thoughtful silence. Suddenly he opened a drawer and removed a brown wooden box. He cut a banderole that had sealed it, extracting gingerly and lovingly a beautiful cigar. He raised it to his nose, smelling it the way connoisseurs inspect expensive, exotic and delicious objects.

"Whether it's food, wine, cigars or perfume, their lovers always savor the object of their passion the same way," thought Dmitri.

Still lost in contemplation, Brandeis removed two more cigars, closing the lid on the brown box. Then, gifting the speechless pair with a cigar each, he said, "Cohibas, finest grade. I hope you enjoy them as much as I do."

He smiled benevolently, "Now that I have opened the box, they must go into my humidor." Saying so, he followed through by pulling a rather large receptacle from a file drawer.

Dmitri and Brent felt they had entered the twilight zone as Brandeis put them through an elaborate ceremony, preparing the cigars for an enjoyable smoke. He acted with the same deliberate, delicate fashion that denotes a Geisha involved in a tea ceremony.

Fortunately, Dmitri knew how to respectfully honor the unexpectedly delightful gift, having smoked on occasion precious cigars with friends.

Although Raphael was Cuban, he had never been introduced to the intricacies of cultured cigar smoking. Brandeis relished the role of patient teacher. He hugely enjoyed bringing another man into the fold of the aficionados.

Almost half an hour passed while the three calmly smoked and spoke about their mission in relaxed tones. Soon aromatic, blue haze filled the tightly closed room. Brandeis elicited information from both men and posed innocuous seeming questions. By the time fire had consumed the cigars, turning them into small, ugly stubs, the official had come to a decision:

"Next Thursday I want you, Raphael, and Angel to be on board of a boat I will provide. Your man Manny together with one of my own agents will watch the house in Coconut Grove, which I will check out in the meantime. They will follow the Russian convey down to Key West. This will be a test run to ascertain that the pick ups are a regular occurrence."

Brandeis thought for a moment, his large forehead wrinkled, as if the effort of making crinkles aided in the thought process.

"The agent I am going to attach to you will be with you all week long, at all times. That is to prepare for the eventuality that they change schedule. In the meantime I will work out a plan with my staff how best to nail the whole gang. I assure you we will hand over Miss Sokolova to the INS."

He sent an endearing grin toward Dmitri, "With you present, of course, and fully credited for her capture."

"Couldn't have gone better," rejoiced Raphael as they were leaving the unlikely office building.

"Hard to believe that the man conducts customs business out of such a dilapidated joint," mused Dmitri.

"Yeah, fancy that. I also wonder where he got the lovely cigars, forbidden Cubans, no doubt."

"Well," surmised Dmitri, "he probably saved them from getting cremated. Better this way."

Naval Operations

৯৶৽৶৽

THE PROMISED AGENT MATERIALIZED two days later when Raphael received a call to pick up agent Anthony Li at the customs office. Henceforth, Li became the detective's fourth man. He alternately took turns with Angel and Manny, guarding the station in front of the Coconut Grove compound.

He had only been on duty for two days when he called Brandeis. "I can't believe what is going on in Avarikidze's manor. You would not believe the comings and goings. I think it is wrong that Mr. Pataklos should have to pay for three detectives. We are obviously facing a criminal gang of great proportions, a menace to the people of the State of Florida. And yet, here this man is facing them with private funds and detectives."

After Li's eloquent plea and explanation of the situation, Brandeis decided that customs, short on men as always, could at least pay for two of the detectives. Anthony Li, son of Chinese immigrants, had been brought up with an intense feeling for what constituted right, wrong, fair and unfair. It bothered him that Dmitri's costs in the pursuit of the law were unjust.

Anthony Li was tall for a Chinese man, well proportioned and muscular. He had an oval face with calm, relaxed features and narrow, almond-shaped eyes. He moved deliberately, as if considering every motion. However, this impression was deceptive because if needed, he could strike as quickly as a snake.

When Dmitri heard of Brandeis' decision he was extremely happy, for his detective agency bill had proved to be enormous. Three men, two on day shift one at night, with extra charges for equipment and sundries amounted to a goodly outlay.

By Tuesday Dmitri became restless. The world felt all out of order. Nothing he tried to fill his day with satisfied him. In a fit of anger he threw one of his favorite patio chairs, a swivel kind, which he was repairing, into the canal. He did this only to dive right after it into the deep, dark water. He finally rescued the chair from the depth, expending exceedingly more energy each time he dove below, because it had become entangled among the coral rocks in the canal bed.

Martha, next door, heard his caterwauling and came over with two glasses of rum, Coke, and ice. For a while he sat with her on the porch, enjoying the sun and a friendly breeze, only to fidget discontentedly again the moment she left.

To change his outlook, he climbed aboard the Estrella. He trimmed her, for no reason at all, as if he were to take her out into the ocean. Deeply involved and pleased with himself, he almost did not hear the phone ring.

"Brandeis here," intoned the mellifluous voice, "I have a request to make. It seems the Russians just left for Key West. Li and Angel are following. I, however, have a dilemma. I could not get a boat allocated at such short notice. Now I do not have anyone to shadow them at sea. I even tried several suitable rental establishments to no avail. I could have had a coast guard cutter, but they can be spotted from miles away."

Brandeis' voice became a soft flutelike instrument as he intoned, "How about the boat you guys used last week? Is that a possibility? We can pay for expenses and a rental fee."

"No, that will not be possible. We used my neighbor's boat and he is working. But," and here Dmitri's voice became superbly cheerful, "I can get my sail boat down there today, and unless they do the pick-up this evening I can shadow them. Better this way anyway. They would surely remember the Jeanette because of the tuna we caught."

"Great, I will send Raphael and Manny to help you with things."

Infused with new life, Dmitri padded about the Estrella getting things into the shape that suited him. He was a stickler for neatness—the keeper of a tidy ship.

"You are anal retentive!" Martha told him once. Because of his neatness tick, getting ready was fairly simple.

He prepared a cooler with food and another with drinks. The detectives were always woefully unprepared. They relied on fast food sources, often the kind of fat-fare that made him nauseous just thinking about.

Just as he carried his supplies to the Estrella, Raphael and Manny appeared in a jalopy the natives called Keys cruisers, and gave him a hand. The men lost no further time. Dmitri took the controls, engaging the engines while Manny untied the Estrella.

Out in the Atlantic a strong wind from the East filled the sails of the ship hastening the boat on its southward course.

Later, arriving at the Boat Basin at Key West, Dmitri was lucky to be given a berth close to the entry. This way they were far enough from the Prekrasnaya Irina to be spied upon by the Russians, but in a great spot to either follow or sail ahead of the enemy.

They repeated last week's program almost to the letter. Angel and Li joined them soon after they docked. They ate in two groups at different times in the Mexican Cantina. Then Angel and Manny took up surveillance stations where they could monitor the Irina. The rest of the crew went below deck where a stateroom and two smaller cabins promised a good night's sleep. After six hours Raphael and Li came up for a change of the watch, giving Angel and Manny a few hours of sleep.

Next morning's wake up call was at five. As the men contemplated going out for coffee and breakfast, Raphael and Anthony Li literally pounced on deck.

"They are moving," they cried breathlessly, "The yacht is moving out. The Cigar boat is staying."

A flurry of activity ensued. Dmitri called out orders instantly obeyed by everyone. They wanted to give the impression that they were out early, ahead of everyone—independent agents unconcerned with time, without interest in other boats.

Dmitri barely had gotten the boat away from the dock and out into the channel when the yacht appeared behind them, looming majestically against the rosy colored background of Key West.

Dmitri wore a captain's hat shadowing his face. Furthermore, he put on broad-rimmed sunglasses, which obscured his features even better. Manny wore, apart from three-day-old stubble, a red knit cap and was unrecognizable. The top prize for a disguise, however, was to be had by Angel. He came up from below, taking the men's breath away.

"What the devil?" cried Dmitri, before it dawned on him. There, right before their eyes stood a gorgeous blond girl in a white sailing dress, a matching knit sweater, and white deck shoes. To the men's hoots and whistles Angel posed, turning from side to side, smiling a silly girly smile.

"Now I don't have to stay below when the Irina is present and we have become just another pleasure sailing ship." He pursed his lips, grinning. "Just look at the owner's daughter."

"Who bought that expensive stuff you are wearing?" inquired Raphael concerned with finances. "Don't worry! I think I can sell it to customs as necessary disguise. Who knows, perhaps later my girlfriend, Manuela, will thank me for the quality of the stuff when I make her a present."

They set their course in the direction of Cuba because they all agreed that eventually the Prekrasnaya Irina was going to the old pick-up point. But not before first leading curious followers to the Marquesas or Dry Tortugas. A sailing ship in the role of spy-boat is at tremendous disadvantage, for its mast can be seen from great distance even if its bulk is obscured.

It wasn't long and the Irina swept by them, passing like a Jaguar leaves a Volkswagen Beetle in the dust. Aboard the yacht no one was visible. Irina's wake was enormous, rocking the Estrella as if she braved heavy seas. From this Dmitri surmised that Prekrasnaya Irina was in a hurry, pressing on full speed.

The sun had not risen yet. Today the sea showed a disgruntled face, reminding Dmitri of a moody, pretty woman unable to make up her mind whether to stomp and storm into the day or have morning coffee in a flounced, pink negligee.

In the East, at the point of sunrise, shades of gold, pink and white alternately vied for attention, promising a nice day. Yet, higher in the sky, packs of black storm clouds bunched together.

Darn, it's hurricane season, thought Dmitri. A sky like this one often announced a storm. He turned on the ship's radio for a weather report. Fiddling with the knobs for the right channel, he heard the monotonous announcement of the prevailing weather conditions.

It was a tape that repeated itself over and over again. It was updated hourly by maritime authorities together with the updates for the shipping lanes in the Gulf Stream.

Satisfied that the weather would be overcast with medium seas yet unthreatened by a storm, he took the Estrella in hand.

So far, they had moved on engine power. Now, he showed Raphael whom he knew to be totally reliable, how to steer by the compass in a southwesterly direction as he went to rig the sails.

The Estrella was a sloop; her main sail was hoisted automatically, otherwise one would have needed a large, trained crew to work the rigging. With help from Angel, Manny and Anthony, Dmitri was able to put up the main and the jib sail to make the best of the breeze, tacking as they went.

With the wind in her sails the Estrella ran like a busy girl, giving the impression that the people on board were nothing but pleasure sailors. Soon, they lost sight of the Prekrasnaya Irina. As before, she seemed to be destined for the Dry Tortugas. Unconcerned, since they knew pursuit was fruitless, they kept to their course. For one reason, they could not catch up to her, for another, they were to remain unnoticed. Lastly, they hoped that she would come to them eventually and that such a meeting would look innocent, indeed.

They reached the previous coordinates of Irina's rendezvous an hour after sunrise. After the stirring morning hours, the wind had subsided and they ran the last stretch on motor power. They had taken the sails down and now cut the motors too. The sea had become oddly calm—flat as a mirror. What had happened to the lively seas experienced earlier? The air had become abnormally cool. Angel in his light girl's dress, rummaged through the cabins until he found a heavy seaman's sweater to cover himself. Steam began to rise off the water, enveloping ship and crew in nebulous fog. Becalmed, the Estrella floated lazily upon the ocean.

The eerie fog drifted slowly in swaths as if moved by invisible hands, opening temporarily glimpses of a stretch of water, only to close again like a curtain after allowing a teasing peek.

"I don't like this," said Dmitri to Anthony Li standing beside him at the wheel. Li, too, looked unhappy.

"Rarely do we encounter fog in these waters this time of year and nothing this morning foretold of fog. For fog to occur, a layer of cold air, much cooler than the surface water must be present. The weather service had forecast nothing of the sort."

The men were uneasy, subdued. They spoke quietly, almost in a whisper, as if an enemy waited in the foggy wings. Their silence was all the more strange because the fog muted all sound.

"It will be a damned daunting task for the smugglers to find their boat in this soup," ventured Li irritated. "We will be lucky if we don't get hit by another ship."

"Not to worry," said Dmitri, calming such fears. "Any ship of size can see our mast sticking out of the fog, and anything moving must sound its horn." Li, however, was not comforted by such thoughts.

"I don't think the Cuban smugglers have any intentions of sounding horns and thereby attracting attention to themselves. The same goes for the creepy mob of the Irina."

As if to prove his point, by perverse coincidence, a channel opened before them, dividing the gloom. Angel, afraid of missing the enemy, had sat above in the crow's nest. Now he flew down to the deck with simian speed, making his way to the wheel.

～≪

"THERE IS AN OBJECT floating out there in the water before us. About twenty to thirty yards port side. I think we should have a look."

There was no debate. Dmitri switched on the auxiliary motor, a small quiet affair that gently nudged them toward the floating thing.

"Wouldn't ya know," Angel sang out, "It's one of those floating bales the Irina picked up last week."

"The Cuban's must have made their delivery already. Darn, we don't know if they are still hanging around. Let's gaff this bail and disappear quietly. We don't want to be seen and give the game away," suggested Dmitri, almost whispering to Li who was the authority on board. The men were clustered about agent Li, their faces filled with expectation. His decisions would direct what actions would be taken. If he was incautious they could face danger.

Li looked calmly at the men. "Bring the bail aboard and put it out of sight as quickly and quietly as possible. Meanwhile, I will confer with Miami."

He walked to the stern of the Estrella, carrying with him a black case containing a radio that worked on a special frequency. While Li talked to Brandeis, Dmitri pulled a gaff from its hold. Looking for a likely place to insert the gaff he noticed that the bale was tied with cord. "Splendid," he thought, "we don't want to puncture anything."

They had barely manhandled the awkward package onto the ship when Li came flying across deck.

"Let's handle this thing very carefully. Chances are it's booby-trapped in a way that only a knowing recipient can open it without getting blown up. Brandeis said to gently put it on a mattress or such and cover it with a few heavy tarps just in case it does go off. He presumes the charge will not blow a hole in the boat, but damage bodies close to the charge."

Since the cord had proved safe for lifting, Manny and Li gingerly lifted the bale, holding it by the cord, and carried it below. They placed it on a bed in the smallest cabin, heaping blankets and finally a heavy tarp on top.

Having completed this delicate task the two heaved a sigh of relief and went up to join the others. Now Li could finally give them the rest of Brandeis' instructions.

"He wants you to set your course for Miami and get there with all possible speed. He does not care if we shadow anything, or if we witness a pick-up. In the bale we should find enough evidence to start an operation."

Silently saying a prayer to his maker, Dmitri set about the business of getting them away from this treacherous spot. He was relieved that they would not have to hang around here any longer. However, he knew that they were not out of danger by a long shot. He knew that he should begin to sound the foghorn the moment the ship moved. Yet he could not bring himself to give away their position.

As if the fates had aligned themselves in his favor, a light breeze began to blow once again from the east, sweeping the nebulous veils westward. Angel in the crow's nest reported a speedboat far away to the south.

"They must have left before we came," he crowed happily. The men on the Estrella were invigorated by the open water, the view of the horizon, and the freshness of the breeze.

However, they were still driven by the unvoiced fear: If the Irina were to appear now, and someone made the connection between the Estrella and one missing bale of contraband, it was a small thing to establish the ownership of the boat and find Dmitri to be the villain. The mob could find him and squash him, long before any government agency began taking action. He could be dead, shark-bait, miles out in the ocean weighted down by a sack of cement, before anyone even missed him.

These frightening internal deliberations sped Dmitri to work at frantic speed. Not only did he put both sails up, but before they could catch the wind, he also ran the engines in his haste to leave the dreadful coordinates of the rendezvous.

Flying along, the compass set on north, north/east, Dmitri was the only one aboard steeped in misery. The rest of his company was in high spirits. So far they had gotten out of danger—perhaps only by the skin of their teeth—but they were in the clear. To add to their pleasure, the clouds were moving off, clearing the sky.

A pod of bottlenose dolphins capered around the ship. A few fearless individuals were riding the bow-wave as the men cheered them on. After the dolphins left, a school of feeding rays passed by. This was a rare sight for most of the men.

Relieved of the earlier strain, the crew now noticed their hunger. Dmitri urged them to bring up the coolers he had packed and feast on his special Cuban sandwiches. He prepared them with white crusty bread, roast pork, tomatoes and onions. He himself could not eat a thing. Earlier, a knot had formed in his stomach, which prevented even the thought of food.

Finally, when Angel once more on lookout announced that land was in sight, Dmitri relaxed. So close to shore, his ship was just one of many, plying the waters. No one would look at her with suspicion.

He gratefully accepted a sandwich, which Raphael brought to him together with a can of Coke. He smiled when a small flock of boobies flew by and laughed broadly when a big turtle he spied off starboard dove into the deep as if attacked by a flying enemy from above.

After a ten-hour run, they tied up late at night at a private mooring. All along Li had kept the radio contact with Brandeis open. They had followed Brandeis' directions how to find the dock. It was a place Dmitri swore he could have never found otherwise. The dock and surrounding neighborhood made the same shabby, neglected impression he had of Brandeis' building. *Well*, he thought, *perhaps at least one agency is concerned with taxpayer's money.*

He could not hang onto his thoughts much longer, for suddenly the deserted mooring came alive. Like an army of ants a stream of men descended upon the boat. Dmitri could hardly believe his eyes. There were at least twenty men crowding onto his vessel, Brandeis in the lead.

For an overweight fellow the man moved surprisingly well. He stood up straight among his men, gaining inches in stature that way. His usually well-modulated voice had the rough edge of command as he introduced the players of this night's game to each other.

"I have called in the FBI. We will need all the help we can get for the next operations." With a wave of his hand he introduced about half of the men as FBI agents. This gesture ended the formalities and work began.

Dmitri, having run the ship for almost fourteen hours straight, collapsed into a deck chair, exhausted. Angel, who had taken a liking to him, because he admired his nautical skills, his common sense and his love for all things Cuban, brought him a glass of Rum and Coke—heavy on the rum. Drink in hand, Dmitri watched tiredly from the edge of whirling activity as two explosives experts brought the suspicious bale, constructed from floating plastics, onto the deck.

They wore protective suits and helmets, holding long-handled tweezers and cutters in hands protected by huge metallic gantlets. As they worked, the rest of the group stayed at a respectful distance. No one expected too big an explosion, just a booby trap to finish off the curious fool looking for an easy prize.

Although everyone knew that the danger was minimal, the men held their breath in anticipation when the cutters were applied to the cord. The blades cut clean through the stout binding and it fell useless to the deck. The explosives experts next inspected the bale from all sides for a hint exposing a trap. As all seemed clean they began to cut the plastic wrap from the big package. The outer layer fell away and nothing happened. Next two layers of air-filled material were removed and still all was well. Yet, underneath, perhaps next to the core, was an oilcloth wrap, which the men with their long-handled probes gently prodded. The moment the probes made contact with the cloth a blinding flash and an explosion shocked the assembled company.

When the men had adjusted their blinded eyes again to the relative darkness of their surroundings, they saw that the demolition men were still alive. Better even, protected by their helmets and special goggles they were able to see. Their probes had been knocked out of their hands and they were looking for their tools. There were plenty of eyes looking and hands to retrieve the needed gadgets, and a moment later the men began working once more.

Before them stood a wooden box, peppered by bits and pieces of oilcloth. They opened a simple latch without incident and began to lift the contents from the crate. There were boxes of cigars, Cuba's finest, and boxes, plastic-lined, containing shiny white powder—cocaine.

When the FBI totaled up the value of just this one floater, the street value was astonishing. Multiplied by ten or twenty times more and it was obvious that each pick-up represented a grand fortune for the mob.

It was past midnight when even the most minute piece of evidence had been gathered by specialists and carried off in plastic baggies for the FBI's forensic laboratories. Every shred could be a clue, yielding important evidence in the war against crime.

Before the teams dispersed, Dmitri could not help but ask of the demolitions men:

"How would the mob be able to open the bales without being blown to bits? Would they be prepared like you are?"

The experts laughed amused, "No, of course not! They have a key of sorts to defuse whatever is under the oilcloth layer. By tomorrow we will know perhaps what they use. Probably something as simple as drenching the package in water or some such thing. There are many ways to set up a flash explosive."

After locking everything securely, Dmitri was the last man off the boat. After all, who knew what could happen in this neighborhood. When he stepped ashore, Raphael was waiting for him as he had promised.

"Too far for you to go home tonight," he'd said. "You will come home with me and have Cuban breakfast tomorrow."

Dmitri protested politely, "Your wife might have other ideas about a sudden guest." Yet, he was genuinely relieved when Raphael insisted that he come with him, that he would be very welcome. Suddenly Dmitri felt every hour of his age. He wanted nothing more than a bed to lay upon with a pillow to cradle his aching head.

Cuban Hospitality

స~৯

WHEN DMITRI AWOKE THE next morning, he felt very much better. He began to think with residual excitement about last night's happenings. He performed his ablutions with a feeling of restoration and after a pleased look into the mirror he walked into the kitchen of his host. The kitchen was done in the colorful style of his host's Spanish heritage. A golden-brown floor of large, thick tile was dotted with a few multi-colored, woven rugs. An island, sitting within reach of the stove, and all other counters were covered with glazed honey-colored tile. A life-sized clay rooster, painted in shades of red, green, yellow and black, stood on the island beside a large basket of eggs. Bunches of fresh herbs formed an interesting bouquet in a sunflower-painted vase. On the other side of the island, a basket filled with lemons, limes, and chilis announced that an avid cook prepared great food in this kitchen.

As Dmitri parked himself on a barstool by the counter, he noticed the well-executed mosaic of a matador dispatching a bull high on the wall above the cooking range. Raphael was leaning against the opposite wall, talking rapidly in Spanish into a wall-mounted phone. Raphael's wife, a pretty, dark-haired woman with a pleasing, softly rounded figure and a friendly face, turned away from the stove where she had been stirring eggs in a large pan. She approached Dmitri, her hand stretched in welcome.

"Welcome to our house. I hope you slept well."

"Thank you, I had a very good night and feel very good." Dmitri shook hands with Isabella Mendoza and smiled broadly. She had seen his interest in the detailed mosaic of the bullfighter and explained laughingly, "I had to have him in my kitchen. It is a picture of my grandfather who was a matador in Spain many years ago."

Dmitri commented politely on the quality of the artwork.

"Come over to the table and sit down. Everything is ready and Raphael will be with us presently." She led him to a porch, shaded by Bougainvillea, where a table covered with a plain white tablecloth and set with colorful plates and cups awaited three people.

On his way to the table Dmitri spotted a ceramic clock on the wall, and almost jumped.

"Heavens!" he exclaimed. "No wonder I am so well rested; it is almost lunch time."

Raphael, having finished his conversation, joined him laughing heartily. "Don't worry, amigo. I slept almost as long as you did."

"Why didn't you wake me up?"

"Why should I? No hurry. I do not have to work today, so there is no harm."

Over breakfast Dmitri learned that the Mendozas had three boys—six, eight and eleven years old—who'd been very quiet this morning while getting ready for school. To his surprise, Dmitri learned that Raphael, despite his demanding schedule, coached baseball three nights a week, and spent most weekends in outings and celebrations with his large family.

They feasted on spicy eggs, pulled pork, fried potatoes and Cuban bread. Crusty, yet soft inside, the bread tasted like no other in the world. When Dmitri left, he had made new friends, a good feeling for a man standing alone. Regretfully he thought about his own family, his children and grandchildren who were far away up north.

Later that day back in Key Largo, he missed the company and excitement of the last few days. He missed people so much that he cooked shrimp in spicy sauce, boiled some rice, made a salad and asked Martha for dinner. She accepted instantly, a sign that she, too, had been missing company. From somewhere in his kitchen, he dug up a bottle of rather good Pinot Grigio, light and delicate, that went well with the meal.

"So," asked Martha, when they started the salad, "how does the Irina story develop? You were gone for almost two days, and you took your boat. By the way, where is it? It's not your habit to leave this sail-girl in strange berths."

Dmitri was more than happy to oblige with a tale. In former days, not much excitement had enlivened his days. But lately, dear God, he could talk a long streak about his unwanted adventures.

"You must promise not to repeat any of this!" He made her swear on her husband's grave. "Not a word to anyone until the whole case is solved. Then you might shout it to the sky, but right now, mum's the word."

He took a deep draught of the Pinot, let it play in his mouth, swallowed, and spoke. He told her everything. The surveillance of Russian Irina and the mob, the Thursday runs to Key West. He spoke of the mob's storehouse, the yacht and the cigar boat and the rendezvous out at sea, complete with the pick-up of the floating contraband.

"Can you imagine, they wrap the core of the bale in a material that has the ability to blow-up into your face? We are not certain if it will kill you but it will surely damage your hands, eyes and face severely."

Martha listened, spellbound. Her eyes were huge, shining with excitement; her lips were half open, moist and red, from having been bitten a few times.

"My," she finally breathed, "your adventures are terrifying. I can't imagine what these people would do to you if they knew you are on to their criminal exploits. They seem to be capable of torture and murder." All upset, Martha was wringing her hands so hard that the tendons came visibly to the fore.

Moments later though, upon cooler reflection, her fear and compassion turned to raw anger. Like a mad hen, blowing up her plumage, she grew visibly larger and scolded, "You had a perfectly peaceful life, no worries, no fears and no enemies. With one stupid decision you turned it all into a frightening nightmare!" Dmitri grinned at her like naughty boy.

"Martha, Martha, it's not all bad. I have come to recognize that I was dying then by inches. I was only half alive. Now, with one stroke of luck, I feel anger, fear and joy. My old friends are back in my life and I am meeting new people who might become friends."

He poured for each another glass of Pinot Grigio. Sipping the wine, and reflecting on his motivation to send for a foreign woman, he admitted, "I had such a deep feeling of dissatisfaction. It was, as if I were caught in a nebulous web, hanging there suspended like a blind bat until someone would free me."

"Maybe you felt like this because you lived without purpose. Having stared death in the face, you might have realized that you are not leaving much of a legacy. Perhaps you viewed your declining years as a waste. Did you ever consider that with Theresa's death, your service came to an end and with it the feeling of usefulness to which you had become accustomed. I believe that you are dreaming about possible fatherhood again because then you were needed, the way you were needed on one of your ships. In those days you were serving, forming minds, shaping your children's future, and with that you were fulfilled."

He stared thoughtfully into the silky, silvery night. It was one of those moonlit, twilight nights that compels men to take their boats onto the water to fish or dream. After a long silence he finally addressed her valid comments.

"You could be right. Perhaps I should become more involved in my community. I could be teaching navigation and marine safety to young people. I could volunteer at the library. I am there twice a week anyway. And yet," he hesitated long enough for the thought to form, "there is more that I want and need. The last weeks have been great. I would not trade one minute of the experience. And that includes even the miserable things, the disappointments, the anger, the fear, and the scolding by the ICE."

"Well, you must know what's best for you," conceded Martha, rising to leave. It was late and as always, she had a slew of plans for the morrow.

The Professional's Scheme

≈∽∿

ALTHOUGH DMITRI PUT a positive spin on his adventures, his sleep was plagued by night terrors. In one episode, he dreamed that the Estrella was pursued by a huge, black warship. Its cannons were pointed straight at her while he stood helplessly at the wheel. He knew that they were doomed. He and his ship were all alone awaiting the onslaught of the monstrous boat that seemed to be grinning through its portholes.

In another dream he was swimming, far away from shore. Behind him a huge shark was gaining on him. Every time he turned the triangular fin of the beast was closer than before. Other dreams, thankfully, were only chimeras. They hinted at danger but only vaguely and veiled.

Next morning he tried to analyze the reasons for his horrid night. Perhaps it was the moon shining into his bedroom. Or perhaps his mind was just overactive with over-stimulation. Could it be that he just was not used to new and exciting experiences anymore? Whatever caused these dreams could be just the Pinot; maybe he should just stick to the rum and Coke. He was used to this potion.

Deprived of rest, he spent his day automatically going about his business but accomplished little. In the evening Raphael called.

"Just thought I'd let you know that we have been ordered off the case. Looks like from now on only government agencies will be involved."

"Why on earth would they do this? I thought Brandeis liked you guys and the work you are doing. After all, we brought them the case. Without us they would know nothing."

"They probably think that we could give the game away because we are not trained professionals by their standard."

"I don't care what they think! I want you to remain a part of it all." Suddenly an unpleasant thought hit Dmitri, "What if they won't put Irina into my custody so that I get right with the ICE again? Maybe they are cutting me out of the deal too?"

"You better find out. I think Brandeis will play fair with you. Why don't you just give him a call? Let me know what's going down."

"I will! Regards to Isabella. I fondly remember her food."

Dealing with Authorities

꩜

A LONG CONVERSATION WITH Brandeis produced a game plan that Dmitri thought he could live with. The agency man insisted that Dmitri's men lay low for the next days and stay away from the gang and house in Coconut Grove.

"The FBI is adamant that they have the lead in this investigation. There are more sinister issues than smuggling at stake here, and we have to defer. However, I will try to involve you guys when we bust this gang. Nothing has been decided yet. The FBI boys thought you guys had done a rather nice job by not mucking things up and reporting the case. So I think I can make them see it your way. Even if they don't, I will make sure you get straight with Immigration."

Dmitri informed Raphael. Deprived of action once more, and uncertain about future involvement, he threw himself into an orgy of yard maintenance.

Weeds were a constant to be counted on always. Pesky green shoots pushed their heads everywhere through the white, immaculate surface of the coral rock.

The inhabitants of the Keys had different ways of dealing with the tropical lushness of the flora. There were those with the motto, "if you can't fight them join them!" This group installed coarse lawns of African pest-resistant grass that they chopped down regularly. Others used weed killer on anything that shoved its head above the rock, and still another group used a combined assault of spray and pulling the offenders from its white bed.

Dmitri, a natural man, belonged to a unique group that pulled weeds only. This brotherhood abstained from dousing the weeds with Roundup. As he looked about his yard, this time he groaned with frustration. He had paid little attention to his property and green was visible everywhere. He could have hired help to do the job, of course. Yet he had sworn that rather then run to a gym in Miami to get exercise he would not avoid physical labor and keep himself in shape by working the grounds of his property. He gritted his teeth and began to pull out the green devils. After an hour the heat and humidity wearied him. It was one thing to work standing upright in a tropical environment yet quite another to do a job head to the ground. As he contemplated leaving the job in search of water, another reason to leave the weeds offered itself in the form of Brent.

As was his custom, the big man visited via the canal. Brent had gone for his usual swim down the canal and into Florida Bay. There he would swim to his heart's content or until he had worked the kinks out of his muscles. Since he sat in the cabs of big rigs for long stretches of the day, he worked his body in the water until it felt right again.

As always, he pulled himself onto land, disdaining the ladder. He boomed at Dmitri, "Are there any refreshments to be had at this cantina?"

"Glad to oblige. Need a break anyway. Just give me a minute. I need to cool off in the canal."

Dmitri stripped off his T-shirt and jumped in the canal with a splash. When he came out of the water, he followed Brent. They used the outdoor shower to get the salt off their bodies. Rubbing themselves dry with large, severely used beach towels, they began to exchange the latest details of their lives. When Dmitri's turn came he said, "Too damn much has happened. I will fix us a sandwich and bring a couple of beers and we will talk then."

Minutes later, he came back with a tray heaped with sandwiches, potato chips, salsa and the promised beer. They settled comfortably into his cushioned patio chairs and attended with gusto to the business of drinking and eating.

Brent had been up north in Georgia for the last few days and was glad to be back in his beloved Keys. When he was properly relaxed, Dmitri began the tale of the mob's pursuit aboard the Estrella.

"Have you ever come across fog out there this time of year," Dmitri asked when he reached the part where they awaited the Prekraznaya Irina.

"Can't recall. Sometimes in winter when a cold front moves down from the north, but this time of year, no. Heck this sounds almost like a miracle. Dmitri and his ship obscured with the help from unearthly forces." They laughed sheepishly.

"Strange business that. I still have not figured it out and I have been thinking about it for days. However, it sure saved our bacon and allowed us to get a bale."

The part with the explosion intrigued Brent mightily. I hope the FBI boys can figure out what it is; how to stop it from blowing up at all."

In this neighborhood, when someone sits long enough on their porch enjoying a snack and drink, others come calling. Although these people drop in without invitation, Key's etiquette allows for this; it's a perfectly proper way to act. For down here, if someone was coming at the wrong time, or people were too busy to see to guests, they candidly said so. Because of such easy manner, the feelings of either party were never hurt.

Therefore, it was not unexpected or unusual that Brent's wife, too, swam across the canal. She held one arm high in the air, holding a dry swimsuit over her head so she could change on arrival. Although middle aged, Jan had kept her figure trim, and her blond hair short. She had taken great care not burn her skin the way many people were wont to do in Florida.

As she stepped away from the outdoor shower, dripping warm water, Dmitri handed her a dry towel as proper Keys hosts do. His duty done, he rejoined Brent while Jan found a quiet spot to change in the house. They were a congenial group of friends who treated each other like family. They knew each others houses intimately, knew their tastes in foods and drinks, their likes and dislikes of books, boats, clothes, art and weather. They could be relied upon to remember birthdays, anniversaries, important doctor's appointments, and were handier in an emergency than family.

Joining the men, Jan had barely helped herself to a lobster sandwich and iced tea when Martha appeared, walking along the dock. Traipsing carefully, watching out for treacherous ropes, she balanced a covered cake platter and a large, comical dolphin beaker filled with her special blend of tea.

Once more, for Jan's benefit this time, Dmitri was obliged to tell the latest tale of encounter with the mob. Jan was a delightful listener. At the appropriate spots she sighed, cried out in horror and commiserated with Dmitri's travail.

Martha, having heard it all before, dripped a little poison, by mentioning that all the trouble could have been avoided if a certain man had not insisted on crossing a foreign bride's path.

"Forgive him, Martha, he is just a man. Their thinking is never quite straight where women and romance are concerned," cried Jan. Thereafter, both women pursued their own interests in a private conversation, while Brent and Dmitri discussed how the strange situation might develop in the future.

"Whatever happens, cut me in on any action. I could not stand to be left out. If I am not working out of town, I will be your man."

Glad to have such generous, true friends, Dmitri thanked him and promised that any adventure, if possible, would include Brent. It was decided that sitting about waiting for phone calls was unacceptable, that instead they should go fishing.

Their fishing trip next day was a failure. It was as if every mangrove snapper in Florida Bay had decided to go on a diet. Nothing tempted them. They caught purely by mistake two small barracuda and Brent, undeservedly blaming their bad luck on the young hunters, decided to eat them that night for dinner.

"I can't see why you would deal with these miserable, bony things," protested Dmitri. Brent, however, had developed a taste for this ferocious fish as a Boy Scout, when the boys ate everything they caught, camping out on some of the unpopulated, mosquito-infested Keys in the bay which were subject to occasional flooding at very high tides.

"The small ones are good," he now defended his choice as if Dmitri didn't know, "it's the big ones that are poisonous, having absorbed over the years the impurities of their food."

Three uneventful days passed. Dmitri went to the library to get books for the evenings. He liked to read in bed, propped up, a glass of wine within reach. Next day, he obliterated every last one of his weeds; he cut the brown fronds on his palm trees and sprayed the foundation of his house against cockroaches and palmetto beetles.

On Sunday he went with Martha to Jan and Brent's for a steak dinner. Every so often Key's folk had the primitive urges of cave-men for meat and this hunger had to be assuaged. Often they ate seafood four or five days of the week, so change was welcome and steak dinners were a treat.

When he returned late to his abode, he noticed the red eye blinking on his answering machine.

"Brandeis here! I have good news. The FBI has agreed to let you and your people be a part of the operation. In a minor, supportive role, I might add. It may console you to know that customs will be involved in a supporting role also. Since you are not home right now, I will give you all details tomorrow morning, early."

Dmitri could not help himself. Late as it was, he had to call Brent, who would be still cleaning up after the very extensive dinner.

"We are in. The FBI is throwing us a minor supporting crumb, but we are in," his voice cracked with excitement.

"Good going, finally the uppity Russian bitch is getting some good American justice," growled Brent, scraping his grill with more vigor than before.

"Let me know the details. I will be out of town for two days, but the rest of the week I'm free."

In the morning Dmitri called Raphael and informed him of the new developments.

"Whatever transpires, I have talked with my guys and they want to be a part of the action. This will be a freebie. No agency fees for this one. They just want to see the tail end of their most exciting case ever. Man, how often do we come across a gorgeous woman, the mob, cigars, dope and blow-up bales?" He answered his own purely rhetorical question, "Never! For us it's always straying husbands, missing loony adult children and, you would not believe it, stolen toy poodles."

Dmitri promised to call with details as soon Brandeis delivered the particulars. To his surprise, he didn't have to wait long.

Brandeis must have had a great day, for his voice vibrated contentedly and he spoke more eloquently than he ever had before.

"We are acting this week. The day and the time, however, will be determined by the denizens of the Coconut Grove mansion. This means that everyone has to be ready and able to spring into action at a moment's notice. It will be your part to come up with two or three boats, the faster the better; it saves the taxpayers money and it is your enterprise, after all. Every man involved in the caper must know that there could be trouble and they might get hurt. We assume no responsibility and they will have to sign waivers to this effect." He paused, consulting his notes, Dmitri surmised from the noise of paper being shuffled.

"Furthermore, you will be directed in all aspects of the operation, and never act on your own!"

By now Dmitri was ready to burst and could not contain himself, "All right, all right. We will agree to all conditions you impose, but what is the plan? Are we to get ready and are on standby as of today?"

"Patience, patience, friend. I'll explain presently. Yes, we want you to immediately get ready, summon your friends and go down to Key West. We want you to take station in the boat basin where you have been before. I will get a special radio to you that only has one frequency, secret, of course, with which you can send and receive. The FBI boys will stock you with a plethora of clandestine gadgets. For that they will contact you on their own. I am not at liberty to discuss the details of the plan or how we envision things will go down. Sorry, but you will be fed details on a need-to-know basis only. I think this is all."

"I know for a fact that Raphael and his guys are going to come and help. So perhaps you want to send the radio down with him," suggested Dmitri. He thought for a moment and added, "Well, I better get cracking and get down to Key West."

The moment he hung up the phone he remembered with dismay that Brent was going to be out of town for the next two days. Damn it all, he had counted on his boat to be one of the boats used. Musing on the matter, he thought that with a little luck, perhaps Brent could be reached wherever he was. He dialed his number in hope to get his permission to take the Jeannette down to Key West where Brent could meet up with her on Wednesday. He was astonished when Brent himself picked up at the second ring. That in itself was more than luck—more like a miracle.

"Where are you? I expected to raise you on your cellphone. I was just calling Jan to get your number," Dmitri shouted, surprised.

"Well you got me. I am home. My run got cancelled. They are having machinery trouble and until they have things fixed, I am shelved here. What is your burning problem?"

"Stuff is hitting the proverbial fan. You and your boat are sorely needed like right now. We are instructed to go to Key West and wait for the action to start. Are you still willing and able?"

Without the slightest hesitation Brent shot back, "How much time do I have?"

"Perhaps an hour. I have to call the others and Raphael has to come from Miami with the special radio they are outfitting us with."

"All right then, I'll pack some clothes and grub. Then I'll get the boat filled up; when I am done with that, I'll pick you up."

"Don't you have to prepare Jan for what you are about to do? Maybe you will be gone for a week."

"Oh, I think she'll be fine with it. I thinkshe made some plans thinking that I would be gone, and I would have fouled things up for her by being here." Brent hung up in a big hurry, leaving Dmitri to his phoning and the preparation of provisions.

Dmitri's luck held in a most marvelous fashion, for his very first phone call to Dan Heminger brought him a double winner. Dan was willing and could be ready in a couple of hours. But best of all, he would bring the second boat that they might need. It was a Pro Line 35 Express, one of the finest boats on the market. In size, a vessel much like the Jeannette, give or take a few feet. But it was fast, as boats go, and Dan was chomping with excitement to take her out of her berth and run her for a good stretch.

"Hell, this girl is gathering barnacles. She needs fresh ocean water and a good airing. She smells a little below.".

"Don't let Ada hear you say such a thing. She might get a might steamed," laughed Dmitri, for the boat was named Ada-May.

"I will take care not to say such a thing within Ada's hearing." Dmitri could imagine Dan grinning from ear to ear.

The friends agreed on a meeting place in the boat basin at Key West, for they wanted to stay close to each other for the operation.

"I'll make sure the harbor master will give us the same moorage as before, close to the entrance."

Buoyed by the ease with which fate arranged his adventure, Dmitri gathered the rest of the old Intrepid crew. In his conversation with Dan it had been decided that the men of the Intrepid were to join Dan at his house in Jackson, where his boat was berthed.

Dmitri raided his freezer and the refrigerator for food, and the garage for cases of soft drinks. His arms loaded, he heard the kitchen phone ring with annoying persistence. Impetuously, he hot-footed it out of the garage to answer the ringing. He bumped a shelf and a case of corn dropped from up high, smashing his toes. Limping and yelling unpleasant things about vegetables he raced on, reaching the phone on its last ring.

"It's Raphael. I have some bad news. Two of us will have to take a new case this week. It's important. So we drew straws. Manny and Ignacio lost, so you will get Angel and me. I hope that will be enough men in your boat."

"I think it will be fine. There will be four of us on our boat, because Brent was miraculously furloughed."

"Ok then! We get on the road in five minutes. You can expect us within the hour."

Dmitri took his responsibilities as host of this party very seriously. He had raided his larders until they were bare. Although he could depend on the others to bring supplies, too, he wanted to do well by his friends who so selflessly came to his aid. He looked around, proudly assessed his efforts, and began to move the provisions to the dock.

He had barely begun to haul the supplies down to his dock where Brent would pick him up shortly, when the pesky phone shrilled again. He fumed and frothed, being angry with himself for misplacing the portable unit. Once again he raced to the kitchen to hear Brandeis' voice.

"What luck that you have not left yet, Pataklos. I want you to take Anthony Li with you. I gave him the choice of a ride with our fellows or with your guys on a boat, and you won hands down."

"Be glad to take him. We have become quite fond of Anthony. He is a good man in a hard place; even if I suspect you are sending him to keep an eye on the dilettantes."

"No, no, I trust you to perform. However, I quite agree with you, Li is a good man.

By the way, he left the agency half an hour ago, so you should see him soon. Bon voyage."

Hmm! Dmitri thought he detected a note of enjoyable excitement in Brandeis' voice. *It's the thought of the hunt. It's the gathering of an Orca pod determined to take out a Great White Shark for stalking their young. Orcas, too, communicate avidly, advising each member of their position and the right moment when to move in for the kill.*

Still thinking of pursuit and confrontation, he was torn from his musings by the horn of Jeannette. Dang it all, Brent was already here. Well, that was all to the good. The big fellow could carry four cases of provisions to his two.

The palm trees threw ever-longer shadows upon the white gravel and the house while the friends stocked the boat. Angel and Raphael, arriving by car, had appeared in such unobtrusive manner that the two friends did not notice their arrival until they stood on the dock.

"Watch it, you guys!" yelped Brent coming from below deck. "You can give a guy a heart attack. How about a nice hallo?"

"Is that how you watch out for your crew? You'd be dead buddy if I were a nasty man," laughed Raphael. Angel grinned from to ear to ear over his handsome face. They wore regulation Keys wear—shorts, T-shirts and loafers. Each carried a sports bag with a week's supply of clothes, including a warm-up suit in case a stiff, cold wind should blow.

Not much later Anthony Li joined the group, looking like an ad for a work-out-program. He and Brent rivaled each other for the title of best-developed body. He, too, carried the obligatory bag and a small case, which he handed to Dmitri.

"Little present for you. I enjoyed your scotch so much the last time that I thought we needed to revisit the experience. Hope we have at least one quiet night to do so."

Raphael, Angel and Li brought in more supplies from their cars. "Contributions to make this a memorable, exciting enterprise," smiled Raphael.

Dmitri's new friend Isabella sent his favorite dish, a huge paella stuffed with shrimps, crabs, mussels, sausage and lobster, and an accompanying note, wishing the men a pleasant voyage. Another package of hers contained Cuban chicken, pork, and, of course, also enclosed was a loaf of the bread that they all loved.

"Madre de Dio, Raphael," Dmitri sang out with joy, "we can live out there like kings for a month. I will have to catch a fine fish to thank Isabella." Raphael, never shy to sing his wife's praises agreed.

"Yes, my Isabella is a great cook. She takes care of her friends. I think she would love a nice fish. I happen to know that grouper is her favorite."

"I will make sure that I catch a fine one for her this season."

They stowed their gear in no time and pushed off from the dock. The weather, so pleasant and fine all day, had suddenly turned grim. Far out over the Atlantic a thunderstorm gathered rain clouds, turning the sky black. Now the storm approached the islands with a vengeance.

"We will get soaked," predicted Brent. He pointed at the ominous aggregate of clouds, which were herded by the wind like sheep by a dog. As he spoke, the wind picked up even more, blowing strongly from northeast, roiling the water. Because of the foreboding brew over the Atlantic, Brent decided they would take the Intracoastal, a channel in the bay, and ride alee of the islands. Dmitri agreed with this plan.

Brent slowly maneuvered the boat through the connecting canals until they were free in open water, where he fully opened the throttles until the Jeannette fairly flew over the waves. Not long into their journey the storm broke. Its veritable fury unleashed gusting winds, a deluge of rain, thunder and lightening.

One after another the men disappeared below deck, closing the hatch, leaving Brent and Dmitri to cope with the elements. Protected by the wheelhouse, they stared into inky darkness, which was periodically broken by streaks of lightening, while the boat was buffeted by the wind, which drove sheets of rain into its side.

Brent stood behind the wheel, occasionally checking the instrument panel that softly glowed in the gloom. His legs were firmly planted absorbing every roll and toss of the waves and the wind. He curtailed the boat's speed severely because it was impossible to see in the deluge. Lightening now struck uninterruptedly all around them, making the men wish they were safely on land under cover.

Unable to see the buoys marking the Intracoastal, Brent slowed the boat to a crawl. He didn't dare stop altogether because he needed engine power to maintain his place in the middle of the channel. He could not chance getting stuck in the shallows and then spend the night mired in the muck.

Fortunately, the first vicious onslaught of the storm lasted but a short while. The storm, together with the water-laden clouds, thunder and lightning moved deeper into Florida Bay.

"Don't think it's over yet," cautioned Dmitri. "This whole thing can start over again in no time." Meanwhile the boat was once again moving at a good clip.

Dmitri got on the radio and checked on Dan Heminger and his crew. It turned out that Heminger's boat fared far worse than the Jeannette.

"We made great time and were approaching Isla Morada, when the squall hit us with such force that we had to run before the wind. We managed to enter Snake Creek and hid in one of the canals tied up to a nice guy's dock."

"So, are you still in Snake Creek?" Dmitri wanted to know.

"Yes, we are still clearing out debris and water."

"That's all to the good. When you are through cleaning up you might just come through the creek and join us on the Intracoastal. This will not be the last of the bad weather."

A short while later the two boats met in the bay. There was no time for a reunion, no matter how short. Time was of the essence. And so it happened that after a short exchange the Ada-May followed the Jeannette on a southern course. Dan's wife, Ada, had given him enough cash to buy the very best in ocean going boats. The cabin below was endowed with a master suite to sleep five comfortably. The kitchen was amply endowed for the production of gourmet meals. The amenities on Dan's boat were luxurious, to say the least.

Without further incidents, both boats arrived in the boat basin at Key West in deepest darkness and were assigned their berths. The harbormaster, motivated by Dmitri's handsome incentive, allocated both boats desirable spots at the entrance of the harbor. Safely moored, the two crews met aboard the Jeanette. No one expected any action during the night hours. Dmitri broke out beer and scotch. After introductions were made, libations followed. The Intrepid fellows regaled the detectives, Brent, Anthony Li, and Louis Ranger, with ancient stories that had become more daring and dangerous with each telling over the years. Ranger, a gangly fellow sent by the FBI, endured a goodly amount of ribbing because of his name. At last, they called it a night. They posted watches who were responsible for maintaining constant contact with the two agencies in charge of the operation.

The weather was glorious the next morning, but unpredictable, as always this time of year. The crews awoke to a cloudless sky, mild temperatures and, a rare event for the Keys, very little humidity. Last night's deluge had freshened the air and removed the cloying tropical moisture.

The report from the FBI told of only minor movement at the Coconut Grove manor. It advised relaxed readiness.

"What the hell do they mean by that?" asked Angel.Louis Ranger laughed, explaining, "That means that you can enjoy yourself just as long as you are ready to move when they call you, which means do nothing."

Anthony Li and Louis Ranger, despite cheerful comments to the crew, doubted there was cause for enjoyment. Filled with foreboding, they began industriously to outfit both boats with reflectors and spotlights. Both men were superbly capable of rigging the boats with devices capable of lighting large surfaces. Once they completed their job they were willing to take it easy with the rest of the crew.

Hungry, the men took turns going to the Mexican Cantina. They ate their fill and swam in the waters surrounding their boats. These exercises were not entirely free of trouble. The harbor bottom was sandy and loaded with stingrays, which buried themselves in the soft sandy bottom. Often, as if curious, the rays rose off the sandy floor and followed the men. By afternoon the crews were fully assembled on board. Most of them found a place to take a nap, sleeping off passionate debates about the mafia, illegal immigration and fishing. In half-dreams, they wished for something grand to happen soon.

෴

NOT MUCH LATER, a call came in. "The Coconut Grove contingent is moving. A large group, fourteen strong, is getting ready to move out, perhaps to Key West." This, an FBI call, caused action in both boats.

"Please let me talk to the FBI guys," clamored Dmitri. Louis Ranger obliged, handing him the special-connection phone.

"You only mentioned men. I need to know if Irina Sokolova is among them. Without her the mission is without value to me. I need her to get caught." Panicked, he almost begged for affirmative news.

"Pipe down! She and Avarikidze are among the group. It seems Petros does not trust his goons to act alone. So he and Irina are in the lead car."

Dmitri breathed a sigh of relief. Now the mission made sense again. It was one thing to be part of an operation for the good of the country, quite another still to see your own goals accomplished.

Now that they knew the Russian mob was creeping down the Overseas Highway, which, as usual, was stuffed with traffic heading toward Key West, their attitudes changed. Their talk was sparse and abrupt; their movements were precise and deft; their senses sharpened. Although every man involved in the adventure was eager to stake out the mob's headquarters or stand watch for the Prekrasnaya Irina, at the moment they were restricted to their boats. Those were their stations for observation or operations. The highway was off limits. Such were the dictates of the federal agencies.

At sunset, they saw a swarm of men take over the Russian yacht. The Russians manned the stations, tested the generators, ran motors and stowed gear. After this frantic assault, all stations were shut down again and quiet settled once more over the Irina and its berth.

Aroused by the Russians' activities, the men had a hard time falling asleep. They played cards, they talked, and discovered that Angel, besides his many other talents, also played guitar. He had brought his instrument aboard, hidden among his clothes, and now amused himself and the others by playing their favored tunes.

As a poor Cuban boy Angel never owned a guitar, never mind been able to afford lessons. Raphael noted the boy's musical abilities. He bought him the instrument shortly after Angel came to Miami and the boy taught himself to play. As the night wore on, he sang and played so well that the crews from neighboring boats came to visit.

Gray-haired women, slender girls and deeply tanned men crowded close to hear him play. His best renditions were Cuban love songs that made the young girls admire him. They looked up to him, soft-eyed as the does in a forest.

Although the men enjoyed his popularity, they took care not to be identified. It would not do if any Russian creeping about should make out Dmitri's or Raphael's face that they might have seen at an earlier encounter. No one worried about Angel, for the young man, like a chameleon, changed his looks constantly. Even now, hunched over his instrument, a slouching hat hiding his forehead and eyes, no one would have known him to be the young man, who had delivered supplies to the Prekrasnaya Irina.

Louis Ranger, tall, slender, of oval face with observing, intelligent eyes and winning demeanor, called for an end to the entertainment.

"You need your sleep, gentlemen. We have no idea what tomorrow brings and we want you sharp as razor blades," he said only half-kidding.

As before, they set watches following a schedule they had agreed to beforehand. According to this plan Dmitri had the first watch on the Jeannette, while Dan Heminger was first on watch on the Ada-May.

Dmitri sat alone in the stern of the boat. He was fairly comfortable in a padded chair with a Coke in his hand while he contemplated the vagaries of life. Many daunting, difficult and dangerous situations had presented themselves over his lifetime. He found it amusing that during the later days of his existence he was once more involved in the unfolding of an unusual tale that he could tell his grandchildren.

His unfair treatment at Irina's hands still festered in his mind; he was still immensely annoyed. All his life he had played by the rules. Fairness could be his second name. For the few times when he had broken the rules of the game he had been unmercifully punished. Here, he thought of the time he had an affair, a meaningless incident that cost him plenty.

It was for such righteous thoughts that he wanted Irina punished. Oh, he had pondered her motivations. Perhaps her life had been without a great purpose and meaning in Russia, without the ability to acquire wealth or a chance to become somebody of consequence. However, this reasoning did not count. It was nothing but baseless justification. Because in the end, the kind of person she was, would become a soulless materialist in any setting. There was no thought or concern in this girl for others, for their welfare, their emotions or their rights. But was this not exactly the human being that communist culture would produce? When the rights and feelings of others are constantly violated and callously destroyed by those who govern, the lessons learned by their adherents are that only total egotism serves in the fight for survival.

As he followed this train of thought he suddenly became very curious to find out how his nephew Jeremy was faring with his new

Russian wife Tatyana. He fished through the pockets of his shorts for his cell phone and typed in his nephew's phone number. Because it was only eleven o'clock Miami time, he knew that he might catch Jeremy right after dinner. It was only eight o'clock in Riverside, CA.

To his surprise a female voice loaded with sexual dynamite answered. When he asked for Jeremy, she asked with a peppery snarl, "What do want? He sees no patients after hours."

"I am not a patient. I am his uncle and I want to talk to him if it's no trouble." He added the "if it's no trouble" part with as much sharpness as he could load into his voice.

There was silence on the other end. He already began to suspect that the unpleasant woman had hung up on him, when Jeremy suddenly answered.

"Uncle Dmitri, what a surprise. You are not in town by any chance?"

"No, I am still on the other side of the country. Just could not help myself wondering how you were faring in your marital bliss."

"Well, you heard her sweet little voice, didn't you? Actually not too bad, we still are getting used to each other. She is beautiful, loving and very intelligent."

"Well I am glad that, at least for you the foreign bride has turned out well," commented Dmitri a little sourly because deep down he had expected something else.

"Yes, it's going well." Here Jeremy's voice fell a few notes, showing a certain strain. "However, at times it seems that we both have different expectations of married life. I expected her to cook and keep my house, which isn't much and for which she has help twice weekly. I also hoped she would learn how to play tennis and become my partner in doubles. But she's not doing that well yet. Conversely, every weekend she expects me to take her into Los Angeles to grand hotels, dinners, and events with the movie crowd in Hollywood. It's a little tiring, but I hope to cure her of these ideas eventually. Her clothing bills from shopping on Rodeo Drive are ridiculous."

"That doesn't sound too trying," said Dmitri with a lot more warmth, for he could smell trouble in the wind. Since Jeremy had thrown his advice and warning so casually into the wind, Dmitri could not help feeling a little glee that he might have a few problems.

"So what is new with the bride that fled her groom?" Now it was Jeremy's turn to revel in sarcasm. Of course, he had detected Dmitri's only slightly concealed satisfaction with his bride's expensive tastes. At first it had occurred to him to outright lie and just present the marriage in a rosy light. But then he felt if he gave a bit of the truth he might get back more juicy tidbits about uncle's troubles. He was correct in that assumption.

He had given Dmitri enough feeling of connectedness to make his uncle want to confess to problems of his own. He could not, however, know that sitting alone at watch in a deep inky tropical night might bring up feelings of abandonment and unfairness. They were stronger at night than a man would allow coming to the fore in bright sunlight. Because he was vulnerable, Dmitri talked.

He spoke of his current adventure with a certain bravado, making it sound as if this was the greatest adventure of his life, thereby turning his defeat by a woman into an asset.

"I cannot reveal how this thing is going to play out; it's all top secret. But you can believe me: I will get her back and take her to the ICE-offices even if I have to drag her there by her hair."

"I wish you all the best, Uncle Dmitri. You know what my Greek mamma, Alcesta, always said, 'No one will ever get the better of a Greek.' "

"Now that you mention it, she did say this often. A good woman is your mother."

The conversation at an end, his thoughts turned to his sister. Two years younger than he, she had been astonishingly beautiful in her youth—a beauty that matured pleasingly later in her life. But in her youth she had been tall, slender, with full breasts, black hair and flawless skin, tinged slightly olive. She had a great sense for comic situations and jokes, and loved to laugh with her full, generous mouth open, exposing perfect white teeth.

What an amazing girl she had been. When she entered a room at a party, came to church or to a dance, a stillness descended upon the congregants for a moment; every eye followed her every move as if to sate itself on beauty. Yes, Alcesta was beautiful, smart and funny. But for reasons not discernible to her brother and the rest of the family, she fell in love with the town doctor. He was a dour man, well advanced in years and without a shred of humor. And yet, she had married the man.

That old doctor became Jeremy's father. Unfortunately, the son embodied few of his mother's charms, but all of his father's dourness. Well, Jeremy was what he was and one had to accept facts.

Earlier, the FBI called for Louis Ranger with a report detailing the Russian deployment. They counted ten men at the Key West house, which everyone assumed to be also a storage place of sorts. Located in a residential neighborhood and looking just like the surrounding wooden homes, colorfully painted, with a huge, shaded porch in front, it was an ideal warehouse for the mob, because a more respectable place could not be found. No one would suspect gangsters in this fabulous place.

Irina and Petros were installed on board of the Irina, together with another eight or ten men.

"Hard to keep count of them," complained the agent who was tracking the mob. "Traffic in front of the house is so thick that the Georgians duck in and out almost at will. We finally nailed them down by taking pictures of them, comparing the pix."

By two in the morning Dmitri heard a stirring in the cabin below. Angel climbed on deck a moment later, stretching his long body in many directions. Rubbing his eyes he sighed, "Anything of interest happening?"

Satisfied that all was calm, he asked where the sandwiches could be found. Raiding the indicated cooler he also discovered home-made lemonade, his favorite drink. Fully supplied with fuel, he relieved Dmitri who was glad to be released. He barely caught himself a few times before almost falling asleep. He kept himself awake by taking little walks on the planks leading to the dock.

Now he yawned, his mouth a dark cavern surrounded by a white picket fence of teeth. He wished Angel a good watch, and went below. Not much later Angel observed a small object quietly drifting toward the entrance of the harbor. Closer observation with the special night glasses they had been given revealed that it was the Russian cigar boat. The speedboat was ludicrously propelled by two men using oars.

Soundlessly, Angel crept below. The first room he found, granting privacy, was the head. He entered. Perched on the toilet lid he dialed his special connection to the FBI coordination center.

"Hey there, good buddy," he intoned, "Are you aware that the Russians are trying to pull a fast one? I just saw them go by oaring the cigar boat out of the harbor. These guys do not want to be observed; they are very quiet with oars in the water."

"I read you loud and clear, Jenny. Jenny was the call name they had agreed upon earlier. Yea, we have noticed that they are up to something. However, at this time of night we cannot send a boat after them without instantly arousing suspicion."

"What are you going to do? They can go for a pick up and no one would be the wiser."

"Don't worry, Jenny. We will send a coast guard boat instantly to the coordinates of the last pick up. Might I mention those are coordinates available to us thanks to your earlier fine work. We will also send a copter up to monitor the area. If the bird tells us that stuff is happening, we will allow all goods to be brought into the harbor for transport to Miami. That's when the operation begins in earnest."

"Thanks, I feel much better now," sighed Angel into his transmitter. He realized that the agent in question had been kind, providing much more information than they were entitled to. This fount of knowledge helped Angel to understand much better what to expect. Knowing a bird was up there with heat-seeking gear taking pictures of the scene was a comforting thought.

The rest of Angel's watch passed calmly, uneventfully. He was relieved by Brent at six in the morning and told him of the night's incident. They were still trying to make sense of the cigar boat occurrence when Anthony Li appeared on board.

"Oh, it's good to see you, Li," Brent whispered, trying to keep his voice muted, like a student in front of the teacher. "A little problem has arisen during the night." Angel and Brent informed Li of everything that had transpired during the night. Li felt duty-bound to contact Brandeis immediately.

"I know. I know," came Brandeis' reassuring reply. "I am closely attached to the FBI's chest. These guys are top-notch. They are not the usual glory snatchers. They want this to be a successful undertaking. They know that the best results can be achieved by total cooperation. So you guys have nothing to worry about. You will know every little detail."

Hardly had he stopped speaking, when the FBI rang in with a report. The cigar boat was sitting in the previous pick-up spot doing nothing. The boat just sat as if anchored, waiting for action.

An urgent call came in. Everyone listened breathlessly. "Jeanette, Jeanette! Get moving! We want you to follow the Irina out into the sea until we give you a signal to return."

"What about the Ada-May?" asked Brent, excitement making his voice tremble.

"Nothing, the Ada-May will stay here until further orders." The FBI man's voice sounded almost cheerful, as if he could foresee the positive outcome of the planned action.

Angel hustled below and awakened Dmitri and his uncle Raphael. "Get up sleepy heads, the FBI calls us to action!" he sang out, barely containing the joy in his young, loud voice.

Moments later they pushed off the dock and headed for the open ocean. Their radio contact never stopped from the moment they began moving. Brent on the wheel was supplied with a constant stream of information about the whereabouts of the Irina. When she left the harbor, she set her first course as anticipated. Later, she changed her direction, as she had before.

Brent was at first far ahead of the Irina. He cleverly disguised his intentions by pretending to test previous fishing coordinates.

No one ever was quite clear about the reason, why at a certain point in the cat-and-mouse-game the Jeanette was called back to the harbor.

"Let the Irina sail unencumbered," was the order. "We have her well under control."

And so, by noon, the Jeanette lay in her berth, with her crew free to go and enjoy lunch. The crew of the Ada-May, never having left port, was already well watered and fed. Her crew sat fat and happy at the agency's disposal.

To everyone's surprise, the Prekrasnaya Irina did not come back into the harbor that day. Both crews sat idly and bored for the entire afternoon and the following night. Without so much as an action report to keep their adrenalin high, they played poker, told jokes and drank beer.

The next day, at noon, an urgent call came in.

"Get ready, Jenny! Get ready Ada-May! You must be operational at a moment's notice to move out. The Irina is coming in from her tryst and we have no clue what she will be doing. Some venture a hypothesis that she might go straight to Miami; other, cooler heads, surmise that she will come to the harbor and unload her cargo. Whatever the scenario, we want you to be prepared to either follow her, or follow a convoy of cars."

"I bet that she will come to the harbor," surmised Angel. "She will come back here. We have seen it before." He underpinned his guess with a bet of twenty-five dollars.

"I take your bet and raise you fifty that she goes to Miami," declared Dmitri.

As if to verify the truth of Angel's argument, the blatantly extravagant, shiny cigar boat entered the mouth of the boat basin, going straight for its berth.

"See, she will be coming soon," laughed Angel. "I will be having lunch soon in the Mexican Cantina."

"Don't!" called Brent. "The FBI will be royally pissed if you don't obey orders."

As if to mock Dmitri, the prominent bow of the Irina entered the mouth of the harbor.

"I am going to lunch! Amigos," yelled Angel cheerfully. His normally good humor was reinforced by the appearance of the Russian boat.

After a satisfying lunch at the cantina and a few Margaritas, both crews lay about their boats awaiting orders. Nothing happened. At night, once again, they set watches. The next day also passed uneventful. The crews were bored and edgy.

However, at nine o'clock the next night a call came through on the radios of both boats. A determined voice commanded, "As of this moment I want you ready at a moment's notice. I want everyone acting in concert. Both boats and crew will get exactly the same instructions and will act as one unit."

Two hours later the call came in, "Get ready to fly. We are going to Miami in a few minutes." Shortly thereafter, the same voice instructed the crews sharply and succinctly.

"I want both of you to parallel the Overseas Highway. The Ada-May covers the bay side, while the Jeannette follows the ocean channel. Anthony Li is assigned to the Ada-May. I need him there as liaison"

"So, that's it then," thought Dmitri. His heart beat a little faster and his breath came in shorter bursts, as he started the engines and took the wheel. His crew flew about, untying the boat, stashing and lashing loose items.

"Move out!" came the command from voice control. The Jeannette detached slowly from its moorings. The Ada-May followed closely in her wake. The entire procedure commenced in almost total silence. Brent came up from the cabin below and took the co-pilot seat to the left. At the mouth of the harbor the boats separated. The Jeannette veered east into the channel, following the course into the Atlantic, while the Ada-May went west into Florida Bay.

Few persons traveled the Intracoastal channel through the bay by night. Only a seasoned captain with good headlights would attempt such a feat, for the channel is narrow and ill marked. Even the slightest navigational mistake would be instantly punished by getting the vessel stuck deep aground in clinging sand and silt. Everyone navigating the bay has experienced, at least once, the indignity of being grounded and in need of help from strangers.

"I pity the poor sods on the Ada-May," said Dmitri with deep feeling. This led Brent to reminisce. Once, at sunset, he had the misfortune of taking a turn too fast, ramming his small, shallow-bottomed fishing craft into a sand bank. It was late. No other boats where about anymore. Brent did not even contemplate spending the night in the boat. He stripped off his clothes and jumped into the muck and began pushing his boat into the channel.

"I was sinking deeper and deeper into the ooze. The more I shoved, the deeper I sank until I was buried well up to my thighs in primordial debris. The boat was now floating free in the channel, my hands glued to its nose. But try as I may I could not free myself from the ooze." Brent laughed self-consciously as he revisited his predicament. The guys listening to his tale grinned appreciatively. They all had similar tales and envisioned his discomfort.

"At last, when I thought I would be stuck in this most unenviable place, a ready victim to the mosquito swarms, the tide began to come in, running fast and furious. It tugged on my boat so hard, I could hardly hang on. Wouldn't you know, I suddenly felt the sucking sand around my knees give a little. Inch by inch my boat, straining to be free and be gone with the tide, pulled me from the muck. There was a last struggle and I floated free behind my boat, stern first, toward Florida Bay." That seemed to be the right moment for a break in the tale. Brent reached for beer.

"The hell you do!" exploded Angel, tearing the can from Brent's grasping fingers. "Have you lost your senses, man? We are on a mission! Lemonade for you and the rest of us."

"Sorry," Brent apologized. "I was all caught up in my tale."

"So what happened then?" queried Dmitri.

"I made it home a little later. Jan was about to launch a rescue mission by calling out the Coast Guard. I prevented that embarrassing detail, but it was much harder to explain the sand and debris in my underpants to her. I had to talk for a long time before she calmed down."

A while before Brent began his story the night had become inky-black. Nights in the Keys are usually well lit, with the whole sky visible and the moon prominent. But ever so often, the moon is hidden beyond the horizon and a velvet blanket obscures the sky. The small flotilla following the Prekrasnaya Irina and the cigar boat had ventured far into the Atlantic Ocean, at least a mile off shore. The instrument panel indicated more than thirty feet of water below the boat, a reminder that the shoreline of the Keys had been left behind.

All of Florida and its surrounds are the remnants of a giant coral reef. Eons ago this land had been under water, the fertile environs of an ancient eco-system. Plate tectonics and other geological forces raised the reef, the islands and surrounding sand flats, creating an unusual, amazing ecological environment unrivaled on the planet. Coral and calcified deposits were ground into sand and silt by storms and tides, leaving the Florida Keys and other small islands, surrounded by acres of sand and mudflats, many of which are left to dry in the sun during low tides. They are the feeding grounds for egrets, herons, gulls and other shore birds. In the early morning sunlight these flats shine with a pearly, purplish hue, christening one of the keys—Isla Morada

Approaching the island chain from the Atlantic, the sailor has to navigate with attentive circumspection. The sandy mudflats surrounding the Keys extended far into the Atlantic. It is therefore imperative to find the designated, well-marked channels when approaching land. The islands are connected to each other by bridges. Especially the last bridge—The Seven Mile Bridge—linking Marathon and Key West, is an engineering marvel. Over Moser channel, providing access to the Bay, the bridge rises in an arc to allow passage of large boats with a 65-foot clearance.

Well away from the shore, the Jeanette made good speed. Far ahead, going north at a good clip, they saw the positioning lights of the Prekrasnaya Irina. Farther still, flashing like a glowworm as it rose and fell with the waves, was the cigar boat. Dmitri could not figure out why a boat so obviously used for its speed should be bobbing along at such a pedestrian pace for its class. He was soon enlightened.

The special FBI phone vibrated noiselessly. Dmitri listened to the message meant for the crew in the bay: "Ada-May! Ada-May! Watch for the cigar boat. We have harassed it. We assume the crew will seek the next large channel and run into the bay. Let them pass unmolested and continue on your way to the Moser channel. You will station yourself there with another of our boats, blocking the channel."

Dmitri heard Robert Butweiler and Angel ask the same question simultaneously. "But what if the cigar boat carries the load? What happens then?"

"Not to worry," came the reassuring reply. Dmitri believed he recognized Anthony Li's voice.

"We are on top of it—literally. We have a copter waiting and two coast guard boats ready to pounce. It will be your job to block the Irina, and remember, stay out of the fighting! I don't want you guys to become casualties. We get paid for these things. So don't try to be heroes!"

As if on cue, the tiny bobbing light of the cigar boat became a straight flash as the boat begun running under full power. Not much later it veered left into a smaller channel leading to the bay and became lost in the mangroves edging the channel. The Irina, too, picked up speed as if she wanted to do the same. However, her size prevented her from duplicating the maneuver.

"Hot damn," remarked Dmitri with appreciation to Brent. "The powers-that-be have it all figured out. They are going to begin pressing the Irina at any moment now. She will have to make a run for Moser Channel and we are going to trap her in the channel."

"I think you figure right," acknowledged Brent. Excitement began to build among the crew gathered around the wheel. To a man, they wore dark sweaters and swim trunks, ready for action. It was a strange night. A mélange of smells composed of seaweed, saltwater, mangrove and decaying matter hung densely over the water as if a ceiling above prevented the ocean to air its surface. The darkness had deepened even more, if such a thing was possible. The eyes of the men made out only the lights of the other boats and the occasional white crest of a wave rolling in.

"Odd," mused Brent, "I have seldom experienced a night quite as black as this." Raphael agreed. Dmitri grumbled that he was navigating by instruments only.

"Let me take the wheel for a while," offered Brent, who had been itching to lay his hands on his boat. As much as he liked Dmitri and trusted his seamanship, it was another feeling altogether if he was running his own boat. Perhaps Dmitri sensed his eagerness to captain, for he quickly relinquished the captain's seat.

When the call came—they were ready. "Pick up speed and get as close behind the Irina as you can," ordered John Brandeis. He was in the lead vessel. "We are coming at her with two boats from the side; a boat from the Isla Morada coast guard station is ahead of her. She cannot go anywhere but into Moser Channel."

"You reckoned right!" exulted Brent, slapping Dmitri's shoulder.

"I did, didn't I" boomed his friend happily. However, they had to suppress their hunter's adrenal rush, because another half hour passed before they approached Moser Channel. In the meantime they tried to reach maximum speed, which was hard. High tide was running fast and heavy toward the bay, pushing on the right side of their boat. Furthermore, the surf was rougher than usual for this time of year.

Not far from the channel the Georgians on the Irina seemed to realize that the channel might become a trap for their boat. It had become obvious that the harmless fishing vessels surrounding them were acting too purposeful and in accord to be harmless. The Russian captain, suddenly desperate, threw the Irina's engines into reverse and, with a forceful right turn, tried to break through the semi-circle of hunters. In a frantic burst of speed he almost succeeded and reached the open ocean. But the mind of the crew was changed by a volley of gunfire across the Irina's bow that left a respectable hole in the windshield of the wheelhouse.

The Jeanette's crew watched the Irina's lights with wonderment, as the hunted boat violently reversed its engines again, turned short and headed straight for Moser Channel.

The moment the vessel entered the carefully set trap, Lewis Ranger called the hunters on the special frequency.

"We have the Georgians where we want them." He could not conceal a slight gloating tremolo in his voice.

"The plan is as follows: the coast guard's and our boats are going after them into the channel. The Jeanette and the Ada-May, fortified by two coast guard boats, will block both ends of Moser Channel."

And so it was that the Ada-May was stationed in the bay blocking the exit escape route, while the Jeanette followed the enemy boats into the channel.

A slight break in the transmission allowed the disappointed grumbling of the crews to be heard the very instant the frequency cleared. Both crews wanted a part of the action and complained bitterly about being left out.

"Easy fellows! Easy! I never promised you a piece of the action. On the contrary, we have always said that your pristine, intact condition is our uppermost concern. We must return you to your wives and loved ones without major damage."

Lewis Ranger chuckled, pleased with his oratory, and continued conciliatory, "We promise though that any Mafiosi swimming in the water will be yours to capture. We suspect a few might rather go swimming instead of getting nabbed by us. Be very careful though, because they will be armed. So knock 'em cold before you rescue them."

His instructions were interrupted by violent crackling noises in the radio channel. An angry voice screamed. "Mosquito to Guard: The bastards are shooting at me with an effing sub-machinegun. The first blast almost took me down. I am out of harms way right now, shining my lights at their boat. So go and get 'em guys! Over!"

There was more crackling on the frequency. Then a young, eager voice yelled jubilantly, "We are on them like ticks on a dog. Your lights make it easy. We have two boats. We will get them!"

To the chagrin of the listening men, the transmission of the guard's site report was interrupted.

"Damn! It's getting hot in the bay and we sit here on the tail end of the action," groused Brent.

"That's all right, big buddy," grinned Dmitri. "The bad guys seem to have really lethal weapons at their disposal and we want you to stay hale and hardy for your wife."

"Yea, thanks for nothing," grumbled a chastened Brent.

Brent, sporting night-vision goggles, somehow made out all the channel markers. He drove the Jeannette squarely into the middle of the waterway. Ahead of them, they saw the lights of what they believed to be a coast guard vessel, rolling in the wake of the Irina. The boys from the Coast Guard had all the fun. In the normal pursuit of their duties, they intercept would-be-immigrants intent on reaching US shores. They came on all sort of floating matter that could hardly be called boat. The Guard often saved the lives of Cubans, Haitians and other South Americans. Interception on the high seas means that the illegal immigrants are returned post haste to their country of origin.

Furthermore, the Coast Guard also tangles with drug smugglers. They chase the smuggler's fast boats and recover the dope thrown overboard during the chase as evidence for court cases. Standing before a judge, the bad boys always claim that they have only been fishing. Without the goods, there is not much of a case for the prosecutor. The men of the Guard also search for the victims of boating accidents, rescue endangered mariners, swimmers, entangled marine wildlife—you name it. If there is help needed on coastal waters, or the law to be upheld, the Guard is sure to be there.

If you happen to visit the Coast Guard station at Isla Morada, you will be welcomed and treated to a tour and a lecture about the young men who come to this place from all over the country to serve. The welcome extended to the visitor, depends, of course, on the training schedule and emergencies. The brass likes it if one calls ahead and makes an appointment. That small courtesy also prevents disappointments.

The station is ideally located at the entry of the Venetian Shore Development. It has access to the Atlantic and to the bay via Snake Creek, a deep channel between islands. A three-sided dock, facing two canals and the creek, sports an array of boats. Some of them are substantial, ocean-worthy vessels; others are smaller, fleet boats, capable of transporting ten men. Other boats are flat bottomed for use in the bay.

One section of the coast guard dock is studded with an array of odd, floating devices. Visitors marvel as they envision that people have used these fragile, cobbled-together floats to cross the Atlantic. Most of the floats were carried here by the current from Cuba with little help from their sailors. On their various visits to the coast guard docks, Dmitri and Brent looked with wonderment at assorted barrels lashed together with hemp cord. The resulting float could carry two to three paddle-wielding people, who, depending on current and weather, had a chance to travel across the ninety-mile span between Cuba and Key West, Florida. In disbelief, they once examined a float of lashed-together small tree trunks and branches, about six feet square. From its middle sprang a five-foot post with a dangling sheet—poor excuse for a sail. At the rear of the improbable contraption, a paddle jammed into the lashing served as rudder.

"Hell," remarked Brent as he was looking at the fragile, odd thing, "I would not like to sit atop this floating trap if there was a Great White around."

"Never mind sharks," mused Dmitri, "just imagine a really stiff breeze. It would take you straight into the Atlantic. The Gulf Stream would probably grab you and carry you north forever. As small as this thing is, no one would ever see you in the shipping lane."

"All this is true. And yet, the guy made it over. It had to have been just one guy. The miserable thing couldn't support more than one person."

Looking at the assemblage of contraptions, which reminded one more of flotsam and jetsam than seaworthy vessels, Brent ventured, "Can you imagine the poor bastards sitting behind their shacks in Cuba, stringing these floats together, worrying the entire time that they could be discovered."

His face was taut with indignation. "I can see them working on their miserable devices, wondering if their neighbor had seen them collecting floating stuff and would report them."

"Great God! What a crummy life. One has to admire the courage of the guys trying to come to the US under such conditions. I can't even imagine what it must be like to live in a place where the government controls every aspect of your life."

"Just ask Angel. He told me that from the time he was born strangers determined his life. Although he was a healthy baby at birth the nurses kept him from his mother for days, saying he needed special care. Later, his mother was forbidden to stay home and nurse him, because she was needed in the factory in which she worked. His grandmother wanted to look after him, but no, the party put him into a commune nursery where they taught him little communist songs and rhymes as soon as he could speak. His story about government control went on forever."

"Poor buggers, all of them! Same thing with the Haitians. They keep on having children until the island bursts at its seams. Add to that a socialist system and they all want to leave. No jobs, no money—starvation in regular intervals."

While speaking, Dmitri scanned the floating devices along the broad concrete dock of the Coast Guard.

"Oh, Jesus! Look over there!" He pointed at a large blotch of yellow and white bobbing like a jellyfish in the water of the canal branching off Snake Creek. Upon closer inspection the patch of large plastic tubs, plastic gallon bottles and blown-up air mattresses, turned out to be another ingenious Cuban craft.

"I don't believe it," exclaimed Brent. "No one could have used this thing and survived." He was wrong! Two young guardsmen had strolled over to check out the visitors. After introductions, the coast guard fellows confirmed that, indeed, the improbable float had carried a man and a woman across the sea. The two had made it onto land below Duck Key, where they found themselves stranded on a sandbank at low tide. Someone from a cruising boat had called the Coast Guard. The two bedraggled, dehydrated young Cubans were rescued and allowed to stay in the country because they had made it to dry land.

Reliving these experiences in the dark of night did not keep Dmitri from closely monitoring Brent's every move. The crackling of the special communications channel caught everyone's attention.

"We got them. Hot damn, we got them," rebel-yelled a young male voice excitedly, before he even identified himself. He corrected his omission instantly.

"This is Tommy Kruse, co-pilot coast guard helicopter." They heard him swallow hard as if to clear saliva, released by the adrenalin rush of the action, from his vocal cords. His voice resumed clear and sharp. In the inky black night, moonless and without stars, his words echoed eerily between the mangroves.

"We have lights on the Irina! They are ditching the stash!" Tommy Kruse was yelling now. "They are firing at us, at the coast guard cruiser and the other boat. Oh, my—now it's a battle. We are firing back. Our stuff is better!"

As if on cue, transmission stopped. Then Lewis Ranger's calm, composed voice came over the radio.

"They are ditching their stash and are jumping overboard. I can see Petros Avarikidze in the water. I can see Irina Petrovna in the water. They are all wearing diving suits and gear and are trying to swim against the tide toward the pylons of the new bridge. They are armed, of course. I want no heroics from you guys!"

Dmitri's heart pounded like the pounder of a pile driver. This was it. His chance to get even. He could almost taste the sweetness of pulling Irina from the water and handing her to Mr. Rogerson of the ICE. Justice would be served—he would be exonerated.

As if hypnotized, the men aboard the Jeanette stared into the dark depth of Moser channel. It was impossible to make out anything below. Suddenly they heard the rotor of a helicopter above. Floodlights from above revealed the rushing waters of the tide below. A moment later Brent spied a black-suited body, struggling violently against the fast running tide. The swimmer was obviously bound for the bridge pilings, where he could hide and rest, while trying to outwit his pursuers. For one moment the tide pushed the swimmer toward the boat. Without thought of consequences, Brent flung himself over the low metal railing on top of the black shape.

The force of Brent's jump, combined with his two hundred forty pounds of solid muscle, took the body of the Russian diver, with Brent clinging to his back, to the bottom of the channel. For a moment both men were a physical unit—stunned, unthinking, caught below many feet of dark water. An instant later they both reacted with the precision of their training. Gripping the neoprened body of the other man by the oxygen tanks with one hand, Brent tore the face mask with the breathing tube from his adversary, who reached back and gripped Brent's hair, painfully trying to remove his scalp. The man's other hand reached for a weapon strapped to his thigh. As natural buoyancy floated the two toward the surface, both were overcome by the urge to rid themselves of the other body and thereby rise faster for a breath of air.

But here, Brent, unencumbered by diving gear, had the advantage. Squeezing the gangster between his legs from behind he held his neck in a strangle hold. As the other man tried to extricate himself from Brent's lethal embrace, by kicking and clawing, the pressure on his neck increased.

Slowly rising upward, the men struggled frantically. At one time Brent thought he had overcome all resistance of his adversary, only to find that the other man, none other than Petros Avarikidze himself, had managed to pull his gun from a leg holster. Half strangled, Petros pulled the trigger as he jabbed the gun viciously backward toward Brent, who felt a burning sensation in his right thigh. He gave it no thought and instead increased the force of his strangle hold. Petro's body went limp and a moment later Brent's head broke through the water. He coughed, and sputtered as he filled his lungs with much-needed air.

"He's got one!" rejoiced a voice from above in the helicopter. The coast guard bird above still illuminated the Jeannette and part of the channel. Helping hands and a gaff were extended over the railing from above the Jeanette. They lifted Petros from Brent's tired arms onto the deck. The Georgian lay flattened in a puddle of water like a large fish, his right hand still clutching a gun. With a lunge, Angel was beside him. He pried Petros' hand open and with quick motion pushed the gun toward Li, who stuck it into his belt.

By that time, helping hands pulled Brent aboard via a ladder beside the propellers. He hoisted himself to a standing position. That's when Dmitri, looking up from the screen he monitored, exclaimed, "Damned, Brent, you are bleeding like a stuck pig."

"Hot damn, so I am," grunted Brent with amazement.

It took only moments for Li and Angel to put a tourniquet around Brent's upper thigh. "You've been shot, man. The son of a bitch must have hit you in the water."

"I did feel a sting and some burn," acknowledged Brent. "That must have happened right before he passed out." Anthony Li scrambled below deck and returned with a first aid kit and began to tend Brent's leg. While all eyes were on Brent and Anthony's tender mercies, Petros began to stir and groan. He painfully sucked air into his lungs and spit up gulps of water

"Time to tie him up," said Li." Moments later he and Angel had the Georgian securely trussed.

"I used my best sailor's knots on him," smiled Angel. He looked down on Brent, whom the men had propped up in a deck chair with a stiff drink in his hand, which someone had hurriedly concocted.

Throughout all the excitement Dmitri never left his place. He stood as if glued to the railing and stared into the water. For him the drama in the back never happened. He had neither heard nor seen any of Brent's heroics. The world around him had ceased to exist. Since the alert reached him that Irina left the big boat and was swimming in the water, he had only concentrated on the swirling, dark flood below. His fellows had called to him—he did not hear them. The crackling of the ships radio with its interesting voices and comments was a mere buzz in his ears.

His eyes swept up and down the channel as far as the lights from the copter above allowed him to see. He knew with certainty that he would spot the fair Irina on this side of the vessel. How he knew this no one could say, least of all he himself. But deep in his gut he knew.

And then—he saw her. First he noted her long, blond hair swirling, trailing behind her. It was so odd a sight in the dark water that, for a moment, he thought a bit of flotsam was floating about. When the water parted and her face became visible, although obscured by a face mask and the mouthpiece of a diver's apparatus, it was obviously Irina. She was wearing a black neoprene wet suit, making her appear to be a streamlined fish. She frantically used her large flippers, stirring the water.

She was fighting the fast-running tide as hard as she could. Swimming at the very edge of Moser channel, she was not making much headway. Looking up at the Jeanette, she suddenly became aware that she now was visible, illuminated by the lights from above. She dove down deep. According to plan, she and Petros had attempted to meet at the same pilings. Now she revised her plan. She knew she could not make it unobserved past the Jeanette. She had seen the intent faces of the men, staring like pointing hunting dogs at the water. She could not count on chivalry or mercy from that lot. They would hand her over to the FBI and she would go to prison for a long time. She was certain that, with her charms evaporated, she would be scrubbing floors for a living after she got out. Perishing the thought, Irina shuddered in her wetsuit. Perhaps the men aboard the Jeanette had spotted her already. Well, if she could not go forward, she'd float back with the tide.

Aboard the boat, Dmitri sensed what she was about to do. They had been idling the boat when Irina became visible, with just enough power to hold her against the tide in the middle of the channel.

"Give her some juice, Brent," cried Dmitri afraid to lose his prey, as if Brent had never left the wheel to jump on a strange mobster.

"Straight down the channel. I have my quarry in sight."

The beauty of men's friendships is expressed in their reactions to each other. Brent, although wounded in his leg and mellow from a drink—more whisky than ice, reacted instantly and never questioned the call. The boat slid languidly into the middle of the channel. Brent tried to assess the presumed speed of the swimmer. The tidal pull accommodated his endeavor. The moment the boat moved forward the helicopter above also changed its position. The men aboard the copter had heard every word spoken below and knew what they needed to do.

After a breathless moment, Brent saw Irina again in the light of the spotter. Or, to be precise, he beheld her strongly kicking long legs. She was a courageous woman, not easily to be discouraged. However, the unusual conditions of her situation had begun to influence her psychic equilibrium. It was one thing to swim with her lover to pilings where they could hide from pursuers. It was quite another matter to swim alone at night in an ocean channel while being pursued by men who wished to capture her.

She knew that her ship, the Prekrasnaya Irina, had been boarded by federal agents. In the ensuing gun battle her crew suffered two deaths and a number of injured. Everyone aboard had sought to escape by jumping ship. The prevailing notion was that it was better to take one's chances in the water with the sharks than to fall into the hands of the law. For any swimmer, the way to the pilings was blocked by the Jeanette. So, the group of Georgian outlaws split up to avoid attention. In the ensuing frantic attempts to avoid detection, Irina was separated from Petros and had no earthly clue how to find him. She only saw one chance to escape capture. If the cigar boat was waiting for instructions at the other end of Moser channel, she might escape yet. If, however, the boat had left, she would be all alone in the dark expanse of the bay. Perhaps, with luck, she might be able to swim to one of the many mangrove islets and spend the night clinging to one of the higher branches.

After deliberating her fate, Irina decided that she would try to stealthily bypass the boat of the Feds and the Prekrasnaya Irina and swim for the bay. In the commotion of the battle, shots were still fired by both sides, she might slip by undetected. Although most of the crew of her boat had instantly jumped ship when confronted by the boat of the government agents, they were obstinately defending their untenable positions by shooting from the depth of the mangroves that edged the channel in which they were hiding.

Determined to escape her pursuers, Irina swam strongly but cautiously into the middle of the channel, where the current allowed her to move with great speed. She assiduously avoided splashing. She had turned off the oxygen, breathing normally, because she was concerned with her uncertain situation and wanted to conserve the resource. The dank air contained a mélange of smells, of seaweed, of mangrove, of shrimp and brine, a smell strangely frightening to her. It reminded her of death and decay—a long weary, slow, watery rot.

Twice she had encounters that would have frightened tougher souls than hers. Diving to escape from the helicopter lights, a large fish brushed up against her, and a little later, a curious bottlenose dolphin gave her a playful bump with his snout before looking for better morsels. In her eagerness to avoid the perils before her, she paid scant attention to her pursuers behind. Perhaps it was too much of a challenge to watch two fronts at once. Or maybe Irina thought that the Jeanette was only empowered to function as rear guard. Whatever she might have been thinking, she never looked back once set on her path to the bay.

It would have well served her to look back, for Dmitri, once having spied her, never lost sight of her. And so it happened that the Jeanette, with her engines at a fast idle, came up beside the hapless woman only moments later.

Dmitri had instructed the crew. Every man aboard, except for Brent, was on the lookout for Irina—gaff in hand. Even his buddy Robert, who had been saddled to facilitate the overall functioning of the operation, and Li, they, too, were looking for Irina. It was simple—all they had to do was hook onto her neoprene suit and pull her on board. But it was one thing to talk about this feat and quite another to execute it.

The moment their quarry noticed what was happening, Irina dove under the boat. She willingly risked injury from the engines. Her action prompted Robert to jury-rig his gaff to a long pole, to be able to hook her suit when she was visible deep under water. Unfortunately this tool proved too unwieldy. It broke at his first big pull. He cursed a blue streak. She dove again. After a long interval she reappeared on the port side. The mouthpiece firmly between her teeth, she once again breathed oxygen. Although she could dive and stay under water for hours, she was afraid of becoming disoriented. Her diving training had commenced only recently and hastily. Most of her crew faced the same predicament.

Only two of Petro's men were master divers and even they dreaded prolonged night dives without the aid of lights and a boat as base to return to.

Angel had kept a close eye on Brent. Calculating how long Brent could stay on the wheel while suffering from his injuries, he decided to err on the side of caution and relieve him. He was amazed to see Brent still standing strong, handling the boat perfectly.

"Let me spell you while you take a rest," he offered.

"No way, good buddy! I am okay," bugled Brent.

"Let me have turn," clamored Robert, who wanted a more exciting part in the adventure.

"Sorry, this is my girl. I am okay, I can handle her." Robert clutched his gaff and moved back to the railing.

A small cry from Angel, his face pale against the darkness, moved Robert's gaze. Following Angel's focused stare and looking into the swirling water, he, too, saw her.

In an instant Angel and Robert were bent over the railing, intent on hooking the black suit covering Irina's lean body. Sensing their efforts to capture her, she dove once more under the boat.

"Dmitri, cover the other side she, might surface there!" During the entire proceeding Angel provided constant shouted comment to everyone on board. Sitting above in the the crow's nest, he aided the action. Apart from Brent, every man aboard the Jeanette lined the railing, gaff in hand.

When Irina disappeared under the boat once more, Angel could not stand the tension any longer. He reached the middle of the forecastle with one elastic jump from above. Halfway to port he heard Dmitri cry out, "There she is at the edge of the light."

Despite his obsessive preoccupation, Dmitri had heard every word. Like a pointer hunting game birds his motionless body was tense, coiled like a snake ready to strike. The water in this part of the channel was not very deep, ten perhaps twelve feet. The lights from the helicopter illuminated the depth to the bottom. A rock lobster and a few crabs scuttled furtively out of the bright circle; a few fish shot through the circle of light and vanished in the dark beyond. Then he saw the small movement at the light's edge. Her hand, parting the water, gave Irina away.

"I see her," rejoiced Angel. "More speed ahead!"

Brent answered Angel's call with a quick surge of the engine. Suddenly the woman's body floated up beside the boat. Without a thought Angel leaped atop the madly swimming woman. Their bodies plunged to the bottom in a frantic tangle. Brent heard Dmitri's shout that Angel was overboard. He stopped the engine. There was no telling where the fighting couple would come up. No reason to mince them in the propellers.

The thought of turning people into chum had barely touched his ken, when he heard the unmistakable zing of a bullet striking a metallic surface. Simultaneously he heard the rest of the crew shouting, "Duck! Down on deck! We are under fire. Some assholes are shooting at us!"

Above, the helicopter had also taken fire and executed evasive maneuvers. Flying higher and moving away, its crew consigned the Jeanette to total darkness.

"Damn, oh, damn," moaned Dmitri, "this could not have happened at a worse moment. Angel is in the water fighting Irina and her bloody goons are shooting at everything at will!"

Sometimes in life miraculous events determine the outcome of impossible situations. And so it happened seemingly against all odds, at the horizon of the western sky, the moon rose over Florida Bay. Not only did it rise but, almost full, it shone so brightly as to illuminate the water in the canal, the Jeanette and the mangroves in silvery light.

Further down in the canal, about halfway to the bay, the outline of the Prekrasnaya Irina and the coast guard boats were darkly outlined against the brightening sky. On the canal bank to port of the Jeanette, perched two goons, now clearly outlined in black.

In the helicopter above, the sharpshooter took careful aim and fired. One of the black shapes collapsed with a terrible cry. The other dove into the canal.

"Oh, hell, I hope he does not go to help Irina," groaned Raphael. "He has a gun and Angel's got nothing." The terrible odds set him to curse a streak of Cuban specialties, of which the crew only knew caramba. He could have saved a good part of his verbal arsenal, if he had known that the Georgian gangster was only concerned with saving his own broad stern.

The goon was heading toward the Atlantic with all the speed his flippered legs could muster. Little did he know that the helicopter crew had him in sight. Flying in a large curve over the mangroves toward the ocean they banked the copter and returned flying low over the channel. Their quarry swam straight on to meet them. Earlier, when shot at by the goons, the sharpshooter had been overheard to say that he was terribly pissed off and would exact a pretty price for this bad behavior.

No one was surprised, therefore, when he began firing his HK semi-automatic into the water as if gunning for a shark. A moment later the black body of the quarry floated upward. A young guard, the third of the copter crew, jumped into the water near the floating man. He was tethered to the copter by a line. The pilot pushed the copter to gain height in an effort to minimize the impact of the rotor blades on the water. Quickly and efficiently the Coast Guard Officer searched the body of the immobile Georgian for weapons. He found in the pockets of the villan's vest a small arsenal. Then he tied the inert man to his own body. Lashed together in this fashion they were winched into the helicopter.

"I gotta go away for a moment and deliver this body. Be good and don't get hurt while I am gone," announced the cheerful voice of the pilot over the intercom. Flying over the Jeanette, as he zipped toward the coast guard boats.

Unaware of the shooting further up in the canal, Angel struggled with Irina. The desperate woman realized that her advantage lay in her ability to breathe under water. Angel was strong and agile, but needed air in intervals. Knowing that, Irina tried to grab onto Angel and take him down into the depth of the canal. Angel was well aware of her plan. As soon as she took hold of one part of his body he freed it with vigor. By contrast, his stratagem was to remove Irina's oxygen tanks, for only by depriving her of unlimited air could he defeat her.

The uneven struggle went on. She pulled him deep under and he dragged her kicking and punching back to the surface. He finally got a hold of a sizeable chunk of her hair. That made her more compliant. The moment they reached the surface for more than just a gulp of air, Dmitri spotted them. In an instant he was leaning over the railing wielding his large gaff. A vicious slice hooked Irina's harness to which the oxygen tanks were attached.

"Good job," bellowed Raphael. "Hang onto her. Let me give you a hand." With a great jump he was beside Dmitri. Seconds later he, too, was pulling like mad to heave Irina into the boat. But that was not to be the end of the struggle. Irina had freed her hair by biting Angel's arm so savagely that the young man loosened his grip in order to free his arm from her ferocious jaws. Who would have surmised such power in such a delicate, pretty creature? Irina was quite an enigma to most of the men who got to know her. Not one of them had suspected so much power and strength contained in her lithe body. It had taken Petros Avarikidze a long time to learn of Irina's capabilities, and even he was amazed when presented with new feats by the woman.

At first, when he flung himself upon the girl, Angel had relished the contact with her body. He delighted in the sport of trying to subdue her. Soon, however, his delight in this conquest turned into a bitter struggle for survival. Now that her hair was free of Angel's excruciatingly painful grip, she used both arms to push him away. The force of the gaff had lifted her upper body out of the water. Soon she would be pulled onto the deck of the loathsome boat. She kicked frantically at Angel, who was renewing his efforts to contain her. With one quick motion she zipped the vest open to which the oxygen tanks were attached, and slipped out of the harness. Immediately the horrible pain of the yanking gaff ceased and she slipped under water.

Freed of the tanks and the pull of the gaff, she felt relieved, almost happy for a moment. But then Angel's arms and legs imprisoned her from behind. A bitter fight ensued. Irina bit, kicked and punched. In a tangle they went down into depth, only to rise momentarily in a frantic bid for air.

On the deck of the Jeanette Dmitri could not stand the tension any longer. The helicopter had returned, providing illumination all the way to the sandy bottom of the canal. When the fighting pair came up once again for air, Dmitri allowed Angel a few gulps to fill his lungs before throwing himself into the melee. Although advanced in years, Dmitri was still in excellent shape. It was not to the fight's detriment that he could put two hundred and ten pounds into the effort, when he jumped on top of the pair.

Predictably, the knot of three bodies went under once more. Angel, glad for the help, relaxed his grip on the woman and kicked his way to the surface. He had been expending lots of oxygen while trying to subdue Irina and needed a few good breaths.

Freed of Angel's grasp, Irina concentrated her full fury on Dmitri. She lashed out with her legs, turning the hard plastic of her flippers into sharp scrapers.

"Oh, no," groaned Dmitri silently, "let's not draw blood." The different struggles in the channel must have attracted the attention of at least a few large sharks. Add blood to the equation and you might get attacked. He tried to hold Irina firmly but at a distance while he kept her under water. Without her oxygen tanks she would succumb sooner or later. A turn of events initiated by Angel changed everything to Dmitri's advantage.

The young man was tired of games and futile struggles. He returned to the fray a gaff in hand which he used to puncture and hook Irina's diver's suit. He now held her securely at a distance while pulling her to the surface. In this endeavor he had Dmitri's full cooperation because he, too, needed air. Dmitri had seized Irina's arm, pulling hard. A moment later helping hands dragged the unwilling Irina on deck, where she writhed, clawed and kicked. It took every bit of muscle on the boat to subdue her.

However, as the sailors say, even the devil must sleep sometimes and, at last, Irina gave up her struggles with a mighty sigh. A moment later she was securely trussed up and locked in the cabin below.

Breathless and spent, the crew felt to a man that they had been an integral part of the struggle. Irina's capture had become a very personal thing for all of them. They eyed each other with pride, wide grins on their faces. Dmitri especially positively glowed with the pride of accomplishment. "We did it, by God, we did it. We went and captured that Russian wench."

"Yep! And not only that, but we stirred up a whole nest of drug hornets. Man, oh, man. What a great day!"

From above, as if from heaven itself, a loud voice boomed, "Good show, guys! Looks like we got the lot. If the guys in the Bay were as lucky as we were here in the channel, we should have all of them."

The ship's radio began crackling. Lewis Ranger's voice came roughly over the ether.

"Jeanette, Jeanette, rendezvous at your earliest at the Prekrasnaya Irina. We will put all prisoners on board and proceed in convoy to Miami. The guys from the Ada May, and everyone operating in the bay have left already for Miami. So let's mop it up and get going."

The radio crackled some more and then he said, prideful emotion coloring his voice, "By the way, this was a damn fine operation. Well executed and smartly finished, men." There was a short pause. He began once more, laughter in his voice, "You finally got your woman, eh, Dmitri?"

"Yes, sir! And well tied up this time."

Arriving at the Prekrasnaya Irina, the trussed Russians were heaved onto her deck and into the hands of the men from Coast Guard and the FBI. "Do I need a receipt for Mr. Rogerson from the ICE to prove that I delivered one Irina Petrovna Sokolova into the hands of the authorities?" Dmitri asked with a mixture of humor and bravado. He looked up to Lewis Ranger from the deck of the Jeanette.

"No, that won't be necessary," replied Ranger. "You have enough witnesses for the collar." He smiled rather pleasantly, "Matter of fact, I will recommend that you fellows get a commendation, and perhaps something tangible out of this affair. You all performed intelligently—splendidly." He singled Angel out for special attention.

"Why don't you join me on deck of the Irina," he proposed, sounding avuncular. "I have a lifechanging proposition for you. Fellows like you are always welcome in our ranks."

Angel, who only moments ago had given a detailed performance of his struggles for the benefit of the men on the Prekrasnaya Irina, now looked sheepishly from man to man, as one hoping someone would tell him what to do.

"Well, go up there," bellowed Dmitri. "This might be the best offer you will get in years."

"Yes, Angel, go talk to the man," urged Raphael. For a moment the young man stood motionless. Then, energetically as he did everything, he climbed aboard the Irina. At the same moment the chopper reappeared above the Jeanette, having returned from delivering bodies to a speedboat. The pilot announced that a harness would be lowered for Brent, who had been booked for surgery on his leg at Jackson Memorial Hospital in Miami, and would be flown in. Brent did not like the ensuing fuss at all.

"I can go to my doc in Key Largo," he complained. "It's just a scratch. I can hardly feel it."

"Sorry! Orders are orders, and we all must follow them," intoned the cheerful voice from above. And so the men fastened a harness around Brent and a moment later he was lifted into the air.

"Take care of my boat!" he yelled, before he disappeared in the belly of the copter.

"You damn well know that I will," shouted Dmitri, trying to overcome the sound of the rotor blades, while the copter already banking, was flying off.

With the last of the bodies taken care of, the convoy set out for the waters of the Atlantic. The men on board were in a jubilant mood. Everyone had done his part in the operation; everyone played an important, integral part. Adrenalin was ebbing slowly, while they returned to their regular duties. Anthony Li, aboard the Ada-May, was bending over his computer. He was reviewing reports from other agents. A substantial recovery of cocaine, hidden in bales, was announced by the crew of the Ada-May. The coast guard boats reported towing the cigar boat, filled with contraband, and the Irina, too, was loaded with drugs. The later report came from his boss, John Brandeis, who was brimming with pleasure, together with an unusual accolade: "Atta boy, Li!"

"Well," said Li to no one in particular, "sometimes it pays to be a customs agent!" And he hummed a little tune.

Dmitri was on his cellphone to Jeanette, Brent's wife. "Jeanette," he mused, "such a pretty name but no one ever uses it." Everyone addressed her plainly as Jan, and she probably would not have answered if anyone had called her by her full appellation. Jan came on line in an instant. "What's up, Dmitri?" she said perkily, and then with suspicion in her voice, "Why are you calling me? Why isn't Brent calling?"

"Jan, dear girl, there's been a small accident, and Brent was in it."

"What kind of an accident. I knew you guys could not be trusted. I knew he'd get hurt. So what is it? And give it to me straight. No softening of the edges. I will find out soon enough anyway."

"Calm down, Jan. Of course I will give you the whole story. So sit down and I'll tell you everything. You see, we were after this Russian mob, drug dealers. The leader was swimming beside our boat, and Brent got excited and jumped on top of him and the fight was on."

"Oh, my God," came a moan from the unhappy wife. Dmitri used her intake of breath, caused by a sob, to continue his tricky narrative. He did not want to make the report sound too easy and matter of fact. He had to give his friend his due; on the other hand he did not want to distress Jan unnecessarily.

"Well, yes, they struggled fiercely. But you know what a fighter Brent is; every one of his many pounds is muscle. He got the upper hand and was pulling the guy up to the boat, when the Russian, almost passed out, managed to pull a gun." Dmitri's hearing was almost destroyed by Jan's earsplitting scream.

"Is he dead? Oh, my God, tell me he is alive!"

"Jan, girl, calm down! Didn't you hear? I said small accident?"

"Yes, but now you say gun and things are serious. So hurry up and tell me what happened."

"He got shot in the leg. Nothing serious. The guys put a tourniquet on him and he felt good enough to captain the boat for a while because we were having problems. They just air-lifted him by helicopter to Jackson Memorial, and I just wanted to tell you that you can see him there."

Jan, much calmer now, heard the rest of the story. She listened raptly to the whole glory tale, especially the valor of the participants. Dmitri ended his account: "So Irina will go to prison first, and then be deported to mother Russia."

"Serves her right," exclaimed Jan grimly before hanging up on him.

All is Well That Ends Well

⋐⋑

THE SUN ROSE AS the small convoy finally arrived in Miami. In a special section of the harbor, complements of police and immigration officers were already waiting. The cigar boat, its escort of coast guard boats and the Ada-May, were the first to be received. The moment the boats were tied up, they were boarded and relieved of contraband and prisoners. Then the arduous bureaucratic processing began. It was almost mid-morning before the men were able to finally go to bed. That is not to say that they were released to go home. No, the mills of government mill slowly and produce voluminous amounts of fine grist—paperwork

The men from the Jeanette, minus Brent, and the crew from the Ada-May were put up in a nearby Day's Inn, courtesy of the authorities, and had to hold themselves available for more debriefing.

After a couple of hours of much-needed sleep, both crews went in unison to Joe's Stone Crab on South Point Drive. They ordered Land & Seas and Surf & Turfs, the biggest things on the menu. Only some great whisky, and some great wines would do justice to such wonderful fare, and the men did not stinge on their drink orders. Dinner was the perfect thing to relive the last few exiting days. Dan Heminger recounted how he had regaled his wife with the deeds performed from the deck of her boat. Butweiler was hailed as the hero of the boat; cut from the same cloth as Brent, he had flung himself upon a Georgian gunman, disarming and subduing him.

This particular Georgian had been shooting at the helicopter in an attempt to destroy the searchlights, while his nearby colleague fired at the Ada-May. The latter had been subdued by a young Coast Guard Officer, jumping upon him from the helicopter. While the furor of battle raged, the Ada-May had been alternately captained by John Morell and Dan Heminger. Dan had distinguished himself by pulling two extremely reluctant Georgians aboard while ruthlessly wielding his gaff.

Some tales of daring were told with more glee than others. Raphael was remembered for a grand new invention—the breakaway gaff, Dmitri for his concerted effort to keep Irina away from his body.

"I never knew him to be so shy of a woman," trumpeted Brent, turning the heads of many diners in their direction.

The call came during the grand finis of their banquet, which consisted of coffee, liqueurs, flan and Key Lime Pie. Once more they had to face the questioning authorities for the final time.

Back in the Keys

❧

AFTER A LONG, GOOD night's sleep Dmitri awoke with the pleasurable feeling one derives only from sleeping in one's own bed. He stretched to his full length, pleased that his morning pains were minimal. Some mornings it was harder than others to get the kinks out; age, what an annoyance. He still felt as young as ever in his mind—if only the body would comply. He suddenly realized with overwhelming glee that he had done it—Irina had been captured. Now she was sitting in a jail. He sighed with palpable relief. Irina would be sent back to Russia—under guard—once she had served time in prison. The entire Georgian mafia was awaiting trial. He and his friends had been assured by the FBI agents that the sentences for the gang would be stiff, especially for Petros Avarikidze.

What a remarkable time this had been for him and his friends. Every one of them had enjoyed the adventure, been proud to be a part of it.

Brent was already back at home with his wound stitched up, and a firm bandage, his hero's badge, around his thigh. Jan had forgiven him his crazy stunt, forgiven Dmitri for having provoked the trouble. All was well, but there still was no wife in his house. As he did every morning, he trod in the kitchen and began to make breakfast. He did not mind fending for himself—he rather liked cooking. It was the eating alone part that he hated. Well, at the present, there was nothing he could do about that. But he was not one to give up easy. He would find a way to meet the right woman. Just wait and see!

Part Two

Precious Jewel

❧❧

IN THE MONTHS FOLLOWING the exciting Russian adventure, Dmitri divided his attention and energy between the house, his neighbors, the boat and fishing. As time passed, however, a disillusioned but undaunted Dmitri decided to seek romance in foreign lands once more. He had been repeatedly told by different men of his acquaintanceship that the real hunting grounds for willing, pliable women were in Asia.

"Go to Hong Kong," said one friend.

"Go to Thailand," said another. "The Philippines, Vietnam, Korea; these are the places where women still listen when a man talks!"

Provided with such sage advice and many colorful prospectuses, Dmitri began his studies of the feminine sex of Asia. To his surprise there were thousands of women from which he could choose. All were young and willing to marry an American; whether the man was young or old, appealing or sordid, it mattered not. As long as they could come to America and leave their miserable circumstances behind, they would marry anyone.

In this manner, by catalogue, he found Precious Jewel. She was offered in a glossy Thai publication and efficiently described like a new winter coat in the Sears catalogue. Already at his first glance he liked her sweet, round face and innocent doe eyes. He was slightly disturbed by the fact that the girl with the unpronounceable Thai name was twenty years younger than his own daughter.

"So you are going to fetch her from the airport? The previous horrid experience has taught you nothing?" asked Martha, sending a questioning look at Dmitri. For months after the Irina affair the female complement of the neighborhood had plied Dmitri with sly jokes and ridicule. And although they employed every one of their crafts and wiles in an effort to inoculate him against foreign women, in the end they were helpless in the face of raging hormones. They fruitlessly used injections of wisdom and venomous antidotes, as if he had contracted the flu.

The two neighbors were standing on this perfect day in November on the concrete dock connecting their properties, which bordered a canal. The temperature had already risen to a balmy seventy-six degrees, with a forecast of no more than eighty degrees all day. The sky above them was clear and blue, furrowed with wispy, wind-driven bands of clouds high in the altostratus.

In the coconut palms lining their properties, mourning doves and green parrots rustled about in the gently undulating fronds. Martha was the only neighbor to approach him this fateful morning. As every day at home, she was dressed most casually in an ancient white blouse, gathered at the waist in a tie, and a pair of dark blue shorts that also belonged to earlier decades. A spanking new pair of Nikes finished off her apparel. She ogled Dmitri with obvious interest because she had seldom seen him dressed so well.

"Yes, today Precious Jewel arrives," he replied stiffly as he sometimes did when he tried to be formal for a special occasion. Once more he had undergone the transformation from casual Key's man to dressed-to-kill suitor. His shirt was blinding white; his hair gleamed with pomade.

Pleased with himself he smiled at Martha as guileless as a sixteen-year-old boy going to the prom. Martha, a seventy-year-old widow, and therefore much more compatible in age to him than his new Thai entanglement, smiled back with a hint of pity in her sunburnt but still pretty face. In her youth Martha must have been a beauty. To this day she looked from afar like a young girl. She was trim, still comely shaped. Only close-up did one notice the uneven harshness of her colored hair and the spider web of creases in her skin. Her figure was still firm, for she had never refused the hard work on the hundreds of projects which her husband forced upon her. Most of the jobs concerned construction on the house, a hobby with which her husband occupied their retirement. When she smiled, she became pretty with white shining teeth in a generous mouth made for laughter.

As she now beamed at Dmitri, her face reflected genuine fondness and a glimmer of amusement. For a while, after his wife's death, she nursed the notion that he might turn to her for companionship and a bit of home cooking. But that was not to be as she soon found out. They'd gone fishing a few times, even cooked dinner for each other on occasion. But despite their compatibility and their evident enjoyment and ease in each other's company, his obvious belief that his youthful superiority merited a much younger companion, destroyed all possibilities of a relationship.

Martha vetted him with motherly attention, thinking, *They are all the same—stupid—ruled by the dictates of their little members. There he is in all his put-on glory, middle sixties looking like fifty with his strong, compact Greek peasant body. His face is still firm and olive brown, as is his body. His wrinkles are few and the gray in his hair is "becoming."*

Martha was very apprehensive about this whole new thing that he got himself involved in. What did he really know about this Thai woman except that she was young and fairly pretty. He'd gone to Thailand to meet her and came back all in a dither. He admitted to Martha, however, that he had been unable to have a real conversation with the Thai girl.

"What about the differences in your cultures and your life styles?" Martha had asked. "How will you communicate what you want her to do outside your bed? She may not even know the simplest appliances in your home."

"Oh, I will show her by example. Precious Jewel will learn." That was his standard answer to her reasonable questions. "She is young and bright, she can adapt."

Poor Dmitri, Martha thought, as she watched him eagerly jump into his car. The old fool had purchased a brand new SUV in honor of "Precious Jewel."

If he says Precious Jewel one more time I will be sick, thought Martha as she watched the shiny Chevy Yukon disappear among the palm trees. In this small development on Key Largo, consisting of a main branch to US 1 and of five side roads and ten canals, Dmitri had been her neighbor for thirty years. She knew him since the day he came with his now-dead wife to purchase the property next to hers, and built his house.

His wife, Theresa, a blond, fair, blue-eyed Swede soon became her best friend. Together they had shopped for food, clothes and sundries, given dinner parties, gone on picnics and watched each other's grandchildren. They celebrated birthdays, weddings and holidays together and trusted each other with the keys to their houses. Now, Theresa was dead and Dmitri had a Thai bee in his bonnet.

At first, when he told her that he wanted to marry again, she understood. A same-age companion is a good thing to have. However, she changed her mind when he resorted to all this nuttiness. What an absurd idea, wanting a young wife who was able to give him children.

"Be serious, Dmitri," she cried, "You will be seventy five or eighty when your kid is ten and you will be hopelessly in your dotage when he is a teen. It's not fair to the child you would father."

He laughed and positively roared.

"Who talks just about one child? I want a crew! Those were the happiest days of my life when the children were small and I taught them."

He looked at her with the most soulful expression, so innocent and sweet it could have melted a stone. Martha, however, kept a cool head and reminded him that the odds were fifty-fifty that when his first child wanted him to throw a baseball he would be unable to even chew his own food. Seeing the picture of Dmitri as a tooth-less old fool in her mind, she laughed delightedly. Soon she came up with another concern.

"And what about your new wife? If you suddenly were to die she would be helpless and all alone in a foreign country with a passel of little children."

"She will have money to raise them," retorted he. "She can pay for help."

"Be serious Dmitri! Just forget for one moment your own wishes and think about the girl. Do you think she will be happy for long being married to a rather older man? Do you think that a girl mar-rying for money and citizenship will fall in love with you and be-come the wife of your dreams? People after all have their own feelings and secret thoughts and motives. Has it occurred to you that you might be nothing to her but the means of escape from the third world? Don't you remember the horrible adventure with the Russian?"

"Of course, this has occurred to me. I am not totally the idiot you think I am. I knew that even when I invited Irina to come here." He once again grinned, amused at her in a certain boyish way that was so winning.

"Precious Jewel is different. When I was in Thailand I talked about these things with her through an interpreter. She told me that in her culture girls are prepared from childhood to marry as their fathers tell them. The men are often older, she said, because by a later time of life they have acquired enough money to raise a fam-ily." Dmitri eyed Martha hopefully, anticipating that he had dispelled all her arguments.

"Well, that makes it alright then," she sniffed, put off by the ca-sual way he approached something as serious as marriage. She had married her high school sweetheart at seventeen, and although they had loved one another passionately, there had been very rough times when they stormed and raged against each other.

"I hope you know what you are about to do. I, for one, wish you the very best."

Already turned to leave, she stopped to throw her last rock into the mechanics of his mind.

"So, what about her religion? How does that compare to your own? Will you be married in church? Will she want you to change to her religion? What is she anyway, if anything?"

"Oh, come now Martha, as if this will make any great difference. But if you must know, she is a Buddhist, however, not a serious one. She does some things with prayer wheels and flowers on small altars. I really don't know."

Whatever argument Martha used to change his mind, to bring him to reason, it mattered little. His mind was made up. He selfishly only wanted to go forward driven by his burning desire, and he walked away.

Standing alone on the empty dock, she contemplated the futility of her oratories on reason and sense. Upon this reckoning, she firmly decided that this was a matter for God. For, as she told herself, *This is nothing an earthly creature can handle.*

Placing the problem named Dmitri into her Maker's hands, she walked back to her own house along the concrete dock lining the canal bank. Every home in this development was built to the precise specifications of the county. No matter how elaborate, elegant or pompous the structures on top, they, like their less prosperous cousins, stood below on steel and concrete pilings. This design allowed a huge tide or storm surge to pass harmlessly below the main house, at least according to the building code. But human beings what they are, flaunting the code of the county, endowed many of the structures with visitor's quarters where once a void would have allowed storm floods to flow through.

A hundred years ago, there had been only fertile mangrove swamps at the edge of the narrow Keys. This development, like many others, had been raised to its present height by the digging of canals. The resulting coral rock was used to make the land for the building sites. Huge machines cut the coral, depositing it on both sides of the emerging canals where it was compacted into buildable land. These waterways, giving access to Florida Bay on one side of US1 and to the Atlantic on the other, were the lifeblood of the Keys. To save space, the staircase of most houses wound along the side of the house. Martha's own house was an uninspired concrete rectangle, finished with everlasting, blindingly white coating. The most redeeming features of her simple home were the huge tiled balcony enclosed with screens, and her magnificent living room. It looked upon the blue-green waters of the canal, with its docks, beautiful yachts, boats and, of course, palm trees, hibiscus and bougainvilleas. The flowering bushes adorned her house and the houses of her neighbors. Martha's happiest hours were spent on this balcony or in her boat on the water.

The Arrival of the Oriental Gem

෨෪෭

BEFORE MARTHA BEGAN THE steep climb upstairs, she harvested a jumble of clothes from a line that stretched from her house to Dmitri's fence. Having collected the clothes, she released the line from the hook on the fence, seeing it automatically spool back into its case by the house. By unspoken agreement one could dry clothes outside on the line, but it was not proper to leave the line hung with clothes too long.

She entered her spacious living room, which, except for a dividing counter, was open to the even larger kitchen. All rooms in her home were beautifully tiled and appointed. Her own, and her deceased husband's constant labors had kept the home beautiful and in style.

She had barely set her heavy clothes basket down when she felt soft fur rubbing against her calves. Her cat Lucifer, looking like a miniature black panther, claimed his mistress' attention softly at first, then more insistently.

"One moment my pet," placated Martha, briefly petting her gorgeous cat. "Let me get a cool drink and I will sit with you a while." Going to the refrigerator, she filled Lucifer's food dish in passing. She poured herself a tall glass of pink lemonade. The moment she sat down in her favorite rattan chair, a big, handsome resting place, softly cushioned with fat pillows covered in flowered chintz, the big cat was in her lap. He purred as if his life depended on a good purr. Peacefully, companionably they sat for a while, almost drowsing off. A loud, demanding call from across the canal disturbed the peace.

"Martha, Martha, are you awake?" The disturbance was created by a tall, jolly looking woman who yelled across the water, using her hands to make a megaphone.

"As if some one could sleep with you around," laughed Martha, just as volubly as her friend.

"So, did he go to get Precious Jewel?" Martha's neighbor, Jan Sorensen, strongly overemphasized the Precious Jewel thing. It was obvious from her ridicule of the name that she felt about Dmitri's bride the same way Martha did.

"Yes, I saw him leave. All excited he was, polished and slicked. It's very comical to see him so foolish."

Martha interrupted herself and looked at her wristwatch, "You know, it is almost time for him to return. We must eat. Why don't you come over and I'll fix us some lunch. It will give you the opportunity to meet the bride when they arrive." ·

It was understood by all, of course, that Dmitri would bring the bride for Martha's inspection before taking her home.

"Sounds like a great plan. I will be right over," hollered Jan.

Moments later Jan arrived on her ancient bike, a contraption suffering from rusty patches where salt water and ill treatment had left their mark. From one of the handlebars hung a small blue cooler. Jan casually leaned the bike against one of the square, white stone columns, close to Martha's parked car, and ascended the staircase, cooler in hand. Her flowered shorts, cut loosely like a short skirt, swung about her shapely, long legs with every step; while a white cotton blouse revealed the curse of the menopausal woman—an amply endowed chest. Her blond hair was cut in a short bob because in the Keys no one wanted to mess with fussy hairdos. For that same reason Martha got perms, which she pulled into shape each morning with a long, forked styling comb. When things were really bad she tamed the frizz with coconut cream applying it liberally with the palms of her hands.

Halfway up to the front door, Jan announced her coming sotto voce, even though Martha could hear her clearly through the open kitchen window.

"Let yourself in, dearie. I am almost finished putting our salad together. I will just make us a crab sandwich and we are ready to go."

Jan knew that Martha must have been crabbing the day before or early in the morning, because she only prepared the freshest seafood. Everybody in the Keys knew that seafood a few days old was not worth having. That's what the people up north had to eat, but no one would ever eat it down here.

Jan walked over to the kitchen sink where Martha was working and gave her a peck on the wrinkled cheek. "How are you today, my girl?"

"Oh, I am fine. I am dying with curiosity to see what the mail-order-bride is like."

"We shall know soon. I figure by the time we are done with lunch they should arrive." Jan had placed her little, blue cooler on the counter. She now lifted the lid to reveal a promising looking jar, containing a light green liquid. She deftly extracted the jar from the cooler and held it up for perusal.

"I made us some margaritas. They should put us in the proper mood for the bridal inspection."

They both laughed delightedly. Somehow the idea of ordering a bride by mail still struck them as very odd and amusing, although this was Dmitri's second go-around. From the very moment they had heard of this business they had thought it was a crazy idea.

Martha and Jan were women of the sea and the earth. From their earliest days they were connected to water and soil through their fathers and grandfathers. They had raised their families, learning along the way many truths and secrets of the human mind. Now, in the retirement cycle of life, they looked upon worldly matters with the wisdom acquired through long living and pain. Therefore, the idea of ordering a wife from a catalogue appeared to them as preposterous.

"You cannot order people from a book like a dress from the Sears catalogue," opined Martha. "Everyone knows it takes time to get to know a person before integrating them intimately into your life."

"I chose my dogs more carefully, when I still had dogs, than he chose this wife to be." Jan had put this gem forth when first she first heard of Dmitri's plan. Martha could not have agreed more. With practiced ease Jan pulled two glasses from the freezer where she had stuck them to frost up good and dipped their rims into coarse salt.

Jan poured the drinks and added them to the tray with their lunch, carrying it out to the porch where Martha had set the table for two. They toasted each other, holding their green, wide glasses high. Martha, taking a sip, exclaimed, "My, these are good Margaritas, Jan."

Jan was bursting with laughter, "They should be better than good. They should be great! Because for good measure, I put double the Tequila in."

As they ate their lunch, Martha inquired about the health of Jan's husband. Brent had been recently diagnosed with diabetes and his new health regiment was hard on him—a big, powerful man, who had always done anything he wanted to do. He felt indestructible until the insidious illness struck at his very being.

"He is doing much better now that the insulin is adjusted properly and he sticks to the diet more."

Jan swiped at a fruit fly that had managed to penetrate the fine screening.

"Hardest for him is the one-drink-per-day rule. I always make him a good-sized drink right before dinner so he feels it, but it's never enough. I know he sneaks another when I am not looking."

"I know how he feels," agreed Martha. Deep empathy echoed in her voice.

"I wish the golden years would come without the aches and pains we must endure. Also, I could do without the nightly bathroom walks, because I can never go back to sleep once I get up."

They were almost finished with their second Margarita when they heard Dmitri's car pull into Martha's yard. The car door opened noisily; simultaneously they heard his hearty bellow.

"Hallo there, anybody home? I want you to meet someone!"

"We are here, up on the balcony," yelled Martha from the kitchen window, which overlooks Dolphin Drive and her front yard. Driven by curiosity, Jan joined Martha at the window. Side by side they peered out of the window, watching the scene unfolding below.

In the driveway, Dmitri yammered non-stop with happy excitement. He went to the passenger side and opened the door with a flourish.

"Out with you my girl. You are home now. Just you wait and see the palace I have for you."

He reached inside the passenger seat, for the girl still had made no move to join him. From the high seat of the SUV the female passenger looked down as if the distance to the ground dismayed her. Impatiently, Dmitri caught her by her upper arms and lifted her to the ground. The girl stood stiff like a porcelain doll before him. As if annoyed by her unease, he pulled her to his chest with a proprietary air, creating an awkward embrace.

"Come, come my Precious. Here are some nice ladies I want you to meet." Still holding the girl as if for support he beamed up at his friends at the kitchen window.

"He looks like a proud hunting dog, having fetched a duck," murmured Jan, while Martha concentrated her eyes and thoughts on the girl. Oh, yes, and a girl it was. This was not a woman by any measure.

"The old fool looks like her grandfather," she remarked in an aside to Jan.

The latter instantly dissolved in jolly laughter.

"Stop it!" hissed Martha, "He will know that we make fun of him, and I don't like to hurt his feelings."

During their small exchange, the hopeful couple had climbed the stairs to Martha's famous balcony. Both women greeted the visitors kindly at the door. They ushered them into the room, smiling so hard in an effort to impart friendliness to the young stranger that their facial muscles ached.

Finally the party was seated on the lovely balcony and began to exchange pleasantries. However, because Precious Jewel knew almost no English, the conversation limped along tentatively and was hard to maintain. To fill the silent gaps, Martha bustled about. She poured cold pink lemonade into tall iced glasses and served dainty, incredibly delicious cucumber and shrimp sandwiches. Jan, nursing margarita refill number three, tried valiantly to extract comments from the diminutive Thai guest in the next chair.

"Did you have a good flight?" She asked solicitously with exaggerated slowness, as if her indolent speech could bestow upon the stranger the instant power of understanding.

"Oh yes," Dmitri piped up. "She had a great flight. Didn't you, pumpkin?"

Martha, off to the side and out of the guests' field of vision, rolled her eyes heavenward.

"Pumpkin, indeed," she mouthed to Jan who buried her grinning visage in the wide expanse of her glass. Dmitri, unaware of the waggish amusement of his friends, shone his light of happiness at the pretty creature beside him. The girl, understanding nothing at all, smiled dutifully back and nodded agreement. She smiled broadly, exposing teeth reminiscent of pearls.

The conversation dragged on—no matter the difficulty of the question. It was obvious that the girl understood little of what transpired. Jan and Martha thought that, at best, she comprehended only a word here and there. At last, the awkwardness of the lagging conversation was overcome by Martha passing the sandwiches once more. While everyone was occupied with the delicate morsels, Jan and Martha found time to study the stranger more closely. They had eyed her as unobtrusively as possible—after all, one did not want to be rude.

"Easy keeper," thought Martha whimsically. "She certainly doesn't eat anything. Dmitri can maintain her on birdseed."

The thought made a giggle rise in her throat, which she suppressed valiantly.

Martha was usually the kindest of women. However, food played a major part in her life and she frowned upon those who were unable to enjoy exquisite food and drink. Jan, fired up by three Margaritas, was pursuing different topics in her mind.

The girl looks like sixteen, but he said that she is twenty-four. She mused. *She is so thin, yet her arms are rounded and her breasts are full. Interesting.*

Considering this intriguing fact, she posed her next question, miming the meaning while addressing Precious Jewel.

"Aren't you tired, my dear?" she pillowed her head upon her folded hands and closed her eyes. The show and tell approach finally brought the desired result.

"No, no tired," piped up Precious Jewel. "Sleep on plane."

"Damn, she talks!"

The moment the words left her mouth, Jan's oval, tanned face turned beet red with embarrassment. Her blue eyes radiated apologies in Dmitri's direction as she stammered, "Sorry, Dmitri, I am so sorry."

Martha hid a wide grin by turning deftly toward the kitchen, tray in hands, while Jan abjectly continued with her apology.

"Forgive me, I had one too many margaritas and my tongue got the better of me."

Dmitri, far from being offended, just laughed. "No problem, no problem! I know it's hard to converse because she knows very little English."

Soon thereafter Dmitri motioned to PJ, a nickname the women had instantly decided on, that it was time to leave. As the girl stood before them, the women could assess her person better.

PJ was small, about five feet one or two. She was slim—almost as if she was starving—and yet she managed to look healthy. Her skin was flawless, olive tinted. It covered a delicately boned face that sported an exquisite nose and huge, black eyes. Of course, her hair was perfect too. It was carbon black, long and lustrous and caught in a chignon. Her hands and feet matched the delicate body elegantly. The supreme composition was finished off by the black, little silk sheath she wore, of course with matching black, high-heeled sling backs and a string of huge black pearls at her neck.

"Goodness," sighed Martha the moment they were securely out off earshot of the departed.

"How dare he bring such beautiful competition into our laid-back, shabby old- folks backwater. She looks like a model for *Seventeen* or something."

"Yeah," chimed in Jan. "Or something much bigger, like television!" She sighed wistfully, "Did you see her getup? The dress, the pearls, the purse, the shoes—the whole schmier. It must have cost a fortune. How could a village girl from one of the poorest places on earth afford such clothes—never mind finding them and understand how they would compliment her looks."

"Oh, I know about that," said Martha.

"Dmitri told me how he bought her oodles of outfits and accessories in Bangkok. This city is the biggest rip-off place in the world. They imitate the most exclusive designs from Europe and the USA, everything you can imagine: clothes, shoes, watches, luggage, books, DVDs."

Martha sat down beside Jan and poured herself the last margarita before speaking. She had decided that she would have a very long nap today and to that end another margarita might be beneficial.

"Dmitri says they produce everything so cheaply because they pay no royalties. Their workers imitate all products beautifully, admirably so. And you know Dmitri, if he can buy quality cheep he will buy in quantity. He bought Channel dresses and suits for PJ, Luis Vuitton luggage, Ferragamo shoes and purses—on and on. He used an interpreter and a fashion consultant. That is how he did it."

"It still must have cost a fortune. Just the materials and the pearls must have cost plenty."

"Yes, dearie, you are right! He is bewitched by the creature and spent a fortune." Martha looked annoyed.

"After all, he saved plenty on poor Theresa. I know that she never got black pearls—not even the diamond ring he had promised her when they got married. She got a few pathetic jewel things, all not worth much, which he told her they could afford. God, he was quite stingy at times. The business; he always considered the business first. Then he loved his boat for which he had plenty of money, then the house and then—Theresa."

"So PJ reaps the fruit of Theresa's work? This makes me sick. I think I am going shopping tomorrow and buy myself the diamond earrings I have been salivating over for two years now. The way things look here, I could die tomorrow and Brent buys them for the new trophy wife."

Martha laughed uproariously, "Oh come now, Jan. That's not like you! That's margarita talk."

"No, it's not! I am speaking on behalf of woman kind!" Jan rose, collected her containers, and pecked Martha's wrinkled cheek on her way out. As she walked through the door, she emitted the rebel yell, "Toodleloo! That's not the end of the story, yet!"

Intro to the American Home

꙳

MEANWHILE, NEXT DOOR, DMITRI, bursting with pride, showed his bride her new home. His house closely resembled Martha's house structurally, with the exception of the staircase, its position and size. Walking up to the front door, they entered the covered, tiled, broad staircase encased by massive stone sides. The front door was a marvel of glass and wrought iron. Ushered through this formidable gate, the new bride stood benumbed by the opulence displayed in the entry. It was a space created by stealing footage from the oversized living room through the use of cleverly placed Japanese bamboo and rice-paper screens. The screens and potted plants were arranged in such a way that the privacy of the great room was preserved.

"Pretty, pretty," cried P J who had never in her life encountered an arrangement right out of *Architectural Digest* or *House Beautiful*. As they walked through a door to the left, the girl beheld a beautiful modern kitchen. Separated from the living room by a large wall and floor to ceiling cabinets, the kitchen was a work of art. Dmitri, with a Greek eye for contrast and stark juxtaposition of colors and materials, had insisted that the cabinetry wood must be mahogany. The counter tops were made from Ubatuba granite from Africa; the appliances and other surfaces were clothed in stainless steel. The effect was gorgeous, riveting.

Not long after Martha's friend Theresa died, Dmitri decided to remodel in hopes of attracting a younger wife. After Martha had inspected the remodeled kitchen, she rushed to Jan's house. She exclaimed her dismay with moist eyes.

"Too bad Theresa could not have seen this wonder. Even more, she could have used this wonderful kitchen. She would have been deliriously happy in this beautiful space."

Later, she confronted Dmitri with the same comment. Thoughtfully he answered, "Yes, perhaps we should have done this years ago. But Theresa was ill for so long that somehow it didn't feel right to put her through the turmoil of a remodel."

As he ushered PJ into the magic kitchen, she stopped and stood as if in awe—wide eyed and silent. Never in all her life had she seen such room. When her eyes traveled upward, caressing the beautiful wooden cabinets, up to the immaculate white ceiling and back down again to the marble floor, she seemed to grow in stature. She stood straighter and taller as if to pay tribute to beauty and functionality, although the meaning of the assembled appliances escaped her.

At last, Demetrius prompted, "Come, come, my girl. There is more!" Once again he held her arm and gently propelled her through the living room into the next wing. Before the remodel this wing had contained three bedrooms and two baths. Dmitri, however, calculated that he would not need the guest rooms anymore.

"Have them stay at the Marriott if they want to come," he said. Thus he dismissed his usual visitors, his children—four sons in their early forties, his twenty-eight-year-old daughter, and eight grandchildren in one fell swoop—casting the lot of them into the role of stranger visits.

"Dmitri," admonished Martha when he spouted such sacrilege, "this is not like you. You were always such a devoted family man. Because Theresa is dead you are not the same man anymore? Do you realize that you just relegated your whole family to obscurity?"

He sagely retorted to her outburst, "I need the space, and I have given them enough money during my lifetime that they can stay elsewhere when they come to visit. Anyway, the grandchildren are spoiled as hell and not that great to have around."

To give him his desired space, the builder knocked out walls and replaced them with load bearing columns wherever needed. Thus, eliminating rooms, he created for Dmitri a palatial bath—all clad in cream marble—with an enormous tub fit for an emperor. Martha took one look at the huge bath and broke out in ringing laughter, for everyone who even remotely knew Dmitri was patently aware that the man only took showers. To add to the utter grandiosity of the bathroom, gold-encrusted mirrors and fixtures complimented the opulence of the breathtaking design.

Also gained by the wall removal, was a space for a truly royal bedroom. Dmitri had kept the design of this room simple. The floor was marble tiled, the walls virgin white, and the walk-in closet was filled with stainless steel organizers.

Except for a huge, black bed, filled with a multitude of leopard-patterned pillows, which rested upon a custom-made black silk quilt, and an ebony vanity with a white fluffy cushioned bench before it, the room was unfurnished and undecorated.

Seeing this room PJ acted the way Dmitri had hoped she would. She was awed, astonished even, in every room she had seen. But when her eyes fastened on the remarkable bed, she screamed something unintelligible in Thai and flung herself upon its pillowed expanse, much as a teenager jumps upon a float in a pool.

"So, what do you think?" asked the old man. The excited girl replied with a flood of Thai gibberish that somehow made him very happy. And so, right there and then, with the help of a dose of Viagra, which he had taken half an hour earlier, the introduction of Precious Jewel into America was celebrated. So far, that was the easy part of the introduction. The girl apparently was well versed in the art of lovemaking, and for his part, the Viagra insured there were no slip-ups. Floating on a Thai cloud of delight, Dmitri could not foresee any problems marring his happiness. He, the old sailor of the Aegean and the Atlantic could weather any storm. Was he not always ready and prepared for every eventuality? It was with this attitude of "can do" that he began his training of Precious Jewel. Having been apprized by Martha that it would be easier for people to call the girl by an abbreviated term, he, too, decided to adopt PJ as the short form of her name; somehow it was appropriate and suited her.

Introduction to Key's Life

꘎ꙮꙮꘫ

PJ'S TRAINING BEGAN THE next morning, long before the poor girl had any inkling of what was in store for her. Dmitri, in his deliciously demented state of mind, thought that the rest of life would just flow in perfection like a beautiful river. As a man of precise habits, he felt that the new bride must soon learn how he liked to live. How he preferred his meals cooked and when they were to be served; how his laundered items had to be folded was of the utmost importance for a wife to know. With that in mind, he set out to instruct PJ in the art of proper breakfast preparation.

During his visit in Thailand he had tasted the awful stuff—rice, vegetables and eggs, she had made for him in the morning. Although he stomached it while being on holiday and all; he was dead set against feeding on it for the rest of his life.

They had gotten up at six, as was his habit; although PJ looked and acted as if she needed a few more hours of sleep. She cheerfully smiled however, as she went into the bathroom, for she had been told a thousand times that "a husband always deserves a pleasant mien, no matter a wife's true feelings, wants or needs." The pleasant smile had become ingrained in her muscles, like a mask cast in a mold.

Dmitri motioned her to follow him to the kitchen. Five minutes later she appeared in the immaculate kitchen where he awaited her with pots and frying pans and a counter brimming with ingredients.

Dmitri's eyes widened in disbelief when he saw his bride. *What the hell does she think she will be doing in here?* he thought wonderingly. That was a good question. Because the girl standing before him in a chic, flowered silk dress and high-heeled sling backs, looked more as if she was going to attend an elegant garden party than work in a kitchen in the Florida Keys.

"Whoa there, girl," intoned Dmitri. "This will not do at all. Don't you have any clothes suitable for a kitchen or a casual day in the Keys?"

"What is wrong?" PJ asked, clueless. Had she not done precisely what she had been told she should do; namely, dress beautifully, seductively in her most pleasing outfits? Why then did Dmitri disdain her efforts and show such obvious displeasure?

"You can't cook dressed like this!" he said emphatically. "First of all, this dress cost me a fortune; secondly, it will be ruined forever by grease and egg stains."

Like a friendly uncle guiding a small niece, he took her by the hand and led her back into the bedroom. There in the corner stood her suitcases, barely unpacked. They were thrown open to reveal a jumble of clothing. In her hurry to join him in the kitchen, PJ had hastily searched through her carefully packed treasures before finally settling on what she thought was a good choice for the day.

At this moment, PJ experienced her first great disappointment in Dmitri. She was prepared to overlook his age, but she was unprepared for the letdown with the dress. She liked it, no loved it, and wanted to wear the pretty thing. Did he not get the clothes for her to shine? As Dmitri pulled various clothes from her cases and placed them on the bed, he mumbled.

"This won't do, and this is even worse. I guess we will have to go to K-Mart to find tops and shorts for the house."

Meanwhile the girl stood pressed against the bedroom wall and watched his odd pursuits with wonderment? What was this strange American man doing with her belongings? However, it would not have occurred to her to feel resentment at his meddling in her private things.

Fortunately, the newly minted husband soon ended his searching, but not before he beckoned her to help him hang the clothes orderly on hangers and deposit them in the spacious closet. In one fell swoop the country child had been initiated into a most important American custom—the keeping of an orderly closet.

No sooner had they placed the last hanger on its appointed rod, than Dmitri announced that after breakfast they were bound for the K-Mart store.

K-Mart was one of the few places where one could buy anything in the Keys. Most things had to be bought in Miami. There was no room for shops and malls on the slender Keys. The few stores that had bought the available building sites in the early years, when no one wanted to take a chance on the very uncertain developments, now held a monopoly.

Hearing Dmitri's complaints, and finally understanding the gist of his speech, it dawned on PJ that no servants were coming to cook and clean the house; that no gardener would rake the blinding white crushed coral in the yard; that no one would clean the huge boat or the many fish Dmitri would catch. She would be doing many of these things, perhaps with his help, perhaps without. At first, this truth devastated her. All her fancy expectations were crushed. The women in her village had clucked and fussed over her, telling her:

"You marry rich American, you work no more. You will have servants. All to do is dress and look pretty. Clap hands and tell servants what to do." The women had sighed with envy.

"Ah, you so fortunate Precious Jewel. Smiled upon by good gods of leisure."

The young woman had believed their tales when she deciphered the first letters from America, believed them even more after meeting Dmitri. And, after having been taken on the huge shopping spree, she had been wholly convinced of her leisurely future. He had bought her suitcases, shoes, stockings, dresses, nightgowns, underwear and jewelry. A man this rich must have servants. Had he not bought airplane tickets and hotel rooms for her—all first class? A poor man without servants could not have done this.

While she, deeply disturbed, sorted out her thoughts, Dmitri noted that she was still wearing the expensive silk dress and he rooted some more through her belongings. Finally he emerged triumphantly with a black pair of cotton slacks and a tiny lemon-colored top.

"Here," he said, presenting her with his find. "Put this on. This will do until we get you some Keys clothes."

By now PJ understood, of course, that she was meant to change and dutifully went to comply. Moments later the happy couple was united in the kitchen where Dmitri introduced the girl to the intricacies of his breakfast. Modern cooking held its own challenges. The electric stove alone required a thirty-minute introduction for someone who had cooked over an open fire all her life. The experience was not helped along by a certain pedantic bend of the ex-naval man. She burned her hand on the hot bacon pan, a burn which he sorrowfully kissed, anointed and ice-packed. From then on things improved, because she was relegated to watching dutifully as he performed joyfully the ceremony of American breakfast.

"Voila, my dear. There it is, nicely displayed on a platter. That's how I like it and that's what I want you to learn."

The next part of the day unfolded painlessly and pleasantly for the foreign bride. After breakfast, which she liked very much, especially the bacon and the pancakes; she followed her future husband through the backyard down to the dock.

Since the properties were diminutive, the walk took little time except for the ceremony of greeting the neighbors, who were busily performing chores on their boats and docks. Today an astounding number of boats were in need of motor maintenance and folks were doing dock sweeping and tackle restoration.

Across the canal two brothers were outfitting their flat-bottomed craft to fish the bay for mangrove snappers. Their hearty "Good

Mornings" contained a goodly amount of admiration for Dmitri's choice.

"Wonder how long he can keep this boat at anchor," said Matt, the younger of the pair under his breath. Equally subtly, his brother Mike answered,

"Oh, I think only until stronger wind can fill her sails."

They laughed with a deep belly laugh that was only slightly tainted by their own sorrow-full experiences. Each one had tried marriage a couple of times and been divorced by wives who wished for more in life than boats, fishing, beer and whiskey.

Martha warbled a "Good Morning," and "Did you sleep well, my dear?"

A question as little understood by the girl in its double entendre as the rest of the greetings aimed at her.

At last, they sat in the smaller of his boats, a small runabout, and cast off. Dmitri babbled happily about the beauty of the canals, the cheerful palm trees, the friendly neighbors—it mattered not to PJ. She sat, wide-eyed and tranquil, enjoying the ride and understanding very little.

This, at last, was a bit of the promised rich life, of doing nothing but sitting still and looking pretty while taking in the beautiful scenes. Most of all she marveled at all the gorgeous, mostly white, shining houses. This was it. She could do this easily.

Not much later, they arrived at a dock where they tied up. They walked leisurely the short distance to the K-Mart store.

PJ's first reaction upon entering the American symbol of afford-able merchandise was one of indifference. Dmitri had taken her to much more elegant and better stocked stores in Bangkok. Further-more, she was used to overflowing Asian open-air markets where, as in any oriental bazaar, a super fluidity of goods stunned the mind with the demand to make educated choices. Yet it was not five min-utes later, after meandering among the well-ordered aisles, that her feminine, deeply ingrained trait of acquisition came to the fore.

Without needing a thing, or even trying to like anything, she fell in love with colorful tablecloths and accompanying sets of napkins, plates, glasses and silverware. The moment she did so, her doe eyes fastened on Dmitri's.

"Please," she aspirated the only word in the English language she was sure of, as a wishful plea. Dmitri understood instantly.

"No," he said decisively. "This is not what we come here for. I have plenty of what we need. Now, dear girl, we must go to another aisle."

And, as he had done so many times before during the last weeks, he took her elbow firmly and steered her to the corner that advertised "WOMEN" with large letters. In his free hand Dmitri carried one of the ubiquitous red plastic baskets, without which he could not imagine to transport his purchases. As they entered the shoe aisle, he spied black rubber flip-flops, an item needed by every Key's person. A little stool beckoned, and he motioned PJ to have seat. Obediently the girl sat, presenting her foot as he demanded. Her friendly, cooperative mien changed to one of cloudy distaste when Dmitri tried one of the black flip-flops on her foot for a good fit.

What was this strange man doing to her now? Did he really think that she would like something as horrible as this peasant shoe? Poor people all over Asia wore this kind of thing. This was not what she expected at all. But, well trained to hold her peace and unable to complain in English anyway, she composed her face and watched Dmitri as if he were an actor in a strange play.

Dmitri, who had neither observed her displeasure nor her puzzlement, continued to act as if he were alone in the store. He smiled contentedly at her small foot, sporting the perfectly fitting black flip-flop. The old eye was still good at sizing-up objects. This was a perfect fit.

"We will take these," he said with satisfaction. As if to forge a connection to the girl he proclaimed, "I think I will get a pair for myself. Then we are matched."

As he searched for a pair of the floppers for himself, he paid scant attention to his bride, who with childish delight escaped into the garden section where she found a red empty basket. Having observed how Dmitri and other shoppers filled their baskets with their hearts desires, she began filling hers with her heart's desire.

A child of Thailand, she loved flowers, plants and trees with deep esthetic appreciation. Of course, she chose only the rarest most wonderful plants—orchids. And of those rare beauties she picked only the most exquisite, those finding favor in her beauty loving eyes.

Meanwhile, as PJ was so pleasantly occupied, Dmitri had begun a frantic hunt for her. Unable to find her by his side, he ran up and down the aisles, calling her name sotto voce at first. He was reluctant to attract attention to his dilemma. At last, he resorted to the humiliating act of having her paged on the intercom.

I am calling her like a lost child, he thought, annoyed. However, this maneuver brought no results, because PJ neither heard her name—so different when pronounced in English—nor did she pay any attention to the noise at all. Why should she? By no stretch of her imagination could she see herself to be the cause for the demanding, exceedingly loud voice echoing through the store.

The errant bridal pair was reunited only moments after Dmitri conceived of the novel idea to look for PJ in the garden section. Already from afar he discerned that his beloved had broken a new boundary.

He did not know much about orchids, but even to his untrained eye it was obvious that Precious Jewel had loaded her basket with a fortune of bloom. How she could have found, of all places in a K-Mart, Cattleyas worth a few hundred dollars was beyond belief. But there she was, her basket loaded with a deep red Sanyang Ruby 'Crowned Dragon,' a purple Chinese Beauty 'Phoenix,' a green 'Ports of Paradise' and a white and purple 'Exima.' The latter alone had a price tag of eighty dollars and the rest of the basket brought the tab up to two hundred fifty dollars.

"Holy Archimandrite!" exclaimed Dmitri, using an utterance his mother had employed in his childhood days when she was in the throes of frustration.

"PJ what have you done? You cannot have these! They are terribly expensive."

"No understand," smiled the pretty Thai sprite back at him.

"Much money! No can have!"

Dmitri mangled the language in hopes to make her understand. To add thunder to his words he began removing the gorgeous plants from her basket, placing them back into the flower-studded shelves. Nothing conveyed the reality of the situation quicker to Precious Jewel than his crude actions. For a moment she stood there, her face frozen in unbelief, her arms hanging by her sides. Then, as if she now understood, she broke out in bitter tears.

Never in his life had Dmitri seen larger, rounder tears as those rolling over PJ's peachy cheeks. The times must remain uncounted that Dmitri withstood the sobs of his wife, Theresa. Many were the times when she had looked at him with a look of enormous hurt. Yet he had always successfully managed to avert his face and walk without qualms away from her sadness. But now that he was almost in his dotage, he could not watch the disappointment of the young girl he had already treated to more luxuries than he had ever extended to the mother of his children.

"Oh stop it! Stop crying!" he groaned. "Here, take the blasted flowers. But God help you if you neglect them and let them die."

With obvious frustration, he pulled out the same orchids he had shoved with vigor into the shelves and placed them carefully into PJ's basket. The young woman's tears dried up instantly. Her face lit up; she stepped closer to him and, raising herself on tiptoe, placed a big, fat kiss on his mouth.

"Thank, thank," she mouthed, and strangely enough for a moment, to Dmitri that kiss was worth the orchid money.

He changed his mind about the flowers when finally, having obtained the objects they had really come for, they were standing in the checkout lane. Besides flip-flops and orchids, they bought blue canvas shorts, a white T-shirt, and flowered tops for PJ. Once in the spirit of shopping, the young woman had discerned the utility of the clothes, because she made very good choices.

By the time they got home and tied the boat at the dock it was already noon. Dmitri motioned to PJ to change into the new casual clothes and join him in the kitchen. When PJ walked toward Dmitri, she was the picture of a young Key's woman. She wore blue shorts and a flowered tank top and her feet sported the ubiquitous flip-flops. Dmitri was frying eggs in a large pan, bacon in another. Beside him on a counter sat two plates. Upon each one two slices of bread waited to be dressed.

"OK, my dear, you are just in time to put mayonnaise on the bread," he intoned. PJ smiled shyly and stood patiently by his side without moving a finger.

"Oh, Lord! You really do not understand anything. Ah forget it. I do it myself," growled the new husband impatiently. He turned off the burners and hastened to the refrigerator, where he extracted mayonnaise and a few lettuce leaves.

Snatching salt and pepper from a stand that held seasonings, he returned to his pans. Spreading mayonnaise and laying lettuce leaves on the bread took only seconds as PJ watched the proceedings fully engrossed. He expertly snatched up bacon slices and one of the fried eggs placing them on one sandwich. He moved the finished plate far out of PJ's reach.

"All right, lady, if you want to eat you have to make your own," he said.

Gesticulating, he told her to repeat the process, which he had so capably demonstrated, on the other sandwich.

The young woman suspiciously eyed the bacon and the fried eggs, swimming in butter. She had internalized all of Dmitri's preparations and repeated them flawlessly, creating a very satisfying sandwich. If anyone had cared to ask her, she would have told them in no uncertain terms that she would have much rather fixed a meal with rice and vegetables. However, once sitting out on the porch, overlooking the sea-green waters of the canal, she enjoyed the sandwich, enjoyed the fizzing Coke in her glass, and was very happy.

Although the new couple had done very little work throughout the morning, great lassitude overcame them after lunch. And so it came about that shortly after clearing the dishes, they retreated companionably to the bedroom where, without further ado, both fell asleep.

Awakening, Dmitri decided the time was perfect for a spot of friskiness. All went as well as could be expected and Dmitri emerged from the bedroom as a conquering hero, followed by his gently smiling companion.

His ardor cooled, Dmitri's rational mind came to the fore and he decided that the language situation had to be remedied. Otherwise, how could he train his wife to cook a decent dinner? He motioned the girl to join him on the porch where he sat at the ready with pencil and paper. PJ had had some training in writing and reading a few English words. Systematically Dmitri began to teach her the most common words and expressions.

He did not want to appear too pedantic and lose her interest. So he ended the first lesson after ten new phrases and told her to study them. By tomorrow at the same time—here he pointed at his wristwatch and made her read the time—they would proceed with the lessons.

Charity

❧⟡

EVERY WOMAN KNOWS HOW much sway or power she can exert in a relationship. More even, she knows within inches how many amicable gestures and personal capital needs to be invested to achieve a treasured goal.

The treasured goal for P J was purely mercenary—money for her mother and her two younger brothers in Thailand. Their family had been deserted by their father, who, after impregnating his wife with the last two of five children, had found her unattractive and left them penniless.

Concentrating on the creation of a mood from which goodness and the fulfilling of all her wishes would be forthcoming, she planned every day for Dmitri with the greatest care. He, who had more than once tied her shoes—because like a child, she had never tied a shoe——was now the recipient of her selfsame service whenever they went walking. Often she knelt in front of him, her pretty head bowing before him, and pulled on his shoes. And as she straightened to rise, she would float her hands over his genitals in a gesture of promise, which kept him anticipating their siesta or an early bedtime.

She learned to prepare his favorite dishes and playfully fed him by the spoonful, kneeling before him on the veranda. At first Dmitri demurred. The servitude of her gestures set the wrong strings on his righteous instrument vibrating.

"Please, don't do this kneeling before me. I feel strange when you do it. You are my wife—my equal."

"But, my love, me want to do this. Me love you so much. Take— is a gift." Well, after she put it in such terms, he felt like a pasha, a khan, a pati—a lord. She wiped the sweat from his brow before he even knew that he was perspiring, brought him cool drinks when he worked outside—often before he was thirsty.

At bedtime she pulled off his clothes, knelt to remove his shoes, stroked his thighs and other things until he thought he would die from pleasure. Over and over he praised himself for his great good fortune and his foresight that had brought her here. The first day of her design left him breathless on his quilted mattress. What a woman! Nothing he had ever experienced before had been so satisfying to his senses.

If he had imagined himself in paradise on the first day, he thought he had gone to heaven in the days that followed. Every day brought him a delicious, delicate or even a slightly perverse sexual pleasure he had never experienced before. PJ had been trained well—that much had been promised to him by the woman who ran the Emigration for Thai Women Service. By the end of the week PJ did not even have to ask for a favor. He volunteered one all by himself.

"My dear girl, you have made me so very happy. Now what can your hubby do for you to make you happy?" he asked, sheepishly grinning like a school boy after kissing the neighbor's pretty daughter and getting caught.

"Ahh, Pappa, make me happy with money. Send to my momma. She no have. So poor! Two brodders, no money. Bad! Bad. Please, Pappa, give money to Momma."

Dmitri's self-esteem took a severe downturn that night. So, the clever minx had slathered him with attention, body rubs, sexual and culinary pleasures to win money for her family? Hell! Hell! He was really getting old to fall for such tricks.

He should have learned from Irina, the Russian witch, that nothing comes to an older man except with a price tag. Well, whatever PJ had done to entice him was well worth the price of some dollars. Although, thinking back to what he remembered of Precious Jewel's mother, those memories did not elevate him to a giving mood. Most of all, her voice echoed unpleasantly through the chambers of his mind. It was high, shrill—unlovely, as the unmelodious ring of a badly programmed cell phone.

PJ's mother was as unappealing as her daughter was beautiful. She was a thin, bony, woman with a sharp face surrounded by strands of blackish gray hair, which stood at odd angles. Her sarong, although of good material and becoming colors, seemed to have belonged to another woman altogether. But the worst thing about her was her unconcealed avarice. Her greed flew nakedly into the face of the observer.

Meeting him for the first time, she had shamelessly assessed his monetary potential. She had fingered the material of his clothes to determine the quality. She touched and stroked his briefcase, containing the papers he would need to marry her daughter. She examined his wristwatch and asked him the price, remarking, he found out in translation, that he had been robbed. He could have gotten the same watch in Bangkok for $300 less.

The Thai people, he soon noted, were a very clean people. They bathed every day, having an almost religious and symbolic relationship with flowing water. PJ's mother, although she probably followed the same cultural rituals, smelled fishy whenever he had the misfortune to come too close. Furthermore, he was appalled at how she coddled her two adult sons and demeaned her daughter.

Ah, well, he thought then, and he thought so now, *It must be unimaginably hard on a woman in a third world country to be left alone to raise five children.*

PJ, her older brother, and sister were in their early teens when their father left. They did not suffer too much from the following deprivation, but the two younger boys were not so lucky. They were deprived of many things the older ones had taken for granted. At this point of his deliberations, PJ's voice broke into his conscience sweetly and plaintively like an injured bird, "Please, Papa, send Momma money."

"OK! How much do you want?" The young woman had thought for days about the right amount to ask for, and so she answered without a moment's hesitation, "Send three thousand. Be good for five moon times."

"You mean three thousand dollars, not baht, eh?" he asked just to be difficult.

"Yes, no baht."

"Three thousand, my girl, translates into thousands of satangs. Are you sure she needs such an exorbitant sum in Thailand?"

"Yes, boys need school, clothes, doctor—ver, ver spensive."

Dmitri knew, of course, from the beginning of the request for money that Precious Jewel would get her way. Well, after all, it was only money and what the girl did for him was special. He folded his cards—and gave in.

Henceforth, every five months, a money order went to Thailand into the hands of a Mrs. Ragoongong. And, therefore, every five months, during a very special week, Dmitri became served as if he were the caliph Harun al-Rashid, famous subject of many a Thousand and One Night stories.

The Fishing Trip

❧❦

"HALLO, OLD BUDDY, ARE you up and about?" shouted a voice on the phone, nearly bursting Dmitri's eardrum. "Damn you, Brent! You woke us with the damn phone and should have known better, me having a new bride and all. Why would we be up at this awful hour?"

Brent's laugh was loud and delighted.

"That is exactly the reason why I am calling. You have kept the new bride all

to yourself and it's time that you bring her out of hiding. Jan and I have loaded up the boat with a few goodies and want the two of you to go fishing with us. Martha is coming, too. So get yourself dressed. We will be by in ten minutes to pick you up."

"Jeez, Brent, I have not even had a cup of coffee yet. This will take a little longer."

"No way! Ten minutes. We have a huge container of coffee made and we all will have breakfast together once we have left the channel."

Dmitri knew it was useless to protest, useless to swim against the stream. Once Brent's mind was made up it was wiser to just go along with the program. Also, it would be charming to show off sweet, delectable PJ. All of his friends had been having way too much fun, painting him to be an old, demented fool. Well, now he would like to see Brent's jealous face and gloat a little. This thought stimulated him to jump into action. He pulled a half-comatose PJ from under the covers.

"Up my girl! Up! Up! We are going fishing today."

Precious Jewel understood none of his words, save one command, "Put your clothes on!" Sleepily, she brushed her teeth, washed her face and pulled on her outfit from the previous day. Why not? It had pleased him then, why not also today. And she was correct in her assumption. Dmitri deemed the outfit perfect. And why would shorts and a top not be perfect for fishing. He did, however, object to the flip-flops, which she had come to believe to be a premier item for daily life in the Keys. Contrary to her expectations, he made her wear a pair of deck shoes, which he had purchased in anticipation of boating trips.

As she rushed to the kitchen, there were to her immense surprise no fires lit on the magical stove. Instead, Dmitri busied himself tossing ice into a large blue and white cooler, upon which he deposited cans of soft drinks, a bottle of vodka, a flock of lemons, sandwiches and assorted pieces of fruit. Once again PJ watched this strange ceremony with amazement. It was definitely a cultural ritual indicative of an advanced civilization. What was her man doing there, trapped between pantry and counter at this early hour? It must be important—of immeasurable consequences should it be halted—or why would he do this work at such an early hour? Was he not a rich, important man, who should not concern himself with the filling of a cooler—such an inconsequential undertaking?

Dmitri finished his task by the time she had drawn this important conclusion. He motioned her to take the handle of the heavy cooler on one side, while he grasped the other. With great urgency they made their way down to the dock. Dew moistened the white coral rock crunching under their rushing feet. Down by the canal Dmitri plopped the cooler onto the concrete, signaling her that she could let go of her end. At a half-gallop he ran to his fishing shack where he grabbed four of his favorite rods, rods for any kind of fishing he might encounter. A handful of led weights, a few hooks and two spools of different strength fishing line completed his errant. He ran to the cooler, dropped his loot, and leaned the rods against PJ, who had the good grace to grasp them firmly. One more run to the fishing shack enriched the pile on the dock by a bucket filled with ice and bait.

Setting down the bucket, he drew a deep breath and scanned the canal.

"He is right on time. I knew it. There he comes."

His finger pointed at a large boat that slowly, regally made its way to their dock. Now PJ got excited. Oh, they were going out on the ocean, the large expanse of water she had first seen when the plane circled over Miami before landing. Later, of course, she had seen the ocean when they drove from Miami to the Keys.

The beautiful boat, shining white, teakwood trimmed, made fast at Martha's house. The sprightly woman appeared instantly from the depth of the lower level apartment. Martha, too, was loaded down with a cooler in one hand and two folding chairs in another.

"I did not bring a rod!" she yodeled, loud enough that anyone within two hundred yards could hear her. "I assume you brought an extra rod for me, Brent!"

"You assumed right," he retorted with the same vocal volume as his interrogator. Martha, after handing the cooler and the deckchairs to Jan who had come to help her, hopped on board. She hugged Jan, helped her stow the gear, and plopped into a deckchair.

"People, people, must you conduct your business with such ear-splitting noise? Remember there are people still sleeping at this time!"

Dmitri fired off this remark with very little volume restraint himself.

"Oh let's just wake up all the old, retired farts who have nothing to do all day but sleep and drink," yelled Brent merrily.

Promptly, one of the old farts from across the canal fired with precise aim a spoiled grapefruit at his boat, hitting the side where it exploded. It left a large circle of mush, which slowly flowed in runlets down the side of Brent's pride and joy.

"Damn you, Paul. Not only are you awake already, but capable of precision. Now, see what you have done? I have to wash off the mess!"

"Serves you right!" Jan entered the shouting match.

"If you had not been obnoxiously noisy and more restrained, Paul would not have felt challenged." She yawned and shook her head tiredly.

"I think I could have made do with another few hours of sleep myself."

Dmitri was suddenly anxious to get out of the canal and out on the ocean. He scampered down to the dock, dragging a hose behind him. "Here, get the mush off the side and let's be off!"

He helped PJ onto Brent's boat, the Jeanette. "Good morning ladies, here is Precious Jewel ready for her first fishing trip."

"Moning, moning," piped PJ in her high little-girl voice.

"Good morning! Good morning," echoed the ladies.

"Brent, let me introduce you to Dmitri's new wife, Precious Jewel!"

Jan made the introduction with a sweet smile and a sincere effort to make PJ comfortable. She pointed at her husband and said, "Brent, my husband." Then she pointed at her own chest and was pleased when the young woman nodded with understanding. Brent shook PJ's hand a little too vigorously and too long for Jan's taste. Noting this, she shot him a wifely poison-look that conveyed with force, *You are inappropriate.*

Chastened, he turned away and began importing Dmitri's stuff from the dock. The latter reached the items across the railing and Brent stored everything so nothing would roll or slide during a little wave action.

Meanwhile, after releasing the lines from the two bollards they had been attached to, Dmitri stepped aboard. He folded himself into a deck chair beside Martha. Jan and PJ were deeply preoccupied trying to have a conversation. Brent, standing behind the wheel, gave the engines a nudge and edged the boat gracefully away from the dock into the middle of the channel. He performed a perfect turn, kicked up the speed a notch and floated down the canal toward the main channel.

The three women formed a coven at the rear deck, bending toward each other in the moist, cool morning. But to call them a coven would be an inaccurate description, for a coven is a group of like-minded persons. Although they sat in a threesome like three clucking hens, psychologically they were divided two against one. And how could it have been otherwise? Two older, wiser, culturally much more educated women were arrayed against a Southeast Asian village girl.

Oh, the American women were kind and willing to embrace any female. They were willing to help a sister along on her way into the culture. But they were not able to quite subdue all of their feelings of jealousy. Who would want to be cast aside by someone forty years younger? By someone who had the advantage not only of youth, but the adoration of an old rich fool willing to array and present the "Jewel" to its best advantage.

"Martha, I feel I was born at the wrong time. I should be twenty now, starting my life over in this golden age that I fear will not last much longer. I believe that right now our country is in its richest, most opulent period. This little twit does not realize how lucky she is to haven fallen into a nest of prosperity."

"Martha," laughed softly.

"Jan, darling, you have no idea how correct you are with your assessment. PJ not only enters the country during halcyon days, but also as the recipient of a dead woman's, home and money. A woman who worked hard all her life and now that she is dead, she benefits the little cuckoo with the fortune she left behind."

"Oh, Martha! Envisioning the picture of a hardworking Theresa who never fully got to enjoy the money she made, handing piles of the loot to this girl who never raised a finger for it, makes me sick."

"Well, no matter how disgusting it is—that is reality."

To make matters worse, PJ looked wonderful in her little blue shorts and the tight top. As they made their way through the channel into the ocean, the sun was rising among silvery and pink clouds far away on the horizon. The water was calm. One could hardly detect the swells. The tide had been going out for hours, leaving behind muddy sand flats, which looked pearly pink in the light of the rising sun. Seabirds were hunting for their morning's sustenance, flying hither and yon, detecting prey upon the mudflats and in the water.

Talking, laughing and drinking hot, strong coffee, the small group was carried under full steam into the open, seemingly endless Atlantic. Quite a while ago, PJ had stopped following their conversation. That could not be helped, although Martha and Jan tried to be inclusive. Bored, the young Thai woman went to the railing and stared into the turbulent water. Born and raised in a village, she had never been on a boat larger than a canoe—never been out on the ocean. She was thrilled by a mixture of adventure and a little bit of fear. Fortunately she could swim because her village was bisected by a river, and all village children bathed and swam in its warm water.

The men ran the boat full speed to preordained coordinates, where around a rock patch in about twenty feet of water they had on previous trips found a variety of fish. They remembered good fishing here for mangrove snappers. Having found the promising rock pile, Dmitri threw out the anchor, after they ascertained the drift and direction of current and waves.

Dmitri prepared the rods they would need while Brent pulled a bait table upright, which had been hanging attached to the side of the boat. He chose a very sharp, long and vicious looking knife from a sheath beside the bait table. From an ice-filled bucket he produced small silvery fish, which he promptly handed to Dmitri.

"Get the women fishing, while I prepare some substantial bait for our rods just in case there are some big ones around."

Moments later everyone had a line in the water, except for Dmitri, whose baited rod was in a holder while he tried to teach PJ the simplest forms of fishing. The girl promptly fouled her line by getting it wrapped around in the propeller. While he tried to untangle the line he set her up with his own rod, figuring the chances of her getting a hit were nil.

Meanwhile Martha, Jan and Brent alternately cried jubilantly, "Fish on!" time and again.

"Get busy, Dmitri," shouted the latter. "They are biting like crazy and they are big. None of the small fry here!"

Dmitri murmured a hot oath under his breath, because PJ's line was badly tangled. He belonged to the fishing clan that deemed it a sin to discard nylon filament into the ocean where sea life could get ensnared. Because of that, cutting and losing pieces of line was not an option, and he struggled valiantly to untangle the line. Not far from him, staring patiently into the water and catching nothing, stood PJ. She understood perfectly from her lesson that one must hang onto the rod for dear life should a fish bite and exert force in the struggle to save his life.

Every so often she turned her head in the direction of her lucky boat mates, who laughingly reeled in their catch and imported it by scooping it up with a handled net. PJ was not in the least disturbed by the cutting and bleeding of the fish. In the village she had slaughtered plenty of chickens. The niceties of dinners prepared without direct involvement in the food production were foreign to her.

Suddenly, as she dreamily turned to the water again, she felt an enormous jerk on her rod. With both hands she pulled mightily to counterbalance the force on her line. She felt ill equipped to hang on to the monster fish she had on the line.

"Dmitri, Dmitri, help, help! This big, very big!"

Whatever she was doing with her rod annoyed her foe in the water. It answered her efforts with a phenomenally strong jerk. Unprepared, and bending far too far over the railing, the grand force pulled PJ, rod and all, overboard. The splash alerted Brent.

"Man overboard!" he shouted. Meanwhile PJ, holding on to the rod, was hurtling through the water, pulled by the fish, like a fallen water skier.

"Oh, my God, PJ! Let go of the rod! Let go of the rod!" screamed Dmitri, as if the hapless woman could hear him. He was about to throw himself into the water after the quickly disappearing figure of his wife.

"Don't!" yelled Jan, hanging onto him with all her might.

"We will get to her faster with you on board to help. Martha, an old hand at emergencies, had begun to bring all the lines aboard and placed the rods into their holders, while Brent, who had thrown a lifesaver after PJ, was pulling up the anchor. Dmitri stormed to the wheel. He had a very good idea about the direction of the current and figured the fish—big, old and smart—would run for rock, among which to cut the line. Or he would race in to the shallows where the boat could not follow. He engaged the left, the larboard engine and prepared for a quick turn. The moment Brent had the anchor on board, Dmitri powered the engine and turned the boat.

Brent let him have the wheel. He knew that his friend was frantic by now and needed to be in control. Jan, who had the best eyes of all people on the boat, had climbed into the spotting tower, from where she shouted commands for Dmitri to execute. It took her a few moments. But then she spotted the floating lifesaver, which Brent had thrown after the disappearing girl. A moment later she spotted PJ's white T-shirt bobbing up and down in the waves. It seemed as if the girl had finally released her grip on the rod and was now drifting aimlessly in the waves.

It amazed Dmitri once again how quickly a body could be separated from a ship. Even more, how quickly the current could carry an object without the power to resist its pull. Although they had spotted his wife, it required a goodly amount of time to finally catch up to her. What luck that she could swim and keep herself afloat. He had barely uttered the thought to Brent who had joined him at the wheel, when Jan screamed.

"Shark! There is a shark circling PJ." Dmitri panicked and was about to make a dumb mistake. Brent saved him by grabbing the controls.

"Get a marlin spike!" he hollered. "You can pull her in or stab the fish!" Before Dmitri could get to the vicious-looking object, Martha thrust it into his hands.

"We are close to her!" she screamed. "Get her in! This looks like a bull shark in an ugly mood."

From her tower Jan calmly instructed her husband how to approach PJ, who by now was aware of her predicament as attested by her frightened eyes. She swam with all her strength toward the approaching boat. She reached its side seconds before the shark attacked. The fish approached like a torpedo, as PJ floundered in the water below the boat. At this juncture, praise must be bestowed upon good material, for Dmitri, without other options, pushed the gaff into his wife's waistband and pulled.

"Great gods and K-Mart" he jubilated, because the material held. He and Martha managed to pull hapless PJ just high enough out of the water, so that, when the attack came, the shark's large, round head banged against the side of the boat. Not dazed in the least, the beast swam away, circling for another attempt.

Brent, hearing the excited screams, put the engines on idle and joined Dmitri and Martha, pulling PJ fully on board. Dmitri's wife looked a little like a fish out of water sprawled out on deck. Her hair and her clothes were a sopping mess; she had lost both deck shoes to the force of her ride through the waves, and she was spitting salt water. Dmitri knelt beside her. He hugged her to his chest and murmured into her ear. Besides endearments, praises of her courage and strength and perfect behavior, he told her that he loved her.

Around him, the others jabbered amazed, grateful and stunned. The girl on the deck could not care less. At last, she got up and was instantly surrounded by the women. They took her below into the elegant sleeping quarters of the Jeanette. They pantomimed that she should disrobe. Without false modesty PJ stripped off her clothes, dropping them on the floor. Martha picked them up, rinsed them in fresh water, and left for the deck to dry them in the sun.

Jan turned on the shower for PJ. A little later the young woman emerged on deck, turbaned and wearing an oversized, white bathrobe. Sitting in a deck chair, she watched the others who were already fishing again. She realized that she had been a very lucky woman, indeed. But she also knew with deep satisfaction that the people around her were smart, very competent, caring, and could be relied on in times of trouble. She shivered a little, feeling very grateful.

Jan watched her line and kept an eye out for the shark. She remarked thoughtfully, "I think it is possible that the shark out there could be the fish that pulled PJ overboard. This is, perhaps, why he then turned on her since she was the enemy."

"It's a possibility," agreed Brent. "From what I have seen, the fish is about six to eight feet long. Logic dictates that an animal that size would not attack a human unprovoked. But this fish, if it's the one PJ hooked, had reason to be mad."

Reason or not, Dmitri did not care. He was insanely enraged that his little wife had been threatened. She could have lost flesh and bone to the teeth of this shark. He was now doing his best to engage his perceived enemy. He had added a chain to his heaviest rod, to which he attached several fearsome-looking hooks baited with a large, juicy jack and began fishing. Half an hour went by. So far the shark had refused to even look at his bait.

The fish was still around, as his dorsal fin, poking through the waves every so often, attested to. The rest of the party had no luck catching anything with a shark hanging about, and wanted to leave. Yet Dmitri, with a maniacal obsession, wanted to hook the shark.

Shaking their heads, Dmitri's friends reclined in deck chairs. PJ, drabbed down by her swim in the ocean, looked much less the part of a model and more like an everyday housewife. For the moment she was fully accepted by the party. Jan broke out her large cooler of goodies and so did Martha. Out came the lovely sandwiches, the fruit, the beer and the pitcher of margaritas.

PJ was amazed by how hungry she suddenly was. She devoured two juicy roast beef sandwiches, filled up on crispy potato chips and, not knowing what she was drinking, had a Margarita. Fortified by sandwiches and drinks, the party became merry, which did nothing to keep Dmitri from pursuing, or better put, luring the great fish.

Meanwhile, PJ had another margarita and acted very cheerful. Twice she called Dmitri.

"Dmitri, come. Have good time. Come me."

For a village woman who never got a taste of alcohol, because the men never shared their liquor with women, two drinks were an exceedingly large amount of alcohol. It was not too long, when, from one moment to the next, PJ's body seemed to lose its starch and she slumped over passed out in her chair.

Martha and Jan kindly trundled her between them downstairs into the bedroom.

"The poor dear had too much excitement," Martha stated equivocally.

"She must rest a bit." Jan agreed. They put her to bed and covered her with a quilt, whereupon they returned to the deck. Dmitri was still dangling his bait for the shark.

"Oh stop it, Demi," called Jan, using his hated pet name.

"Why should I?" he answered querulously. "I almost had him twice. I am sure he will bite during the next attempt." Brent understood his motivation and zeal. He joined the exchange.

"He will get him next time. What a kick if he succeeds!"

"He might succeed," grumbled Jan. "But in the meantime Martha and I will catch nothing."

She planted herself in a deck chair and retrieved the margarita jug from the cooler. "Might as well join me, Martha," she coaxed. "This fishing trip is over as far as that goes."

"Don't be cross," placated Martha, "we already caught a Lord's plenty of mangrove snappers." With that, she settled herself beside Jan, sipping a drink. As they watched Dmitri's fruitless efforts, they talked about the sleeping young woman below.

"She has grit," said Jan with admiration. "Besides looking like a sweet, little doll, she has other qualities. Watch out Dmitri. This one is no roll-over."

"I agree. She does seem to have a strong character. Will it be enough for her to make a go of this marriage—I don't know."

"Sure she will. Any woman determined enough to hang on to a rod pulled by a shark can do anything." Jan's giggle hinted strongly at an infusion of Jose` Cuervo.

By now it was late afternoon. Large, white clouds moved in from the east and began to cover the better part of the horizon. PJ had never moved from the bed below. Everyone on deck, with the exception of Dmitri, was ready to call it a day and go home. Brent had just uttered this desire to go home, when Dmitri let out a howl that echoed across the water.

"I've got the bastard! Fish on!"

This rebel yell was the beginning of the battle. Apparently, the chain, heavy line, and hooks with which Dmitri had outfitted the rod, had the power to hold the shark. The animal knew that it was fighting for its life. It used force and cunning to free itself. Struggling mightily one moment, having the fish close by, running the line out hundreds of feet the next, he forced Dmitri to be strapped into a fighting chair. The shark was tired out, however, from his earlier go-round with PJ and in need of rest. At times he would allow himself to be reeled in, and come closer to the boat.

A few times Brent helped the fighting Dmitri by running the boat in the opposite direction, forcing the shark to follow the pull of a superior power. Back and forth went the battle between man and beast. Meanwhile, the clouds had thickened, promising a downpour. Daylight was diminishing and still no end of the fight was in sight. No matter how often Dmitri reeled in the shark, close enough to the boat that his dorsal fin, broad head and tail could be seen, the fish always mustered enough energy to break away again. With seemingly undiminished strength, he would repeatedly take many feet of line off the reel.

By now the women were tired of the sport and pleaded with the men to cut the line and go home. Martha, who had been on the ocean with her husband in all kinds of weather, watched the cloud banks with unease. One never knew what these cloud formations boded. They could contain monstrous thunderstorms, breaking over the sea in minutes under the right conditions. In the past she experienced enough bad weather at sea that she fervently wished to be safely in her house if a storm should break.

The very moment Dmitri told Brent that it would be stupid to fight the fish in the dark when landing him would be dangerous, the very moment when he reached for his knife to cut the strong line, the shark gave up the fight and allowed himself to be pulled to the side of the boat. Dmitri held him tight, while Brent thrust a gaff into his gills. Without mechanical help the men could never have boarded the shark. Another hook, attached to a stout steel cable and a pulley, was employed to hoist the fish. As the huge body was pulled from the water, it became clear that he needed to be dispatched instantly. He was about ten feet long and still had the power to kill or injure. Brent went below for his gun. As the head of the fish became visible above the railing he fired a few bullets into its head and upper body.

The shark convulsed. Its body almost formed a crescent, and then it relaxed. Hoisted as far upward as the equipment allowed, the shark's tail was still hanging outside the railing. There was no way to bring the massive carcass into the boat. "We will just have to let him hang and sail home," said Dmitri wistfully. So the men tied the body in several places to the boat to keep it from swinging.

By now it was almost dark. A cold wind was blowing from the east, roiling the water. Jan and Martha donned warm jackets and wrapped a blanket around their bare legs as they huddled together. Now that the boat had turned homeward, there was no more forecastle to hide behind. Their only other choice was to go below and join the sleeping PJ, but that was not an option. Neither woman would have dreamed of going below. They went fishing one way and would return the same way they had left.

The wind forcefully pushed the boat as it picked up full speed, much as it pushed the waves westward. The chains holding the shark rattled and groaned when grinding together and the boat sighed and moaned, heaving through the troughs and heights of the seas. The men stood side by side in the wheelhouse, speaking softly as they steered the boat and checked coordinates and the depth below the keel. A tap on Dmitri's shoulder violently startled him.

Behind him stood Jan. "Troubles, Demi," she yelled. "The shark busted most of the chains and is swinging almost free. The tail is destroying the boat." The men stopped the engines and handed Jan the wheel, telling her the coordinates to steer by. They ran to the hoist where, indeed, the shark swung about, destroying whatever it collided with. Its engines idling, the boat rolled in the waves like a tipsy sailor. Precious minutes passed before the fish was secured once more. Before the last rope was tied, the clouds in the black sky burst and water fell in broad, wind-driven sheets.

Soaked to the skin in an instant, the men swore a blue streak. They scuttled across the slick deck to find their rain gear. Martha had long ago relented. Preferring to stay dry, she had gone below. Curled safe and warm in the large bed, PJ had slept through all travail and noise. Even Martha's arrival did not awaken her. Wrapped in a blanket, Martha sat in a comfortable leather chair, which was anchored to the floor and the cabin wall. Soon, Jan joined her, flopping into the mate of Martha's chair.

"How far from shore are we?" Martha asked concerned. Her husband had been a daredevil, who had gotten both of them in plenty of trouble on the ocean.

"I think we are still a mile out. The guys barely got the carcass tied up again when all hell broke loose up there. Rain began to bucket down and the wind doubled in strength."

"I know. That's when I fled and came down here."

"Did PJ ever wake up through all the commotion?"

"Not for a minute. I am beginning to wonder if the little bit of alcohol could have harmed her—unused as she is to the stuff." Jan laughed.

"Oh, stuff and nonsense. Don't you remember how your first drink affected you? One gets a little silly and then sleeps it off."

"I hope you are right. I do not want Dmitri on our case—corrupting his wife and all."

The women's chat came to an abrupt halt. The boat, pitching into the deep trough of a monster wave, groaned and its engines howled as they churned air. It seemed that tons of water sluiced over the hapless ship. The women were violently tossed onto the floor from their comfortable seats, and looked frightened. They clutched the chairs, as they tried to pull themselves off the floor. The Jeanette bravely fought itself free, righted itself and plowed through the seas as the true champion she was.

Trying to make light of their situation, Jan said, "Oh, boy, the darn shark put a curse on us and here we are."

The women laughed a brave but false little laugh, because they felt very uncomfortable.

"I am going to see what is going on above," said Jan determined. As she made her way to the door she stepped into soaked carpeting. Although the door had special seals, designed to prevent the cabin from filling with water and sinking the boat, some water had found its way in. Shutting the door behind her, Jan stepped into the small stairway, tightly holding on to both handrails.

Before opening the upper door, she waited until the boat was rising on a wave to be sure that the water drained away over the stern. At first glance, craning her neck, things did not look too bad on deck. Everything had been properly stored before the worst of the storm hit. The wheelhouse had been washed by the monster wave and everything gleamed fresh in the greenish light emanating from the instrument panel. Her worry for her husband was allayed the moment she saw him standing behind the wheel. He seemed un-harmed, undaunted, never removing his eyes from the panel in front of him.

Dmitri, standing squarely by his side, also seemed none-the-worse for the tussle with the monster wave. She pulled herself up the steep stairs, holding on to the wet railing and alit beside Dmitri. *Who can know men's hearts?* she thought as she looked into the men's faces. There they both were, square and sure. By God, it looked as if they had enjoyed the trouble—their brush with danger. Their faces shone with the pleasure known to small boys, when falling unharmed out of trees. Brent was beaming and brimmed with contentment. While Dmitri looked much like he looked on the day he had brought PJ home, filled with satisfaction.

"Looks like you two did not go overboard!" she shouted to be heard over the din created by the engines, the wind and the sea.

"I was coming up in case we had to start a search for you."

"You know your old man better than that, Girl," teased Brent affectionately.

"Yes, I do! I always remember the saying your mother had for you: 'weeds never die!'" She turned to Dmitri, "You, too, seem to be doing very well."

"Sure do! When Brent refused to get washed overboard, I decided to stick also. By the way, how is PJ? I have not seen her in an awfully long time."

"She is fine. She has been sleeping through the whole tempest. What happened to your fish? Is it still with us?"

"Last time I checked he was still hanging there, properly trussed up."

Jan did not bother to turn her head to ascertain the truth of the statement. She had other concerns.

"How close are we to home?" she wondered.

"Quarter mile," answered Brent. As if to lend substance to his words, Jan made out the blinking lights of the channel bridge. Not long thereafter the Jeanette was tied up safely at her mooring.

Admiration for the Hero

৵৹

NEXT MORNING THE HUGE shark still hung from the hoist. Its silver-gray skin looked mottled and sickishly dry in the revealing morning sun. Its poor hooked lower jaw, pulled up by the hoist, stretched open the huge mouth as if gulping air, while the triangular dorsal fin, a warning sign of approaching danger in the water, still stood erect. Everyone in the neighborhood stopped their boat in the canal or came by to visit—and everyone heard the amazing story as it unfolded last night.

PJ, after a refreshing night and morning bath, came to admire the fish with the rest of the neighbors. She quickly grasped that the dangling apparition was the ferocious monster that had pulled her overboard; the monster, which she had clung to for too long. As the men told stories, the shark with the help of many neighbor hands, was released from the chains and the pulley and laid on the dock.

They measured its length and forced its mouth open, displaying the rows of large, sharp teeth. The dentition of the monster and its length, eight feet five inches, sent retroactive shivers through PJ. She suddenly realized that she surely would have died of fright if she had known what was swimming in the water with her. She never had a doubt that she had hooked a great beast, but it had not occurred to her that it could be a shark of such proportions.

Furthermore, it dawned on her that Dmitri had relentlessly hunted the beast—the cause of his little wife's distress. Here and there she heard a word amid the crowd that she understood. Slowly she pieced the story of Dmitri's heroic pursuit of the monster together.

Her heart swelled with pride. This enormous fish had to die because it had attacked her.

Instantly Dmitri became a true hero in her mind—her savior, her defender. Oh, the women in her village had been right. He was a great man, a rich wonderful American man.

PJ Model Student

෨ஂ෨

HENCEFORTH, PJ BECAME A model student for her husband the teacher. He wanted her to clean fish? Well, she tried her best to learn. He wanted her to learn English? Well, she learned every day ten new words. When that proved not to be enough, he enrolled her in a language course for foreigners in an extension class in Homestead. This class—a remedial course for the illegal Haitians and Mexicans flooding Florida, seemed at first, the perfect venue for her to learn. Beauteous little PJ was instantly accepted and well liked by the rough farm workers and their womenfolk employed as maids and laundresses in Miami's countless hotels.

Dmitri drove her every evening to school. After two hours of instruction he picked her up at nine thirty at night. PJ was a good student and applied herself in class. Her efforts were supplemented every day by the extra lessons administered by her zealous husband. In a few short weeks her progress exceeded all expectations.

At this juncture trouble began. Among the group of Haitians, they were always more reserved and clannish than the Mexicans, a fellow named Antoine held court like an Island King. Antoine was a tall, bronze-skinned fellow, with a clean, intelligent face. He had black, short curly hair and a powerful physique. In class he spoke in a whimsical patois constructed from French and English words and phrases. With his quirky ability to express himself comically, he endeared himself to the young, female English teacher. She often laughed delightedly when he produced an especially exquisite lingual construction.

People deferred to him, the young women adored him. The brazen among them invited him in French to get better acquainted by lauding their own best physical features and the sexual delights awaiting him—if he would only choose them. Although the girls and women spoke in French, the drift of their address was clearly conveyed to all by their salacious looks and gestures. Antoine held them at bay with wit and charm and the women were never offended by his refusal to be drawn into encounters.

At the very first day of PJ's arrival, however, Antoine was smitten. Savoring her looks across the aisles of the drab classroom, he grew very quiet. It followed, of course, that the day came when he managed to corner her alone in the corridor as she hastened to her lessons. For once, looking serious and stark, he confided to her that his heart became heavy with love each time he saw her and that he wished to know if she, too, could love him. Although the speech was produced in his finest multilingual concoction, the girl understood.

Taken aback by his passionate abrupt confession, PJ was speechless for a moment. He had caught her in a cage built by his body, his arms and the wall behind her. The closeness of his powerful male body made her feel faint. Uncomfortable, flustered and yet strangely excited by the physical closeness of a young, virile body, she managed to stammer, "I am married woman, Antoine. The man who comes for me at night is my husband."

Antoine understood that much English.

"Mon Dieu! On old mon! He be vous Papa."

"No, papa! Husband!" She pushed her finger with the enormous diamond engagement ring and the even larger gold band in his face. Antoine's face fell. Dismay was written over his usually open features. He groaned as if in pain. Pity grew softly in PJ's heart. Who knows what might have happened if the poignant moment had not been sharply interrupted by their teacher's voice.

"Antoine! Release Precious Jewel this minute! Both of you come to class."

Ms. Sandhurst's voice showed concern besides strength of enforcement. She had to deal quite often with situations requiring force. Her Mexican, Haitian, and sometimes Cuban subjects had strong feelings and often acted upon them, leaving her to deal with social, relational and cultural problems. She had discerned at once why Antoine had cornered the young woman. Furthermore, she knew Dmitri, who had introduced himself when he delivered PJ for her first lesson. Dear Lord, what a scenario! There was the old, enamored, foolish husband with a pretty, young wife, and a passionate, young, bursting-with-life lover. She decided to have a talk with Antoine after class and put a stop to the whole unwholesome affair, before this love thing could grow and flower.

Everyone in class seemed to know what had transpired in the hallway. PJ, who entered the classroom with its flickering neon lights first, drew scornful, ugly looks from the girls. They coped well with Antoine's refusals of their favors, as long as no one else received his attention. But the state of affairs had changed the moment he singled PJ out. The carefully maintained balance was thrown out of kilter.

The young, and even the older men, exhibited the sharp interest of hunters on their visages. They identified with Antoine and were keenly interested how far he had gone with the girl.

PJ, although dazed and distracted, noticed the looks on all the faces. In her village, too, even though the culture was different, entanglements were accompanied by the very same looks.

Antoine noticed nothing. Oblivious to the stares, he crashed into his seat. He was drowning in his emotional, androgen-fired misery. Why could she not say the words he so longed to hear? Why did she hesitate until the teacher's voice parted them? So the old man was her husband? Sacre` bleu! Such an old devil—he had believed him to be her father. The old Mon treated her like a child. Not only did he drive her to and from school, but once, when she skipped across the parking lot and tripped over her untied laces, the old man rushed to her and picked her off the ground. Dusting her off, and looking like a buffoon, he tied her laces.

"La princesse!" the women had scoffed, indicating that P J was incapable or unwilling to take care of herself.

Henceforth, the congenial environment of the classroom was no more. Envy had entered, twisting the young women's heads. Now they watched the Thai girl's every move. If she gave a good answer they sneered—sure, sure, she does not work all day like we do. No, she sits at home and preens. When she has done her hair and fooled with her clothes, then she sits and learns the words to please the teacher.

Bitterness crept into their thoughts. Once they knew that PJ got access to a green card by marrying an old man, they despised her. They, conversely, had taken their lives into their own hands. They crossed the ocean in rickety, unseaworthy contraptions which no one would call boats in America. Once arrived, they worked from morning till night, while this one—this princesse—just acted like the whores in the harbor quarter of Port-au-Prince.

While the young women developed venom, the older, married women were sympathetic. They knew what it meant to be a poor, insecure woman with children. In their hearts they could not find blame for a sister who had the good fortune to be pretty and cool headed at the same time. In retrospect, a few of them wished they had chosen their man with their head and not their burning hearts and their loins on fire. Yes, if they could do it over again they would have made wiser decisions and, therefore, they held their tongues and watched. Sometimes watching a reality drama unfold was better than television.

The men, all of them—young and old—made bets: ten to one that Antoine would bed her within the month; fifty to one that the old man would shoot him within two months. No one believed that perhaps nothing would happen. No, that would be impossible, for the air was charged with the special sulfur created by intriguing affairs.

Ms. Sandhurst felt the sizzle every time PJ or Antoine was called upon to give an answer or read from the text. As the days dragged on, PJ accelerated her studies and soon was far ahead of the rest of the class. This only became another reason for envy and derision, a fact keenly noted by Ms. Sandhurst. At this point she decided to have a talk with PJ's husband. She called Dmitri early one morning and explained to him that PJ had become the object of open envy. She suggested that, because the young woman was so far ahead of the rest of the class, a transfer to a more advanced class should take place immediately. Dmitri, pleased with such astounding progress by his paragon of a wife, agreed to the change.

And so it happened that the next Friday evening Antoine sat down in class and looked forlornly at the chair, which formerly supported the pleasing bottom of his beloved.

She will be back! he told himself. *I hope she is not sick. Monday, Monday, surely she will sit here with me again.*

However, Monday, Wednesday, and Friday next came and went and no PJ graced the naked classroom with her presence.

Antoine had already lost all hope of ever seeing the adored face of his beloved again, when Manuel Garcia, a Mexican who had made his way to Florida from the state of Guanajuato, apprised him of the fact that he had seen PJ enter the classroom three doors removed from their own. Manuel, born into an enormously large family of Garcias, living outside the city of Salamanca on a small finca, which could not support the tribe, had learned in the war of survival to note even the slightest changes in his environs.

If a fly moved from its spot in a room—he would see it; if a vulture changed his course in the sky, Manuel would know instantly where the carrion could be found. So it was only natural that Manuel requested a small appreciation for his information. Antoine was generous. This newfound knowledge was like balm upon his soul. At last he knew his adored had not vanished—no, she was within reach.

"Oh, Manuel, Amie, here take this," he proffered ten dollars, which disappeared with sleight of hand in Manuel's deep trouser pockets.

Antoine walked once more with the spring of hope in his step and his good humor flooded Ms. Sandhurst's class once more.

Acculturation

఼ఞ

MEANWHILE, THE PROCESS OF turning a Thai woman into an American was in full swing. PJ had acquired many more plain outfits than the fashionable lot already hanging in her closet. The latter she got to wear very seldom anyway.

For her driving lessons, given by Dmitri, she wore the standard shorts and T-shirt, which she found each day increasingly more comfortable. Dmitri would drive her during her free evenings to the local high school parking lot. With plenty of space around the car, he felt safe to teach her the basics. Alas, the missing language gaps proved to be a problem. Already on her second lesson, when Dmitri told her to turn sharply to the right, she did a quick left turn and smashed his Denali into the only light post within thirty yards. Dmitri cursed. PJ cried. They drove home in silence—sad on her part, disgusted on his.

Tuesday thereafter, they drove to Homestead, where they left the Denali at Blake's Chevrolet to be repaired. While they stood in the showroom of the dealership, it dawned on Dmitri: what he really needed was an inexpensive, small car to teach her. Moreover, he could give her the car upon graduation for independence. And so, the two walked in the bright burning sun with a patient, but determined salesman, through the immense lot of the dealership. Rows upon rows of cars were offered. They came in all colors, small, large, convertible, expensive and affordable. The sheer volume made a choice difficult.

From the onset it was understood that PJ had no choice in the deal. And so she trotted bravely behind the two men never saying anything. But when the clever salesman suddenly turned to her and said, "So, little lady, which one do you like best?" Her answer came like a shot from a pistol, "That one!" She pointed at a sports model a few cars back, a canary-yellow Pontiac convertible.

"Wouldn't you know!" exclaimed Dmitri. "Brand new and expensive."

"Yes," agreed the overweight salesman, wiping rows of standing sweat beads from his forehead. He returned his not-too-clean hanky to the pocket of his sand colored trousers and remarked, "Women are all the same when it comes to dresses, shoes and cars. Give 'em a choice and they will always pick the best."

"Sure, sure," growled Dmitri. "We, however, will stick to our budget and buy a nice used car."

"Well, well! I think I have just the right thing for you. It will please both of you."

Saying this, the salesman led the couple to a back row where, surrounded by a high fence, the lot ended. The hefty salesman breathed heavily, as the extended walk took his toll on him. But he unerringly led them to a yellow Pontiac convertible, just like the one they had seen.

"Hey," objected Dmitri, "Didn't I just rule that one out? What are you trying to do to me?"

"Nothing, friend," huffed the heavy man, "I am trying to please you both. See this beauty here is a repo. Only been off the lot half a year. The young jerk who bought her could not keep up with the payments. We have to sell her cheap, because she is repo."

To make a long story short, Dmitri bought the canary because he could not avoid looking into PJ's expectant, begging eyes. Henceforth, the lessons continued in the "yellow lemon," as Dmitri called the convertible in his mind. Before PJ got her license, she scraped the right side of the canary trying to park by a concrete column. She also smashed the left rear light and got her fingers caught in the convertible's roof. Groaning and gently scolding more like an adoring father than a husband and lover, Dmitri persevered. He had the damage repaired and her hand stitched up in the emergency room.

Finally, after six months of relentless effort, Dmitri thought PJ might pass the driving test. Passing the written and oral exam was another matter. For that to occur they studied every evening for two hours, rehearsing specific driving vocabulary.

A year after PJ had arrived in the USA she was ready to take her driving test. By now the young woman could handle everyday language fairly well. She could clean fish, make spanakopita, dolmathes and pizza—Dmitri's favorite dishes besides pasta Azul and fried fish with lobster potatoes. Under Dmitri's avid tutelage she had learned how to run the washing machine and the dryer, how to clean a modern house, make a bed and wash a boat. That is not to say that Dmitri had turned her into his slave. Quite the contrary, he was helping with every chore and treated her as an equal partner.

For the driving test Dmitri made her wear blue jeans, because he thought it unseemly for her to sit in shorts beside the examiner. Such close contact in a vehicle with too much exposed skin did not bode well, especially if the tester should be a young man susceptible to her charms.

"Why would that be a bad thing?" asked PJ. "He look at my legs, he let me pass."

"PJ, oh PJ, girl! You still do not understand. In this country we like our people to pass their tests because they have the knowledge to be a safe driver. For their own safety and the safety of others we choose not to certify people because of bare legs."

PJ made a pretty moue, which announced in no uncertain terms that she still thought the alternative made great sense to her. Dmitri laughed and assured her,

"You have nothing to worry about, my girl. You have studied

hard and shall surely pass the test."

Mollified, PJ smiled and rewarded him with a hug. But despite her fondness for her elderly husband, she chose not to tell him that her bare legs and tanned arms had badly turned the head of one man in particular. And, that furthermore, this man Antoine had detected her in her new English class and begun to pursue her relentlessly.

Freedom

༺༻

OF COURSE PJ PASSED her driving test with flying colors. The moment she held her driver's license in her hands, her picture prominently displayed, she insisted that she should drive them home. How could Dmitri refuse her? She had taken the driving test in Homestead because the DMV office there was large with few waiting times. PJ had taken her test late in the afternoon. Afterwards they shopped at Costco and then had dinner in their favorite Mexican restaurant. By the time they got on the road, the sun had set and humid darkness encompassed the Everglades.

For that reason Dmitri tried to keep her from driving. But PJ insisted that she could handle a night drive. She swung the car, which she had christened "Yellow Bird," out of the parking lot onto US 1.

From there they were headed homeward through the long stretch of the Everglades where the road separates Long Sound, Little Blackwater, Black Water and Barnes Sound. In the latter, to this day, saltwater crocodiles can be found. The area is designated as Crocodile Lake National Wildlife Refuge. The road through this watery paradise of mangrove isles, salt grass marsh, and black-water ponds is long and narrow, only two lanes wide, and especially dangerous at night and during high traffic hours. More than one person driving through the watery environs reported that they had killed or injured an alligator bent on crossing from Black Water Sound into Barnes sound. But most accidents occurred because anxious drivers, annoyed by the slow poke speed of sightseers, tried to use the other lane for passing.

They began the drive with the top down, reveling in the cooling air. But soon Florida's plague, insects, began to decimate their pleasure. Dmitri told PJ to stop the car by the side of the road, where he closed the top with the help of just the slightest bit of profanity.

PJ was always capable of making Dmitri feel young. The moment she was on the road, she turned on the radio to her favorite Spanish station. This station played a mix of Cubano, Mexicano and Espana twenty-four hours a day. She drove cautiously, but not timidly, picking up speed as the road stretched open before her. Dmitri, delighted with her happiness, allowed her to go faster than the speed limit. The headlights showed an open, clear stretch before them—miles and miles of road without vehicles. The wind rustled in the leaves of mangroves and salt grass on each side, now removed from view. Dmitri had just praised PJ for her good test results, when suddenly the headlights revealed an enormous log thrown across the highway.

"Good God! An Alligator!" screamed Dmitri, reaching for the steering wheel. However, his reaction was much too late. PJ, barely knowing how to handle a car, never-mind how to react in an emergency, pulled the car far to the right without taking her foot of the gas. Despite Dmitri's violent interference, the car headed over the large, grassy roadside bank straight into one of the murky black-water ponds. Fighting for control, Dmitri managed to stop the yellow bird from being completely swallowed up by fertile, black mud, but the front wheels were hopelessly mired in the goo.

PJ had been thrown forward onto the dashboard. Looking into the black depth of the pond, she cried helplessly.

"Just look at mess I did!" she wailed, repeating this refrain to an outpour of grief. Dmitri, shuddering himself, tried to sooth her. He was grateful not to be on the bottom of the black pond, being suffocated in primordial muck.

"It is my fault, pumpkin. I knew better. I should not have allowed you to drive at night. My fault—not yours! He tested the car for stability and when he was reassured that it would not slip further into the pool upon movement, he opened his car door. He gingerly put one foot onto the grass and found firm earth beneath. He left the car and opened the trunk, retrieving a large flashlight that he had earlier deposited there together with a first aid kit.

Barely had he activated the flashlight, when a loud hissing sound behind him made him turn around with a jump. In the light of the powerful torch he saw the open maw of an enormous reptilian. The beast was in the middle of the road, coming for him fast.

Adrenalin is man's most powerful ally in emergencies. In a flash, contradicting the reality of his age, Dmitri was atop the Pontiac. There he was thanking his maker that the car was a convertible that, with its cloth top, prevented him from sliding back into the enormous tooth-rimmed mouth of the beast.

Lying flat atop the Pontiac while clinging precariously to the window rims on each side, he stared at the enormous head of what he now determined had to be a croc. It had to be a croc. He had never seen anything so venomously ugly and large as this crocodilian. The beast had elevated its head onto the trunk of the car. From there, it stared malevolently up at him. Its open snout, illuminated by his torch, displayed a fat, large tongue and rows of three-inch-long teeth. From the depth of its enormous, cavernous interior emanated a primordial stench that made Dmitri want to vomit.

"Damn, damn, damn," he muttered in despair. "What the hell am I going to do now? I need a weapon, anything to defend myself. If the beast gains more ground, he can get me."

Suddenly he noticed the stout antenna sticking proud and straight into the air. This gave him an idea. With one sharp yank he broke it off, providing himself with a fairly long stick. He realized that he would not have many chances to get at the croc. His first try had to be successful. He lay quietly on his belly atop the car, staring at the giant head below him. Yes, if he did it right his plan might work. All he wanted was to make the beast leave the car—or, at least, move away far enough that he could join PJ in the car.

He drew a deep breath, steadied his hands and then, according to plan, he shone the powerful torch into only the left eye of the croc, blinding it, wile he immediately pushed the antenna with a powerful shove into selfsame eye. The head of the reptile jerked back in agony with a powerful hiss, exposing its light-colored throat. Dmitri used that opportunity to stab the exposed throat with his antenna with all the force he could muster without falling from his perch.

The stab to the eye must have been a great deterrent—an exceedingly unpleasant sensation—for the croc slid off the trunk of the small car and ambled off. Not trusting his luck to hold for long, Dmitri, thinking that he had a safe moment, slid down the side of the car. He ripped the door open and threw himself into the car. Sensing the movement, the croc whipped his tail around and was back in a flash. Dmitri was barely able to close the door against the powerful jaws of the beast.

When he finally found his voice, he asked PJ, "Did you see the gator or croc or whatever it is? He almost got me." He aimed the flashlight out the window, shining it all over the beast.

"I can't believe what happened here," he mused wonderingly.

"I thought for sure the beast had crawled away into Barnes Sound. The car should have scared him somewhat." Mumbling, he kept observing the beast, which attacked the car and bit the fender, shaking the car and making him fear they might slide further into the pool.

"Damn, PJ, I believe this is no alligator! This must be one of the saltwater crocs. It is big enough to be one." He thought for a moment and then remarked, "But I thought they were supposed to be shy and retiring, hard to observe. Well, this one knows apparently nothing about its supposed behaviors."

Precious Jewel was silent throughout the entire scene. Her sobbing had stopped, replaced by heart-stopping terror. Her small, oval face was frozen with fear. She had seen enough of the primeval monster out there in the dark that the shelter of the car seemed inadequate. She wanted nothing more but to be in her bed—safe and sound. She understood that were the car to slide into the pond they would have to get out or drown. She prayed fervently to familiar spirits she believed were surrounding them. She asked for their intercession and prevention from going to instant afterlife—reincarnation. If eaten by the monster outside, would she come back as such a one?

Although it seemed ages had passed since the accident, Dmitri was surprised to find, as he looked at the illuminated face of his cell phone, that only a few minutes had elapsed. He called 911 and asked for a tow truck as well as armed help against the croc.

"You are joking, sir, are you?"

"No, no, I am very serious. It had me trapped atop the car and now we are not able to leave the car. There is a reptile outside, at least twelve or more feet long and very angry. Believe me, I did not take the time to ascertain whether it is a gator or a crocodile."

The tension in Dmitri's voice convinced the dispatcher of his veracity.

"I will send someone immediately. So stay put."

"Believe me, we will stay put. We have no desire to go outside."

After about half an hour that seemed as long as half the night, headlights approached their car. Dmitri had been holding PJ's hand, dispensing as much comfort as possible. She was calm, trusting his affirmations that all would be well soon.

The men in the patrol car sent to rescue the hapless couple, had a most peculiar experience. Their work left them vulnerable to the most unusual, not to say weird happenings. But tonight's rescue took the prize for their many years of dispatches. The bright lights of their cruiser revealed an enormous lizard approaching their car, jaws spread far apart. The officers in the patrol car were veterans of the Homestead force. Over the years, officers Hoskins and Borman had come across a fair share of unusual circumstances. They had delivered a baby, rescued people from a burning house, and administered CPR to victims of violence. They were involved in gang shoot-outs and had hunted poachers alongside game wardens in the Everglades. But never had a reptile attacked their cruiser.

"Holy cow! The dispatch was not joking. This does look like a croc!" exclaimed the astonished Borman. At forty-five, he had spent the last twenty of those years on the force. Blond, thin hair crowned his square, large head. Of medium build, he was muscular and fit. His sharp blue eyes appeared to be boring into the skulls of suspects, as if giving him the ability to know their thoughts. His partner, Hoskins, was two years younger, a few inches taller, dark haired and thin. He matched Borman's pragmatic outlook in the way they performed their duties. Both men were married and had children, girls and boys. Hoskins' daughter at fifteen was the oldest of both broods.

"If it's a croc we can't kill it. They are protected here," pointed out Hoskins with obvious regret.

"What now? We have to do something to get to the people over there. I am not leaving this car, because the beast will be on me before I get a good shot at it."

"Well," mused Hoskins, "since there are lives at stake, especially ours, we will bend the rules some."

With that he revved the engine and drove, slowly but straight, at the crocodilian. When the front of the car connected hard with the snout of the beast, it slid back a few feet. Hoskins angled the car slightly and hit the beast's head and upper body hard from the side. The croc raised itself up with a threatening, opened maw. But, having felt the force of the cruiser, it began to slide across the road and into the water on the other side.

The officers grabbed their guns and got out of the car. Looking carefully about, they made their way to the yellow car. They shone their flashlights into the windows and seeing two worried, but unscathed people, opened the doors and bade them come out.

"Let's talk in our patrol car. It's safer there," Borman told the relieved couple. Dmitri and PJ were overjoyed to be released from the precariously perched yellow car.

"Let me get a blanket for your daughter, sir," offered Hoskins. "She seems to be chilled from the dank night air."

He was thinking of his own girl and how she would feel under the circumstances.

"No, officer! Me not daughter. Me is wife," PJ piped up, looking even younger than usual in the defused light of the car's interior. The officers looked at each other with a knowing look that spoke volumes. Of course, Dmitri noticed. He was very uncomfortable to be judged in this manner. To defuse the awkward moment, he thanked the officers profusely, looking more than ever the apologetic father. Hoskins handed PJ the blanket; who, whispering her thanks, wrapped herself into a cocoon.

"The tow-truck should be here soon," said Officer Borman, handing bottles of water to his charges.

"You have been stuck for a while and had a bad scare. The water will help."

Having taken care of the accident victims, the officers began to sort out the facts for their report. Dmitri got a long lecture about his irresponsible permissiveness. How could he a seasoned driver allowing a brand new student to take the wheel at night?

"But conditions could not have been better!" he defended himself. "The road was straight and open, very little traffic. We saw only a few cars. There was enough light from the headlights. Who would have thought that a huge beast would choose to cross the road at this hour?"

"Well, yes, we did see the monster and because of the scare your wife must have received we will not proceed with charges. This could have rattled even an experienced driver."

Late that night Dmitri and P J arrived at their home. The yellow bird was dirty but not too much the worse for the adventure. Therefore, the officers had told them it was okay to drive the car home.

They were dead tired and headed for bed without much ceremony. Before sleep took him away, Dmitri felt very much the way he had when his now forty-three-year-old son, as a teen, wrapped his very first car, a little roadster, around the post of a street sign. The experiences were so much alike. The police, the interrogation, the tow-truck, the shook-up boy, the late hour—the deadly tiredness—erhaps he was a bit too old for so much youth. But then he thought of the children he might have with young PJ, who slept exhausted beside him, and he believed he was young enough.

However, nagging doubts had lately crept in to his thoughts. If he were the same man he had once been, should not PJ be pregnant by now? Oh well, perhaps it was her fertility fault and not his. Her new life in America probably drew too much energy from her to become pregnant at once. Patience! He counseled himself. Patience! Rome was not built in a day. It would happen! Just believe in the dream.

Antoine

⇜⇝

DURING THE WEEKS ANTOINE had been deprived of PJ's
presence, he was pining for a look at her face. Most extraordinary,
too, is how his usually good appetite had left him and he had lost
weight.

"Whatsa matter with you, Mon?" teased the girls. "You gone on
diet? Merican food not good enough?"

"Come home with me. I make Creole food. Plenty good,"
offered one.

"It's not food make him thin," opined another girl. "He tinking
of married Thai woman. Dat make him thin."

The girls laughed and gently punched each other. Their saucy
dark eyes teased Antoine and the other young men in their class.
The latter laughed and joined in the fun.

"Mon, you be stick-Mon soon."

However, once Manuel revealed PJ's whereabouts, Antoine used
Manuel's information speedily. It was easy for him to discover the
schedule of her new advanced class. Most days it ran parallel to his
class hours. For those days he made plans. He awaited her arrival
in odd places and surprised her with sudden appearances. If he
could not corner her to talk with her, he would slip a note into her
hand and walk away. Soon a flower accompanied the notes—a
frangipani blossom snatched from a tree, or a lovely bell-shaped,

large hibiscus flower. These were sometimes replaced by other offerings, a homemade CD of his favorite songs or a chocolate bar.

PJ was touched by so much attention and unadulterated admiration. In her heart she admitted readily that everything about him pleased her: his youth, his bronzed skin, his beautiful, yet manly face and his athletic body. Oh, oh, oh, her heart beat so much faster whenever she saw him. But then, when she was alone again, her twenty-something mind said: no, no, no! You need this marriage and American citizenship. She had been fully informed before coming to America that the marriage contract had to be fulfilled. If she were to be discovered in an affair, Dmitri could send her back to the village, to poverty and hopeless future. Her best years were already over.

In Thailand, men liked to marry very young girls, children really. The girls were given at a very young age into marriage by their fathers. Some were sold by their parents into brothels in Bangkok. She had been lucky, her parents were poor, but had enough money and work for her to do to keep her at home. Even after her father deserted the family, the older children were more of an asset than a drain. When her mother heard about the mail-order brides, her value to the family had increased enormously.

She resolved to be very circumspect and keep Antoine at arms length. How would she explain a dark baby with Haitian features to Dmitri? Although Antoine's skin was bronze, not black, and his face more white in cut than African, who knew which of his ancestors would come to the fore in a baby? She had seen enough interesting surprises in the village when suddenly a Thai baby looked dark as its Indian grandfather, or had the eyes and nose of a Malay past.

She had to be good! Could not cause disappointment. Martha Lenius and Jan Sorensen had kindly taken her under their wings and bit by bit introduced her to the neighborhood, while educating her. She would not have them look down on her. They had shown her where to shop for the best clothes and the best food. They also taught her the time-honored tradition of a lady's lunch. Further more, they had eased her transition and freed her from the constant pressure of a controlling teacher-husband. She would honor them by behaving properly and show herself worthy of their continued friendship.

Although it felt as if she had to put out the fire with her bare hands, she worked to extinguish the flames in her breast. She devised clever ways of foiling Antoines's interceptions. Sometimes she would be late, at other times very early to class. If she was early, she would hide out in the classroom; if she was late, she'd run to class and move even faster at his approach. Yet she did not trust herself totally. Being a woman from a land where pregnancy dooms women's futures, she opted for prevention. Not that she intended something to happen—but if it did, she would be safe. On her shopping trips with Martha, while she asked about the efficacy of different products, she found a variety of interesting things that would prevent getting pregnant. A troubling thought about Dmitri's fatherhood wishes briefly entered her mind. Yet she believed it was more ethical to prevent settling him with another man's child should anything untoward happen to her. Especially, since she was not seeking entanglement.

Soon Antoine knew the kind of game that was being played. He was terribly hurt. But he was a proud young man; if his pursuit must end, he would be the one ending it. By that time PJ's yellow bird had been repaired and cleaned after the accident on US 1. After a few more practice lessons and a few weeks of flawless driving in the neighborhood, Dmitri allowed PJ to drive herself to school in Homestead. She had been begging him, no, beseeching him, for this privilege day after day. Finally he gave in.

Within hours all the evening students knew that the Thai woman now drove a to-die-for gorgeous yellow car. Antoine watched from afar, while others gathered around the convertible after PJ's first arrival—top down. She fumbled for a long time to put the top back up, for Dmitri had lectured her that an open car invited theft of anything in the vehicle, perhaps even theft of the car itself. Antoine laughed at the hubris of the girl. How innocent to think that closing the top would prevent it from being stolen. But he did not want to see her hurt. Acting on her behalf, he called on the Haitian men and a few influential Mexicans, putting out the word that anyone touching PJ's car would be subject to terrible retribution. For himself, he chose to wait and observe from afar—at least for the present.

Captive

∼∽

TEN DAYS LATER PJ was in for a grand shock. She left class at
10:30 p.m. and crossed the badly lit parking lot. Her yellow car was
a bright spot in the half-light put out by the few light fixtures attached to the surrounding buildings. The school parking lot was as
safe a place as one could expect anywhere. She had never known
of any crimes committed here. For that reason she had never been
afraid to come and go from school.

Yet suddenly, she felt high terror. As she opened her car door
the way she usually did, sliding into the seat, strong arms shot out
from the dark interior and pulled her inside. Her mouth was
clamped tightly shut by a powerful hand and a voice hissed. "No
scream, no struggle! No hurt!"

PJ did not struggle. She was frozen into terrified stiffness. It
dawned on her that the interior lights had not come on when she
opened the door. Whoever had awaited her arrival had not only
forced his way in but disabled the lights. No doubt, the strong arms
belonged to a man. That man had pulled her into a backward embrace. Her back was pressed to his chest so forcefully that she felt
the strong beat of his heart against her skin. Her head had been
pulled sideways, away from the attacker and she looked bleakly at
the gloomy, pockmarked parking lot pavement. She suddenly caught
a whiff of the man's scent. He used an aftershave she knew well.

Aqua Velva! Now she knew—the man was Antoine.

She released the breath she'd held confined in her lungs as her muscles yieldingly softened. Feeling resistance leaving her body, the hand clamping her mouth shut was slowly removed. "Antoine? It is you, isn't it Antoine?" she whispered.

"Yes! I frighten you?"

"Yes, you did. What do you want? You know that I cannot be seen with you. You want make trouble for me, so husband sends me back to Thailand?"

"Sacre` bleu! Non, no trouble. You come with me—little while only. Two days then come back to old Mon."

"There will be trouble, Antoine! My husband will call police. I not come home, he will call. You be in trouble, bad trouble."

"Ha, police. That police not know us. I know good hiding place, very beautiful." By that time he had her imprisoned in his arms. "Two days!" he begged. Suddenly he propelled her over his body into the passenger seat and started the car. He peeled out of the parking lot, without lights, and tires screaming. That maneuver caught the attention of the few remaining students and one of the teachers. Everyone was alarmed, for they all knew that P J drove the yellow bird with great caution and attention to detail. Her accident in the Everglades had taught her to be vigilant when at the wheel.

It was not much later when Dmitri began to wonder why PJ had not returned from class. He patiently waited a while; but as the minutes ticked away, he grew concerned. His wife was very reliable. Never did he have to wonder about her whereabouts. When his inner tension made him pace the floor, he could not stand the suspense any longer. He grabbed his keys and walked to his car.

He had not gotten far, when Martha called to him from her yard. "Where are you going at this hour, Dmitri?"

"PJ did not come home. Something is wrong. She is never late. I am afraid she might have had an accident and needs help."

"She would have called you if she were in trouble. She's got a cell-phone, doesn't she?"

"Yes, but it could have run out of charge. Who knows! She is not always taking care of the small things, like plugging the phone in the charger."

"You could be right. Would you like to have company? I would not mind coming along. It is a fine evening for a drive and who knows, you might need help." For a just a moment Dmitri was annoyed. He would have rather gone alone and stewed in his heavy brewing worry. His next thought, however, was caused by the realization that being alone his worry might drive him crazy with imaginings. Martha had a good head on her shoulders and could distract him. They set out for the school at a faster pace than his usual clip.

"Give me your cell," ordered Martha. "Is the school number programmed in? I want to see if someone is still there."

"Hell, why didn't I think of that? I just paced and fretted," groused Dmitri deeply disturbed by his own inattention. Martha was lucky. A female voice answered her call. Dmitri recognized PJ's new teacher's voice.

"Rodriguez here. Yes, I am PJ's teacher. We are very worried. She left under very worrisome, I might even say, suspicious circumstances."

"What do you mean, suspicious?" asked Martha perturbed. She was not prepared for something to have gone very wrong with PJ. She thought that the girl might have a flat tire, or other small mishap. The word suspicious was not auspicious at all.

"Well, her car peeled out of the compound as if the devil were after her. All tires screeched. This made all of us notice, for this is not the way of that young lady. I have tried to call her husband, but could not find the sheet with the contact numbers."

Dmitri had heard Martha saying, "suspicious" and was even more alarmed than before.

"Give me the phone, Martha!" he ordered, short tempered. Martha slipped the small phone into his hand. A second later he shouted into the instrument.

"Yes, this is Dmitri, her husband! What is suspicious with my wife?"

"Nothing is wrong with your wife; but the circumstances under which she left today are somewhat worrisome."

Dear God, thought Rodriguez, shaken by his yelling, *I have to keep this one calm or he will go berserk. He acts as if his wife is six years old.* She explained as gently as possible what she and the students had observed. She insinuated that it was possible that his wife was not the person at the wheel.

"Are you saying my wife was with someone? Is that what you are saying?"

"No, no, that is not what I am saying. We really know nothing about the whole thing. I should not have alarmed you with my own overly cautious concerns."

"If my wife was with a man in this car, she must have been abducted by the creep," yelled Dmitri into the little phone, as if his shouting could kill the "creep" outright.

Inez Rodriguez, five feet of dark, energy-laden, prettiness, decided that her evening was shot. She would have to stay and keep the raving nut calmed down. Her husband would have to eat dinner alone. Not only that, he would have to bathe and put the kids to bed. Luckily, she had fed the children before leaving for evening class. They always messed with their food when Heraclio fed them. The school had never before had a problem with a student disappearing. They had a few brawls—bruises, two broken bones—but never anything serious. For that reason, and the good reputation of the organization, she was willing to suffer and wait. Having made that decision, she said, "I think it will be better Mr. Pataklos if we talk in person. I will wait here for you and then we can decide together what needs to be done."

When Dmitri and Martha reached the school, only a small group consisting of pupils, a janitor, and Inez Rodriguez, were left standing in the parking lot. Dmitri vaulted from the high seat of his SUV and rushed to the clustered people. In his haste he forgot to help Martha alight from her high seat, and she was struggling to follow him. Curiosity had taken hold of her, setting her mind ablaze. What had begun as the story of a possible mishap, a punctured tire, a slip into a ditch or a small collision with another car had turned into the hundred times more exciting tale of a love affair, a car-jacking, or even more delectable an abduction.

Martha was a good woman. Never would she wish ill on anyone. Although she tried hard to think only the best of her fellow men and women, she, like most of us, could not help being entertained and excited by the foibles, shortcomings and, yes, even a bit of bad luck falling upon a neighbor. And so she scrambled to reach the small group, for she did not want to miss a morsel of the conversation.

Belated and somewhat sheepishly, Dmitri introduced her to the teacher, Ms. Rodriguez, and the few Haitian, Mexican and Cuban men and women left at the school. She heard the story of the strange exit of the yellow car from the school parking lot, and the strange fact that no one had seen PJ inside the car.

After a heated discussion, it was decided that Dmitri should call Jan to see if PJ, by chance, had returned home. Ms. Rodriguez insisted on this call before she was willing to alert the local police department.

Jan answered in the negative when questioned if she could see the yellow car in the driveway or lights in the house. To be totally sure, she called Dmitri's number and sent Brent across the canal to have a look—all efforts proved negative. The call to the police department went out.

"We will have a car over at the school in ten minutes," promised the dispatcher.

More than an hour had elapsed. The trail had grown cold. How could an alert for a canary yellow Pontiac do any good now? Any evildoer had an hour to hide the car, or desert it in one of a hundred hard-to-find locations and abscond with the young woman. Those thoughts plagued Dmitri. Suddenly, PJ assumed an even greater importance in his mind and his emotions. She was not only the young foreign wife—nay she had become the representation of everything that was sweet, good and worth living for in his life. The thought of how he would face another day without her caused a heavy ring to tighten around his chest, as if an adversary twisted a metal chain.

Martha saw his face—clay-gray and sick. *Oh, Lord,* she thought. *Don't let the old man drop dead from worry.*

She took his hand in her own, reassuring him, "It will turn out to be nothing, Demi! A stupid prank. You know these young people. They do not think rationally like we do. Perhaps they want to just have some fun and went to a dance or a cook-out on the beach. Think back—you were young not too long ago."

Martha's prattle calmed Dmitri, reassured him. Yes, things could not be as bleak as he made them out to be. He breathed deeply and recovered his color.

At that juncture the police car drove into the parking lot. It stopped close to the assembled. The officers climbed out of their squad car, holding flashlight-torches and notebooks in their hands.

"Hey, we know you! You are the guy stuck in Black Water Sound and threatened by a croc," called out one of the officers, approaching the group. It turned out to be Hoskins from a few weeks ago.

"You got that right! It is me. Trouble seems to follow me wherever I go," stated Dmitri mirthlessly.

"So what's up tonight?" Borman, his partner wanted to know.

"It seems that my pupil, his wife, has disappeared under suspicious circumstances," explained Ms. Rodriguez after giving her credentials to the officers.

The tale of PJ's disappearance was told once more in great detail, leaving the officers puzzled.

"Could be a carjacking or an abduction," ventured Hoskins.

"I hate to put it this way," said Borman, slightly cringing. "How well do you know your wife? Are you sure that she is the faithful person she makes you think she is? Any hint of a romantic involvement?"

"Officer," puffed Dmitri insulted. "Precious Jewel is a respectable, very honorable person. I never had a moment's doubt about her faithfulness. It is only because of her impeccable record of coming and going that I was concerned at all when she did not show up at home at her regular time. I suspected an accident and drove out to aid her."

"Alright, alright, I don't doubt your wife's integrity!" soothed Borman. "I just put forth this possibility to see if we can rule it out."

Although the statement appeased Dmitri, the rest of the severely shrunken group still had doubt written on their brows. Everyone thought, *Yes, we think we know a loved one, but no one can fully know another person's heart.* And in this particular case, the group standing about was speculating about the heart of a young, beautiful woman, whose different culture and origin had to be taken into consideration.

Hoskins got into the police car and put out an All-Points Bulletin for a missing yellow Pontiac convertible and a young dark-haired woman. After that, all persons were dismissed. Their statements had been taken and they were free to go. Dmitri, Martha in tow, followed the police cruiser down empty streets to the police station. Like most buildings in Homestead the police station was encircled by the ubiquitous white gravel lot that gave way to asphalt around the cluster of flat buildings. Dmitri and Martha gave their testimony concerning the case and were dismissed also. Once their statements and the pertinent details of their circumstance had been recorded, they were of no further use to the investigation.

"Call us immediately if your wife should show up at home or if she calls you with a location where she can be picked up," the cops instructed Dmitri and sent him on his way.

Dmitri and Martha dissatisfied and fretful, walked away from the plain dismal offices of the Homestead police station . Now what? What could they do to help a possibly kidnapped, terrorized young woman? There was, however, nothing they could do but drive home and try to get some sleep. Needless to say, they did not talk much on their long way home. Having arrived, they parted quickly, being tired and upset as they were.

Martha went to bed almost instantly. She had begun praying for hapless PJ while still brushing her teeth. Being elderly with an otherwise untroubled mind, she fell asleep almost instantly—her prayers half said.

Dmitri, on the other hand, was immersed in discomfort. He had a headache. His mind could not let go of the horrible pictures he had begun to imagine when PJ failed to show up at the appointed time. His body, too, was experiencing agitation. He was writhing and twitching, because he was painfully aware of the void on the other side of the bed. Most of all he missed the regular, gentle breathing and the almost childlike sounds his wife emitted when falling asleep. Subconsciously, he listened to every strange sound in the house—there were suddenly many. Two hours passed while he twisted, tossed and turned. At last he could not stand it any longer. He walked into the kitchen to sooth his stomach and his mind with a cup of hot chocolate.

He had barely reached the entrance to the kitchen when the phone rang. Dmitri flung himself in the direction of the phone like a tiger pouncing on its prey.

"Mr. Pataklos?"

"Yes, I am Pataklos."

"This is detective Merryl Potter of the Homestead police department. I thought you might be interested to know that we found your wife's car. It is a yellow Pontiac convertible, isn't it?"

"Yes, that sounds like her car. Does the license number match?"

"Yes, it's the number you gave the patrol men earlier."

"Where did you find the car? Any sign of my wife?"

"We found the car parked alongside Alligator Alley, hidden in shrubbery. It was locked. Inside we found a sweater and some books belonging to your wife. We think she might have been an unwilling passenger. There were signs of a slight struggle."

"What do you mean by that?" croaked Dmitri, fully aware that PJ would not be able to put up a forceful defense.

"We lifted a print of her forehead, or what we assume to be her forehead and not another woman's, from the front window. Either she was fairly violently thrown forward into the window or pushed there during an altercation. We surmise the latter case, because there isn't a scratch on the car and the brakes do not show abuse, so we rule out that she slammed into the window because of an accident."

"What do we do now?" Dmitri wanted to know. Potter was a calm, intelligent man who, even on the telephone, exuded a comforting rationality that, in the past, had soothed even the most frantic citizens.

"Don't worry, Mr. Pataklos. We have a team of officers working your wife's case. They are out there this very moment with dog teams, combing the area. I am on my way to location at this very moment. You will be notified if and when we find anything."

"Thank you, detective Potter, thank you!" Dmitri could hardly contain himself. Finally something was crystallizing. Dog teams! It sounded professional, comforting. To give up the worry, allowing the team of professionals to assume responsibility was a temptation that proved to be remarkably pleasant. During the next hours whenever an almost hysterical wave of worry seemed to engulf him, he had the psychological fortitude to defer to authority.

What did he, an ordinary citizen know about abductions, carjackings and other violent crimes? In his most vivid imaginings he could not see anyone doing harm to PJ.

She was so pretty, so innocent and kind. So why would anyone want to harm her? Oh, he could see why some young man might want to extract her from the herd of pupils surrounding her so he could talk to her awhile. But to hurt her? No!Perhaps he just wanted to talk to her for a while.

Had he been able to read the minds of the professionals, he would have been shocked. Detective Merryl Potter, a family man with three daughters at home, was almost sick with anticipation of what the dog squad might find in the Everglades. Bodies could disappear there, dismembered by alligators. In the Florida Keys resided any number of psychotic creeps. They lived in little unrecorded, unlicensed shacks, feeding themselves on part-time jobs, drinking and doping away the nights, ever ready to blow the tentative toehold on their sanity. Potter's last hunt for a serial killer had turned up just such a man.

Potter, therefore, put PJ's safety in the hand of Jehovah. He was not a strict believer, but he believed in a higher power, much higher than man, at least. And until he found the young woman, he preferred to think her fate to be in more sacred hands than his own. From his interview with Dmitri, he believed PJ to have a certain code of honor. She certainly was not one of the young women, so prevalent in today's society, who counted her physical and psychological health as nothing.

PJ is Found

৵৽

WHILE THE WORLD WAS preoccupied with the task of finding
PJ, she had her own battles to fight. Dmitri was alternately crazed
with worry or infused with hope. Because in later times, nothing
factional could be ascertained about the period of her disappearance, and we must employ our imagination and construct our own
story about her absence with Antoine.

For three days operatives, volunteers, and dogs combed through
a certain part of the Everglades. Nothing, not even a small trail was
ever found. The young woman had disappeared as if swallowed by
a force that had pulled her into the bowl of the earth. On the eve
on the third day of the search, a team of dog-handlers detected her
walking sedately along rout 821 from Leisure City to Homestead.

"What happened to you?" was Merryl Potter's first question
when he sat across from the well-composed young woman who
seemed no worse for wear after her ordeal.

"I was taken by force. It was a young man with a crush," smiled
PJ mildly. "He took me away. But he was not bad. He did not hurt
me. He just wanted talk."

"So where did he take you?" interrupted Potter. He felt uncomfortable. He sensed what was coming and knew that this case would
not be solved to his, or the department's satisfaction.

"I cannot tell where it was. He put things over me and covered my eyes."

"So tell me, who was the man who took you hostage. This way we can file charges."

"I know not his name and I am not telling about him. I do not want him hurt. He did nothing!"

"What? He did nothing? Your husband is a nervous wreck. He calls here by the hour—is that nothing? We had teams of officers; officers with dogs, and teams of detectives were looking for you and you say it was nothing? Your young man committed a crime by abducting you. Is that nothing?"

"Yes, I see! But he just loves me. Can he help that?" asked PJ with the most innocent flutter of her eyelashes.

Potter closed his eyes and tried to imagine what it had been like when he was twenty-five, courting his future wife. He was definitely love-struck and reckless then, but abduction? By Jove, that was taking it too far. And this pretty, young thing was obviously doing her best to protect the love-struck idiot.

"Couldn't your young man just talk to you in the parking lot and be done with it?" he asked acerbically.

"No," explained the girl patiently, talking slowly as to one demented. "See, me married. He come and talk to me. I say, "I no can meet with you; me is married woman, my husband would not like.""

Potter noticed that her English grammar deteriorated whenever she became passionate. He wondered if he could get her flustered enough for her to reveal a name or location.

"Do you know, my dear, that it is wrong of you to protect the young man who took you away? We can put you in jail until you tell us who he is and what he did to you. Right now we have police officers coming to my office to take you to the hospital to be examined. We will find out one way or another what went on while you were with him."

Potter's words fell on deaf ears. Precious Jewel, looking like a Catholic schoolgirl, sat quietly defiant, her legs modestly crossed;

her hands were folded in her lap; she looked at the scuffed linoleum beneath her feet. The moment Potter was about to launch a second attack, a knock on the door interrupted the proceedings.

"Detective Potter! Mrs. Pataklos' husband is here and would like to see her." Potter thought for a moment. Then, deciding that her irate husband might loosen her tongue, he called out, "See him in!"

Entering Potter's impersonal office in which a large desk, a few unfriendly chairs, shelves and metal filing cabinets dominated, Dmitri was a study in anxiety. It was an anxiety fraught with anger, fury, relief, insecurity and uncertainty. These strong emotions played on his face as if it were a stage.

PJ slipped instantly off her chair and ran to the man who looked worn and older than she had ever observed. She wrapped her arms around his waist and pressed her head against his chest, her long, black hair falling over her face. Potter's mind recorded that she did all this without uttering a word, making Dmitri break the ice and giving her the psychological advantage.

Clever minx, he thought. *We will have a hard nut to crack.*

His surmise was prophetic. Because throughout the interrogations that followed, PJ's silence about the abductor and the whereabouts of her days in a hide-a-way, was never broken. She stubbornly refused to reveal any of the details that could have led to an arrest. Since she would not file charges, there was really nothing anyone could do.

She held the line with Dmitri, too.

"Nothing happened. Nothing. The man is not bad." She repeated over and over. She always ended with a phrase that infuriated Dmitri.

"He love me. This not a crime." She stoically endured the invasive medical examinations without demur. They all proved negative or inconclusive. No force had been exerted sexually, but that did not prove she had not been a willing participant in sexual activity by having protected sex.

"PJ, PJ," groaned Dmitri in the privacy of their bedroom, "I am your husband and you must tell me everything. Do you under-stand—you must tell."

He even made veiled threats as to her uncertain status in America. Yet the woman, to whom he had become addicted, kept her secrets, cleverly calling on his marriage vow to trust her.

"I cannot put innocent man in prison," were always her last words—unchangeable and forever. When the threat of expatriation did not force a confession, Dmitri gave up. He buried the thing by pressing it as far down in his mind as he could, and decided to stop obsessing. What did he gain by self-punishment, sulking amid sordid pictures and emotions? Nothing. If she had a fling—she had come back to him—the better man.

Detective Potter did not give up so easily. He was annoyed that some young punk could commit a serious crime, riling his police department, and walk away without even one hair on his head crushed. It was not right—it upset the balance of right and wrong. Therefore, he combed through files, interviewed the students at the foreign language night school, and had PJ's car fingerprinted and searched in great detail. To his chagrin, nothing was found. Obviously, the car had been wiped clean before it was abandoned in Alligator Alley. All fibers found in the car's interior belonged to PJ's clothing—and that was it.

The teacher, Ms. Rodriguez, and the students played dumb and deaf. They either knew nothing or pretended not to know. Potter came to the conclusion that the man in question must either be very much loved or feared by everyone.

Ms. Rodriguez, who had a very good idea about the entire affair, had long ago decided to keep neutral. What else was she to do, after finding out that PJ filed no charges and claimed that no crime had been committed. Antoine had returned to his classes, looking sad and beaten. The reality of his situation had defeated his ardor and wishes—the icon of his dreams was just that, an icon he could adore only by sending her prayers and wishes.

Detective Potter almost could have solved the case. One of the lovesick women in Antoine's class would have told all. Everyone in class knew exactly what had transpired during the abduction. But she was the only one willing to talk about the matter. However, she was silenced by Manuel during the first words of her testimony to the police. Sitting behind her, he poked the tip of his knife into her back. It was a gesture she instantly understood, having encountered the tip of a knife before.

"Well," Potter finally said to officer Hoskins one fine day, "win some, lose some—we lost this one. Stubborn woman—what can I say, but very, very pretty. I can actually believe the story of the love-struck fool. But I cannot swallow the line that nothing happened."

"I know what you mean, sir! Her husband is much too old for her. There might be more trouble in store for him in the future."

"Could be! Unless he resigns himself to feed on the crumbs that others leave."

Precious Jewel Gains Power

❦

HENCEFORTH, DMITRI'S CONTROL OVER his Thai woman was much reduced. PJ did the things she thought she ought. She cooked his breakfast, lunch, and dinner the way Dmitri liked it. She made the beds to his satisfaction and kept the house neat and clean. She did, however, balk when called upon to clean fish. "I no like that!" she stated firmly. And that was that. When they, as couple or a fishing party, went out on the ocean, she willingly cleaned most of the boat afterwards. Most of that activity consisted of sluicing it with fresh water to get the salt off, but she balked at polishing the stainless steel rails or the precious wood trimmings.

"Too hard on de hands and arms," she claimed. And Dmitri, emasculated by her abduction with its aftermath, gave in and did the tasks himself.

The neighbors watched their ménage with friendly, curious interest. Martha had spread most of the details of the fateful disappearance to her friends, who, inclined to speculation, had spread their own versions of the event.

By the time the abduction account reached the end of the development, PJ had been turned into a wanton hussy, who had facilitated her own capture because of her relentless, sexually driven personality. Oh, ye gods, how the men and women in this little, boring community loved the juicy gossip resulting from a tale told blandly and trustingly by Martha.

The gossip machine progressed according to the rule posed by a Russian rabbi: "Gossip multiplies ad nauseam. It expands fluffily, like the down of a plucked goose thrown into the wind."

PJ seemed unaware of the demeaning, unflattering things that were said about her. She went about her days with a sweet smile and serene Buddhist demeanor. Dmitri, however, knew exactly what talk was afoot in the community and it bothered him tremendously. Yet outwardly, he showed none of his discomfort and, yes, it had to be admitted, his pain.

Two years passed. Years punctuated by little but doctor's appointments for Dmitri and dental care for PJ. The routine was only punctuated by holidays and fishing, which became almost a boring chore if pursued daily or even weekly basis. For PJ, at least, it quickly lost the special glitter of adventure, the thrill of the hunt. How often did one need to go and kill the denizens of the deep if the freezer was filled already with many packages of fish? Enough fish, so that one would not be able to eat it in an entire year.

PJ's English, completed in a three-year cycle, was excellent. Her teachers pushed her to study for her citizenship exam. Outfitted with the materials needed to pass the exam required by the naturalization board, she began to study what makes America the special place it is in the world.

Dmitri believed she would understand the material better if she knew the historical background of America. So he told her about the Indians who inhabited the continent of America. He progressed to the first settlers and, in passing, touched on the French and British rivalry and the resulting wars. He taught her about the Continental Congress, beginning with the forerunners the Provincial Congresses.

"For example," he said, "it was resolved in the Provincial Congress of Massachusetts in 1774: To resist tyranny becomes the Christian and social duty of every individual! …and with a proper sense of your dependence on God, nobly defend those rights which heaven gave, and no man ought to take from us."

That small paragraph required a lot of explaining to a woman who stemmed from a society where the individual had hardly any rights and their religion left justice to fate, perhaps to be executed in another dimension.

The same Massachusetts Congress reorganized the militia, providing in the statutes that one-third of all new regiments be made up of "Minutemen." These were men ready to fight at a minute's notice.

By the time Dmitri had explained the precarious situation of America's settlers, the British overlords and the onerous tax load they exerted, he was ready to leave the country's early beginnings, and rush into more pertinent stuff—pertinent to the exam PJ had to take. He went straight to the passage about the Continental Congress, September 7, 1774, in Philadelphia on the morning when news of the attack on Boston arrived.

From that famous Congress followed all the other important meetings. In these congregations the measures were decided, which, in due course, led to declaring independence from the British and surviving a war. Dmitri had taken to these lessons with gusto, because he began to relive some of the most interesting lectures he had attended in officer's training. The lecturing historian, a crusty old military man who loved history not only for its own sake, but also for history's strategic and military lessons, had put his very soul into the interpretations of America's Noble Heritage.

"Yes, gentlemen, he used to say, you are the defenders of a Great and Noble Heritage. To be truly cognizant of just how sublime, special and unusual this heritage is, you must apply yourselves and understand the complete work of those who forged these United States."

When Dmitri told PJ that in the beginning there were only thirteen states making up the "United States," the young woman could hardly understand the concept, let alone the Declaration of Independence, signed by Congress on July 4, 1776. It was daunting for

PJ to internalize its foremost principle: the guaranty given to American citizens of life, liberty and the pursuit of happiness, for in her culture, nothing but birth was guarantied. From these, the basic beginnings, the couple progressed in the lectures to tenets guiding American life—the Constitution.

"The overarching tenet of the constitution sets up government and defines the role of government and protects the basic rights of Americans," so read Dmitri. Then he proceeded to explain how this concept works in the daily life of the citizens. PJ marveled at the very idea of such a thing. Her country was ruled by a constitutional monarchy, quite different from the political structure she studied now.

"Remember, already the first three words of the constitution allow self- government to Americans. These words are: "We the people." And because of these principles we have a structure allowing the separation of power. We have the House of Representatives, the Senate, the President and the Supreme Court. And then, of course we have the special laws that every state of the union can make to the wishes of the people in their state."

"It all is very complicated!" complained the Thai woman. "It also sounds very strange. You say the people have self-government and then you elect the same people over and over again. Some are in their dotage and sound senile. They seem to have their own little country in Washington where they do as they please. At least with the King in charge, we know there is only one person controlled by a constitution."

"Smart girl! You put your finger on a sore spot. You are right. Our people are too complacent. They become familiar with one person and the politicians know that and work day and night on their re-election campaigns. They all should be thrown out after two terms. But you in the meantime will have to learn what amendments are."

"I learned that chapter," said PJ proudly. "Amendments are changes to the constitution and the first eighteen of them constitute the Bill of Rights."

She made a pretty moue and commented further, "I think that some of the later amendments should not have been put into the constitution."

"Which one do you think in particular?"

"The Twenty-Third, of course. The District of Columbia should not be a favorite entity. It should either be part of another state, or be treated as such a state instead of being a special entity. My teacher, Mr. Cloude, thinks it is very wrong what government had done there."

"Yes, I guess one could be of a different opinion on that matter," admitted Dmitri.

"Well," groused PJ, "and then there are all the clauses attached to the amendments. Supposedly the government is restricted in its ability to tax and spend but you and everyone I know is constantly complaining about the taxes levied upon them. It seems to me government has finally found out how to put their hands into your pockets. Much like the crime lords in Thailand—but they are more direct by putting a knife to your throat."

Ye gods, thought Dmitri. *What has happened to the village woman? Give her a little more time and she could become a lawyer.* That, however, was not on PJ's mind. She was more or less just complaining about the material she had to study for her naturalization test. Of course, there were easier ways of learning the material the government served up. They were simple, user-friendly study guides. But Dmitri, wishing her to shine and pass with flying colors, had enrolled her in a citizenship class with the aforementioned Mr. Cloud, and was now reaping the results of his foresight.

Mr. Cloud was steeped in the intricacies of the Constitution; he lived, breathed and preached the wonderful sentiments of the founding fathers and insisted that his foreign students become conversant in the best governmental document ever produced in the entire world—the Constitution. He was convinced of this truth, as are multitudes of other thinkers.

For PJ, however, this meant a great deal of study and extra work, which she in turn cherished and eschewed. She struggled mightily with the Federalist Papers, especially the sections written by Alexander Hamilton for which she sought Dmitri's help again and again. When she finally had worked her way through the required material, plus Mr. Cloud's extra measure of material, Dmitri proudly patted her cheek and assured her that she would pass her test without the slightest problem.

"You, my dear, have mastered an amount of American knowledge most natives have never studied in depth. You will make a fine citizen."

Her tutors did not know that at the bottom of her heart PJ believed that one good criminal could in the end destroy their entire system, because it relied on a populace that believed in their Judeo-Christian principles. Destroy this foundation and a dictator could impose whatever rules he liked.

The New American

❧✦

ON A FINE FLORIDA DAY, attired in a sundress—which featured a white, delicate leaf design on a dark blue background—and white sandals and matching purse, Precious Jewel entered the offices of the Naturalization Service in Miami. Dmitri, whose arm she clutched for support, had to stay behind in the waiting room when her name was called.

A friendly, officious lady with flaming red hair, delicate white skin that never saw the sun, and freckles across the bridge of her nose, offered her a seat across from her desk.

"I am Mrs. Mc Ardle," said the redhead. After greeting PJ and confirming her name, she said, "I see from your application that you have been married for over three years to a citizen and have all the requirements to be naturalized. You are of age and seem to be of good moral character—there is nothing against you in the records. So let us see how well you speak English and what you have learned about our country."

She reached across the desk, handing PJ a printed sheet.

"Please read the fourth paragraph on the page," she instructed.

PJ read the text slowly but fluently. She had noticed instantly that this particular paragraph was the most difficult on the page. It began with, "When in the course of human events, it becomes necessary for one people to dissolve the political bonds which have connected them with another…"

"Tell me, Mrs. Pataklos, what does that mean? What is expressed in this paragraph?"

Thank you Dmitri for making me study hard, thought PJ. She smiled, revealing her perfect teeth.

"This paragraph is the beginning of the Declaration of Independence. It says that the people of America want to be free of England. That God created all people to be equal and gives them rights which no one can take from them. Rights like life, liberty, and happiness."

Here PJ paused, for the rest of the declaration was harder for her to put into her own words.

"Well done," praised Mrs. Mc Ardle. She was pleasantly surprised, for she had been prepared for a very poor interpretation. Apparently, the little fashion plate from Thailand had a good brain and had studied besides. She put PJ through the paces of the test. How many senators for each state? How many senators altogether are seated in the Senate?

How many representatives are there in the house? What is the role of the Supreme Court? How many terms can a president serve? Could you, Mrs. Pataklos, become president of the USA? No matter the question, PJ knew the answers with certainty.

After twenty minutes of questioning Mrs. Mc Ardle thanked PJ, shook her hand and remarked that, according to her examination PJ had passed her test. After checking all other requirements, she would be notified if and when the swearing-in ceremony would take place.

There was a glow about PJ when she returned to the waiting room. She almost flew into Dmitri's arms, a wide smile on her face.

"I did it! It went great! Thank you! All the studying paid off. I will be an American!"

Dmitri fairly melted with almost fatherly pride. His wife, his girl, now she could be a good mother to the children he still wished to beget. Pity that. Almost four years had gone by and still no baby.

He certainly was not getting any younger. But…today was today—a day to celebrate. And so, Dmitri drove his jubilant wife to the Miami waterfront, the promenade, where they had dinner in a most expensive French restaurant, sitting al fresco under the stars, drinking expensive Beaujolais.

Not long thereafter the invitation from the Naturalization office arrived for the swearing-in ceremony of the new citizens. This was the year for an enormous foreign class to be sworn in. The usual venues for this purpose, inside buildings, proved too small. Pressured officials put up a covered stage, rows of chairs shaded by beach umbrellas, loudspeakers and a grand American Flag flying high on a steel mast right on the beach for a most impressive, meaningful ceremony.

Under a very large hat, PJ's face glowed with the excitement of the occasion. She nervously clung to Dmitri's hand and followed the proceedings breathlessly. American citizen—she. Imagine! Now she could bring Momma and her siblings to this rich country. What joy!

PJ had to wait a long time before her name was called. Important people, she thought it was a senator and the mayor, spoke movingly about the opportunities and good life in their new homeland. Then, standing, their hands on their pounding hearts, the foreigners took the pledge of allegiance and, by so doing, became new American citizens. Officials spoke and officiated. Their work was complicated by the sheer volume of people to be processed. So large was the crowd that the new citizens were called out in groups by different officials, instead of one by one.

PJ was in one of the R-groups and followed the others merrily to the official who held their certificates. He shook their hands, wished them well, and handed them the all-important document.

That evening, Dmitri hosted the entire neighborhood. A barbecue feast with wine, beer, and other drinks was laid out on long tables by the canal. Torches burned smoky, keeping the annoying mosquitoes and other insects at bay. Everyone, most of all PJ, had a wonderful time.

Jan, the imp, fed the young woman Mimosas, telling her that the orange juice would mitigate the alcohol of the champagne. PJ chose to believe her promises. At midnight, when Dmitri was already quite tired, he found that his wife could not walk very well anymore. She almost fell in the canal. Hoisting her over his shoulder and wishing his guests a good night, he ended the party.

An Unpleasant Discovery

❧❧

AFTER A FEW DAYS on cloud nine, PJ returned to earth and business at hand. It was time to shop for groceries. Shopping for food was always an expedition to be undertaken with preparations. As soon as PJ discovered the great and wonderful power of coupons, there was no stopping her. Never in her life had she been able to get things with newspaper clippings.

Having a practical bend, she snatched the paper from Dmitri's hands the moment he seemed finished with its perusal and began her work with sharp scissors. In the beginning she had ruthlessly removed coupons whether she needed the featured items or not. With Dmitri's guidance she narrowed her searches and only clipped items she intended to purchase.

Before they could leave for the long drive to the nearest Winn Dixie on Plantation Key in Tavernier, or the even longer drive to the Publix Supermarket in Homestead, they followed an involved routine. First the coupons were collected and put into a special pocket book. Dmitri filled coolers with ice for the perishables, for nothing delicate survived the long trip in the hot sun. Lastly, bushel baskets were stashed in the van for handpicking vegetables in the fields outside Homestead.

Outfitted in such manner, the industrious couple set out for the road. They tried to leave the house by 9:30 a.m., avoiding the hottest part of the day. But this did not always work out. Once safely out on US 1, heading north, they began to relax and get into the rhythm of their weekly adventure. After shopping and picking vegetables, Dmitri always allowed them a generous lunch in one of their favorite restaurants. Mexican, Cuban, Indian—there were many good choices.

Looking forward to a pleasurable day, Dmitri was in no way prepared for the onslaught on his psyche that was soon to occur. On the contrary, he was leisurely enjoying the drive. His keen eyes saw the different kinds of waterfowl teaming at the edges of swamp and road. The telephone and electrical poles, with their high wooden supports along US 1, were the favorite perches for different hunting bird species.

Most prominent among them were kingfishers and ospreys. The former, sitting high on the wires, eyed the pools of the Everglade's marshes for the silvery flash of prey; the latter purveyed the lake waters on the other side of the road from their nesting platforms. Their nests were large accommodations constructed from sticks and rushes. Every year the ospreys returned to the same platform and enlarged their real estate. It was the soon-to-be home to two offspring if all went well. Snowy egrets and their smaller cousins, the cattle egret and great blue herons, different species of ducks and stilt-birds foraged close enough to the road to be easily observed.

At first, Dmitri and PJ conversed lightly. But she soon grew unusually quiet. Had he known what was on her mind, he would have stopped with instant dismay his happy low-tune whistling. However, he was in his own remote sphere of thought and noted nothing. Meanwhile, the tension built in the wife beside him. She thought that the moment had come where she had enough ground prepared for the seeds she was about to cast. Seeds she hoped would instantly germinate and come to fruition.

While PJ formulated a speech in her mind, Dmitri congratulated himself on the wonderful choices he had made in the last few years.

A loving, lovely, young wife who was perfect in all respects sat sweetly poised beside him. He daily lived exactly the way he wished; his food was lovingly prepared to his liking; his home was clean and pleasant to the eye—comfortable, too. He fished whenever he wished, enjoyed the shopping trips, went swimming in the early mornings or evenings with PJ and the neighbors who had embraced her and made her one of their own. Oh, life was good! It flowed without eddies and whirlpools in which a man could be caught. Enmeshed in these soulful pleasures, PJ's voice broke into his reveries. At first, he could hardly understand the gist of the flood of words released by his wife.

"What?" he asked perturbed, "What are you saying? Your mother coming here? To live with us? In my house?"

"Yes! Is a good time for Momma to come. I am a citizen now. We have a good house. Momma and the boys can live here and be more happy, much better than in Thailand."

"What makes you think that I would like such an arrangement? You know, of course, I have told you so before that I do not like your mother; and your younger brother is a pain in the ass."

"Yes, but darling, they my family. You my husband—husband must provide for all the family. I promised Momma she could come!"

"Yes, I must provide for my family. My wife, my children, even my mother and father. Your mother and your brothers, however, are the responsibility of your father who made them," replied Dmitri icily. Upon this harsh declaration PJ broke out in loud sobs.

"You know my own Popa left and Momma no has money." Dmitri had noticed that PJ's English deteriorated when she became exited or flustered. He now looked at her tear-stained peachy face and was unmoved.

"Don't even go there!" he warned. "I am sending her plenty of money. Enough to live like a queen in your country. So don't try that spiel on me."

"But I am unhappy without Momma," wailed his wife.

"Well, maybe you should go to Mama for a long visit," ventured the irate husband.

"I am unhappy, too," complained Dmitri, who was all of a sudden reminded that amid his momentary bliss a few items of happiness had gotten lost.

"Where are the children you promised to have? Almost four years and you are not the least bit pregnant. Perhaps your mother can come here for a little while for the birth of a baby."

Oh, ho! PJ suddenly realized that the mission she'd been on was not as easy as she had thought. To the contrary, the mission needed a change of game plan. She had firmly believed that she had the sexual power to make him compliant—she had worked that magic for the money to be sent to Thailand. Now what? She would try the scheme one more time.

Needless to say, the rest of the day went in polite silence. Only the most necessary words were exchanged. PJ realized that she had to tread carefully upon a slippery floor. Life in America was not as easy as she had believed it to be. It was time to reverse her agenda; time to get off birth control. Perhaps she would get lucky and get pregnant by the old fool. Well, she would try—give it her best shot.

A Step Toward Conception

❦

IN THE WEEKS FOLLOWING the fateful shopping trip, the fog of unacknowledged tension hung in the air. The harmonious life of previous times had fallen victim to suspicions that once aroused, would not leave.

Why was PJ not pregnant by now? The question hung in Dmitri's mind. *Plenty of time had passed. The stress of learning and adjusting should long have disappeared. So what was wrong?*

He knew, of course, that he was a virile, active, fertile man. Nothing wrong there. So it must be her! A few times she had again done some of the wonderful things for him that almost made him swoon. Following the exciting treatment, she would bring up the question of mama's visit or her living with them. He got the drift and refused outright.

Predictably, PJ stopped the delightful sessions and punished him with every- day boring sex. Yet, she never lost her sweet smile and submissive demeanor. There was, by all rights, nothing he could complain about. But they both knew the difference. During the time of what he perceived as punishment, the subject of Thai Momma Ragoongong, was never brought up. Despite feeling his deprivation, Dmitri did not break down and give in. No baby—no momma! Basta! As his Mexican friends would say.

At twenty-eight, PJ was seasoned enough to know the score.

Provided knowledge by a hard life, she knew the rules. For one like her—compliance was the game-changer—the winner. She stopped taking the contraceptives that had so fortuitously kept her free of pregnancy. Times had changed. She needed a pregnancy, a child. Without it she would lose her powers. Apparently, sex was not enough to keep Dmitri in line. What had worked so beautifully on her own behalf, held less charm for her mother's benefit.

Although she banned the pills, months passed—half a year even, and she still was not pregnant. She came to suspect that either one of them could have an infertility problem. Since she wanted to pacify her mother, who was hounding her to procure a visa and airplane tickets enabling her to come at least for a long visit, she decided to take action.

"Demi, I feel I must see a doctor and find out about the baby thing. Please make appointment for me," she said, her head bowed a little, in pretty show of sorrow. Strangely enough, she could always use the hated pet name—and he liked it.

"Oh, Precious, I am so happy that you want to do something about this! It has been bothering me for a long time, but I wanted you to make the decision."

They hugged and cuddled for a while and harmony was restored. That night he took her out to her favorite restaurant, Pierre's. It was the most elegant and probably the most expensive restaurant in Isla Morada. Situated on the beach, the huge white and blue trimmed colonial was distinguished by a wide wraparound veranda, upon which deep wicker seats with chintz covered cushions beckoned the patron to rest. Inside, interesting artifacts and beautiful furnishings, together with candlelight illumination, provided a civilized, old-fashioned atmosphere.

Of course, one could enjoy one's meal outside on this veranda under the stars, overlooking the bay. There, everything was so much more romantic and the food and drinks assumed deeper tastes and flavors. Needless to say, PJ loved the place. She would primp for over an hour to appear her best for the occasion. Dmitri was always very proud to take her there, never mind the smug looks and smiles from the young muscle packets who were there with their golden-tanned girls. The evening was a great success and ended with greatly enhanced lovemaking.

The Quest Begins

❦

"WHERE ARE YOU OFF to so early in the morning?" called Martha to PJ as the latter was about to fold herself into the Yellow Bird. Martha had come out of her home on her way to the canal where she was to perform her morning ritual—feed the fish with yesterday's leftovers. At least those foods she did not care for.

"I am going to Miami to see the doctor," answered PJ.

"What for? Are you sick?"

"No, nothing of the sort?" smiled PJ.

"Well, that is good. I would not want you sick, my girl. But why Miami, don't you have a doctor here in Largo?"

"Yes, we do, but this is a special doctor. Make-a-baby doctor." PJ laughed broadly, for she knew of Martha's aversion seeing Dmitri as father. It was Martha who had talked with her about birth control and who had even gone with her to the pharmacy for the first time.

"So the old fool wants to see it through. But it has not been working properly, eh?"

"No, has not!" said PJ mischievously. She stepped closer to Martha and whispered, "I have only stopped the pills a few months ago. I must get pregnant to get Momma here."

"I see," mused Martha. "Well, if you must, you must. Good luck, girl." PJ was about to leave when Martha tugged on her arm and asked her sotto voce, "What if it is him?"

"Oh, then he must see doctor! It can go on forever," said PJ, while a hundred little devils pulled her cheeks into smiles.

Martha laughed out loud. "Oh, you clever minx, good luck to you!" The women parted amid convivial hilarity.

After an agonizing ten days for Dmitri, the tests came back: everything was fine! There was no reason why PJ could not get pregnant. The truth of these results hit Dmitri with the force of an upper cut. Could it be that he was the faulty link? Ye gods! That could not be. He a fertility failure? But what else could he think? It had been years since he married PJ and there had never been even the slightest hint of anything, never even a missed period.

He stewed for days. Then, he decided to confront the problem head on.

"It must be me," he said to PJ. "I will see if there is a chance that I am at fault here. We will find out once and for all."

"Oh, Demi, you are so good!" sighed PJ. "A lesser man would not say this." She hugged him gently, idolizing, while peering ecstatically into his eyes.

Once aroused, Dmitri took action. He made a few phone calls for referrals. The first call was to his doctor. Before giving him the asked for information, Dr. Mergentrau probed his mind.

"Are you quite sure, Dmitri, that you really want to take this step? Remember your age! You are going to be seventy soon. Why do you want to bring a child into the world?"

Mergentrau, tall and tanned with thinning dark-blond hair, was in his late fifties. He could assess and understand all aspects of Dmitri's dilemma. He himself had faced the same problem a few years ago when his wife had found out about his affair with the receptionist and left him. He married the receptionist—why not keep it in the office? And then, the woman twenty-five years his junior, had wanted children. He had been irate, distraught, frantic even because he had three children from his first marriage and was happy to have raised them. The idea of starting over did not appeal to him at all.

Nevertheless, he gave in to the nagging, the tears, the pouting, and sex withheld. The resulting little girl had kept him sleepless for months, because his new, modern wife insisted on shared baby duties. Although he loved his little daughter, who was four by now, he still remembered the first two years with a shudder. That's when he had acknowledged to himself for the first time that he was becoming an old man. Dmitri's voice pulled him back from his flashback and the horrible realization.

"I don't intend on dying tomorrow, doc! I can be a good father for many years. It was not so long ago that you told me I had the constitution of a bull, a man much younger than my chronological age."

"Yes, I remember saying that. However, you must remember that even with the most modern equipment we can never be totally sure what is going on in a person's body. Despite all evidence to the contrary, you could collapse tomorrow of heart failure."

"Okay! So you warned me. You did your duty. Now give me the number of a reliable fertility clinic."

"Well, I can't refuse you a name. Better I send you to a reliable doctor than seeing you end up with a quack."

Mergentrau pulled his prescription pad from a drawer of his overloaded desk. Pharmacy magazines, medical journals, an in-box filled with correspondence, and an array of pill containers and samples in small cartons occupied the top of his desk. He held the pad in his hand while scripting the referral, for there was no room on the desk.

"You should clean your desk, Doc," remarked Dmitri, who was a stickler for order and cleanliness.

"No time, too busy. Not only is there a practice, a wife, and an ex-family competing for my attention, but no —I had to have a little one. I tell you old friend, she can make me feel very old in just one hour. You should think this over."

"You forget, I am retired—no office time for me. And PJ is young. She can chase the baby."

"Don't bet on that! You will find out that reality changes the dreams we have considerably."

Ten days later Dmitri and PJ traversed the Everglades once more on their way to the fertility expert. The doctor's office was located on the outskirts of Coral Gables in an area newly rehabilitated.

"High rent area. The guy will charge a mint," grumbled Dmitri under his breath when they reached their destination.

"What did you say, Demi?" asked PJ.

"Nothing, nothing, Precious."

Their arrival in an elegantly furnished cream and white waiting room, in which a large rubber plant, languishing in a corner, provided contrast, was duly noted by a mode, blond creature seated behind a curved desk. She asked them politely to have a seat. They folded themselves into the comfortable cream leather chairs. Dmitri studied the smart paintings set in gold frames and knew they were expensive. Having annoyed himself with this observation, he turned his attention toward the other "Patients."

Including him, seven men of assorted ages waited their turn for diagnosis or treatment. According to their temperament, they amused themselves with their electronic toys, read magazines, or nervously twisted their hands into pretzels.

Dmitri paid extra attention to two older men, who could have been anywhere from fifty to seventy years in age. As he compared himself to either one of the two he came away feeling superior. One was thin, and, although slightly tanned, looked sickly. The other one was overweight, balding, with a nose glowing like the Christmas reindeer's. It suddenly dawned on him that he was the only one in the office who had brought his wife.

Damn! It looks like I brought her to hold my hand, instead of the outing we have planned afterwards, he mused.

"Darling, this might take a while. Why don't you go shopping until we can go to lunch." He made this remark loud enough for everyone to hear, as if he needed to explain himself to the assembled.

"Thanks, Demi. I have seen some nice shops when we drove here. I will come back in an hour or so," whispered PJ and departed.

After what seemed to be an eternity, he was finally called in to see the great man. The doctor was a handsome man who resembled John Edwards to a great degree. As Dr. Momson greeted Dmitri, he displayed almost the same easy-oily mannerisms as the politician. *More money!* thought Dmitri.

Dr. Momson informed Dmitri about the procedures, tests and possibilities. Thereafter he placed him into the care of a white-clad young nurse, who looked like an advertisement for teeth whitening. Her blond hair cascaded past her shoulders in waves and her golden tan made one dream of Miami Beach, bikinis, and coconut oil. The beach-girl presented Dmitri with the previously discussed specimen cup and directed him discretely to a comfortable small room. There, with the help of spicy magazines and interesting DVD's, he was to perform the required service.

When he finally produced the needed sample and left the odious office, he felt somehow defiled.

"What an awful place!" He groaned. "I felt like a prostitute in there. Performance at command—disgusting," he complained to PJ when they were back in the car.

"Well, Demi, now you know how the working girls feel, and you only had to satisfy a doctor." He sent a nasty look in her direction and spied out of the corner of his eyes a pile of shopping bags in the back seat.

"What on earth did you buy in such a short amount of time?" he asked, naked suspicion tingeing every one of his syllables.

"Not much really. There was not much time. These are only a few necessities. Things I cannot find in the Keys."

Dmitri decided that this was not the right moment to quibble over anything. The farther the car carried him from the unpleasant office the better he felt. He suddenly noted that he could breathe normal again. The terrible strain of performing for a laboratory fell away, leaving him relieved.

He had taken a northern course toward Little Havana, where he soon found the exquisite little restaurant that they both liked. "Buenas tardes!" intoned Dmitri the moment they walked through the door. The tall Cuban waiter standing by the bar was familiar with their faces and rushed toward them with outstretched hands.

"Buenas tardes, sen`or Pataklos, y sen`ora! Como esta usted?"

"Muy bien, gracias, y usted?"

"Muy bien, muy bien, gracias."

Formalities taken care of, the waiter, whom they knew only as Carmelito, led them to their favorite table. They were lucky to have arrived late, for this table by a large sliding door, which was always open with a splendid view of the garden, was much sought after and not often available.

They ordered their favorite dish, Cuban Paella. It took only a few moments and a good glass of red wine to re-establish Dmitri's psychic equilibrium. When the Paella was delivered to their table it was perfect as always, and after another "copa vino tinto" Dmitri thought that this had turned into a perfect day, after all.

A Disconcerting Result

❧❧

WHEN DMITRI SAW Dr. Momson the next time it was to discuss the results of the fateful sample.

"Sit down, sit down Mr. Pataklos," invited Momson, "while I have a look at your file with the results of the tests." Momson fiddled with the pages of the file for a moment, found the right page and sank into intent perusal. A moment later his head popped up and he gazed with concern at Dmitri. Somehow Dmitri had the feeling that the other men had heard precisely the same thing he was about to hear.

"Well, dear fellow, it says here that you are lucky. You have lots of healthy sperm." Momson paused and Dmitri braced himself against what surely was to follow. In that he was not disappointed.

"Yes, lots of sperm, however very little total motility."

"What does that mean—total motility?"

"It means that few of your little fellows display any type of movement."

"Is that a bad thing?"

"Sure is! If they don't move they cannot swim upward to the egg they are to fertilize."

The doctor paused in his explanation. Dmitri's crestfallen face moved even the doctor, who had told this tale many times.

"Now, now, Mr. Pataklos. This is not the end of the affair. Let me explain." Momson perched his behind on the end of his handsome, very organized desk.

"Motility is the ability of sperm to move properly in the direction of the egg and, by reaching it, to fertilize it. This is the main factor in impregnation. The amount of sperm is not that important for that to occur. Sperm must penetrate the zona pellucida, a membrane surrounding the egg. A forward directed strong swimming sperm can penetrate successfully, whereas damaged sperm cannot.

We classify sperm by their actions and differentiate them into three categories. There are non-motile sperm; they do not move at all. You have some of those. Then there are non-progressively motile sperm. They show movement, but often abnormal movement, like swimming in circles instead of the straight path they should take." Momson noticed that Dmitri's face showed a pained expression. His hands combed distractedly through his immaculately cut mane.

"So what you are telling me is that I am an old, infertile husk of a man? Is there nothing that can be done about this? Do you have any pills that make them swim?"

"Well, there are a few things we can do about your condition. For example, if all else fails, we can take samples of your best sperm and technologically intervene in the process."

"Are you hinting at artificial insemination like they do with horses and cattle?"

"Yes, that sums it up correctly."

"God, what a miserable thought. Poor PJ!"

"Oh, you might be surprised. Most women wishing for a baby are not half as squeamish as their husbands."

"So what else do you have in your bag of tricks? Anything else we could do before becoming technological?"

"Yes, there is. We will try some hormonal treatments first and see what we get."

The doctor had become quite serious now. He left his perch on the desk and began pacing about the large room, displaying long legs encased within tan, silk and cotton pants. Dmitri looked with envy at Momson's Italian-made tan and black loafers, which oozed elegance and comfort.

"You see Mr. Pataklos, we men never pay the mysteries of reproduction much of a mind. Most men think that having sex takes care of procreation. They are sadly mistaken.

The production of sperm is a very complicated process involving the pituitary and other glands, as well as a complicated array of hormonal and chemical reactions." Momson faced Dmitri and continued.

"Years ago when I first studied the subject, I was amazed how any human would ever get conceived, for so many critical minute things had to be just right for a baby to be created. The sheer intricacies of reproduction can turn you into a believer of a higher power, if you are not already a believer. At the very least, it certainly makes you marvel at the wonder of a living healthy child."

Momson held up his finger as a schoolteacher would, "So I want you to think very hard about your wish to become a father once more. For as we age, the eggs and the sperm have many more chances to be damaged. If you still wish to pursue fatherhood in a week, I will try my best to help you get a healthy child."

"You were in there a long time," remarked PJ gently when Dmitri picked her up from her favorite store.

"Yes, it was quite remarkable. The doctor became all caught up in his work and talked about the wonders of conceiving children and what miracles they are. He got all soft and mushy in there. I hadn't thought he would be the type."

"But can he help you? Can he make it so we can have a baby?"

"I think so. Not much wrong with my sperm anyway. He can probably cure it with a few pills."

PJ said nothing more about the matter and changed the subject to dinner. Dmitri was much more comfortable discussing food, and they drove to the restaurant chatting companionably.

The Helper

❧❧

DR. MOMSON TREATED DMITRI with hormones. He advised him on an appropriate diet and told him not to stress himself too much.

"Get help with some of the difficult chores so everything works smoothly," he admonished.

Taking his advice, Dmitri looked for a handyman to help with the tougher work around the house and on the boats. There was the raking of the coral when it turned gray, the painting of the woodshed that constantly suffered from the assault of mildew, mold and salt deposits, and the clipping of the huge dry palm fronds.

He placed an ad in the nickel ads, which brought him three candidates. Dmitri knew the Key's characters well. Steeped in this knowledge, he knew by his appearance that the first one was a lazy boozehound who would only work until he had enough drinking money. Moreover, he probably would do a poor job at whatever he attempted. The second candidate was a serious elderly man who impressed him with his diverse abilities and seemed capable enough, but he was seeking permanent employment. He needed at least one full day per week. However, that was something Dmitri could not guarantee. The last man on the list was a tall, lanky Swede, who was spending a year in the US studying marine biology. He needed work to help with tuition while also getting to know the country and its people.

Sven Halvorson faced the world with an open, friendly face. A band of freckles spread across his medium sized, well-formed nose. He had deep blue eyes and short-clipped reddish-blond hair.

Since Sven was clean cut, well-spoken, flexible in the hours he could work and not too expensive, Dmitri decided to give him a try. He set him right away to the raking of the coral, which was a hard chore in the hot, humid air. By afternoon he was gratified that the job was finished and perfectly done. Dmitri was delighted. Now there was more time for him to spend with PJ.

Speaking of PJ, the gentle soul felt sorry for the handsome young worker and kindly served him tall glasses of ice-cold lemonade. When lunchtime came round, she brought him a huge sandwich laden with three kinds of meat, Gouda cheese, lettuce, and tomato slices. She could count herself lucky that Dmitri did not spy this work of culinary art, for he would have been furious—it was better than his own sandwich. But he never knew. He only saw the empty plate being returned to the kitchen, and got an innocuous explanation from his wife.

Soon Sven was irreplaceable in the Pataklos household. He fixed a shelf that had wobbled for a many months, turned their king size mattress when deep valleys developed, and even managed to help Dmitri fix the motor on his boat.

Sven didn't say much but was still personable and friendly. He set to his tasks, did not dabble, and always cleaned up his work's resulting messes. Dmitri, who at first watched the Swede like a hawk to see if he would make eyes at his wife, began to implicitly trust him. The young man never glanced at PJ a moment longer than appropriate. At least outwardly, he showed no interest in the pretty Thai woman.

In the beginning Martha and Jan, worldly wise and skeptical, talked about Sven as a possible snake in the grass. What would be more normal than for two young, beautiful people to fall for each other?

"He is as gorgeous in a blond way as she is in her dark-haired beauty," said Jan. She looked dreamily into the gently streaming water of the canal and, sighing romantically, she added, "When I watch them standing together they are like the sun and the moon."

"How poetic!" smiled Martha, "If Dmitri would hear you, he would dismiss Sven instantly."

Both ladies sat in cushioned wicker chairs under a palm tree close to Jan's dock. The small marble table before them held their lunch, elegant little sandwiches, a mixed salad and a pitcher of margaritas. From this pleasant place a perfect view of most of the canal was to be had and the women made the most of it. Boats came in, floating to their mooring after a morning run of fishing, while other boats, laden with small parties, set off for lunch at waterside restaurants. There were a few of those restaurants in the Keys, sporting docks for boating customers. They served fresh seafood fare, burgers, and buckets of French fries, and were enormously popular.

From their superior location, the women also possessed an advantageous view over most of Dmitri's property—house, yard and dock. Only a small portion of the front yard, blocked by the house, was obscured from their prying eyes. Half hidden under the long palm fronds, they could see everything, but they could be discerned only with difficulty. Today, as so many times before, they were not disappointed.

Promptly, as before, five minutes to twelve, the back door to Dmitri's house opened and PJ stepped into the open. She carried a large tray with three plates of food, glasses, and a pitcher of liquid.

"Lemonade," Martha hazarded, "Dmitri's favorite drink in summer."

"No," corrected Jan, who had better eyesight. "He is having beer today. I see the bottle. Not that he would give any to the Swede in the middle of the day. The guy might loose his zeal and only poke around for the afternoon."

PJ let out a loud, high yell. "Demi, Demi, lunch! Ven! Ven! Lunch!" She could never pronounce the "Sv" in Sven's name and her Ven sounded incredibly sweet and seductive. Both men arrived from different directions and joined Precious Jewel at the table in the screened-in porch overlooking the water.

Jan laughed sardonically. "There they are again, having lunch together as if they are family. Doesn't Dmitri get the drift?"

"Perhaps we are too cynical, Jan. Maybe the whole thing is totally innocent and will not develop into anything. Demi is not a total idiot. He has eyes to see and a nose to smell things."

"Well, we can hope for the best," said Jan, unconvinced.

The Assimilation of Sven

෨∽෧

A FEW WEEKS AFTER their intimate lunch, the women had their chance to form a better opinion. Dmitri decided that the time was perfect for a barbeque. He invited all the neighbors to his place for the event. As custom required, everyone showed up promptly at five in the afternoon, bearing hors d'oeuvres and bottles of spirits. The attire, of course, was Keys Casual—T-shirts or blouses and Hawaiian shirts, all worn over shorts, completed by sandals. One very well-built lady arrived in a sea-green sexy mini-dress that barely covered the essentials. Shell necklaces were draped over her very open décolleté and her hair sported a large red Hibiscus bloom. To PJ's amazement the risqué lady was received with pleasurable laughter and friendly banter.

"She is harmless!" explained Jan when she noticed the young woman's puzzlement.

"I thought she is lady of the night!" PJ laughed out loud.

"No, she just dresses like a tart. If one of the men would take her up on the open invitation she would probably faint."

Everyone in the assembled group had a tan. But some of the older guests, who had been burned by the sun repeatedly, had skin resembling a well-tanned hide.

Two large round tables had been placed in shady spots with waterway views. Service was casual. A square serving table held disposable plates, tumblers and cutlery, as well as the drinks that were also served from there.

Dmitri, covered by a large denim apron, embroidered with large letters spelling "Gourmet Chef," tended to his old venerated charcoal grill. He then joined the party to get a drink and introduce everyone. Few introductions were needed because most people knew each other already, but when Sven arrived, bearing a bottle of Scotch, introductions were in order.

The guests cordially greeted the young Swede with more or less veiled interest. Martha and Jan, under the guise of motherly interest, took him under their wings. They supplied him with a drink and filled his plate with hors d'oeuvres, while shooting all kinds of questions at him. For a moment PJ moved around like a shadow, organizing things. She was utterly lost in the overwhelming exuberance of the Americans. Feeling uncomfortable, she shot a few helpless glances at her husband. Her looks signaled that she wished to be rescued and be made part of the crowd, but Dmitri was busy and never noticed.

But Sven noticed. When he could do so unobtrusively, he looked at her encouragingly. He was almost wholly occupied to satisfy the wishes of the two older women flanking him. God, they were merciless! Like the Inquisition, they interrogated him about his family, his city in Sweden, his schools—everything.

"How many brothers and sisters do you have, my dear," Jan wanted to know.

"Two sisters, two brothers. The boys are older than the girls. I am in the middle."

"Does your mother work?" He had already noticed that having a job was very important to American ladies.

"Yes, my mother is a cardiac nurse in a large hospital."

"Oh, how wonderful!" shouted both his nemesis.

"Why did you want to come to America?" asked Martha.

"I got an opportunity to study Marine Biology at the University of Miami—scholarship deal. Of course I accepted." Anticipating the next question, he volunteered, "My father is a professor of medieval history. In Sweden professors are not paid as well as here. So, there was never enough money to send all children through college. We were always looking for scholarships. My oldest brother got one, playing tennis. He found out that playing professional tennis provides him a better life than he could have made for his family as a historian. So, his being seeded 28th at the tennis rankings is history's loss."

Jan, who played tennis often at a club six miles south, was intrigued. "Do you play?" she asked.

"Of course! In my family we all played tennis, played piano, and sailed on Sundays."

"Oh, that is wonderful!" warbled Jan. "Perhaps you would not mind being my doubles partner in an upcoming tournament?"

"Not at all. I am a bit rusty. But if you want to have me, I will make time in the late afternoon and evenings to play."

Jan was overjoyed. What luck! She had been thinking of canceling her spot in the tournament after her partner, a local dentist, injured his knee.

Barely had Sven arranged a tennis date for next evening, when Martha endearingly asked him if he had more time available to help with projects other than Dmitri's.

"Of course, I have more time. Mr. Pataklos only requires me for half a day or, at most, one day a week. I would be delighted to help you. How would Mondays work out for you? I will finish all your projects and then I will only work as needed."

"What do you charge Dmitri? You know I am on a fixed income," inquired Martha with a slight whine in her voice. Her husband had left her well off. She did not swim in money, neither did she have to worry, but her natural inclination was always to pinch the penny. Sven heard the penurious wheedle in her speech but was not affected in the least. He had learned long ago that if he did not stick to a fixed hourly wage, people tried to take advantage.

"I have to get fifteen dollars an hour or it is not worth my time, because I can get other jobs closer to my apartment that pay ten dollars with time to study." Martha struck her sails.

"Okay, okay," she said hastily, because she realized that at fifteen dollars per hour he was still a bargain.

By the time Dmitri served the enormous rib roast, Sven's life had been arranged for the following two months. All of the dates brought him into the immediate vicinity of PJ's home. *Not bad for a pleasant evening's doings,* he thought.

Meanwhile, the object of his interest brought a large platter of Thai rice to the serving table. It was an offering that she followed up with a platter of beautifully displayed grilled vegetables. Everyone fell to the magnificent spread and returned to the tables with heaping platters. A feast in the Keys turns often into a meat orgy; because seafood could be had daily and was sort of a staple. On the other hand, meat had to be trucked in freezer containers and was, accordingly, much more expensive.

Everyone commented on the fact that PJ's rice was a wonderful accompaniment to the prime rib, instead of being a too-soft distraction.

"I think she put lemongrass in there," hazarded Jan.

"I think you are right. I detect also a dash of coconut milk and, of course, cilantro."

"Yes, it is great. I must have the recipe!" agreed Martha.

Both women did the food the honor it deserved. Somehow in the casual search for a seat, Sven managed to be seated beside PJ. He talked animatedly with Jan's husband Brent, who sat to his right, about boats, sailing and fishing, when he accidentally stepped on PJ's sandaled foot. She did not let on. For some unexplained reason he did not apologize; instead, he slipped his own loafer off and gently placed his naked foot on hers. PJ's expression never changed as she kept calmly talking to the woman in the small sea-green dress.

The night was dark, but starry. Although lanterns and smudge pots had been lit, only the faces of the guests were clearly visible. Soon, under the cover of the tablecloth, male calf joined female calf, and for a stolen few moments, hand joined hand. Dmitri suddenly called for his wife to help him serve coffee and dessert. His tone brooked no dawdling. PJ jumped up and in charming confusion called out, "I seem to have lost my sandal under the table." Sven bent and retrieved the missing item. No one was the wiser.

Later, many drinks later, a few brave souls began to sing and soon everyone joined in. All in all it turned out to be a fabulous party.

The Shining Knight

⁊⤳⤳

WHEN THE MUCH TALKED about tennis tournament was finally held, needless to say, Jan and Sven returned victorious. For days Jan could not help but warble about the neat way in which they had demolished their opposition. She gave a large party at her house in honor of her partner.

Sven gently tried to tone down her enthusiasm by pointing out that he had been the youngest man at the tournament. Most of the opposition had been in their fifties and older.

"Oh, pooh! I am of their age group and you had to cover my infirmities. Don't sell yourself short."

Sven just smiled nicely and let her gloat innocently. Somehow he had managed to sit beside PJ again. Although, by unspoken agreement, they neither looked at each other nor did they exchange more than a few polite words.

In the following weeks Sven became the neighborhood's savior. He mended fences, repaired boat engines, raked coral and mended fishing tackle. For his efforts he was monetarily well rewarded. But the extra perks were the best part of his employment. The ladies fed him the most delicious lunches he could remember since coming to Florida. He was invited to some the best parties in the Keys, played tennis with lovely people, and knew that he was adored from afar by the prettiest woman he had ever seen.

At first he had not been able to understand her marriage arrangement with old Dmitri. Later on he had been enlightened by his friends Martha and Jan, who told him an incredible tale. The worst of it was that the old fool wanted his inamorata to get pregnant. Why would such an old man want to father a child? Sven could not fathom Dmitri's mindset. Did he not care that he would leave the darling girl to raise an infant by herself if he were to succumb to a heart attack or a stroke?

At present, things stood not too badly. It seemed that the old man's plumbing did not work satisfactorily. P J seemed happily resigned to the fact that he was lacking potency.

"Seems his little guys do not swim," grinned Jan, discussing the situation.

"They seem to circle around and around instead of going where they were meant to go."

"Oh! Very unpleasant for the couple," said Sven feelingly. Secretly he hoped the old man's swimmers remained stationary or circling.

All Things Get Hotter

❦

THE END OF APRIL brought summer to the Keys. The temperature climbed into the nineties and the humidity rose accordingly. The weather, and his studies, forced Sven to change his work schedule. He dropped a few clients, keeping only the best of the bunch, and started work at six in the morning. By nine, when it became unpleasant to perform physical work, he was on his way to Miami or he worked from his apartment on Key Largo online with his professors. If he kept up the pace, he could finish his PHD in two more years; that is, if he did not break down or get sidetracked by a certain woman. However, he sensed it was too late for the latter—he was already hooked.

While Sven mapped out his academic carrier and his working schedule, Dmitri obsessed about the little swimmers. Once a week he showed up in Dr. Momson's office, gave a sample, and experienced the same horrible disappointment when his sperm still refused to become motile. Another treatment was discussed and implemented and he was sent home to wait another week or fourteen days for a change in his condition.

After the first few weeks PJ had insisted that she stay home.

"I am tired of shopping, Demi. The waiting room gets boring and I can do more things at home that should be done."

Reluctantly, he agreed. One day, when the humidity was especially oppressive, she asked his permission to use the Boston Whaler to go snorkeling with Martha. Martha, although up in age, could still hold her own when it came to swimming, snorkeling, fishing and working. Dmitri saw nothing that should prevent him from giving her permission to use the boat. She had learned over time how to handle different boats and was very proficient in the use of the Whaler. And if she should encounter trouble, Martha was great in an emergency.

"Sure, darling, go ahead and use the boat. Have a good time and stay cool out there."

PJ hugged him and murmured, "Demi, you are so good to me!" He smiled as he went on his long, boring way to Miami. Yes, he had to finally admit the truth to himself, for he had always loudly praised the beauty of the drive to Homestead. But at last he had to say it: the commute to the doctor had become atrociously boring.

He and PJ, although she was not always the ardent participant he wished for, were still trying hard to make a baby. Sometimes he thought her heart was not in the endeavor.

"Don't you want to have a child?" he asked her with bitter frustration.

"Of course I do! You deserve a child, husband, and I would like to give it you!"

"Well, if that is so, can't you show a little more enthusiasm? Remember all the nice things you used to do? Let's do some of those and maybe things would work." Then he remembered how all the intricate little bed games subsided when he did not allow her mother to come. But now she should have an incentive to be fervent. Should she not? Had he not granted her mother a visit for the birth of a baby? So what was holding her back? Temporarily, PJ's sexual involvement returned. Yet it ebbed fast after only a week had passed.

Once he had given PJ permission to use the boat, he could not rescind his word. She now used the Whaler freely whenever a whim struck her. She would hop into the boat and zip out into the bay where the water was shallow and fish for mangrove snappers close to a mangrove isle. She would anchor the little boat, allowing it to drift and jump over the side and swim for a while. Sometime she'd hang onto a line and let the boat pull her along in the slow current. Most times no one had a clue where she was and what she was up to.

"Don't go out by yourself," warned Dmitri time and again. "Although the bay is shallow, it holds dangers. You can get stuck in the mud-flats, the tide can strand you and one can get lost among the little isles and channels."

"Oh, come on, Demi! By now I know where to go and not go. The little boys in the neighborhood, twelve-year-olds, ten-year-olds even, go out there all the time in their boats."

"Yea, but have you noticed their fathers only let them go out there in pairs. And then, if you have not noticed there are sharks about. Big ones, too. I have seen fifteen footers in the bay. They come in with the tide. Did you know that the bay is one of the biggest shark nurseries? Many species go there to give birth."

He reminded her of an incident that had happened only half a year ago. Sven, the marine biology student had asked Dmitri if he would allow him to do an experiment from his dock.

"I want to see what kinds of large fish come into the canals at night," he explained.

"I would like to see what hunts here and in the bay. My hypothesis is that many large fish come from the Atlantic through Tavernier Creek and the boat channels to hunt in the canals and the bay. But what species do the hunters belong to?"

"Sure, please yourself. I will give you a hand with that. I am intrigued by the subject myself," Demi agreed.

Following that conversation, they met one evening on the dock. Dmitri provided tough, thick filament, rope, chains and hooks of different sizes. Sven came with a scientifically prepared bucket of bait. On top of the bucket rested a large sheep's head. The department head of the marine biology department had advised Sven on the suitability of bait for different fish. The bucket held chunks of meat and horse innards, also fish and fish heads. Apart from the content of the bucket, Dmitri brought live fish and shrimp.

Then they baited the hooks. The sheep's head was impaled on a huge hook, which in turn was attached to a strong three-foot chain that was lashed onto a thick rope. Positioning the bait in the middle of the canal at about fifteen feet of depth so a large grouper would not be tempted to take the morsel proved more of a problem than the rest of the entire enterprise. The sheep's head, weighted down even more by the chain, tried to sink straight to the bottom. As the two fiddled with the tack, they were hailed by Brent from the other side of the canal.

"What on earth are you trying to do Dmitri?" When the problem was explained to Brent, he came up with the perfect solution. They strung a heavy rope across the canal, fastened on both sides to large posts that were cemented into the ground. That accomplished, they floated to the middle of the canal with their baited line, shortened to fifteen feet, and tied it solidly to the guide rope.

Sven arrived at five the next morning. With coffee cups in hand, they walked to the canal and checked their lines. Already from afar they saw that the guideline was sagging ominously. They had obviously caught something large. A moment later a body floated up; it was visible for a moment before sinking back.

"Dear God, we have hooked a monster. The fish is enormous! Now how do we land him to measure and evaluate him?" Sven looked worried. Dmitri scratched his head in deep thought. Suddenly his face lit up, "We cannot do this alone. We need help. We will get Brent. I hope he is not working today. And I will call Joachim."

"Who is Joachim? The name sounds biblical."

"Oh, it is, the name is. The guy is a crazy German who lives close to the end of the canal. He came ten years ago for a visit to Florida, fell in love with the Keys, sold his house in Germany, cashed in his bank accounts and bought a house here."

"So why is he crazy? He sounds rather normal?"

"Believe me, he is either nuts or the most fearless man I have ever met. He thrives on danger!"

As they walked to the house to make their calls, Dmitri recalled a story everyone in Tavernier and Key Largo was familiar with.

"So imagine, crazy Joachim goes out a mile into the ocean with a group of divers. They anchored the boat. The divers attached themselves to floats and lines, so that they can be found if there is trouble. Then they dive. A good while later some guys run out of oxygen and come up. The dive master goes from float to float and signals everyone to come up. They all do. The master counts the floats and the people and there is one missing."

Dmitri stopped and slid open the glass door to his living room. The twosome entered and walked to the phone.

"I will tell you the rest of the story after calling," announced Dmitri and began dialing. Brent was at home. When told about the morning's surprise, he said he'd be right over. Joachim, or Achim, as they mostly called him, also promised to come right away. Dmitri had barely hung up the phone, when the shrill sound of a ship's siren pierced the air. After a startled jump, the duo ran to the dock and found a boat idling in the canal, blocked by their guideline.

The skipper, eager to get out to sea to fish, let go with a few more shrill blasts, and greeted Dmitri with a flood of unkind unprintable words.

"Damn you, Dmitri, what the hell have you dreamed up now to make my life miserable?" he yelled, furious and red in the face.

Dmitri kept his cool and explained exactly what was going on. He ended by promising: "…and until we have the damned fish out of the water you will be going nowhere!"

Ron, the skipper, was a reasonable man, although a bit rash.

"All right, we will help you make short work of it."

Ron had his son-in-law, Burt, an ex-football player, and his twenty-two-year-old son, Jason, with him in the boat. Both men were instantly keen on the idea of landing what was probably a shark or a monster fish. For fishermen, the shark never loses its mystique. They love encounters with the great hunters even when they steal their catch and ruin rods and tackle.

"You know, I think you guys showed up very providentially," mused Dmitri. "Do you think we could use your boat to winch up the shark? I think that's what it is."

"Sure, why not?" agreed Ron, who was immediately hooked on the venture. A shark, hopefully a large one—and right here in the canal—what luck! Brent and Joachim, who had also arrived, joined Ron and his crew on the boat. They all knew each other and could work in concert without uttering many words.

"Get your camera, Jason!" barked Ron at of the top of his lungs, while he, ever so gently, turned his boat around. His bow was now positioned to look at the end of the canal, while the stern firmly pointed at the guideline and its still-struggling object.

Ron's boat was a serious affair. It sported two fighting chairs for combat with marlins or large tuna. On its right rear a vicious steel beam rose into the sky, topped by block and tackle. It took no time at all to attach the catch rope to the block and tackle. As the winch began reeling in the rope, the fish began to fight. Although the monster had been struggling for quite some time against the hook and the horrid bait stuck inside his throat, he was not yet ready to give up the fight. If it had not been for the agonizing pain caused by the triple barbed hook, the great animal would have torn itself lose a along time ago. Yet no matter how valiantly the great hunter tried to pull free, at a certain point he always relaxed and gave up the struggle because he knew instinctively that to pull beyond a certain point would mean certain death.

So when the tugging on his head began, he threw his body about in protest, but moved forward with the pull nevertheless. Minutes later, engaging the engines, the monster of the canal was hoisted, foot by foot, into the warm air.

"Damn, it's a Tiger!" roared Dmitri. "Damn, it's a Tiger," roared Sven, deliriously happy. The more the skin of the fish was exposed to the air and the sun, the more his striping disappeared. At one point, Ron could not stand watching the agony of the animal any longer. He went below. Returning with a high caliber rifle, he put a bullet through the animal's head. The body of the fish slackened perceptibly. Higher and higher they lifted the fish. Soon it became apparent that their catch would be a record for canal catches. Never had a fish of such enormous proportions been caught in a canal before.

"Mother of God," roared Ron's son-in-law, "our women swim in this canal almost daily. A monster like this could have them for a snack."

"And he would, too. Tigers are notoriously aggressive!" Sven was almost delirious with joy. Combined with the other study objects he had caught, this was the crowning glory for his thesis. The others nodded their heads sagely. Even Achim, who came up against sharks all the time, was impressed.

"I am glad I never met him when he was alive. Hell, I dive for lobster all the time in this canal."

The consensus was that—oh, yes—by pure chance they had probably avoided a tragedy. Sven, who had previously recorded the data on every line, for strength of filament, bait and location they had chosen, now recorded the date of the monster they had caught.

"Jesus, the thing is almost sixteen feet tall!" he screamed into Dmitri's ear. He could not wait for the autopsy of the monster. When Ron shot the beast, he almost had conniptions, for he thought that the precious head would be destroyed. However Ron had placed the bullet with such precision that most of the head, the mouth and the great jaws were left intact.

When, at last, the shark hung as high as the steel post allowed, his size was so awesome that his tail remained submerged in the water. There was no way that Sven could deal with the fish on Dmitri's dock. Also, since this proved to be a record-setting catch for a canal, an enormous amount of publicity would be generated. The large hordes of reporters arriving could not be accommodated on Dmitri's narrow dock, never mind the public.

Frantic calls to different outfits resulted in a slow journey to a professional fishing and docking site, where Sven, with the help of many enthusiasts, could start his research. As the boat slowly left the canal, drifting into the main channel, Sven suddenly remembered the unfinished story of "Crazy Achim." Since the very man was at the stern, lashing the shark to the boat with Jason and Brent's help, Dmitri could speak freely.

"You must understand that I am not exaggerating a word of what I am about to say. By the way, where was I?"

"I think you left poor Achim in deep water in the Atlantic, his diving buoy almost certainly gone. By now the man must be drifting free."

"Yea, that's what the diving master thought too. He got all frantic. He himself went down—all the way to the bottom. They were at depth of about one hundred fifty. Couldn't find anything, of course. They called the Coast Guard, measured the direction and speed of the current, and hung about till dark in the hopes that he might still come up."

Dmitri's face had become unusually alive. He kept his eyes on Achim's powerful body as he tugged and pulled, securing the shark.

"Well, to make a long story short, the boat went back to shore as darkness set in. There was no reason to expose a group of tourists to an accident in the night. Everyone thought that Achim was a goner anyway. A lot can happen while diving in deep open water. A shark or other creature might have a go at you. Your air runs out and you cannot come up fast enough, or you get a cramp, a seizure or a heart attack. If you stray from your group or lose your buoy, you are all alone in an awful lot of water."

"So what happened then?" interrupted Sven, because Dmitri did not make the story any shorter.

"A couple of coast guard boats looked with powerful beams all night for him—nothing. And then, in the morning, the coast guard guys were already on their way home, a sharp-eyed lad saw a very strange crab pot in the water and insisted on taking a closer look.

Lo and behold, when they came close there was Achim clinging to the float. They plucked him off and brought him home. Can you guess what the strange son of a bitch said to them when they handed him a water bottle?"

"No, what?" Sven felt he needed to contribute.

"He said, 'Don't you have anything stronger? I have been in this stuff all night long!' They made damn sure that he drank the water anyway. We asked him next day what exactly had occurred, how he had saved himself." Dmitri swallowed some of the coffee they had forgotten to drink in all the excitement.

"It was pretty much the way everyone thought it happened. Apparently his buoy became detached and floated away. Achim came up and looked for the boat and there was—nothing. Water—as far as he cold see. It was late afternoon and that cool, old sea dog knew that on this day the tide was going toward the bay from early afternoon to later in the evening. He calculated that the tide would give him a good power-saving pull. If he did not panic and swam with the tide, saving his energy as much as possible, he should sooner or later be reaching land—some part of the Keys."

"How could he know what direction was land and that he was swimming in the right direction? The wind and the waves could have just as well taken him into the Atlantic. Couldn't they?"

"I agree that someone unfamiliar with the oceans, the tide tables and that certain feel of the water could very well have had a bad end. But Achim had been diving, swimming, fishing and boating the waters around the Keys for ten years and knew them well. But then, and I give him that, he is the coolest son of a gun I ever met. As you heard, he did reach land. He made it to the crab pots by nightfall. Then the tide started to go out and he was afraid he would be swept back. Also, it got dark, which is not a good time to be splashing in the water because all predators are out hunting. So he grabbed on to a crab pot and floated on his back much of the night."

"Did he tell of any frightening encounters that night?" asked

Sven with a deliciously morbid twang to his voice.

"He said there was something large nosing and probing him once or twice. He suspected bull sharks—notoriously dangerous. He had a spear with him in his diving belt. He said he pulled it and stabbed a few times in the direction of the nudge—that stopped it."

"I am no coward," ventured Sven, "but out in the water all by myself? I wonder if I could be that cool."

"You do what you have to!" said Dmitri with conviction. "You could survive."

Entertaining themselves in such fashion, they arrived at the large accommodating dock in the harbor and paid attention to their work.

Having recalled the incident once more for PJ, Dmitri said, "Have you already forgotten this affair? It happened right in front of our house, at our own dock."

Dmitri reminded PJ once more how dangerous an encounter with a tiger shark in the bay could be for her.

"But Demi, that was at night! I go during the day when I can see things and I do not swim that often."

"But still! I would rather that you take someone with you, anyone at all."

"Ok," said the ever-obliging PJ. The next time she went out boating during one of his trips to Miami she took Sven, who by now had passed his exams and had much more time.

The Baby

༒

BY MID-SUMMER DMITRI'S "little swimmers" still did not perform to norm. The doctor decided much more drastic measures were needed. He informed him that artificial insemination was the next step.

"You must go home and discuss this with your wife. She has to agree to the procedure, sign papers and releases. If she does not like the idea, you are up a creek. We cannot do anything without her consent."

"Oh, she will go along with it alright. She, too, wants a baby. Trust me, I will see to it." Dmitri was sure of his position.

"All right then, you give me a call and get everything set up. After that you bring your wife for the event."

Dmitri left Momson's office, feeling exceedingly uneasy about the whole affair. It all sounded so technical, cold and sterile—not at all like the natural process in bed. How would PJ feel about the whole thing? Oh, the heck with her feelings. He had been doing so much for that woman. Just the rescue from the hellhole of a village where she had lived should make her grateful enough to become the mother of his child.

When he came home he breached the matter very gently and persuasively. PJ listened attentively. When it came to the description of the artificial stuff though, he could feel her stiffen and a shadow flickered over her face. She did not meet his eyes, keeping her eyes directed toward the blooming hibiscus in front of the house.

At last, she said sadly, "I will do it Demi." She walked out of the house down the paved path to the dock where she sat deeply in thought, dangling her naked feet in the water. A while later he joined her.

"What is it PJ? Don't you want to have the baby?" he asked.

"I do," she replied simply, "But I must think. Please give me a little time."

A week later Dmitri made the appointment, or tried to.

"You waited a little too long, Mr. Pataklos," informed the office help, Maria Josepha.

"Dr. Momson will be gone for two weeks to a conference in Switzerland. He will be giving a hallmark speech on his specialty." Maria's voice reverberated with pride.

"So, when will he be back then?" Dmitri wanted to know.

"First week of September. All else is filled before he leaves. I have September ninth at eight o'clock open. Do you want that date?"

Dmitri almost groaned, "Yes, yes! We will take it. You are sure there is nothing earlier? This is almost four weeks in the future."

"Yes it is. I am so sorry, Mr. Pataklos. But we will do our best." They left it at that. When he told PJ about the late date, he seemed to detect distinct relief in the way the air left her lungs. A few days after he received notice of the remote date for the insemination, Pataklos received a call from his banker.

"Been spending a lot lately, have you?" asked Burt Peterson from Bank of America.

"What do you mean? My expenses are the same as always. I have not changed anything!" objected Dmitri.

"Well, my records show that you have spent $10,000 this period and we are only five days into the new month," explained Peterson calmly. When Dmitri heard the amount of the transactions he jumped straight out of his chair.

"You are kidding, buddy. What's it for?"

"You made one transfer to Thailand in the amount of three thousand dollars, and purchased airplane tickets for another seven."

"I will be damned! I did not! I assure you. I've got to talk to my wife. Perhaps she can clear this up."

"Well, good luck old buddy! See you at the fishing contest."

"Yeah, see you there," mumbled Dmitri disturbed. The moment he was off the phone he roared with the strength of a lion.

"PJ, PJ! Where are you? Come here now! This moment!"

"Yes, what is problem?"

She stood before him sweetly smiling, her cheeks mild and pure as freshly fallen snow.

"You know damn well what is! The bank just called me and reported that you bought airplane tickets for seven thousand dollars and sent your mother another three thousand!" bellowed Dmitri.

Not for a moment did PJ deny this accusation. Looking him calmly in the eye she said, "You said that when baby comes I can have the family here for visit. So I arranged it!"

Dmitri screamed. His face was red as if he were about to have a stroke.

"Are you insane? You are neither pregnant nor about to give birth. That's when they were to come, anyway—not now!"

"But I will be having a baby soon, you made the arrangement for the insemination. So it will be. Why not have them come now?"

"No way!" yelled Dmitri, shaking with anger.

"Until there is a living baby they are not setting foot into my house. Now give me back those tickets and the money transfer slip. You know damn well that I sent the old witch her quarterly allowance already."

Precious Jewel, for the first time in their marriage stood defiantly before him and looked very unfriendly. Her lips were clenched; her eyes shot daggers at the floor. Her skin had blotched as if she had the hives; her brow was wrinkled and her fists were clenched. Dmitri did not know the woman standing before him. Anger made her hideous in his eyes. She reminded him of the most fearsome shrews he had ever known. She lifted her eyes to him in defiance and said, "No! They come!"

"They do not come!" His reply came with the same deep raw anger in which her defiant words had been spoken. He left the room in a furious rush for his office, where he instantly called Burt Peterson.

"Put a stop on both transactions. I will talk to the airline and explain. Just make sure the old hag does not get the three thousand."

"Will do! I did not allow any transfer to be made without your approval. What the hell got into PJ? Isn't she the most docile, lovely creature ever?"

"For some time now she's got it into her head that her mother and two younger brothers should live with us. Live in the milk and honey USA where everyone is rich and never has to work."

"If she has gone so far behind your back, you better contact our authorities. Notify them that you deny all responsibility for the family's upkeep. You know, of course, that as a citizen she can ask to be reunited with her family."

"Shit!! I am going to check it out. Thanks, Burt, you are a pal! I owe you one."

Next Dmitri called the visa office. Sure enough PJ had filed papers for her family to come to the USA. Dmitri explained the situation. He made it very clear that the Thai woman had neither an income of her own, nor did she have a job. Her family would be going on welfare, for he did not intend to provide for them. The agent agreed with him and everything was put on hold—into the proverbial drawer.

The moment PJ discovered that all her plans had been foiled, her demeanor changed once again. After immersing the household in dead silence for two days, she dropped her defiance and emerged from the bedroom the third morning mild mannered and sweet as before. She used, however, every opportunity to go out by herself. She went shopping in the little yellow bird—all the way to Marathon or Key West—and was often gone all morning or afternoon.

Dmitri tried to prevent her trips by taking the keys for the car and for the Boston Whaler away from her. However, she must have had double and triple keys made up, which she had hidden all over the property, for she escaped him every time she made up her mind to leave. He outright forbade her from leaving the house without his permission or presence, to which she answered in honeyed tones,

"If I am doing wrong then you must call the sheriff and have me arrested. But I believe, as a citizen I am free. You cannot lock me up."

Dmitri was so disturbed by her behavior that he resorted to what for him amounted to an appeal to the highest authority: he consulted with Jan and Martha. Under their sharp eyes and precise, prying questions he told them everything; even the most embarrassing thing, the insemination thing. What a blow to his ego! The women thought the idea was preposterous.

"How would you like it if the doctor would shove an instrument up your belly and inseminate you with someone's egg so you could incubate it for nine months?" they asked rudely.

"Would you go along with all the things you asked your wife to go along with?"

He had no answers to their questions. His defense lay contained in the thesis that she wanted to come to the US to become a wife, a mother, and a citizen, all according to a previously arranged contract. In order for her to come to this great country and become a citizen, financial and diplomatic arrangements had been freely agreed to by both parties.

"She was an independent agent in the agreement," he said.

"I never withheld anything from her. She knew I wanted children! She had the option of staying in Thailand if she did not like the terms."

Dmitri was angry now. He looked at the women and pounced.

"You speak with the tongues of feeling and mush! This contract between us was a business contract! I never said I love you—until much later. And our government looked at the transaction the same way. If she did not like me in three years' time, she could have chosen to not become a citizen and had the right to go back to the poor, backward third world nation and live there according to her own high standard!

"Hell, I have bled money to make things nice and special for her. Paid for her English lessons, got her teeth fixed—they had cavities in the back—bought her clothes, the god-darned first pair of shoes she ever owned, bought her a car, let her have the boat, taught her cooking and a few other things she needed to know to live in this country, and now she goes behind my back and steals money for her family; a family, which I am supposed to totally support and feed? You call that gratitude and good behavior? I have a good mind to send the little bitch back to Thailand and be done with it!"

Dmitri was so angry he pounced up and down Jan's wooden balcony; the floorboards groaned and threatened to snap under his weight.

"Oh, of course, from your vantage point you are quite right. But try to look at it from her point of view."

The women believed that PJ was acting out. Too many things were happening to her, done to her without her express consent. The secret affair about her mother and the visas was probably just her reasserting herself.

"She never had a voice in any part of her life—never—all of her life," said Jan. It was obvious with whom she identified and sided. In the end—of course, neither party was right. They could not see into the mind of a cultural entity that was totally different from their own cultural mindset.

Precious Jewel looked at the world from a view much more practical, less philosophical than her American counterparts. She was not burdened with any of their honor concepts, their moral and ethical concerns. In her universe, one took care of one's own no matter what. She felt that she paid with her body for anything she had received. Love was a practical matter—the stronger one won the contest. So, for the moment, she was in the weaker position. Without rancor, she reassessed her position and decided what she had to do was to stay in a position of power. The concepts of love, fealty and faithfulness were not concepts to be applied to marriage.

All of those pretty constructs diminished one's power and were notions to be contemplated outside marriage. PJ had known many a girl who had fallen violently in love with a callow youth. They lost their virginity, sometimes got pregnant—and then they sat with their babes, beggar poor by the wayside collecting alms. Or they ended up in the brothels of Bangkok, doing drugs and foreigners. No, she wanted no part of that. If she was being paid for sexual services, the money might as well be good and plenty. She parceled out love when she felt like it—to men she wanted to love.

Readjustment of Power

సౌ౼ఌ

AFTER RETHINKING HER OPTIONS, she quite suddenly stopped the "abnormal" behaviors as if nothing had happened. Once more she appeared to be the compliant, pleasant wife. Dmitri tried to make up to her. He promised that her mother could visit as soon as PJ was pregnant. As to her brothers, they might be able to come for a short visit—say three weeks—when the baby was born.

"That is reasonable," she agreed, as if this arrangement had been all she had ever asked for.

Suddenly time ran fast like a runner on a track. Within a week of the Momson appointment, PJ prepared a grand dinner one night. She served it amid a wonderful setting, with candles, wine served in fancy goblets, a shining white table cloth and soft music in the background.

"Boy, oh boy, this is nice, my girl!" exclaimed Dmitri when she led him to the prepared room.

"What is the special occasion?" he wanted to know.

"Sit down and enjoy. In time I will make an announcement that you will like. But until I am ready, you must be patient."

With that she left the perfumed room for the kitchen and returned with a Thai seafood curry, steaming with fragrant herbs, lemon grass and lime. She departed, only to return with rice, a vegetable dish and condiments. What a meal! Dmitri thought he had gone to heaven and there his angelic, obedient wife had been returned to him. He leaned back in his chair and sipped the oaky Chardonnay she had poured with the meal and thought that life was good again. He would win again! He would have the wife and the child he wanted and a life arranged to his liking, just as he had planned it.

For dessert PJ had concocted a mango rice pudding that sang. Dmitri sat, enjoying the smoke of a Havana, which Achim had smuggled into the country a year ago. At precisely this moment PJ said, "Here is my surprise for you, dear husband. I have not bled at my monthly time. That has never happened and so I think that I am pregnant."

"What are you saying, my dear, dear girl? Can it be possible? Could we become parents?" Dmitri jumped off his chair and gathered her in his arms. He lifted her off the floor and shouted like a fool. PJ was sure the whole neighborhood would hear him.

"I am going to be a father again. Lord, oh, Lord, a child to love— a child to teach!" Dmitri went slightly crazy with unexpected joy. For a moment PJ felt almost bad. He was so much in love with the idea of fatherhood that he drew her, too, into the whirlpool of joy. Henceforth, joy and light reigned in Dmitri's house. Ten days later, the tests at PJ's gynecologist confirmed the pregnancy. The official pronouncement led Dmitri to inform the neighbors, his estranged, grown-up first family—the world.

To the great consternation of Dr. Momson, the insemination appointment was of course cancelled.

"How the hell did he get his wife pregnant?" Momson asked his nurse. "His little swimmers still do not have motility."

"Beats me!" smiled Maria Josepha wonderingly.

"Do you think the old fool had a little help?"

"From all I have seen in this office, I would say all things are possible! I have seen that God has a sense of humor and kindness and sometimes he arranges for things—but more often than not, I have seen outside help at work."

"I almost feel duty bound to tell the stupid man to have a little test taken, just to be sure!"

"Unethical! Not our business! God and the couple must sort it out!" Maria Josepha said wisely.

And, therefore, the pregnancy continued, uninhibited by ethical concerns. PJ grew a slight belly. Her appetites changed. She suddenly took a liking to fried foods, pickled herring and oranges. Of the latter she consumed several every day. It was left to Dmitri to peel them because she could not be bothered anymore with mundane chores that frustrated her.

Dmitri, in a frenzy of expectation bought a crib, a changing table, and wanted to "do" the room. However, one could not "do" a room in the wrong colors and décor if the sex of the baby was uncertain. Dmitri waited and fretted. The moment PJ's gynecologist, a small brown woman from Ecuador, said an ultrasound would be a good thing Dmitri made the appointment.

All the while PJ showed little interest in the fuss he made over the baby or her own condition. Dmitri remarked that her disinterest was unusual. Was she not the least bit intrigued by the mystery taking place in her body?

"No, not really!" she said. "It is just nature doing her thing. I have seen hundreds of women pregnant and they all dropped their babies without trouble. Most of them did it in the rice fields, got up and cut rice stalks half an hour later."

"Yes, but it is a wonder, a miracle that you are privileged to perform."

"Yes, of course," she concurred sluggishly and walked away.

The special day came and the ultrasound was performed in the facility of Magdalena Porfirio, the doctor PJ had chosen for her prenatal, birth, and aftercare. Dmitri did not think highly of the woman. She was much too tiny and unimpressive, he thought, to perform such strenuous a service as lifting a child from a womb. PJ, however, liked her and did not think of switching. Magdalena always greeted her with an outpouring of warmth. She enfolded her in an embrace and called her "My Precious."

Dmitri almost fainted with emotion when he saw the small body of the new child on the ultrasound screen. PJ looked almost bored.

"Here look," the doctor said, waving her small hand over certain parts. "This is the liiittle nose. Here is an arm with a small hand; here is the small body…oh, and look, here is—it is a liiitle girl!"

By now even PJ had become involved in the discovery. Good, happy emotions spread through the otherwise sterile room.

"How marvelous!" exclaimed Dmitri.

"What a great invention! When I had my first set of children there was nothing like this. We had no clue what we were getting until the babies were born. Now I can paint the room. We can buy small dresses and girl things!"

Dmitri was beside himself with pleasure and perhaps, or so the doctor thought, a touch of early dementia. Be that as it may, the small family went home wreathed in bliss. Henceforth, Dmitri treated PJ, whom he had always handled with certain adoration, like she was a precious Meissen Porcelain Figurine.

Meanwhile, Dr. Momson simmered in a hell of his own making. Tortured by his conscience beyond the bounds of the endurable, he confided to Maria Josepha:

"It is not right that I allow the old fool to have a cuckoo grow up in his nest. The man has grown children who should be the recipients of his legacy, not this woman and the child she conceived to rip the old man off."

"Oh, oh, oh!" groaned his faithful helper. "I think you should close your eyes and ears and let nature take its course. The demented fool did not listen when you told him not to go there. Instead of taking your words to heart, he pushed and pushed until she decided natural insemination was more to her liking than what you had to offer."

"Yes, yes, you are right! But still, when I come down to the right and the wrong of the thing my blood boils. I put myself into the old man's shoes and the whole thing stinks."

"Well, if you are so chagrinned by the preposterous affair go ahead. By all means, tell him the truth. By now we know that even with artificial insemination his chances of fathering a child would have been miniscule."

And so, within the hour, Dmitri received a call from Dr. Momson to please come to the office—urgently.

"Come into my laboratory," invited Momson when the puzzled Dmitri arrived at his office. Momson's laboratory was a large, well-lit room, its walls studded with marble tables, microscopes, and centrifuges; little color-coded plastic stands that held slender phials of different lumens. On the walls were charts of reproductive organs; they were displayed along many cupboards. Three plastic roller-swivel chairs stood before three workstations.

"So, what is all this about? Is my wife not really pregnant? I must inform you that she is—I saw the damned ultrasound for God's sake!" intoned Dmitri aggressively.

"Sure, sure she is pregnant alright. That is why I want to show you something. I feel it is my duty to make you aware of anything that is of importance to you as my patient."

Dmitri's back bent slightly, as if he felt the heavy impact of Momson's words. Momson had decided to let him down as easy as he could. With that in mind, he invited him to roll his chair over to the enormous electron microscope on a special, broad workstation that took up the middle of one counter. He, too, rolled his chair over to the microscope. With a pipette he dropped a minute amount of a liquid onto a glass object carrier. He placed the slide under the microscope and looked through the ocular. He adjusted the vision field by fiddling with different round controls and then, having reached proper visibility, invited Dmitri to put his eye to the ocular of the microscope.

"What do you see in there, Dmitri?" Momson asked kindly.

"A bunch of sperm, much like those you showed me before."

"Right! That is exactly what they are. Now what do you notice about these particular sperm?"

"They do not move much. Some are bunched up." Dmitri hesitated. "Some zigzag rather listlessly."

"Right again. Dmitri those are your sperm. The only way your wife could have gotten pregnant from one of those fellows would have been with a lot of help or a miracle. I assume no miracle has happened in your house?"

"What are you saying, Doc? Are you implying I cannot be the father of the child my wife is carrying?

"That is exactly what I am saying, Mr. Pataklos. Please think for a moment. You tried for four years to have a child before you came to me seeking help. Why would a miracle suddenly have occurred when we are dealing with defective sperm? A miracle that did not happen before?"

Dmitri's shoulder had slumped even more than before. His face was a grim mask of doubt, suspicion and fear. True to his being, he came out swinging defensively.

"What business is it of yours to meddle in my affairs? Did it bother you that we got it done without your professional interference? Are you lacking in business that you must drum it up this way."

Momson buried his handsome head between his hands in obvious despair. When he looked up, straight into Dmitri's eyes, he said, "Do not make me regret that I called you, Dmitri! Maria Josepha warned me it would turn out this way, and yet, stupidly I had to follow my honorable impulses and call you." He breathed hard.

"Do you know why I called you? Do you really want to know? It was less for you and your sake. But I thought about the children and grandchildren you already have. They are your legitimate offspring and deserve to inherit your legacy. Better they benefit than the child of some adventurer who got your wife pregnant."

Momsen paused, controlling his breathing and then continued calmly, reasonably.

"If I were you, I would at least do a paternity test and find out reality. Then you can address the matter, informed and logically."

Momson rose to his feet indicating that the visit was over. Dmitri got to his feet, slowly, almost painfully. He crept toward the door rather than walked.

"Think about what has transpired here, and then make a decision. Good day, Mr. Pataklos."

The Worm of Uncertainty Gnaws on the Mind

৵৽

ON THE INTERMINABLY LONG way home, Dmitri's mind was assailed by hundreds of pictures and thoughts—many of them featuring Sven. It was entirely possible that he had put excessive trust in PJ. Perhaps his own wishes had addled his brain and kept him from thinking straight. Had he just made assumptions about her thoughts and feelings—about her as a person? When it came to PJ, he saw himself as the knight in shining armor; the hero who had saved her from poverty, mediocrity and boredom—the one bestowing citizenship of the greatest, most sought-after country in the world upon her. Had she learned nothing, understood nothing? Where was her concept of faithfulness, of gratitude? Did she even have such a concept?

It became appallingly clear to him all of a sudden that he had never talked with his wife about the constructs and certainties in his own mind. He had selfishly and ignorantly refused to inform himself about her culture, her belief system. He had just assumed that she would come to love him—good man that he was, or thought himself to be.

Oh, what pain to be born, to see himself as cuckolded fool—unloved and disrespected. Damn her! He had been an officer commanding men on a ship—in war. How could she have done this to him? He stopped himself short: how could he have come so quickly to a judgment of her guilt? He had not even asked her, yet he was thinking of her infidelity as certainty. In the deepest recesses of his being his mind must have gathered small bits, evidence of wrong-doing. Now they came to the fore, weaving a quilt of guilt with more guilt.

And what about Sven Halvorson? He had carefully watched the young man before allowing him access to his house. He had never seen him behave even slightly improperly or show any interest in his wife. He had, however, often felt jealous pangs when he had seen him standing close to PJ. Jealousy, which he had pushed away as feelings unworthy of his manhood. And yet, oh, agony, they had looked so perfect standing beside each other. The blond, blue-eyed, well-built young man, and his wife—the perfect foil for him, in her slender, peachy, dark-haired way. He groaned and smashed his fist into the dashboard, busting his knuckles open so that they bled.

He pulled a white, freshly laundered handkerchief from his pocket and wrapped it around his hand. It comforted him, in a strange way, to see the blood seeping through the white cloth; as if the blood restored his manhood; as if he had just cracked Sven's jaw open. God, yes, he would like to do that. The thought of violence and revenge had barely entered his conscience, when other horrible bits of memory floated up and registered.

There had been, of course, the episode with the Haitian young man, who had kidnapped her. At that time, he implicitly believed her when she told him that she was innocent of the affair. Nothing to prove otherwise could ever be found against her. He had even believed her when she resisted divulging the man's name; believed that she was just protecting a young, impetuous fool who had done nothing wrong with the exception of a two-day abduction. Now, he looked at the incident in a different light. Perhaps, even then, she had been a willing accomplice to the scheme.

His whole world had been turned upside down in Momson's office. Nothing was real, solid, or worth believing in anymore. Oh, hell and agony. What a thing to put him through! He did not, no, did not deserve such betrayal. This was treason—of the highest order! She should be shot, the damn traitress. Too bad she was not in Saudi Arabia—they would show her how one dealt with treachery, adultery.

Time flew as he drove, seemingly on automatic pilot. He was pulled from his unhealthy contemplations when forced to brake sharply at the first of Key Largo's traffic lights. What was he going to say to her—his wife? Was she going to deny it, necessitating a paternity inquiry? Oh damn! He did not wish his present situation on a dog.

Tragedy

❧✦❧

HE ARRIVED HOME WHEN the sun was low on the horizon of the bay. He had no idea why he should notice such things, that, or the purple coloring at the edge of his vision.

Although the air was balmy and beautiful as always in the Keys, he felt hot, as in a fry kitchen or standing before his barbeque grill. The house looked deserted and he stormed inside. He crossed the living room, entering the bedroom. The air in the bedroom was heavy, moist, and strongly scented. The bathroom door opened and PJ stepped into the bedroom. She had washed her hair. A fluffy, peach-colored towel was wrapped around her head. The same sort of towel covered her body.

She took one look at his angry, distorted face and raised her hands as if to ward off a blow. The towel floated to the ground, leaving her naked, exposed, vulnerable. In another life she would have been terribly appealing to him. In the life he was living now, her protruding belly disgusted him. "Cover yourself!" he growled. Shaking like a leaf, she bent and pulled the towel about her body. The action allowed her to find her voice. With an effort requiring enormous courage, she forced herself to utter, "Demi, what's wrong? You are so different, so angry."

"Sit!" he commanded. A command barked as at a dog. She sat on the edge of the bed.

"So, whose kid is in your belly?" he hurled at her.

"I know it is not mine. I spent a very interesting afternoon with Doctor Momson. I am quite clear now that I cannot be the father of this."

He pointed with ill-concealed fury at her bulging abdomen.

"But you are the Papa!" PJ whined, somewhat unconvincingly.

"Do me a favor, you slut. Do not add lies to deceit and betrayal. Who is the father? Sven? You might as well come clean, because I will find out one way or another!"

A long moment of silence brought him to a new boil. He clenched his fists, and as she still looked at the floor, seemingly thinking of a way out of her predicament, he lost control. In three large steps he was before her. Ripping the towel from her head and flinging it into the middle of the room, he grabbed her long, wet hair and pulled her upright. Staring menacingly into her face, he repeated, "Who is the father? Out with it?"

By now PJ was crying. More from hurt than from contriteness, he thought. That thought made him pull even harder. He began to shake her head back and fro until she burst out:

"Sven. It is Sven's baby!"

Dmitri pushed her away. She fell onto the bed, curling herself into a defensive position. The very act repulsed Dmitri.

"Slut! I trusted you, wanted the best for you!" He left the room for his office. Suddenly he felt very old, defeated, unlovable.

In his office he sank into his padded, comfortable CEO's chair. For a moment he was shaking with rage, frustration and weakness. He collected himself and called his lawyer's home number. At least he could trust the men of his acquaintanceship. Irving Morgenthaler was the most honest, most trusted lawyer in the Keys. Once a week, Dmitri played golf with him, another lawyer, and a dentist. It was an event that always left all of them feeling good about the world. Now he felt better hearing the warm, reassuring voice of his friend.

"What's up Dmitri? Must be important; you never call in the evening."

"Irving, I need to change my will. I have to cut P J out. The kid…" Morgenthaler heard a horrible sound at the other end of the line. It was an awful, deep, groaning noise, followed by torturous breathing and the crashing of the phone onto a hard surface. That was the last sound Irving heard, and he became terribly concerned. He tried a few times to rouse his friend by calling, "Dmitri, Dmitri!" But it was to no avail.

Dmitri's words came to his mind: "I need to change the will! I have to cut PJ out. The kid…" Had his friend discovered what others had hinted? They speculated that the child PJ carried might not be his. And had that sudden knowledge caused him to have a stroke or a massive coronary. Irving knew he had to find out. Immediately!

During the next few minutes he kept calling Dmitri's number in the hope that PJ had found him. Every time a busy tone announced the phone was still off its cradle. When he could not raise PJ, he called 911 and told the dispatcher to send an ambulance to Dmitri's house.

"Tell the guys the man is in his office. The wife probably does not even know that he has had a stroke. And hurry, this is my friend."

Little did he know that PJ knew very well what had transpired. She had silently followed Dmitri to his office and listened through the partially shut door. She had listened to the interrupted phone call and heard the cessation of Dmitri's functions.

Carefully, scared to death, PJ entered the study. She saw Dmitri slumped over in his tall chair. His head was tilted to the left side, hanging over the angled shoulder. His left arm dangled so far down that his fingers touched the floor, seeming to support his body. His eyes were open, unfocused, and crazy-wild. Bloody spittle oozed from his slack mouth.

She stared at her husband for a while, transfixed with horror. Finally the idea to rouse him, or to get help, entered her mind. However, she was terrified and confused. Therefore, she stood inertly, staring at the body. Never in her entire life had she encountered such a horrific situation.

I need to get help! she thought. But the next moment, looking down, she realized that she was naked. Panicked, she ran into the bedroom to dress.

When the ambulance arrived, PJ came to the door wearing her favorite apricot colored silk robe. Her hair flowed around her head in pretty disarray and she was becomingly pale and distraught. She showed the men into the study. She was shaking, concerned and frightened. It was obvious to the young men that she was pregnant. Although they rushed into the house laden with equipment, looking for the patient, they felt immediate concern for her.

"Save him; please do something!" she cried, obviously distressed. She thought it was quite natural for the ambulance to have arrived. She never gave it a thought. Never doubting for a moment it could have been otherwise, or that she should have initiated the call for help. She walked to Dmitri, laying her hand on his right shoulder, which was pointing at the ceiling, as if the pressure of her hand could straighten him.

The medical technicians gently moved her out of the way. They placed the lifeless man on the floor. One of them took his pulse.

"I cannot feel a pulse!" he cried. A moment later another young husky operator said, "Hey! There is no discernible blood pressure."

The ambulance crew worked on Dmitri in a desperate, concerted effort. They used different equipment and methods available to them. For a long time they tried to resuscitate what they secretly knew to be a dead man. At last they gave up.

The leader of the ambulance crew walked up to PJ, who had watched the proceedings, tearfully, wringing her hands. The tanned, dark-haired young man looked grim as he put his arm around PJ's shoulders.

"Mrs. Pataklos, I am very, very sorry, but your husband died. We could not resuscitate him. He probably died from a severe hemorrhagic embolism and was probably dead before we arrived."

PJ shook uncontrollably. She turned and buried her head in the man's broad chest. He stroked her back, murmuring how sorry he was.

"Can we call someone to be with you for the night? Do you have a friend you can spend the night with?" he asked.

"You should not be alone."

PJ collected herself and let go of the young technician. With the sleeve of her silk morning gown she wiped the tears off her face.

"You will take my husband away?" she asked.

"No, that we cannot do that. We will call the police they will arrange for the coroner to view the body in your home, or tell us to take him to a hospital."

Surrounded by his sad-faced crew, he said, "We are so very, very sorry. Let us give you something to calm your nerves. Can we make calls for you? Anything we can do to help?"

"No, thank you, I do not need medication," sighed PJ with sudden understanding. It dawned on her with ugly certainty that the protection she had enjoyed through Dmitri was lost to her forever. Henceforth, she would have to live by her wits and the good will of others. She roused herself and asked with a breaking voice, "Would you please call my neighbor, Martha? She is a widow and will come. She will know what I must do."

The ambulance crew was very concerned for the young widow. They thought of their wives and girl friends and wished to alleviate some of the shock she had received. One of them called Martha on his cell phone.

"I will be right over," was her reply, whereupon she called Jan.

"I will come over later with Brent. We will bring food!" she said, ever the practical wife.

Two ambulance technicians held PJ's arms as they led her into the living room. There they tried to place her in the most comfortable easy chair they could find.

"No, no," she cried to their astonishment. "This is Demi's chair!" Easing herself from their hold, she walked to the large rattan couch and eased herself into the soft, colorful chintz cushions.

One of the young fellows put a pressure cuff on her arm and took her pulse.

"Not too bad," he announced, easing some of their concern. Martha arrived then. She had already been briefed by the group's leader, outside in the dark yard, before he had allowed her to enter. Seeing PJ on the couch, she went straight for her, enfolding her in her motherly arms, hugging her tight. After sharing a very emotional moment, she sat down beside PJ, and asked the young men in attendance, "What can I do right now to be of help?"

The dark-haired, handsome crew-leader entered the room at that moment and heard Martha's question.

"Give me a moment to get my guys collecting our gear. Then we will listen to the heartbeat of the baby and check Mom out, too."

Death's Aftermath

୶୶

BEFORE THE AMBULANCE CREW LEFT, they placed Dmitri respectfully upon a bed in the guest bedroom, covering him with a sheet. When they were alone, Martha led PJ into the kitchen. She put the almost-lifeless form of the young woman in one of the padded chairs in the breakfast nook, and went to the large stove.

"We better have some tea," she suggested.

"That would be nice," PJ answered automatically. Martha, attired in a soft pair of plum-colored sweats, measured efficiently three teaspoons of PJ's favorite Thai tea into a small porcelain pot. She had rinsed the pot beforehand with hot water to "excite it."

"One for the pot—two for the people," she murmured, as PJ had taught her. She filled the pot with hot water, covered it with a quilted cozy, and allowed it to steep. In the meantime, while she waited for the tea to flavor the water, she pulled cups, saucers, a sugar and a honey pot from a cupboard over the back window. By the time she was ready to pour and serve the tea, she searched for and found a bottle of Dmitri's best Scotch and poured a good inch of it into each cup.

For a moment, the women sipped their tea in silence. PJ finished her cup and asked if there was more. Martha fixed her another cup, laced with Scotch just as strongly as the first.

Poor thing, she thought, *what a thing to have to endure.* She sat across from PJ, looking at her as her hands cradled the teacup on the small marble table top.

"So, my dear, tell me how it happened."

Precious Jewel brushed the hair away from her face and sat up straighter. She breathed deeply and began hesitantly.

"Demi had an appointment in Miami in the afternoon." She sighed and Martha thought she might begin to cry. But she contained herself and began to speak once more.

"When he came into the house he was very angry. He came in the bedroom and shouted for me. I had just taken a shower and rushed to him from the bathroom."

She stopped and shook, reliving the scene of the afternoon.

"I have never seen him so furious—so livid. His face was red, his lips were blue and his eyes were black with fury."

"What happened to him in Miami?" interrupted Martha, who knew that Dmitri was a most reasonable man. He was almost always calm, slow to rise to anger. She surmised for that reason that something monumental must have happened for him to fall into such an enormous tizzy. PJ hesitated for a moment. There was no way to tell the truth and still keep the friendship of Dmitri's friends and neighbors.

Prevarication, if ever so slight, might serve her. So she said, "I do not know whom he saw in Miami, but that person told him terrible things about me. Things not true!"

She put strong emphasis on the latter sentence.

"After shouting at me and calling me bad names, he rushed into his study. A moment later I heard a horrible crash and a strange noise. I rushed into the study and there he was. The phone had crashed into the desk's glass cover, alarming me. Demi was slumped to the side in his chair; he looked awful and made gurgling noises."

PJ drank more of her tea and thought about the sequence of events.

"I think I noticed then that I was naked and rushed to put something on."

"Why did you not call 911?"

"Oh, I was going to, but I needed clothes. Good thing, too, because the ambulance was here a moment later."

She again went in her mind over the events and said distractedly,

"Demi had stopped making that gurgling noise. Could it be that he was already dead then?"

"Oh, dear!" sighed Martha. "You should have called the ambulance immediately. Perhaps they could have saved him if they'd come earlier."

"It only took a moment to put on the robe—and then they were here!" wailed PJ, her eyes wide with horror and guilt.

"Someone must have called 911, or why would they have come?" wondered Martha. "Who could have known that you needed help?"

Just then Jan and Brent walked into the kitchen. Jan carried a yellow straw hamper. Brent lugged a large cooler before him, which he hurriedly deposited on the kitchen counter.

"Oh, honey, we are so sorry!" cried Jan as she rushed to PJ, enfolding her in her arms.

"How did this terrible thing happen?" she wanted to know.

"Yes," Brent joined in, "what happened to Dmitri? He was such a hale and hearty fellow!"

"I will explain all in a minute," said Martha. "But right now I am trying to solve a mystery. Did you guys call the ambulance to Dmitri's house?"

"No, why would we?"

"We had no clue what was going on here," confirmed Jan.

"Well, someone did, and it wasn't PJ. She was naked when it happened and instead of calling for the ambulance, she thought it necessary to put on clothes." Martha rolled her eyes toward heaven for the benefit of Jan and Brent.

"So who called 911?" wondered Brent.

"Where was Dmitri when it happened?"

"In his study. At least that's what PJ said," volunteered Martha.

"Give me a moment," mumbled Brent thoughtfully. He left the kitchen and disappeared in the study. The phone rang and was answered in the study. The women silently listened to the murmur of voices. Brent returned after a while. He looked sad and worn.

"Okay! The mystery is solved. I put the phone back in its holder and it rang instantly. It was Dmitri's lawyer. Apparently Dmitri was on the phone with him when he had a stroke or a heart attack. Irving Morgenthaler heard it all. He tried to call PJ, to no avail. When he got no response, he assumed that confusion reigned in the house and called 911."

Brent opened the cooler and removed a glass and a pitcher of drinks. He poured himself a large drink of a deep yellow liquid and parked himself on one of the small kitchen chairs. He drank deeply, wiped his mouth with his forearm and, sighing deeply, said almost groaning, "I had to tell Irving that Dmitri is dead. He suspected as much. He said he could hear a terrible moaning for a while and then it stopped. He said the silence was more dreadful than the moan."

Brent put his head between his hands, elbows on the kitchen counter. He sat there, slumped over, his broad shoulders bent as if in defeat. It looked to his wife as if Dmitri's death had only just now become a reality to him.

"Demi was the best buddy a man could ever have. What am I going to do without him?" he groaned.

"Fishing is never going to be same again."

"It finally sank in. He had to hear it from another man," whispered Jan to Martha. PJ sat stone-faced, empty-eyed in her chair, as if she were not present.

"I gave her two stiff drinks," remarked Martha, motioning in her direction.

"I think she is done for the day. That would be too much for anyone to bear and she is pregnant on top of it."

"I think you're right. Let's put her to bed," suggested Jan.

PJ came alive with a start. "No, no!" she wailed. "I cannot sleep in the house with Dmitri dead close by!"

"You shall not!" said Martha. "Come Jan, we will take her to my house. She can stay there until after the burial."

The Funeral

☙❦☙

MARTHA WAS AS GOOD as her word. She kept PJ with her for the next few days. It was Martha who notified Dmitri's children and grandchildren. PJ had no connection to Dmitri's other family. Dmitri's four sons, large, fine-looking men came as soon as they could. His daughter refused to be in the presence of the Thai woman.

"He abandoned us for her!" she had hurled at her brothers.

Two of the sons were put up in Dmitri's house; two were taken in by Jan and Brent. The oldest of the four, Dorian, forty-eight years old and gray at the temples, with high forehead and stern demeanor, took charge of all the necessary arrangements. He contacted the funeral home, the coroner, and Dmitri's attorney, Morgenthaler.

"After the funeral I need to have a talk with you!" said Morgenthaler with emphasis. "Do not forget! It is important."

Although Dmitri had not been in a church for almost forty years, Dorian sought out a Greek Orthodox priest for the last rites and a proper service. The sons arranged for a large dinner at Pierre's following the funeral. Between the four of them—they were very close, for their mother had kept a tight family—they saw to everything that needed to be done.

They were kind, but distant in their treatment of P J. Her distended belly was obviously an annoying distraction. All four of them were considerably older than their father's new wife. Some of their own children were of her age. Dmitri's grandchildren came later with their mother's for the funeral and so did his friends from all ends of the US. In the end, the funeral was a grand affair—Dmitri had many friends. Off to the side, far removed from the family, stood Sven whose eyes were fastened on the slender, black, veiled figure by the casket.

Dissolution

༄ৎ

AND THEN IT WAS OVER! All the visitors left for their homes all over the country, and PJ moved back into the house that was now her own. Dorian had an interesting meeting with Irving Morgenthaler after which, he, too, left for home.

For the first few days PJ walked through the house almost afraid to touch anything. After the first hours alone she could not bear the lonely feeling. She went out, driving her yellow car. No one knew where she had gone.

During the second night alone in the house she got out of bed, dressed and drove away. She came back fairly soon. Martha, keeping an eye on PJ because she worried about the effects of Dmitri's death on the baby, saw her return and park unusually close to the rear entrance. So close in fact, that the rear of the car was visible from her window. No one had real privacy in the development. The properties were closely linked, and if nosy ones wished, they could spy on the comings and goings of their neighbors. PJ's bedroom lights went out soon after her return.

"Good," thought Martha, the gentle soul, "she must have gone for sleeping pills."

When Martha, the early riser, looked out the window next morning, the rear of the yellow car was not visible anymore. For a moment Martha was puzzled by this development. But minding her own business she put the thoughts from her mind.

Soon PJ developed regular habits. Everyone in the development was pleased that she was doing well. Ten days after the funeral, on a Saturday, Sven's small beat-up Toyota truck drove in to PJ's driveway. Sven parked under a palm tree and jumped from the cab in his usual exuberant fashion. He picked a rake and a shovel off the carport wall and, as he had done many times before, began to rake the coral rock.

Two hours later, also as before, PJ appeared from the house with a pitcher of iced lemonade and joined him for a short cool drink. Lying in a hammock under the palms, Jan watched the interaction of the two young people and saw nothing peculiar in the way they behaved. Following this, the first official work appearance, many more followed. Not much more time elapsed, and Sven came to pick PJ up to go grocery shopping. As she was very pregnant, no one gave a thought to propriety. Instead everyone found it very natural that someone should help her with heavy tasks. Sven began to stay sometimes for dinner or for drinks when the neighbors congregated—it was all as it had been before.

The Summons

ॐॐ

PJ AWAKENED TO THE ringing of the doorbell. It was a Monday morning in late October and the cooler night temperatures facilitated deeper sleep. PJ looked at the clock at her nightstand and was jolted fully awake. Good gracious! It was already nine o'clock. The doorbell rang impatiently again and again while she slipped into a robe and slippers. She quickly moved to the door. Without first checking the visitor through the little round spyglass, she opened the door and stood before a uniformed, large man who handed her a summons.

"Precious Jewel Pataklos, you have been served papers to appear before Judge Alex Hemming on the thirtieth of October at ten o'clock in the morning." He read from a paper.

"But, but…" stuttered PJ, "why? Why am I to see a judge? What have I done?"

"I cannot tell you why. I am just here to serve you these papers." Saying this, the man turned on his heels and walked to his car.

In the living room PJ, deeply troubled, sank into her favorite chair. She began to peruse the pages before her. But her mind had not cleared from deep sleep and she was confused by what she read: a hearing to clear up paternity issues; claims on the estate! On and on the writ went talking about Dmitri's estate. Other claims on the inheritance? Had she not inherited everything Dmitri left? She was the wife. Who was doubting paternity?

No one knew that she had seen Sven on the side. She had always been so careful when she had met him. No one had known about their affair. For heavens sake, they had not even so much as looked at each other in the company of the others—not beyond what was natural and fitting. Dmitri never had a doubt.

Almost crying with frustration and daunting fear, she slunk into the kitchen. She had to make coffee—she needed to think clearly. As the coffee was brewing in the shiny, silver Krupps coffee maker, she knew that she must seek help. Now, as soon as possible. Frantically she pulled the phone from the charger and dialed Sven's number. Fortunately, he had left her bed at five in the morning or the server might have encountered him at the door. The neighbors had stopped paying attention to her private life. No one was going to hold it against her if she sought solace and companionship in her difficult situation.

Dmitri, although beloved, was dead. He had put her into this sorry state despite the warnings from his friends and neighbors. So, why should they now act prudishly? With his own actions he had precipitated the scenes now played out in his house. Some even went so far as to say, it would be blessing if Sven were to marry PJ. He could be a good father to the innocent babe. With the exception of two seasoned ladies, none of the neighbors suspected or speculated that the babe might be Sven's. Everyone thought that Dmitri had always had a firm hand on his wife.

"Haldorson!" PJ sighed with relief when she heard Sven's voice.

"Darling, we have problem! A man came this morning. Give me paper to go to court. Paternity things. Estate things." Whenever PJ got frazzled she still made hash out of her sentences.

"Whoa, slow down, PJ! What is going on?"

"Can come over here? Have a look at the papers yourself. I not know what they mean. Paternity question—someone doubts that the baby is Dmitri's. Who would think that? We have been so careful."

PJ sobbed with anger that someone could have found out about their affair.

"It really is not so far fetched, PJ. He was an older man and people are always suspicious." He laughed aloud.

"Especially when the woman in question is as young and as pretty as you are."

"Do not laugh!" spit his irate inamorata. "I don't need hilarity! I need help. So, can you come over?"

For a moment there was silence on the other end. Then, when doubts about his sincerity rose in her mind, Sven spoke.

"I will make it by lunch time. I have to finish a test in the laboratory and sign out. As soon as this is done I will start driving."

PJ knew it would take Sven over an hour to drive to her house and she resigned herself to a frustrating wait.

When Sven finally arrived, he found a distraught, highly agitated woman pacing the living room floor. When she saw him, she ran to him and encircled him with her arms. He felt the child in her belly pressed against himself and was flooded with ambivalence. Was this really his child? Or did the old man still have some viable sperm circulating at the right time? He stroked PJ's back and murmured some nonsense, remembering that such behavior always calmed his much younger sister at home in Sweden.

His kindness worked. Once PJ calmed down, she became quite rational and business-like. She took his hand and pulled him to the couch, where she sat beside him. For a moment she looked adoringly into his tanned, narrow face, fastening her eyes on his—so deep blue, so true. The moment passed and she reached for the sheets of paper, resting in front of her on the glass-covered coffee table.

Sven began to read the summons. Although he, too, was a foreigner, his English was much superior to PJ's. Everyone in his area spoke English as a second language from the time they were toddlers. He understood very well what the summons entailed.

"We have a problem," he said, assuming responsibility for his part in her dilemma.

"Dmitri's family has challenged your right to the inheritance on the grounds that the child you carry cannot be Dmitri's. They cite proof. And because there is doubt as to the paternity, it follows that you have no right to claim the estate for the child. Also, there seems to be reason to believe that Dmitri was about to change his will and cut you out."

PJ heard the explanation stone-faced. Then she objected violently.

"They have no proof that this is not Dmitri's child. I will defy them. I need the money for us, for my Momma and the boys. He is dead! He needs nothing! And his kids—they are all rich as he is. They need nothing."

Sven felt suddenly very cold. It was as if he did not know the woman beside him. She had always been so warm, so sweet and tender. He had never seen PJ's new face. He shook himself as if he could rid himself of the unpleasant feeling.

"PJ, if this is our child then you have no claim to his estate, except what the court will provide for you as the wife of five years. You see, Dmitri's first family has a much larger claim. There are grandchildren—they deserve, at least, some of their grandfather's money."

"Still, I will say that it is Dmitri's child."

"Darling, you can say whatever you want. But the court will order a paternity test if the family has strong evidence against you."

"Can they do that? Can they test me, test the baby?"

"Yes, love, they can! It looks like they have begun with the proceedings. The summons is to determine all that in court."

"What are we going to do, Sven? What can we do? This is terrible, terrible."

PJ wailed. She was wringing her hands. Her hair dripped wildly around her face. Her generous mouth was distorted, then it clenched into thin lines surrounding a narrow slit. Sven was deeply affected by the unflattering change of his beloved. He came from a kind, well-to-do family in Malmö and had been raised with a strict, ethical Lutheran code.

He realized too late and regretted now, that in his relationship with PJ he had already broken many a taboo. He had felt like a heel when he began the dalliance with PJ, for he had truly liked old Dmitri. It bothered him enormously that he impregnated the man's wife. A sin he tried to ameliorate in his thoughts, by rationalizing that he had provided the child the old fellow so desperately wanted. Now this moralistic house of cards came crashing down around him. He felt worse as time went on. However, what was he to do? He would be ten times the heel if he were to shed his responsibility to PJ, leaving her to pay the price.

He shook himself free of the depressing thoughts and tried instead to focus on a solution.

"You need to hire a lawyer and explain the whole thing to him. He, at least, will look out for you and get you the best deal."

The word "lawyer" revived PJ.

"You are right; that is what we must do."

Sven noticed with a sour taste in his mouth that he was to be a part of this. He decided to call his father as soon as he left here. He, too, was in great need of advice. Dmitri's death had ended his free, simple existence and made him into a family man, complete with future wife and child. Suddenly he felt very depressed. As soon as he could decently extricate himself from PJ's embraces he left, staring glumly into the golden, perfect day.

Family Convocation

Sven's family, to a person, insisted that he stay with the mother of his child.

"If the kid turns out to be the old man's you are free, but if it is yours you are honor-bound to stick it out," pontificated his father.

"Is she pretty that Thai woman?"

"Oh, yes, very. You would like her looks very much," sighed Sven.

"You can always come home and bring her and the baby. Your mother would love that. She feels that you have stayed away too long already. She wants grandchildren. So you see nothing is lost."

Despite these encouraging, definitely hopeful words, Sven did not feel good at all anymore. He knew that he wanted the old P J to return. He did not like the new one.

Seeking further enlightenment, Sven talked with his adviser, Peter Botkin at Miami University. He explained that he needed a sharp lawyer for a friend.

"What kind of trouble is he in," asked professor Botkin, a mild-mannered biology expert.

"It is a she and she is in a paternity and inheritance dispute."

"I do not mean to pry, but are you somehow involved with the lady?"

"Unfortunately I am and I feel responsible for some of her grief."

"In that case, since you are part of our team, I would suggest that you go and see Aaron Marcus. He will give you a great defense that is financially affordable for you."

Sven's adviser wrote the name and phone number on a yellow pad, sending the young man, who had become his favorite student, to meet with Aaron Marcus. Sven had already crossed the threshold when Peter Botkin worriedly called after him, "Let me know how things come out! I will help if I can!"

"Thanks, prof.! I will tell you how things develop."

Aaron Marcus was a pleasant but pudgy man in his forties. A receding hairline let his forehead appear more pronounced than it must have been in his youth, giving him an exceedingly intelligent look. He had bright, water-clear eyes, which despite little coloring had a penetrating quality. His office, with the exception of a large desk and captain's chair, was furnished with plain standard furniture. The wall cabinets were of a modest wooden grade, and hard plastic holders and trays separated a profusion of folders and papers.

Sven, leading a suddenly very timid PJ into the office, noticed that Marcus was a kind man. He stood when they entered and came forward to greet them. He shook PJ's hand and exclaimed jovially,

"Good afternoon, Mrs. Pataklos. No need to be shy! We shall sort out your problems in no time."

That's when Sven noticed on the desk a large photograph of a pretty dark-blond woman and four children. *Ouch, A great family man. What will he think of our sordid story? Will that prejudice the man against us?*

He looked about for a moment and reassured himself with a silent observation.

"Money is money and the five in Marcus's care must eat!"

At first PJ and Sven presented their situation rather awkwardly. As they progressed they became more assured, more competent, putting forth all pertinent facts. Aaron Marcus listened most patiently. He never interrupted. When they were finished, he summarized their case.

"So you both think that the child Mrs. Pataklos carries is yours, Sven. The family wants the paternity of the child established to claim the larger part of the inheritance. Of course, you and Mrs. Pataklos would like to retain as much money as you can get."

PJ and Sven nodded in unison.

"How can you be so certain that the child is not Mr. Pataklos' offspring?"

"My husband tried to get me pregnant for almost five years—nothing worked. Then we went to a doctor Momson, in Miami. He said something was wrong with my husband's sperm. He treated him for months with hormones, concoctions of minerals and vitamins—things I really know nothing about. And then I happened to get pregnant."

She stopped her recital of woes. Looking worried, daunted by the impossibility to explain the shamelessness and callousness of their relationship, she hemmed and hawed as she continued.

"Sven and I, we sort of thought that... That it might make Dmitri happy to have a baby. Any baby... He wanted one so badly that we did not feel badly giving him one."

Aaron Marcus had listened, his face impassive. No disdain or any sort of judgment was discernible in his physical demeanor. Here and there, he had taken notes. It was done in an unobtrusive way that did not interrupt the flow of narrative from his clients. Now he said, "I have a copy of your summons and will get in touch with the judge as soon as he grants me a hearing. Perhaps we can avoid the entire public hearing and the washing of dirty linen in public. I think that would be in your best interest."

"Oh, yes!" agreed Sven and PJ, nodding their heads vigorously.

The Law At Work

❧

AND SO IT HAPPENED that within three days a private hearing between the concerned parties took place in the judge's chambers. Dorian had returned to the Keys to represent the interest of the first Pataklos family. Accompanying him were Dr. Momson and Irving Morgenthaler.

Aaron Marcus had spent a long afternoon explaining the intricacies of the law to his clients and how it applied to their situation. It had taken a while for PJ to totally understand the precariousness of her position.

"The best thing you can do, Mrs. Pataklos, is to avoid the question of impropriety at all. To avoid the paternity test and the appearance of your wrong doing, we stipulate that you will accept any reasonable settlement of the estate; that you will not make extraordinary claims for the unborn child. That will allow for you to take the high road, a reasonable attitude and the avoidance of the possible discovery of your infidelity. When the informative session ended, Sven and PJ agreed that this would be the most equitable, fair, and the least dishonorable path that could be taken.

When the judge's hearing commenced, most things had been settled beforehand. Much better for the clients concerned, because the lawyer fees were kept to a minimum. The judge placed before Sven and PJ the overwhelming amount of evidence in favor of the plaintiff. Evidence, solidified through Momson and Morgenthaler's testimonies, rendered any resistance obsolete.

"However," said the judge, "everyone concerned with the case feels that Mrs. Pataklos has been placed in a position of great vulnerability. Therefore, it has been agreed upon to protect her financially in a fair manner."

He then praised the attorneys of both parties, who "….had in an unusual effort of cooperation, served the cases of both clients in the best, unselfish way that he had ever seen in his court room."

"Both parties can walk out of my chambers with their heads held high, for fairness won out over baseness."

The verdict amounted to quite a generous parting of the ways between the Pataklos clan and Precious Jewel Ragoongong. She would loose the luxury house in the Keys, the large boat, and the grand sedan, together with most of the moneys in several bank accounts. However, she was provided with 250,000 dollars to purchase a new home somewhere else in Florida, perhaps not in such an exclusive enclave as Palm Shores, but quite respectable.

Added to this provision was another 200,000 dollars for the birth of the child and living expenses until she could find a job, marry Sven, or get herself settled in some other fashion. She was also allowed to keep her Yellow Bird and the Boston Whaler.

When it was over, everyone walked away from the hearing feeling relieved and satisfied with the way things had gone. Sven especially felt as if a load had been removed from his shoulders. It had been hard on him to be cast in the role of a home wrecker and perhaps, partially responsible for the death of a much beloved man. PJ, too, seemed satisfied, feeling rather glad that she had been treated most generously. Aaron Marcus had drawn a terrible picture for her by showing her what an appalled jury could do to her financially.

Yet, already a few days later, when she had to look for another home to purchase, because her luxury nest was slated to be put on the market, she felt rancor rising in her breast. Unreasonable thoughts plagued her. She almost had had it all. The house, the grand boat and the humongous bank account. Could she have persuaded a jury that she should be the sole inheritor? Told them the extent of her sacrifice, her great effort to make an old man happy? Would they have listened to her? Who knows! Perhaps she should have fought for what was rightfully hers.

When Sven heard her utter such sentiments, he became irate.

"Don't you understand what happened in the judges chambers? These men, the lawyers, Dmitri's sons and the judge, acted in the most gentlemanly, benign way toward you and the child. They could have made you have a paternity test, put you through the ringer and then left you with practically nothing. Don't you understand how bad you would look in front of a jury when the plaintiff's attorney could paint a picture of an adventuress who married an old, gullible man for citizenship and his money? And then, to top it off, placed an illegitimate child in his home for him to raise? The good people on a jury would despise you. You could have ended up with nothing."

His hot speech somewhat cooled PJ's greedy ardor. She simmered down even more when he took her hands in his own and confided, "Do not worry. I will look after you and the child. I will not desert you."

A New House

⋙⋘

IT TOOK TWO MONTHS before PJ found a home that she liked and could afford. Dorian had been most kind to her by letting her use his father's house during this time. He had decided to purchase the house himself and split the money between his siblings. This way she had more leeway in finding a new house while occupying the old one.

The new house was located outside Titusville in the neighborhood of Mims. It did not, of course, have ocean frontage, but was within walking distance of the beach. She had to pay fifty thousand dollars more than she had intended, but the good points of the purchase outweighed the negative aspects. Easy access to many venues she might need in the future was one of the plusses. Furthermore, it was easy for Sven to reach her there from Miami.

Sven had been very helpful for her to achieve new goals. He had helped with the real estate broker, advised her how to invest the money allocated to her. Finally, he facilitated the move to the three-bedroom, two-bath Key West style home. Once she decided to buy her new home, she was filled with the first flush of ownership. This was her house! The first thing of great worth that she had ever owned. She would not have been female if she didn't instantly want to transform the beautiful shell with her personal style into a very individual home. She decided to paint, and swore that the house needed curtains if she was to live in it. Especially the master bedroom cried out for window treatments.

Over the three day span of a long weekend Sven drove her about—from department to specialty stores. She was very close to her due date now. Her belly was heavy and extended. Apparently the child she was carrying was large. There were times when she sat in her best chair and could not get out without assistance. The chair and an assortment of other furniture had been a further gift of Dorian's. But even gifted with such largess, she never fully understood how generous Dorian had been.

When she found out how quickly the money was running through her fingers and how expensive draperies and accessories were, she bought a sewing machine and began to create. Sewing was a discipline in which she was well schooled. It spoke for her good taste and imagination that she was able to purchase inexpensive, neglected fabrics and forge them into stunning decorative items. The white, flowing muslin curtains she had fashioned for her bedroom transported the visitor to tropical islands with gentle breezes.

Sven was astonished when he beheld what she could do. He praised her efforts highly and even remarked that she could feed herself with her decorations should she ever run out of money.

"Oh, that will never be," she smiled. "I will have you, my dear."

He was touched by this simple trusting statement.

"Yes, darling, you will have me."

He came almost every evening, living with her in the new house. There were days though, when he could not make the long drive up the coast. Those were the evenings and nights when PJ called her mother and talked for hours, running up horrific phone bills. The closer she was to her due date, the more she began to fantasize that she needed her mother—that she could not birth the baby without her mother. Sven talked her out of this dream, many times.

"PJ, together, even you and I, cannot afford to have your mother come and stay with us. You know she wants to bring your brothers and settle here for good and that is unacceptable. Alone the cost for the visas, passports and other expenses are prohibitive. You must be reasonable and wait until you can afford such a journey."

After each such effort at reasonable, thought provoking considerations, PJ seemed contrite and willing to set aside her wishes. Disturbed by the phenomenon of mother obsession, Sven called his own mother and asked her if this was normal behavior for a pregnant woman.

"Oh, my dear, women always want to have their mother's close when they give birth. However, we know usually what is affordable, reasonable and possible to accomplish. Your PJ sounds a little unbalanced. In the past she made very important decisions without the benefit of her mother's advice, as is evidenced by her affair with you. I doubt her mother would have advised her to sleep with you behind her rich husband's back. I cannot, therefore, understand this nagging push for her mother's presence right now."

As always, Sven's mother was very cerebral in her look at the world, which was not to say that she lacked emotions. To the contrary, she had always been a very loving, affectionate mother and friend to her children. She heard Sven's sigh on the other side of the world and remarked, "By the way, when the child is born, have a little swab done for a paternity test. Just to be sure. I would hate for you to give up your research for your doctorate, just to raise another man's child. But, should it turn out be yours, I will gladly welcome the baby into the family."

"Och, Momma! You are the best. In times like these I miss you terribly. Perhaps you can come and visit."

"No, no, my son! It would cause problems. It would strengthen her case, although I would pay my own way. We will save that for later."

Paternity?

৵৵৶

TEN DAYS ELAPSED AFTER this conversation, when PJ awakened Sven in the middle of the night. I think the baby is coming. I feel these terrible pains. The nurse told me to time them. Suddenly they are five minutes apart."

She stopped obviously dismayed and cried out, "Oh dear, I am all wet. Help me Sven! Get me out of here!"

Sven jumped from the bed as if stung by a scorpion. In haste he pulled on his shorts and a T-shirt, and while so doing stuck his feet into tan sandals. He rushed to PJ's side, helped her out of bed and pushed her arms through a maternity dress that buttoned along the entire front—a creation of hers.

"Don't button the thing now!" he yelled. "A few are done and you can do the rest in the car." He snatched the small suitcase they had prepared many days ago. Leading her firmly by the arm, he conveyed her into his Toyota Truck.

"You would not fit into Yellow Bird!" he grinned.

PJ was not laughing. She moaned and groaned every so often and massaged her belly. At times she pressed her hands into her lower back. They had been driving for a little while when she suddenly relaxed.

"Ahhh! Much better!" she sighed. The drive to hospital was relatively short. Twenty minutes—twenty-five in bad traffic. Perhaps the knowledge of her approaching delivery induced PJ to come clean and be truthful with Sven. Perhaps she was afraid he would be even more angry if he were surprised, but she suddenly breathed deeply and confessed, "My mother will be arriving in Miami tomorrow at ten in the evening. I wanted her so much that I sent her the money for a ticket, the visa, everything. I arranged it all. If you love me, please go and get my Momma and bring her home."

Sven heard unadulterated defiance resonate in PJ's words. She was just spoiled and willful. He was a calm, benign man, although exciting sex had led him to become rash and unthinking. He had, however, a boiling point. Anger made him see red. Like a goaded bull he wanted to ram his head into an adversary. His fury drove him to slam his foot on the accelerator and steer the car straight towards one of the many palm trees lining the street.

"Svenny, Svenny! No! No!" PJ pulled on the steering wheel, forcing the car back in to the lane. "Don't kill us!" she wailed. "Don't kill us!"

Sven shook like a tree in strong wind. He took his foot off the gas pedal. The car came to a complete stop. He said nothing. Fortunately it was nighttime. Hardly any traffic was on the road. For that, and no other reason, they were not hurt.

Eventually Sven collected himself, breathing deeply. He drove the car silently to the hospital, ignoring PJ's whining entreaties to talk to her, to be good to her. He helped her into the hospital. It was a low, flat building stretching from the emergency department in the middle to two wings—right and left. Its naked flanks were softened by the ubiquitous hibiscus and palmetto bushes. He checked PJ in with a bored, worn-out desk nurse, acknowledged to be the father, and then left her.

"Don't leave me! Please, please stay with me!" PJ's cries echoed after him, causing the staff to measure him with strange looks. He did not care.

Traitor! It echoed in his mind. *You are nothing but a damn traitor. You always have to have your way. And you get it, too, with softness and manipu-*

lation and outright deceit. But who was he to complain?

Had he not been a willing accomplice in all of her plots? From the very beginning PJ had dominated their relationship. Once she decided that she wanted more in a man than her old husband, she had ever so subtly given him the nod to approach her. And he—mesmerized as by a snake—had only been too pleased and eager to do her bidding. He rushed to any place she ordered him to go the very moment she called.

"Meet me at the resort, at Duck Key, for lunch," she would say, and he would cancel his classes and drive fifty miles to be with her.

It never was just lunch, or the swim in the bay for that matter. She had money—an unlimited credit card, which Dmitri the trusting fool never checked. He trusted her to pay it off herself without looking. They had lovely rooms in different resorts, where she taught him the art of intricate sex. One time, in defiance of all reason, she had him join her in a room of the Chica resort, a place where many of Dmitri's friends went for golf, lunch and dinner. No matter where or when she wanted him, he would comply. He could not have explained to anyone, even to himself, what had transformed his Nordic temperament—from cool observation to faulty thought and flawed justification. How did it come about that he now acted mindlessly like a bull ramming his head over and over into a fence?

As he thought of her machinations behind his back, he thought of his beloved PJ as a gorgeous spider weaving nets around unsuspecting, rather stupid men. Are we ruled only by our penis? he wondered. It was incomprehensible to him that this lovely, butter-would-not-melt-in-her-mouth girl could have gone ahead and against all his wishes and advice, invited her mother and brothers into the country.

What could he do? Nothing! It was her money—money he had fought for. In the end, she was a citizen with all rights, able to do as she pleased. It irked him, however, that she wanted him to be the father of her small family, wanted him to be the future provider.

Yet she robbed him of all decision making. She rode roughshod over every word he said, every bit of advice he gave her, much as she had done with Dmitri. It wasn't as if he ever asked for anything. So far he had been just happy to support her, been grateful for her love. So, what did that make him in the end? A nothing! A bit of human personage that could be manipulated like a marionette for the advantage of Precious Jewel—Thai puppet master.

Well, he wanted out of the marionette drama! He wanted to be plain Sven, marine biologist, again. He wanted be down in forty feet of water with the moray eels and the sharks. He knew those creatures and their behaviors—he was lost above the surf.

Thinking daunting thoughts, he rushed along the corridors. His father's voice was ringing in his head—if you are the father do the right thing. But what if he was not the father? He had just assumed that because he was young, healthy and horny, he had to be the creator of the baby. But what if his hubris was misplaced and the old bull's seed was still potent? The idea of another paternity than his own seemed suddenly to be a wished-for alternative.

His head was filled with angry repudiations of PJ and her child. As he was racing along the corridor of the maternity ward, he came upon an older nurse with the sweet face of an older aunt. Seeing the woman, he blurted out a strange request.

"Mam, please tell me what I must do to get a paternity test done on a baby that is about to be born?"

"What seems to be the trouble?" asked the kind nurse. Her wide-open face and friendly expression, mixed with kind concern, invited an unburdening of the mind. As if she had done the same thing hundreds of times, the mature woman took his arm and steered him into the cafeteria. She bought two coffee's, whether he wanted one or not, and deposited them on a table in a corner of the bright, large room.

"You seem to be in need of good advice," she said smilingly. "That will take a while. It will be best if you start at the beginning."

A monumental feeling of relief flooded Sven the moment he

began to speak to the stranger. She was a godsend, someone who would listen without bias and prejudice to what was troubling him. He told her everything. Beginning with the moment he was attracted to PJ, so long ago. He explained about his job, her marriage and how, at first, they touched accidentally and liked the connection.

"There was definitely a current flowing between us," he said. The nurse, who had told him to call her Marianne, laughed delightedly, "Yes, I know. We call that current sexual attraction."

"No, no, there was more, so much more." Marianne just smiled and let him proceed with his confession.

"A few days after we touched, I did a job for her husband. She came out and brought me lemonade. While she poured the liquid into the glass, she said, "Meet me this evening at six at mile marker 65."

That was all she said and she never changed the expression on her face. No one would have been the wiser watching us together. Well I went, of course, and she was there. The mile marker stands in a barren spot on US 1 going to Key West. The road takes up almost the entire breadth of the Key. Both sides of the road are overgrown with shrubs and stunted mangrove. She had pulled her car onto the shoulder of the road and I parked behind her, blocking it from view. It is bright yellow and easily identifiable. There was a little beach below the road—perhaps three feet of dry sand. It was enough for us."

Sven drank some coffee and, looking into Marianne's calm, interested face, continued his tale. "Well, once we drank from the liquor of love, there was no turning back. We became obsessed with each other. PJ especially could not get enough. She wanted to see me all the time. It became very difficult to meet her without anyone seeing us together. To my surprise, I found soon that I felt like a heel whenever I worked for her husband. He was older but a truly nice man. When the affair began I justified my behavior by telling myself that the old fool deserved to be cheated on, because of his audacity to marry someone so much younger, and so very beautiful.

How dare he chain youth and beauty to an aged, failing body? I now realize that I was very callow, despicable even. And then the pregnancy happened. I had urged her to let me use protection, or, failing that, for her to take precautions herself. But she said dismissively, "It would make Dmitri so happy to have a child and he cannot."

"What an idiot I was. Frankly, we both were so besotted with each other; I think we just did not care. And then—he died! Just had a stroke or heart attack and just died. Suddenly, she depended on me for everything. I did not mind, but then she changed. Now I am not sure that I even like her anymore."

"How did she change? Is it because of the baby? Is she insecure?"

"No, that I can deal with. But now she has become a big spender. Whether I stay with her or not, she cannot afford that. She does not listen to any advice or the warnings I give her."

He recounted all the times when PJ just ignored anything he said. The last of the tale concerned the story of her mother's visit. Having relived the entire sordid affaire, he slumped down in his chair and drank the rest of the coffee, which had become cold, for the tale had been so long.

Marianne who had been most patient volunteered a suggestion.

"I think that you are entitled to be sure who the father of the baby is. I recommend that you talk to the department head of the maternity ward. He will advise you how to proceed."

Being the truly nice person Sven thought Marianne to be, she then took his hands into her own, and said, "No matter how this thing turns out, you have responsibilities. If you wish to look at yourself in the mirror in the future and feel good about yourself, you must fulfill these responsibilities. I think you must stick with your woman until she is safely out of the hospital, even if the child is not yours. You must, furthermore, convey her mother to her house and see her settled in. Then—if the child is not yours—you may disengage yourself. I do not see a good future for the two of you if she ignores your advice as a partner."

PJ's Family

❧❦

RENEWED BY MARIANNE'S SAGE words, Sven did as she said. He initiated the paternity test, and visited PJ after the baby was born. It was a most precious little girl by all appearances. Then, feeling diffident and engorged in animosity, he drove to the Miami airport to collect her mother.

The scene at the airport could not have been more preposterous, although he had imagined the worst. PJ's mother arrived—her two sons in tow. Mrs. Ragoongong envisioned herself in the role of queen mother. Apparently PJ had entertained her with pictures of riches, power and wealth. And though, although shriveled and well past her best days, the woman presented herself outrageously attired: in a flamboyant red silk sari with open mid-riff. How she arrived at the conclusion that this would be fitting attire in America was anyone's guess. Between her, and her two fish-eyed sons, they brought with them an array of ten suitcases.

Before Sven could enlighten her on the subject, Mrs. Ragoongong had instantly relegated him to the realm of domestics.

"Take these cases to the car, driver," she declared imperiously, waving her hand as if she had lived among royalty all her life. She spoke English well, but her son's spoke none.

Sven smiled slightly sourly and told the boys to grab their share of bags.

"If you don't they will just remain here!" He said ominously. He was fuming. But he told himself that this rude treatment made the split from PJ much easier. He loaded the bags in the back of his shabby truck, incurring Mrs. Ragoongong's scathing remark that her wealthy daughter should have sent a better conveyance for their reception. Sven remained silent.

The drive to Titusville was punctuated by Mrs. Ragoongong's disparaging remarks about the quality of Sven's truck, its seats and Florida's humidity. Sven perceived her sons' stony silence as sheer hostility.

PJ had insisted on an early release from the hospital because of her mother's visit. She left the hospital only six hours after giving birth, over the protests of the attending physician. She was awaiting the arrival of her family at home.

She was so overjoyed to see her family that she did not notice Sven's anger and discomfort. Nor did she thank him for the great effort he had put forth on her behalf over the last three days. To the contrary, she paid him so little mind, that the defeated man collected all his belongings from the bedroom of her house and, although deadly tired, departed unnoticed for a dorm room at the university.

The next morning he rose early from the lumpy mattress in the dorm room and wandered into the cafeteria. He was as hungry as a barracuda at nightfall. He had not eaten since lunch the day before. Was it only yesterday that he had been present at the birth of a child? The darling baby girl had arrived at two in the morning. When he saw her in the nursery, waves of ambivalent feelings washed over him. Was this his little girl? Was it someone to whom he owed a decent life, a future? Or was this the offspring of a dead man whose wife he could not stand anymore?

In the hospital bed he beheld PJ's beautiful face with ambiguity. On one hand, she still held a strong attraction for him—the indefinable exotic draw of a different cast, a different culture—so diametrically different from his own sturdy, blond genes. On the other hand, he felt as if a poisonous, nebulous veil was overlaying her features. Looking at her, he remembered her face distorted by avarice, by the hunger for control, by the spoiled look of one who had to have her way. In the past she held her self control, maintaining a mellow face at all times. All that had changed with Dmitri's death. After a few weeks of living by herself, a new person emerged. A certain calculating person, residing deep within her, was now visible.

While he devoured scrambled eggs, bacon and mounds of buttered toast, drowning all in several cups of coffee, the above considerations were turning over and over in his mind. What to do, what to do? Sven knew that punctually at 8:30 a.m. Peter Botkin would open the door to his office. Without fail he would be the first person walking through this door. He needed Peter. Professor Botkin was a great adviser to his masters and PhD students in more respects than one. He steered the young men and women in his care, often without their knowing, along career paths and through the thorny weeds of their personal lives.

Punctually at 8:32 Sven sat in Botkin's office, filling him in on all that had happened in the last few days.

"I don't know what to do," he sighed, at last.

"With her mother and her brothers there, I don't want to be in her house, even if the child is mine."

"There is no reason that you should be there," reassured Botkin.

"Until the paternity thing is cleared up you can keep your distance. Later, if you wish, you can negotiate a relationship on terms acceptable to you. In the meantime, talk to your parents and concentrate on your studies. They are more important than PJ's family."

Surprise Voyage

❧❧

WHEN SVEN LEFT BOTKIN'S office he felt much better. It was as if his head had been cleared of severe congestion. His parents gave him, almost to the letter, the same advice as Botkin had. So, by ten in the morning he was back in the laboratory, checking on his specimen. By noon he got a summons from the department: get your gear together, prepare to be gone for a week to the Turks and Caicos, and drive to the harbor. The department was sending a research vessel into the water of the islands to determine the deterioration of the water quality close to populated centers, and the degradation sustained by the coral reefs from the tourist industry.

Sven almost fainted with relief—a whole week during which he could not be reached, during which he was responsible only for himself. Bliss oh bliss! He called PJ on his cell phone and explained that he would be gone and unavailable.

"Oh, no," exclaimed PJ in her best whine.

"I need you here! I cannot drive yet. We need so much stuff for the baby and I need food for the family! You cannot just take off and leave me here."

"Oh yes, I can!" he pushed back mulishly.

"This is important for my future, and if I marry you it is important for you, too. As to the supplies you need, you know very well that your mother, who, by the way, speaks English very well, can take your useless brothers and walk four blocks down to the nearest Winn Dixie on north Singleton Avenue. Good bye and have a good visit with your family."

He hung up with the satisfied feeling that he had gotten the better of her for the first time.

Be Careful What You Wish For
For Your Wish Might be Granted

ॐ

MRS. RAGOONGONG HAD BEEN reunited with her daughter for only a few hours, when strife was imminent. After viewing every room in the house, PJ's mother decided that, of course, the master bedroom—she being the matriarch—would be her private domain. Precious Jewel was appalled by the way her mother went about apportioning her house. Mother relegated her and the baby to the smallest bedroom, while giving her brothers the other large bedroom. Slowly, dimly, memories of her home in Thailand came back to PJ' mind.

There, she had always deferred to her mother. According to custom and culture, she was forever the least member of the family. With the father departed, her mother and then brother's were the dominant members of her family. She always placed last whether it came to a place to sleep, the food at the table, or the allocation of clothing.

That had changed when her mother perceived her as a valuable commodity. Henceforth, she was clothed with care, received better food and was treated to magazines and books about foreign countries. Her education had been the standard eighth grade schooling, which had been paid for by a Christian mission, requiring lessons in Christian teaching.

But, having lived in the US with a very liberal man who was besotted by her, a man who had allowed her every freedom and furthered her education, she had become accustomed to act as her own agent. She instantly resented the fact that Thai culture was reestablished in her house—her very own house. To be ordered around by her mother, for whom she had provided through her husband's generosity for years, and whom she had now gifted with visas and airplane tickets for the family, was just too much for PJ to take.

"The master bedroom is mine. I have arranged it for myself and the baby. You can have the larger bedroom which you allocated to the boys," she said with darkling brow, and tight lips.

"What? Are you ordering your own mother around? The woman who brought you into this world and raised you without a father's help? Have you forgotten your upbringing? Do we need to teach you respect for your elders?"

Dithakar, her older brother, although he was in his early twenties, still had not managed to find and hold a permanent job, closely listened to his mother. He got off the couch, on which he had seemingly been lollygagging and approached his elder sister. Dithakar was unusually tall, broad in the shoulders and muscular for a Thai man. With his forearm he shoved PJ violently against the next wall. For a moment she felt as if her head had cracked open.

"Respect your mother, nothing person," he said menacingly. He went back and lay down on her pretty couch, placing his greasy head upon one of her favorite silk pillows.

In a corner, by the window stood her younger brother, Alak, grinning broadly. He had observed her punishment. All over his attractive face, with its long effeminate eyelashes, golden complexion and strong chin, she read only scorn for her. Why on earth had she wanted so badly for these horrid people to join her? Had it been that mother made her swear to bring them all to the USA? How could she have forgotten her inferior position in the family? A position made tolerable only by smiling all the time, bowing and scraping, and serving everyone?

She had not forgotten! But she had changed in America and thought that things would be different. Her brothers had never mistreated her, as had been the case with girls in other families. In those families, forced incestuous relations with brothers and the selling of girls to their friends for sex was common. It was for this kinder treatment that she had liked her family.

Her mother imperiously told the boys to remove PJ's and the baby's things from the master bedroom and place them into the tiny room which she had chosen. Moments later, PJ found herself secluded there. She cried softly, helplessly into the blanket in which her baby was wrapped. She had truly believed that her mother would be a help to her during the first weeks after the birth.

However, her mother had already abused her of that notion by saying categorically, "If you think that I will get up at night to take care of the baby, you better think again."

That night PJ cried for a long time. Then she realized, crying would not help her. What she needed was a plan to rid herself of these people who had become strangers to her. They let slip that they expected to remain in the country. They believed that she could facilitate this. Furthermore, they assumed that she was rich and would feed and clothe them. All at once she bitterly regretted having been so beastly to Sven. It dawned on her that he probably understood her situation better than she did.

"Sven, oh, Sven! I need you so!" she thought. But he was gone for a whole week.

The morning following her rude awakening, PJ fed and changed her baby and placed her in her crib. She had named the girl Kamala—born of lotus, beautiful. In the kitchen she found her mother and brothers sitting around the round, rattan and glass table. For the better part of the afternoon she had explained the functions of the toilets, the laundry, the kitchen and the refrigerator to them. Instead of fending for themselves, they were greeting her with their requests for their breakfast. They wanted rice, vegetables, seafood or eggs.

Silently PJ checked her cupboards. "I don't have Jasmine rice. Because of the baby I have not been to the store. Perhaps you can try some other food. Things we eat here in America."

"What do you eat here?" Her mother at least showed an interest. Her brothers scowled. PJ brought boxes of cereal, milk, and bowls to the table. She also pulled out bread, jam and peanut butter, making sandwiches for them to try. They did not like anything. The baby began to cry and she rushed to her bedroom, where she changed the mite and began to nurse her. Her mother came into the small room and said, "You better get real food for your brothers. They are angry. They want rice. That's what they are used to."

"I have to feed Kamala, and I cannot drive a car yet. The doctor said to wait a few days. But you speak English. You and the boys can go to the market and get what you want. I will give you money for the purchase."

PJ silently thanked the Christian God for her foresight to have placed a small amount of cash into her purse. She had hidden the larger amount and the credit cards in the small attic, a place her family would not know about. She could not explain why she had done this. Distrust must have already plagued her before they arrived. Her mother left, but was back instantly, reporting that the boys refused to walk and carry groceries. They wanted the keys to her car to drive to the market. Feeling harassed, PJ returned Kamala to her crib and joined her family in the kitchen. Her brothers slouched indolently at the kitchen table. She challenged her brothers instantly.

"You cannot drive my car."

"Yes we can!" they said in unison.

"That is not possible," said PJ calmly. "You have no driver's license. Here in America you must carry such a thing with you at all times. If the police find you without, you go to prison."

Her brothers laughed. They said no one would catch them. No one in Thailand ever had. There, they often drove other people's cars without papers. With horror, PJ remembered how her brothers had destroyed several vehicles. She thought desperately how she could prevent them from driving her car. She looked at her mother beseechingly.

"Moma, believe me, if the police find them they will send all of you back to Thailand."

Somehow her mother believed her. There was no way she was going back to the hut she had left. She was here to stay.

"You go then," she ordered.

"I am not supposed to drive yet," said the young woman tiredly. It was not yet ten in the morning and she was already totally exhausted. Her mother and the boys did not let up. Relentlessly they hammered her with requests. She finally gave up.

"I will go! Moma can come. The car holds only two people."

A new argument ensued. Her brothers insisted that, with the top down, they could ride their legs inside, sitting on the rear of the car.

"Absurd!" she said. "This way the police will find us instantly."

Finally she negotiated that, apart from herself, only mother would go to the market. She picked up the baby, Kamala, placing it into her mother's arms.

"Leave Kamala with the boys!" objected her mother. "I do not want to carry her!"

"You must hold her while I drive."

"Leave her here with the boys," repeated her mother with strong distaste in her voice.

"I would rather die this moment than leave helpless Kamala with these two imbeciles," hissed PJ.

"Don't call your brothers stupid!" yelled Mrs. Ragoongong and slapped her daughter's cheeks right and left, leaving red marks. She had underestimated her daughter. The obliging girl from her days in Thailand was no more. Instead she had grown into an American girl, who was now fully awake. PJ controlled her temper, got her mother and Kamala into her little car and plotted.

At the Winn Dixie supermarket, her mother took her time. She touched everything that intrigued her, smelled it and held it close to her nose. She tried a few things and rejected them. In no time mother and daughter had become the focus of watchful eyes. It was unavoidable. A manager, stirred by the annoyed comments of customers, joined the two women in the green grocer's section.

"Forgive me, but you cannot put the fruit and vegetables so close to your nose, nor can you open containers of previously weighed berries and cherries and taste them!"

He looked at P J as he spoke, figuring she was the saner of the two.

"I have told my mother that she cannot handle things here as she does in Thailand because of hygienic concerns, but she will not listen to me."

"What wrong with looking for good food?" glowered Mrs. Ragoongong.

"Everything!" said the manager forcefully. "Our customers are objecting to your behavior. We will have to turn you out before we lose customers."

"She will stop now, won't you Momma?" PJ looked at her mother penetratingly. "We will finish our shopping and leave momentarily."

As soon as the manager left PJ said, "You almost got us thrown out of the store. Let us buy what we need and leave. You are in a new country. You cannot behave as if you are in the market at home."

They finished gathering what PJ's mother wanted and went to the check out. The nice manager asked PJ, who had carried the baby all that time, to please join him for a moment. When they were safely out of her mother's hearing, he said, "My dear, you are bleeding profusely and should seek out your doctor or go to the hospital. You recently gave birth, did you not?"

"Yes, not fully two days ago."

"Let me call you an ambulance," he offered.

"No, no thank you! I will drive there. It will be better this way." The man's eyes were sorrowful.

"If that is what you wish. But hurry!"

And hurry PJ did. She paid and let a young man take the groceries to the car. Now this was the service her mother expected. And she remarked on it a few times, too. PJ knew that she was in deep trouble. It was because of possible bleeding the hospital staff had wanted her to stay for a few more days.

She did not tell her mother where she was going, but drove straight to the hospital. Arriving at the emergency entrance, she took Kamala from her mother and walked to the entrance. Her mother, stunned at first, got out of the car and ran after her, shouting, "Precious Jewel, what are doing here? Where are you going? Have you gone crazy?" and then more demanding, "Take me home right now!"

"Are you so blind that you have not noticed that I am bleeding, you monster?" cried PJ in English.

"I told you that I should not have been out driving! The doctors had forbidden it! You forced me because you care more about two useless boys then about your only daughter."

Shouting thus at each other they arrived at the admitting desk. The nurse took one look at the young woman and called for a gurney. She grimly pointed to a chair in the waiting room and said, "Sit," to Mrs. Ragoongong, commandingly enough to make a vicious dog obey. And so Mrs. Rangoongong watched with astonishment as her daughter and granddaughter were wheeled off to where she could not go. For the first time in many days she felt powerless. What was going on? Perhaps she should have listened to PJ? What now? She sat in her chair for a while, but grew bored and furious because no one paid any attention to her. She stomped to the front desk, verbally assaulting the duty nurse with demands to see her daughter.

For once, however, she had met her match. A good emergency duty nurse has dealt in her time with the dregs of mankind and knows how to handle even a drugged psychopath. At first, Mary Knowles, the sign at the desk announced her name in large letters, tried to patiently explain PJ's situation. She talked about the need to allow the doctors to stop her daughter's hemorrhaging. But when she was rudely pushed by the Thai woman to let her see PJ, she resorted to the same tactics she used on the dregs of society.

"Sit!" she shouted, "or I will have you removed from the premises!" Mrs. Ragoongong understood that language very well. She meekly slunk back to her chair.

An hour passed and a doctor came and sought her out. "Your daughter is in very bad shape!" he announced.

"She should never have gone shopping. You are lucky that we were able to save her. She is a very nice lady and said for you to go back to the house. She will be here for a few days."

He gave her a note with the address of the house, and sent an orderly with her into the parking lot, who opened the trunk of PJ's car. The orderly told her to take the perishables and start walking. He gave her directions.

"It is not very far. PJ said that you can come back with your sons to pick up the rest of the groceries. My name is Ian. You can ask for me when you return and I will open the car for you."

Ian had offered to drive PJ's mother home with her groceries. Yet PJ insisted that her family be inconvenienced.

"They are the reason that I almost bled to death," she said. "Let them work for their food!"

A moment after opening the trunk of the yellow car, Ian agreed with PJ's assessment of the situation, for Mrs. Ragoongong raged at him that he, an unworthy underling, should have nothing better to do than convey an old lady safely home. He smiled, turned his back on her and left her, her arms filled with grocery bags, squawking.

Safe

❧

IN THE SAFETY OF the ICU, her baby by her side in a small crib, PJ had enough time to consider her situation. She was hurt by her mother's outrageous behavior. She seemed to care little for her grandchild, and was much more interested in cementing herself and the boys into PJ's household. This was not to be.

PJ still mourned the loss of her beautiful bedroom with its white, ethereal curtains, its luxurious bed covered by the silk spread she had sewn herself and its clean, marbled bathroom. The thought of her brothers alone with mother in her house made her nauseous.

They are uncivilized! God only knows what they will do to my kitchen. Strangely, all these thoughts floated through her mind in perfect English, as if her mother tongue had evaporated.

As every scenario replayed in her tired mind, a new, previously unthinkable, impossible idea came to her mind. The words from an old movie she had recently watched came to haunt her. The actors so perfectly said what she wrestled with—the truth she did not want to acknowledge.

Throw the bums out! She smiled wanly, but as the idea took hold of her mind she grinned wickedly. Yes! That was it! She had to throw them out. Get them out of her house, out of her life. They had become ogres in their belief that she was rich and had to take care of them. She would never be able to explain to them that the settlement money was really a modest amount for a woman with a child. If Sven deserted her, she would be forced to work in a few years, depending on her spending habits.

"I must make up with Sven," she thought.

"How could I have been so mean to him? What will I do without him? I need a father for my child."

PJ knew that without a man, life could be complicated. Despite all the talk about feminism and women's power, she had seen with her own eyes how differently Dmitri had been treated when negotiating at the bank for a loan that had been roundly denied her. Even at the gas station the guys always wanted to pump the most expensive gas when they were helping her. Yes, she would try to make things well with Sven.

What could she do in the meantime to get rid of her family? How could she go home to these nasty people? The way her brothers had taken hold of her minute daughter still made her wince when she remembered the event.

"Well," she talked herself into a decision, "I brought them into the country—I can get them out." And then she came up with the perfect scheme. It was really quite simple.

Three days later she was released from the hospital with the express understanding not to do any work that required the lifting of heavy objects. As the nice male nurse, who had dealt so well with her mother, wheeled her and Kamala to the Exit door, she completed her plan. She had asked the young man the day before to park her car in a fairly safe spot on the street where it might sit until she was well enough to drive. He had done so, taking her there. Now he gave her the car keys and wished her a good recovery.

With the car safely out of the reach of her brothers, she entered a cab and was delivered to her house. No one answered the ring of the doorbell. Fortunately she had a key, because her mother, Dithakar, and Alak had temporarily deserted her abode. This suited her to a tee. She put the sweetly sleeping Kamala into the crib in the small bedroom and went into the master bedroom. Her mother had lived there like a pig. Dirty clothes littered the floor. The sink in the bathroom had a dirt ring and so did the white porcelain tub. PJ almost cried with disgust. She and Demi always kept an immaculately clean house.

She pushed her vanity stool to the middle of the room and stood on it. Stretching upward she opened the trapdoor to the little attic. Reaching into the void she found and opened an old suitcase. Feeling with her fingers she felt what she was looking for. She closed the suitcase, secured the secret attic door and slid gently to the floor. Sitting on the floor, she was breathing hard for a few minutes. This had been a much harder job than the doctor would have allowed. But, oh, it was so worthwhile the effort.

She returned to the small bedroom via the kitchen. What she beheld there kept her frozen in the entrance. Flour and pancake mix was strewn about. Her shiny stainless steel pans sat greasy and blackened on the stove, which itself was plastered with grime from top to bottom. And the floor—she gasped when she saw the mess.

"Ahhhh, so you are back," said Dithakar, standing behind her.

"Now you clean up the mess. Time that someone did that," he said in the familiar Siamese language.

PJ turned around. She saw her mother and Alak entering also.

"Will you finally cook us a dinner?" she heard her mother say.

"We have all the food needed for a good meal."

In that instant PJ's veins pulsed with ice water instead of blood. She watched closely as the three of them arranged themselves into a closed adversarial group. Watching her family arraying themselves as if for an attack on her, she steeled herself. Then she hissed more than spoke.

"The game is over. Throw the bums out!"

"What did she say?" asked her brothers. Her mother translated, looking furious at PJ. The young men heard the Thai translation of a good Americanism and laughed.

"What does she think she is going to do? We will stay as long as we please." Both men advanced upon her, with the plain intent to put her into submission.

"Stop!" screamed PJ.

"Not one more inch, or I kill you!" Her brothers laughed and kept on coming. PJ's hand came up from behind her back. A blast erupted from her hand and Dithakar fell to the floor. For a moment, deafening silence reigned. Then PJ's mother screamed.

"She killed him! She killed Dithakar." She threw herself over the prostrate body, wailing like a banshee. Alak was about to move forward, when he heard PJ call out in Siamese, "Don't move, or I shall shoot you, too."

Her hands were shaking, but she was otherwise terribly cool and in control.

"Stop your screaming!" she ordered her mother. Her mother stopped, silenced by her daughter's commanding voice. Pressing her advantage, PJ coldly said, "I did not shoot to kill. Dithaker is not dead! Tell him to open his eyes; he will live." She turned to her brother Alak.

"Go to the bathroom and get a towel. Don't do anything stupid; I will surely kill you if you do not follow my orders."

All the while she stayed with her back pressed against the kitchen wall, gun at the ready. Alak returned with the towel and she ordered him to press it against the flesh wound in Dithakar's upper arm. The treatment resulted in the latter's sitting up, howling with pain.

"Control yourself you coward. You never thought twice about pain when you smacked my head into the wall when you strong-armed me. Did you see me cry, you baby?"

She smiled. Things were progressing much as they had in the movie she had seen. She began to enjoy herself immensely. From deep within in her psyche came long-forgotten pictures of insult endured by her at the hands of brothers, of family. The compliant Thai girl—ever at the bottom—existed no more.

"Get up, Dithakar!" The sharp command emanated as PJ's voice was cracking like a whip.

"Mother, take the boys and get your things together—you are leaving. Now! I do not want you another minute in my home!"

Her mother let out a high-pitched scream.

"No! You shameless, thankless creature of the night! You cannot send us away! We have rights! Family rights! I have mother's rights. I made you—I own you!"

She howled terribly, all to no avail. The more she carried on, the more PJ realized that her past was long gone that she would never return willingly to what she had left behind.

At the height of her mother's noisy dissent, when she could not make herself understood, PJ raised the gun and fired into the ceiling.

"The next shot will not miss you," she told her mother. "So take the boys, get your things together, and leave."

She never let go of the gun as she fished her cell phone out of her trouser pocket. She pressed a number previously processed into the device. Her voice firm, she said, "I need a cab to take three people to Miami. We are located at 234 Beach Street."

She turned to her mother, "You have twenty minutes to pack your things. Then the cab will be here and you will leave. The cabbie will take you the Intercontinental Hotel at the airport where you can book a room. The cabbie also can take you to the emergency room at Jackson Memorial Hospital. They will treat Dithakar's gunshot wound without charging you. Don't ask me why! They do it all the time for free. They also give free transplants to victims of shooting violence. You can see that you will be in good hands."

PJ followed the members of her family around as they gathered their many things. She watched with hard eyes as they shoved their belongings willy-nilly into suitcases and bags. All the while, the gun, a Smith & Wesson six-shot revolver, treasured by Dmitri since his officer's days, remained firmly in her hand. She paid close attention to the distance between herself and her brothers, never quite trusting them. When they were packed, PJ said to her mother and Alak, "Now go into the kitchen and clean up the mess you made." She sent Alak ahead into the mess, retaining her mother for a moment.

"Here," she said. "Here are eight hundred dollars. That will allow you to stay for a few days at the airport hotel so you can explore Miami. Then you will board your plane and go back to Thailand. I have already talked with the airline. You are booked to go back in three days. Here are the revisions for the tickets, the names and numbers to call, and the dates of your return. I paid the penalties for your early return, so you are okay."

At this juncture, Madam Ragoongong put up violent objections.

"This just is not possible! I have prepared to stay to see my grandchild grow up! And I will surely stay in this country and live here." She suddenly screeched, "I must stay—I sold my house."

"So you decided to do all that for the sake of my baby?" PJ asked facetiously.

"All that—without ever looking at your granddaughter twice. You don't care one whit about her, or me, for that matter; all you ever wanted was to come to America. Well, too bad! Now you are going home. We have already enough people like you in this country!" preached PJ righteously. *Wow*—she wondered, *where did that sermon come from?* The thought disturbed her but for a moment. Then she concentrated again on her problem. She directed her mother firmly into the kitchen, waving her, by now, ubiquitous gun.

Throughout all the commotion Dithakar rested comfortably on the couch, the towel firmly pressed against his shoulder. He fancied himself to be a star in an American gangster movie. One of those films in which the gangster moll shoots the innocent, valiant hero by accident. He was rudely torn from his dream by the honking of a horn. A moment later PJ stood before him waving her gun.

"Get up, get up!" she said, pointing her silver cannon at his chest.

"Out, out," she yelled at her entire family, shooing them with their baggage through the front door and into the cab. At one point, when she thought the cabbie might spot her weapon, she made it disappear, sticking it into the waistband of her jeans. By pulling her top over it, the gun was hidden from view. The gun had disappeared from sight all right, but it was most accessible should she be in need of it. She had told her family of this possibility.

"I will tell the police how you treated us. That you have a gun!" announced her mother viciously, only moments before they left the house.

"Please do!" answered PJ. "I will tell them that you and my brothers attacked me because I would not be a part of your drug operation. Believe me—you will be deported within the hour after being branded criminals!"

At that, Mrs. Ragoongong folded her sails and accepted defeat. In her brown, wrinkled face a question was plainly written, "What has happened here? What has become of my pliant child? The one I could control?"

PJ stared after the yellow cab. It looked to her like a golden chariot. She never wavered, never regretted her decision. She went back into her house and locked the door firmly behind her. Slowly she walked into her wonderfully silent living room, where she sank blissfully into her favorite chair. After sitting quietly for a while, she heard Kamala fussing in the small bedroom. She picked up her baby from the crib and cuddled her, feeling wonderful.

Later, when her satisfied baby peacefully slept, she fixed herself an enormous Mai Tai, strapped on an apron and conquered the mess in her kitchen. When she went to sleep that night, she was amazed that she had never once thought about Sven, Dmitri, doctors' orders—anything at all—only about herself and what she wanted.

The Test

ॐ

AFTER A MARVELOUS WEEK of diving and taking samples in the Turks & Caicos, Sven returned to Miami. Before calling PJ, he went to his cloistered abode at the university. He stored his gear under the hard, wooden bed with the lumpy mattress, and went to the cafeteria. It was dinnertime. The food on the boat, except for the fish, had been so-so and he looked forward to a good meal.

As he sat, his laden tray before him, he checked his messages. He found it decidedly odd that PJ had not called him even once. She could not have known that he had never turned his cell phone on, not even once. She was an excessive caller; often she called him four times a day. And now—nothing? How strange. Perhaps she was so happy and busy with her family that she had forgotten all about him.

The notion that she could have cut him from her life without so much as a "Nice knowing you!" suddenly bothered him immensely. How could she be so callous? This was supposedly his child that she'd borne a week ago. Automatically putting food into his hungry maw, his mind was racing. How did he feel about being totally free, unchained to responsibility? For many months he had thought about his role as a husband and father. On the whole, the idea had not been unpleasant. Not until she had gone against his wishes and advice, bringing her family to Florida, had he wavered.

Ah, hell! What was he going to do now? He actually was eager to see her, see that little girl, which by all laws of probability should be his. He finished his meal, French fries, fried mangrove snapper, green beans, salad and an enormous chocolate milk shake. He went back to the ugly cubicle, lay on his bed and called his father. He had checked the time on his computer and it was 5:00 a.m. for most of Sweden, 5:18 in Stockholm. Not a bad time as far as that went. His father would be up by now, working in his study or sitting in the kitchen having coffee. Morning coffee was a ritual for him and his mother. They always made a huge pot; had a simple breakfast, toast, jam and fresh fruit and, of course the *Svenska Dagbladet* and the *Dagens Industri*.

He had no problem raising his father. By the third ring his father answered the phone.

"Well, well, if it is not Sven the seafaring Viking back from the Turks and Caicos. How was your trip?"

"Good, very good, Papa! We found a lot of interesting stuff, but more about that later. How is you morning progressing? Can I bother you with a few more questions?"

Assuring Sven that any son of his could pose as many questions as he wished, Sven's father told his son to "shoot!" Sven did exactly that. He told his father the situation with PJ's mother and the brothers. He told him about the strange silence coming from PJ, his ambivalence concerning the relationship, and feeling torn.

"I want to go and see her and the baby, but I am afraid to face her awful mother."

"Do nothing until tomorrow," said his father thoughtfully. "Call the laboratory in the morning and find the true genetic status of the little mite. The results of the paternity test will clarify your feelings and with that your responsibilities."

"Aye, aye, professor Haldarsson. Now I can go to bed with a light burden. It will all be clear in the morning."

"As to the mother and the brothers, refuse to meet with her if they are in the house. Meet somewhere neutral instead, like the park or the beach."

"Thank you, Papa! You are the greatest!" Sven heard his mother's voice in the background.

"Not greater than the woman who created you, you ingrate!"

As always he felt better joking with his parents. They managed to impart warmth—enough warmth to heat a rock.

Waking early next morning he dressed and went to the cafeteria. Then he hopped into his beat-up truck for the trip to Titusville. Most mornings in Florida are mild and glorious. As he was traveling the scenic route 95 through Boca Raton, West Palm Beach and Palm Bay, he cherished being alive. Often he had a clear view of the Atlantic and the rising sun. Cloud banks, colored rosy, touched by the sun's rays, seemed to have been placed into the sky by a mild-mannered painter. Sven felt good about the world. No matter how things turned out, he could be a winner. The very thought made him want to sing. Instead, he turned on the radio and found a station playing Spanish pop.

By the time he reached Titusville it was late morning. He rushed to the hospital because he wanted his business finished before everyone went to lunch. This fine day all stars were aligned in his favor. For one, the doctor he had to see about the paternity results was in his office.

"Good to see you, Mr. Haldarsson," he exclaimed. "I just instructed my secretary to mail you the results, now that won't be necessary."

"So what's the verdict?" asked Sven, his heart beating fast. Suddenly he realized that either result could have a negative connotation. If he was the father his life was decided one way without many choices—if the paternity fell to Dmitri, the old devil had one up on him.

"There remains no doubt—you are not the father of this baby, Mr. Haldarsson."

Despite earlier ambiguities, Sven felt tremendous relief. He suppressed an urge to hug the doctor. His life was still an open book before him. He could inscribe the pages with some control about

416 | *The Old Man and the Mail-Order Brides*

the outcome of the story. As the feeling of relief ebbed, he suddenly thought of PJ. Boy, oh boy—she had been robbed of a fortune. The lawyer's good advice had turned against her. He said as much to the doctor.

"She can still try to establish the Pataklos paternity and take it up with the family, but I doubt she can go back on the settlement because she agreed to certain terms. I, however, am not a lawyer."

Revelation

❧❧

FIFTEEN MINUTES LATER, the results of the test lying beside him on the truck seat, Sven set out for PJ's house. He called her from the parking lot of the hospital. The conservation was stilted and very awkward.

"Hi, PJ, this is Sven. I am back from the Turks and Caicos."

"Sven, I am so glad to hear your voice. I have missed you! Will you drive up from Miami and see me?"

"I am already in Titusville and can come within minutes. Is you mother there?"

PJ let out a full-throated laugh, something he had never heard before from her, and so he winced.

"No, don't worry! My mother and brothers are gone. I threw them out."

"You did what?"

"Long story, come over and I tell you. You can see your baby girl, Kamala. She is very cute."

"Hmmm, you see, well, I think we better talk about that when I see you. Be right over."

"Bye!"

They hugged, as awkwardly as they had spoken before on the telephone. PJ asked Sven to come in, taking him to the living room. He noticed at once that she had rearranged the furniture. It was a pleasant change. In front of the large sliding door leading to a concrete patio surrounded by a cozy, enclosed yard, stood a pretty, white, frilly crib. In turn, the door was framed on each side by light cream voile` drapes. The furniture had been placed in a seating arrangement with the door and the patio as the focal point.

Sun light streamed in unobstructed. The room now looked twice as large and light as before. Sven walked to the crib and peered in its hooded confines. The baby Kamala was sleeping. She looked more like a dainty doll, with a tiny tuft of black hair, than a human baby.

"Is she not beautiful?" asked PJ.

Sven looked her fully in the face and said wistfully,

"Yes, she is. Very much so! But P J, she is not mine. She is unequivocally Dmitri's child."

PJ's face turned beet read. For a moment he thought she would choke on the very air she inhaled.

"That cannot be. He could not! Nothing worked. They were going to do this artificial stuff to me—the stuff I did not want to do!"

PJ almost fainted. She trembled and quickly sat in one of the close-by chairs.

"I know! It is incredible. Perhaps some of the medication and hormone treatments he received worked a miracle. Here is the report from the Genelex Laboratories. It states that I could not be the father under any circumstances."

PJ's hand shook as she reached for the document that certified Kamala as a fatherless baby. She read in a focused, concentrated manner, as if she had difficulty understanding the meaning of the writ.

Suddenly she began to laugh fully-throated. It was oriental mirth, reminding Sven of little brass bells tinkling, while her hand covered her half-open mouth.

"Oh Lord, how funny! He has the last laugh. From the grave he fulfills his wishes." Then she grew serious, looking pretty and thoughtful at the same time.

"In retrospect, I was an idiot not to take the paternity test, wasn't I?"

"Yes, but how could anyone foresee this? You know that our lawyer tried very hard to solve our dilemma and allow both of us to save face."

"What can I do now? Kamala is his child and she could be better provided for. Can I go back and reverse the judgement?"

"I have asked a few people that question. They all seem to think that you are still viewed as an adulteress and, therefore, were dealt with in a generous way. A jury might not have been so generous."

They sat in silence as she allowed this information to sink in. Suddenly she raised her eyes to his and Sven read her thoughts. It had to be—sooner or later. She would now ask him to stay and help raise Kamala. And he still was not sure how he would answer the question. Would he ask for time to make a decision or just fall into the role? Without seeking for a diversion, the question of her family's disappearance came to his mind.

"Not to change subject, but what happened to your family? Where are they now?"

PJ, looking like a mysterious temple dancer, moved her hands gracefully. She told him what had happened the day after she came home from the hospital.

"They took over my home as if it belonged to them and I was nothing but a tolerated servant. My own mother threw me out of my bedroom—my own bed—and relegated me to the smallest corner of the house. They tormented me, made me drive to the store. I began to bleed and ended up in the hospital."

She described the sordid details of her brother's behavior and her mother's cruelty.

"She did not care one whit for my baby, although she said that her birth was the most important moment in her life. Now I know mother only wanted a rich life in America."

A few lonely tears sprang from her eyes.

"I loved Kamala from the moment she was born. I do not care

who her father is. She is mine and I do not want her to be treated like I was by my family. It is strange, but living in America I came to view the role I had played in Thailand in a different light. Until I saw my family in my own home assume their old places of importance, I had never thought about my life as deprived and oppressed. Many girls in my country could expect much worse than what I lived through."

"So how did you get rid of the pests? It sounded as if your brothers could have prevented you from kicking them out."

PJ smiled at Sven. He looked so deliciously handsome—tanned golden, blond, with his clear blue, sympathetic eyes. Her adoring look changed to a sinister expression. Then, Sven stopped breathing, because PJ suddenly had a lethal looking gun in her hand. "Holy shit!" he cried. "Precious, put that thing away! You might hurt someone!"

PJ laughed wickedly. "You are scared, worse than my brothers. Dithakar did not believe my threat. He came for me and I had to shoot him."

"You shot your brother?" Sven was incredulous. "How could you?"

"It was easy. It was either me or them. And I only gave him a flesh wound. I tried to shoot by him, but instead the bullet went into his upper arm."

"What then? Did you call the police?"

"No! They would have taken me to jail and left mother and the boys in my house with my defenseless baby. I called a cab and told the cabbie to take them to the airport in Miami, after dropping Dithakar at the emergency room at Jackson. I gave them money for a hotel where they could stay a few days to see Miami and then they have to go home."

"But your mother speaks enough English to make trouble for you. She can go to the authorities and talk about the shooting."

"I told her if she did not do as I told her, I would tell the police the reason for the violence. Namely, that they had forced me to send them visas and now that they were here, they intended to run a drug business out of my house. Of course, I could not allow them to force me to be a part of such a thing, and with the baby and all I had to act."

"You are precious Precious Jewel! What you did took enormous courage." He looked at the gun still in her small, beautiful hands.

"Please, put that away. It makes me nervous!" She laughed. "I will never let it out of my reach; it makes me feel safe." Looking suddenly very serious, she said, "Perhaps I will use it to make you marry me!"

Sven felt as if the air was being sucked out of the room. A shotgun wedding? Is that what PJ had in mind? His head spun. Suddenly the idea of marriage did not appeal to him at all. Clarity flashed through him, removing all ambivalence. No wedding for him!

Shoot me then, flew through his mind, *because I do not want to get married at this juncture.* Yet before he could say the words, PJ put away her lethal gun.

"Don't fear, dear Sven! I am not going to force you to marry me. I don't want to marry you at all."

He looked at his longtime lover as if she had gone mad. They had talked about marriage for so long that he thought neither one of them would change their mind. For the two years, when they made love at odd hours and occasions, they both dreamed how they would one day, freed of Dmitri's presence, get married and live happily ever after. He remembered when they lay on a miniscule strip of beach beside the road, sheltered by mangrove shrub. How, sated after ardently making love, they had talked about their dream of being legitimately together forever. And now? What had happened to them both?

"PJ, what's gotten into you?" he asked in unbelief. "Marriage, wasn't that what you always wanted? To be taken care of. Secure, with lots of money to spend. What has changed?"

She did not say anything for a long time. The baby began to cry. She went to the crib and lifted Kamala out of her little nest. She carried her to her seat, holding her in the crook of her arm. Satisfied, the baby fell silent.

"Until a week ago everything you said was true. I wanted to marry you more than anything—a young husband, a child—my dream. Then my family happened and I realized that I have changed. If I want to I can take care of myself and a baby. I have the means that I can live worry-free until I find a job. This is America. I know if I try I can find something that I can do well—perhaps better than anyone else."

The World Turns

❧❧

AS SVEN SAT IN seat 8A of the number 2027 night flight of Scandinavian Airlines to Stockholm, he relived his final leave-taking from Precious Jewel. It had been sad. They did not even for old time's sake make love one more time. They hugged, and he promised to come back and see her. Perhaps in a year, perhaps later after he was grounded in a job with a future. And then, if they still liked each other, well…who knows.

"Can I bring you an after-dinner drink, Aquavit perhaps?"

The cheerful voice of a pretty, pert stewardess brought him back to the present. With her blond hair and rakishly set blue cap, she looked like a cheerful angel. They began to make small talk in their mother tongue. When the girl, Helge, left his side, Sven began to think of his two years in Florida as a heady, much-perfumed dream.

The Notice in The Miami Herald

☙❧

PRECIOUS JEWEL RARELY READ the paper thoroughly. She did not understand American politics; neither had she understood Thai politics. Although she skimmed the paper for ads and coupons, she missed the small notice in the Herald, which would have been of interest to her. The minute article mentioned three Thai nationals, an older female with her twenty-something sons, who were forcefully deported to Thailand. Apparently the trio had lived in the Hampton Inn & Suites for several days. They had presented cash instead of a credit card. Therefore, when they stayed past the prepaid days, the manager pressed for the bill to be settled.

The Thai nationals had no more money and were told to settle the bill by noon or leave the hotel. An hour later, the older of the two males was arrested by hotel police after leaving another guest's room with cash and jewelry in his possession. Authorities were called. After a court hearing, the Immigration service took custody of the three foreigners, who were later deported.

Questioned by the authorities, they stated that a family member had invited them to come and stay with them, but had later reneged on the offer. The reporter finished the notice with the personal comment that one can hardly blame the family member for wishing to be free of such undesirable company.

The Business

❧❧

THREE YEARS WENT BY. Precious Jewel had never gone back to the community in the Keys that once welcomed her so warmly. She was ashamed and realized that her behavior had been unworthy of her position. After all, they had all been Dmitri's friends—not hers, and therefore they would feel her betrayal of him as their own. She vanished from their presence. After many speculations and the meager explanations presented by Dmitri's son, the neighbors lost interest and forgot her. Sometimes in their conversations her name appeared again, but on the whole—she was no more.

❧❧

ON A MOST DELIGHTFUL Florida spring day, Jan visited an elderly aunt in Titusville. Betty's husband had died two years ago, until then the couple were often visitors to Jan's house in the Keys. With Herbert dead, her aunt Betty at eighty-two did not get around much anymore. So, for a treat, Jan drove her along the coast. The coastal drive is dreamily pleasant. Ocean views and mini-communities entice the visitor to stop and dally. One can easily spend a most wonderful week traveling from Miami to Jacksonville while discovering the Atlantic side of Florida.

Wherever you drive along the scenic Florida routes, you will find small enclaves of shops selling art, antiques, jewelry and nautical items. The two ladies had barely left Titusville behind when just such a tourist magnet beckoned.

"Oh, look at the darling boutique," enthused Aunt Betty.

"And look over there: Chinese antiques! Can we stop for a moment? I live so close to this area and yet, I never knew this precious place existed. When Herbert still lived we always drove the big, fast highways."

Of course, Jan obliged the old dear. However, she had to park quite a distance away from their goal. As they leisurely wandered along the side streets, which sported businesses of various kinds, Jan's keen eyes suddenly were drawn to a peacock-colored sign above a shop window. Flanked by a law office and a shell shop, a house with a large display window featured the many-colored sign. Black lacquer letters, in intricately drawn cursive design, protruded from the iridescent colors and read:

The Orchard Palace

෭෨

Find Your Flower, The Right Woman for Life
We will help you to choose the right wife from
hundreds of women!
We arrange your visit to meet them, and even
arrange your wedding.

BUT WHAT REALLY CAUGHT Jan's attention was the proprietor's name. There it was! She could not miss it: Precious Jewel Ragoongong!

"I know that woman!" cried Jan.

"Betty, this must be the same one that married Dmitri and disappeared after he died!"

She dedicated a moment to refill her lungs with air that surprise had depleted, and continued undeterred.

"You remember the Thai girl? The one he got from a catalogue? We always wondered if she took off with her Swedish young lover. Gorgeous, nice boy! We all could see why she would fall for him. Dmitri, although he was my friend and may he forgive me for saying this, was rather old for such a young woman."

"Yes, I do remember her. I am not totally daft yet. I met her a few times when we came down to visit. She was quite something to look at, I remember. I had to keep Herbert from drooling by kicking his shin a few times," Betty replied somewhat dryly.

"She had that effect on men," laughed Jan.

"If she could have handled a large boat and been good at fishing, I think Brent would have been her next victim."

"What ever happened after Dmitri died?"

"The family hired a lawyer. The oldest boy came down and handled the whole business. All parties concerned, including even the Swedish boy, had a big meeting after which she disappeared, from one day to the next. She never even said good-bye to anyone."

The women had arrived in front of the intriguing store. They stared at a window, displaying the map of Thailand and a huge artistic arrangement of exotic flowers. It was a remarkable work of art: the flowers seemed to grow out of a carved wooden tree trunk. Taking in the oriental flavor of the display, Jan said, "Martha, who had spent a lot of time with her, especially in the beginning when she was ignorant of our customs, the stores, the food—everything, was very hurt by her disappearance."

"PJ was probably in shock and ashamed of her situation," ventured Betty. Both women stopped talking, for Jan had pulled the door open and allowed Betty to precede her into the shop. For a moment they stood transfixed. This looked nothing like any business they had ever seen.

The desk or counter, usually the focal point of any business, stood lonely off against a wall. It was a dainty black and gold Chinese affair with a matching delicate chair. A large circular cream-colored couch took up most of the room. It had been placed against an upholstered wall of cream silk imprinted with flowers and greenery. A large glass coffee table stood in front of the couch. Thereupon, the most interesting, heavy volumes of picture books were displayed. The décor was completed with a few chairs, matching the couch, a low Chinese table featuring travel brochures, and a few large green plants.

A beautiful, elegant woman in sea-green silk pajamas, her shoulders draped with a cream shawl that glistened with gold embroidery, sat on the couch engaged in conversation with an elderly gentleman. Both women had the impression that the man had been ill-used by life. He reminded Betty of a sickly plant always deprived of optimum light, while he reminded Jan of a boy in high school who was always too shy to ask a girl to dance. The elegant lady looked up from a thick volume of photographs.

"How can I help you?" she lilted, with a sweet oriental accent to her words. Her eyes grew large as she recognized Jan.

"Oh, oh, Mrs. Jan Sorensen!"

She almost squeaked, her voice went so high.

"PJ, is it really you?" cried Jan, with pleasure.

"I am so glad to know that you are still in the country." PJ turned to the elderly gentleman, who seemed thoroughly rattled, stunned to be discovered by women in this particular shop.

"Excuse us for a moment, Mr. Smith," apologized PJ. "I will be back with you in a moment."

She rose from the couch and went to greet Jan and Betty.

"Can you stay a while? I am almost finished with Mr. Smith, and I would like to have tea with you if you can spare the time."

"Of course we can stay a while!" breathed both women as one. Titillated by the rediscovery of the Thai woman, the shop and its circumstance, a team of horses could not have dislodged them. PJ led them into a room in the back. It was a modest office with filing cabinets, a proper business desk and chair, a substantial computer and printer arrangement, and two folding chairs. Jan and Betty positioned themselves on the folding chairs, facing the desk.

The focal point on the desk, apart from the computer was the portrait of a little girl, displayed in an elaborately cut crystal frame. The girl was astonishingly beautiful. Her dark eyes were exceedingly large, with a hint of an Asiatic slant. Her hair was very full and long for one so young, which made her small elongated face look ethereal. There was a serious set to her small rose-bud mouth.

"That must be the child she was pregnant with when Dmitri died. I wonder if it's Dmitri's or Sven's."

"She looks too dainty to be Dmitri's," hazarded Betty.

"She is too dark to be Sven's," speculated Jan.

"There is nothing, neither in the eyes nor the hair of Sven's in her." They began an animated discussion of the intricacies of genetics, which was soon interrupted by PJ who came to join them.

"He is gone!" she said cryptically. "Let us go into the other room and have tea in pleasant surroundings."

She excused herself, took a teapot and tea tray from a cupboard in the office and left, while Jan and Betty walked to the outer office. PJ returned presently. She sat the tray with its three cups and saucers, a plate of pastries, sugar, lemon, milk and the teapot on the table before them.

"I have to get the hot water from an office in the back," she explained, walking away once more. When she returned, Jan blurted out, "PJ is the beautiful child in the picture in your office your daughter? Forgive me for being so forward to come out with it like this, but she is a most attractive child."

PJ's smile conveyed great pleasure at this remark.

"Oh, yes, she is my daughter. Her name is Kamala."

The women congratulated her on being the mother of such a sweet, perfect daughter. They warbled on and on about children and this and that, while they were aching to find out who the father was. Perhaps their roundabout questions tipped PJ off to their desire to know; perhaps PJ just wanted to clear the matter up once and for all, but she suddenly said, "Yes, she is Dmitri's and my daughter. They did paternity tests in the hospital and she is definitely Demi's child."

She added almost sorrowful, "I wish he could see her. He wanted a child so badly and she is glorious."

The tea had finally steeped to PJ's satisfaction and she poured like the perfect hostess she was. The women sipped in silence for a moment, enjoying the wonderful flavor of the tea.

"I import it from Thailand." PJ said proud of its quality. After a while Jan brought the topic around to PJ's business. The Thai woman was only too glad and proud to reveal the source of her independence.

"After Dmitri's death I was left by his family with a generous settlement. But you know how life is. Very soon I had to think of a new way to take care of the two of us." She sipped some of the excellent tea, smiled deprecatingly and continued her story.

"I was searching for something I could do without putting Kamala into a nursery. Another difficulty was that I was not trained for anything. I do not even have a high school diploma. You can imagine that my job search was very daunting. Just when I began to despair, I accidentally ran into a Thai woman in Miami, a Mrs. Shinawatra. We talked a little about Thailand and America, particularly Florida. Because we enjoyed each other's company, we met a few more times for lunch and once for dinner. I brought Kamala one time and Mrs. Shinawatra liked her very much. Of course, I told her of my job search. Then, after she'd heard all about Dmitri and seen Kamala, she offered me a business deal.

"You see, I am in the bridal business," said Mrs. Shinawatra.

"I am located in Miami and business is good. However, my clients from further north must come all the way to Miami to see the catalogues, to make the personal visits and the flight arrangements. Sometimes that involves numerous trips and no one has time anymore. You know how that is. I could use an office further up the coast. Titusville is ideal—almost in the middle between Miami and Jacksonville. We could give it a try. If you work out, you will have an independent little office that you can run on your own schedule."

By now, PJ's cheeks glowed with pride.

"I was thrilled with the proposal. This was a tailor-made opportunity for me. I spoke the Thai language and had taken computer classes after Dmitri's death. I remember taking Kamala with me to school in her car seat for those lessons. Another plus was that I am an American citizen and speak English fluently."

She tilted her head toward her visitors in an aside.

"Thanks must be given to Dmitri. He pushed me to learn and always corrected my speech. So it came that I possessed most of the requirements needed for the job."

PJ poured more tea and passed the tray of delicate pastries to each lady.

"I lived for six months in Miami in one of Mrs. Shinawatra's flats. She is an amazing business woman who owns apartments, a store with Oriental furnishings, an art gallery, and many enterprises I do not know about. In Miami, in her main "bride store" I learned everything I needed to know to run this type of business; how to treat clients and how to find them, how to set up appointments with the family of the bride, how to arrange visits and make travel arrangements. Best of all, I knew firsthand how things are done in Thailand."

Jan and Betty sat mesmerized. Seldom did they have the occasion to peer into another person's life so penetratingly. They were kind, benign voyeurs, in sympathy with PJ and yet a bit appalled by this unappealing business that mated young women, barely out of girlhood with older men. They were men, who Jan believed to be slightly suspect in character, harboring fantasies that American women were unwilling to fulfill, or who were plain old and wanted youth in their beds.

Earlier, on their short walk to the shop, Betty commented that men with their mail-order brides reminded her of the Islamic men she had read about in the paper. There had even been stories of Arabs, who went to India to buy slave brides. Was PJ's business any different from that? Both women thought about these things while they silently listened. PJ looked a little sad.

"By your faces I know what you must be thinking. The idea of men practically buying young women for marriage is abhorrent to you. You are so thoroughly steeped in your own culture that this business must appall you."

Confronted thus, Jan and Betty squirmed uncomfortably in their seats.

"Yes," admitted Jan, "As much as I liked Dmitri, I always felt a bit peculiar when I saw you beside him. I knew he was good to you—as good as one can find in a husband—but you blossomed when you stood next to Sven. By the way, whatever happened to Sven?"

PJ smiled an almost motherly smile, it was so benevolent. "I set him free," she said simply.

"When the paternity test showed that the child was Dmitri's, I felt it was wrong to tie him to me. He would have stayed with me had I pushed, I think. But what would that have meant in the long run? Most importantly, I have discovered that I have power. I can do things independently—America has set me free." She reset the clip holding her long hair out of her face.

"You see, the reason why I can work in this business is that I know all aspects of it. When I go to Thailand or Cambodia, I tell the girls exactly what to expect. They all want to come—they'd do anything to come. As for the men, they could hire prostitutes if that were their desire. They choose instead to legitimize the girls and treat them honorably as wives. Most of them are also very well off. We have lawyers, stockbrokers, doctors and many other professionals, who look for what they call an old-fashioned woman who treats them with respect. The financial advantages are much more than most of our girls could hope for in their homelands."

"You make it sound very wonderful—this "bride" business," objected Betty. "But there must be personal tragedies occurring in these marriages—what then?"

"Yes, I also have tragic happenings. I learned so much from my marriage and my mistakes. I had to grow up immensely before I fully understood my own shortcomings. I did not always act properly and responsibly. I see that now. At the time I was just selfish. I had made the contract and then allowed myself to get tempted. I talk about these things with clients. If a girl is not treated well by her husband, she has recourse with us to complain."

"If the men you provide brides for are such wonderful specimens, why can't they find women in America?" asked Betty stubbornly.

"Some of them are looked at as odd in your culture but they are accepted in ours, which is much more tolerant of people's shortcomings. Some are shy because of a physical defect; some waited too long to get married, chasing a financial dream. Suddenly they are in their forties or fifties and want a family. Oh, their stories are as varied as the stories of our girls."

There was a knock on the front door, which PJ had locked for an uninterrupted teatime.

"I am coming!" called PJ, as she quickly moved to open the door. In the frame of the door two figures were revealed. A young woman with a ponytail, and a small child stepped into the room. Jan and Betty instantly recognized PJ's daughter, Kamala.

"Thank you for seeing her safely home!" PJ directed her thanks at the young person, who patted Kamala's head and left with a "Good-bye!"

ॐॐ

MUCH LATER, AS JAN and Betty finally began their search for the "darling antique store," they still debated the pros and cons of mail-order brides. Betty summed it up with the wisdom of old age.

"I don't care how great a thing the mail-order-bride business is for both parties. I will never get used to a marriage arranged like a business. It is like buying an object. I remember the suffragette movement. We fought exactly against this thing, because it puts a woman in an inferior position, or on an unequal footing, at the very least."

"I agree," concluded Jan.

"But perhaps it is better to be unequal in the USA than starving and being controlled by your own family as PJ was."

She paused thoughtfully, then she continued, "Or worse yet, to be sold into marriage to a poor old goat in your home country."

Betty smilingly agreed, "Oh, yes, it is much better to be in our country where you always have the opportunity to even things out!"

Having concluded the matter satisfactorily, they erased it from their minds as they arrived at the antique shop, where they covetously eyed the treasures displayed in two large storefront windows.

THE END